Kane

Also by Jennifer Blake
in Large Print:

Bride of a Stranger
Fierce Eden
Shameless
Silver-Tongued Devil
Surrender in Moonlight
Wildest Dreams

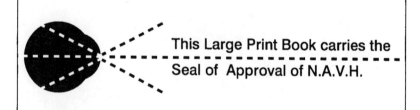

This Large Print Book carries the
Seal of Approval of N.A.V.H.

Kane

Jennifer Blake

Thorndike Press • Thorndike, Maine

Published in 2000 by arrangement with
Harlequin Books S.A.

Thorndike Press Large Print Basic Series.

The tree indicium is a trademark of Thorndike Press.

The text of this Large Print edition is unabridged.
Other aspects of the book may vary from the original edition.

Set in 16 pt. Plantin by Al Chase.

Printed in the United States on permanent paper.

Library of Congress Cataloging-in-Publication Data
Blake, Jennifer, 1942–
    Kane / Jennifer Blake.
        p.   cm.
    ISBN 0-7862-2611-0 (lg. print : hc : alk. paper)
    1. Grandfathers — Fiction.   2. Louisiana — Fiction.
    3. Large type books.   I. Title.
    PS3563.A923 K36 2000
    813′.54—dc21   00-060570

Kane

1

Regina Dalton snapped awake the instant the coffin lid closed.

Darkness pressed around her like a smothering blanket. Not a sliver of light penetrated. The dense air smelled of old dust and ancient velvet. The side walls seemed to contract, so she was supremely aware of her left shoulder wedged against padded wood while her right nestled beneath unyielding solid flesh and bone.

Warm flesh and bone.

Horror exploded in her mind. She gasped and jerked up her free hand. It came in contact with cloth-covered wood that was heavy, immovable.

She was imprisoned in the antique coffin she had seen, only moments before, in the front parlor of the old Louisiana mansion. Set in incongruous display on a base skirted with wine red velvet, its polished walnut surfaces and ancient brass fittings had gleamed in the warm summer sunlight falling through tall windows. She had been fascinated by it, drawn to it.

Now she was locked inside. And she wasn't alone.

"Surprise, honey."

The deep, purring voice, the brush of warm breath against her temple, sent a shiver along her nerves. Relief and dread clashed in her mind. The man who lay pressed against her was alive. It seemed, however, that he might have a direct connection with how she'd come to be in the coffin.

"Who —" she began, then stopped abruptly as her teeth came together with a distinct chatter.

"Who I am doesn't matter," the man answered. "Who you are is what's important. That, and just what you're doing at Hallowed Ground."

Hallowed Ground was the name Mr. Crompton had given the old, white-columned mansion as he'd welcomed her at the door. It had seemed perfectly appropriate for a house that had been both funeral home and family dwelling for years.

Regina remembered, with the haziness of a dream, being left alone for a few minutes in the sitting room where Lewis Crompton, her host and owner of the old house had received her. The graceful proportions of the room and its air of abiding comfort had fascinated her, as did anything antique. She'd got to her feet and wandered here and there, looking at the faded yet lovely prints on the walls and the pieces of interesting bric-a-brac on every flat surface.

At the crack between heavy sliding doors leading into the next room, she'd paused to peek inside. The coffin had caught her attention as it sat on display, surrounded by a brocatelle-covered parlor set and tables where wax flowers and mourning ornaments made of human hair were protected by bells of glass. Intent on the oddity of it, she'd opened the doors a bit more and stepped inside.

Something had charged between her feet, she thought. She'd tried to sidestep. The fat, furry creature had squalled. Regina had stumbled, started to fall. There'd been a sudden flare of pain at her right temple, then gray, star-lit dimness closed in on her.

"I asked you a question," the man said, his voice hardening.

"Business. I'm here on business." The words came with difficulty from her tight throat. She felt as if she were suffocating, unable to get enough air into her lungs.

"What business would that be?"

"I don't see how it concerns you. Whoever you are." He definitely was not Lewis

Crompton. This man was younger, a stranger.

"I'm making it my concern."

She couldn't think for the angry desperation rising inside her. A part of it was the close confinement, something she hadn't been able to stand for years. The rest was the trapped position in which she was being held, welded against this man from shoulder to ankle, almost beneath him as he lay on his side. She was overwhelmingly aware of his superior strength and weight, of his clean scent of starched cotton, citrus aftershave, and overheated male. Her breathing was also constricted by the muscled arm across her chest.

"Well?" The question was rough and dangerously impatient.

She said hastily, "I — I came to see Mr. Crompton."

"Mr. Crompton is an elderly man, one too nice for his own good and too easily taken in by a beautiful woman. I'm none of those things."

He was trying to intimidate her. That recognition brought a flash of defiant scorn. "Good for you! But since I'm not trying to take in anybody, you can let me out of here right now."

"Not likely."

"Why?" she demanded. "Why are you doing this?"

"There are things I want to know. It seems a good way to find out."

She moistened her lips as she searched her mind for some way to gain her freedom. "Where is Mr. Crompton?"

"I wouldn't count on him coming to your rescue. He'll be a while."

"You're the reason he was called away in the middle of our discussion, aren't you?"

"Is that what you were doing, discussing things?" He shifted his arm slightly where it was centered between her breasts, directly above her pounding heart.

She drew a taut breath and clamped her hand on his hard wrist to move it. It didn't budge. Through stiff lips, she said, "If it's the jewelry you want, it's in the other room. Just take it and go."

His laugh was abrupt and glazed with irony. "That's funny, coming from you."

"I don't know what you mean."

"Theft seems to be more your specialty than mine. I saw you pawing over it, figuring out how much it was worth down to the last garnet and seed pearl."

"You saw me?" She stared wide-eyed into the dark.

"Exactly," he said. "Now I want to hear

how you got your hooks into Pops."

Regina breathed in short gasps as she tugged at his arm. She even sank her nails into his taut wrist, but still couldn't move it. At the same time, she said in something less than full coherence, "I haven't. I don't think —"

"I do," he replied, cutting across her words. "My grandfather has the exalted idea that most women are ladies, so he doesn't understand greedy, grasping females. I, on the other hand, understand just fine, and I'll be damned if I'm going to let you con him out of a collection of heirloom jewelry worth thousands."

"Your grandfather?"

"Exactly. How did you get on to him?"

If he was Crompton's grandson, then he had to be Kane Benedict. That put an entirely different light on things. He was all wrong, though he could be trying to trick her with this misunderstanding over the jewelry. How much did he really know, and how had he found her out so quickly?

Perspiration beaded around her hairline. The press of warm bodies and the sun falling on the coffin made it entirely too hot inside, in spite of the air-conditioned coolness of the old parlor.

"I'd advise you to talk to me, and talk

fast." His voice was a low growl near her ear as he tightened his grasp.

"I don't know what you expect me to say," she cried, stung into an answer. "I barely know Mr. Crompton."

"A one-time deal, that it? Who set it up?"

"He called me, asked me to come here."

It was a moment before Kane Benedict spoke, and then it was with taut scorn. "I don't think so."

He was right. In an effort to correct her instinctive falsehood, she stammered quickly, "I mean I d-don't know exactly. He must have called someone who knows my work. The message was relayed to me. These things are handled discreetly."

"Christ Almighty!"

His obvious revulsion, and the tightening of his hold that went with it, sent dismay rippling through her. "Let me out, now. Please. I can't stand —"

"Get used to it. This could take a while."

"Are you saying you can't open this thing?" The question was half-strangled.

"I played in it as a kid. Opening it is not a problem. But you're going to have to do a lot more explaining before I trip the latch."

His touch, his voice, his sheer physical presence, were having the strangest effect, in spite of her spiraling distress. His every breath seemed to shudder through her body until it was hard to tell who was exhaling, who inhaling. Where her shoulder pressed against him, she could feel his heart thudding against his chest wall. And if she wasn't mistaken, the lower portion of his body was prodding her thigh more firmly than was acceptable under the circumstances.

She didn't want this intimacy, couldn't handle it. It triggered a dark cloud of distantly remembered helplessness, the fear of forced compliance, ultimate violation.

"What do you want from me?" Releasing his wrist, she fumbled blindly along his arm and pushed at his shoulder to put more space between them.

"Are you just a little gold digger, or are you after something else entirely? Do you, just possibly, have something to do with the case going to trial?"

"Trial?" The word was a wheezing whisper. She could hear the wild drumming of her heartbeat in her ears.

"Is it purest coincidence that you've turned up now, or is there a connection with the funeral home syndicate trying to run my grandfather out of business?"

Panic exploded inside her. In instant, automatic denial, she exclaimed, "You're insane!"

14

"I might be at that," he agreed in rasping irony, as he shifted his grasp to the back of her neck, dragging her closer again. "Especially since I have a crazy notion to see how far you'll go. Maybe you'd like to try your tricks on me instead of Pops?"

"No! *Don't!*"

"Why not?"

"I'm not like that. You can't —"

She got no further. He slid his hand to her cheek, brushed her lips with his thumb, then eased closer to settle his warm mouth on hers. He shifted, enclosing her more firmly in his arms, using his weight to still her struggles.

It was a heated possession fueled by anger and rampant desire. An act of blatant persuasion, it was also an invasion as he tasted her, urged her to abandon resistance and join him in sensual exploration. The flavor of his mouth was sweet, drugging. For an instant, Regina felt the leap of unbidden response, felt herself losing her grasp on reality in the dense, lulling closeness. Her body seemed melded to his, as if their essences were blending, combining into a single current of powerful, urgent life.

How easy it would be to give in, to accept the hovering pleasure, answer the faint intimation of delight. It might even be best, her mind whispered, the easiest way to get what she needed. What she had been sent to find.

She couldn't. Not now, not ever.

With an anguished moan, she twisted her mouth free and shoved violently away. The abrupt movement caught the man who held her off guard. He rocked back, hitting the side of the coffin behind him so hard the whole thing jostled on its velvet-skirted base.

Regina screamed and stiffened. The man cursed under his breath as he rebounded off the coffin wall. He caught her arm again, snatching her into a hard, stiff embrace as if he could steady their prison with his own rigidity. His knee came up, holding her immobile.

Suddenly, something snapped inside Regina. Beyond thought or control, she lashed out, fighting, clawing in blind, terror-stricken rage. She arched away from his hold while every muscle jerked in spasmodic revulsion and her breath sobbed in her throat.

She felt his grip loosen, heard him exclaim in quick concern, but she was past caring, far past heeding. She flailed at him, felt her hand strike his cheek, her nails scrape the bony protuberance of his nose. There was no satisfaction in it, no reason,

16

nothing except recognition of a vulnerable target. She struck again.

He grunted, muttering a soft expletive. An instant later, he rolled to pin her body to the cushioned velvet, using his weight to subdue her movements while he clutched her other wrist and hauled it above her head.

Abruptly, she stopped fighting. Bitter tears sprang into her eyes as wrenching shudders coursed over her. She moaned in despairing defeat.

"I'm sorry," he said, his voice low, abrupt. "Be still. I'm not going to hurt you. I'm truly sorry."

Her shivering died away by increments. Her breathing quieted as she sought for control, almost found it.

"Are you okay?" he asked. "Do you hear me? I didn't mean to take it so far."

"Let me go." The words were jerked from between her set teeth by a final convulsive tremor.

"I'll do that, I promise. As soon as I'm sure you're not going to hit me again."

"No, I . . . I won't."

"You're sure?" There was a trace of grim humor in his voice as his hold eased a fraction.

That evidence of the lightening of his

mood reassured her. It seemed he meant what he said. She managed a tight nod.

"Fine. Easy does it, then. Nice and slow." He let her go, shifted backward.

It was then that a sharp click sounded, like the spring of a metal catch. The coffin's lid swooped upward in a rush of fresh air. The sudden wash of golden light was blinding. In its glare, like a halo around some divine deliverer, she saw a white-haired gentleman holding the coffin lid open.

Lewis Crompton.

For a frozen instant, no one moved, no one spoke. Then Regina drew a deep breath and exhaled in shuddering release. Lifting a hand, she wiped surreptitiously at the tears that rimmed her lashes.

The elderly gentleman, leveling a grim gaze on his grandson, said, "If you have an excuse, Kane, I'd like to hear it."

The man beside Regina pushed himself to a sitting position with an abrupt gesture as if he felt at a disadvantage lying down. He raked the fingers of one hand through his hair. "Call it an experiment."

"Of what nature?" There was no relenting in the older man's tone.

"I had the idea that your guest might have some connection to the trial."

Crompton extended his hand to Regina, helping her to sit upright, also. "In other words, you were butting in where you don't belong. I hope you've discovered your mistake?"

Kane Benedict frowned before he shifted a shoulder. "Maybe. But I reserve the right to look into it further. Anything that might touch on this case concerns me."

With a glance from under bushy white brows, the older man said, "I'm not certain we agree on that, though I can tell you I don't care for your methods of investigation."

"I can explain —"

"So I should hope, but another time. I doubt the discussion will entertain our guest."

The emphasis placed on the last word was slight yet effective. Amazingly, Regina saw a dark red shading appear under the sun-darkened skin of her captor. She would have said he was well past caring about anyone's reprimand, much less that of an older relative.

For the first time, she gave him her full attention. He was darkly attractive, with iridescent highlights glistening in his black hair, chiseled strength in his facial bones, and jutting authority in the shape of his nose. The deep, royal blue of his eyes held shifting currents of cogent thought and suspicion. In a blue dress shirt and navy pin-striped slacks, he had the surface appearance of an executive, perhaps a banker or stockbroker, allied to the indefinable patina of old money and effortless success. Beneath that outward impression, however, was something else entirely, a hint of reckless assurance and a devil-may-care grace that he wore like a second skin.

There would be few people this man held in awe, she thought, few things that could embarrass him. Still, he avoided her gaze now, and she had the distinct feeling he disliked having her see his fleeting susceptibility to his grandfather's disapproval.

He recovered quickly. "I suppose," he drawled to the older man, "that your guest has a name?"

"She does. Miss Dalton, allow me to introduce Kane Benedict, my daughter's son. He also happens to be my lawyer, and a good one. The lady you've been mistreating, Kane, is a visitor from New York. Miss Regina Dalton is here in her capacity as an appraiser of fine jewelry."

The man beside Regina turned slowly to face her. His gaze was intent as he took in the indeterminate hazel of her eyes behind turquoise contacts, the disheveled, coppery abundance of her hair, and the scattering of freckles that masked the bridge of her nose.

"A jewelry appraiser," he repeated in blank disbelief.

"She was giving me an estimate on the collection left by your grandmother before we were interrupted."

"Is that what she was doing? And she came all the way from New York for it." Kane's firm lips curved in a slow, enigmatic smile. "It explains the accent, at least."

Wariness squeezed Regina's throat as she met his steady regard. It was habit that made her put her hand to the heavy pendant of Baltic amber that she wore there, still she drew confidence and courage from it.

She was used to sizing up people at first glance. From both intuition and practice, she was good at estimating their strengths and weaknesses so she could guard against them, keep her distance. This man was different. He had gotten dangerously close before she could throw up her defenses. She didn't like it.

He was dangerous, period.

He was a man who believed in the law he defended, she thought, one who expected the truth, the whole truth and nothing but the truth, so-help-you-God. He spent his

21

days with absolutes, guilt or innocence, right or wrong, no excuses allowed. He would cut little slack for someone who feathered the edges of facts, skirted the peripheries of legality. It was all there in the hard lines of his mouth and the razor-edged alertness of his gaze.

He would make no allowances for someone like her.

She scrambled away from him, rising to her knees at the coffin's edge. Lewis Crompton reached out to place a hand under her elbow. Even with his help, however, clambering down in her suit skirt was going to be about as graceful an operation as a toddler escaping its crib.

"Wait," Kane commanded. "I put you in. The least I can do is get you out."

"You don't have to —" Regina began.

It was too late. As his grandfather stepped back out of the way, Kane put a hand on the high wooden side and vaulted to the floor. Turning at once, he slid one arm under her knees and the other around her shoulders, then lifted with easy strength. He swung around, lowered her feet. The toes of her sensible pumps touched the floor while she rested against the taut, unyielding body of Lewis Crompton's grandson.

She glanced up, and her gaze was snared

by the mesmerizing blue of his eyes. His hold was firm, possessive. In his face, marked by the red flare of her handprint on his cheek and the scratch left by her nails across the bridge of his nose, was a host of inclinations only half-suppressed.

He was a man who knew women, she realized, knew their reactions and weaknesses and wasn't above using them to make a point. He was well aware of what he was doing to her and deliberately prolonging it. She pushed away at once as she recognized another attempt at intimidation.

"Thank you," she said in tones as cool and measured as she could make them.

"My pleasure, ma'am."

He tilted his head briefly as he released her. That gesture had the same careful courtesy and hint of deferential charm that had so impressed Regina in Kane's grandfather when Crompton had first welcomed her into his home. Regardless, she felt her hackles rise. She was being mocked by Kane Benedict. Why, she wasn't sure, still she didn't doubt it for a second.

This man had kissed her. It was a stunning thought. The smooth, sculpted contours of his mouth, bracketed by slashing indentations that just missed being dimples, had touched her lips. He had sampled her as a wine connoisseur might taste a new vintage. And she could not help wondering, for a flickering instant, just how he might rate her. That brief vulnerability was even more disturbing than his touch.

Turning to her host, she said crisply, "I'm afraid the whole thing was as much my fault as your grandson's since I let my curiosity get the better of me. Forgive me for snooping?"

Kane made a soft, startled sound under his breath. It helped Regina's feelings to know that she could throw him off stride.

"That's very generous of you, my dear," Lewis Crompton answered, his gray gaze twinkling as he divided his attention between her and his grandson.

"Not at all. Could we get back to the jewelry you were showing me? It makes me nervous to think of it lying around where anyone might find it."

The older man gave a genial shake of his head. "No one here at Hallowed Ground would think of touching a piece of it. Anyway, I believe we should postpone our discussion. I don't imagine you feel up to it just now."

"I'm perfectly fine," she said. "Time is important to you, or so I understood, and your collection is such a large one that I don't think we should waste —"

"Now, now, there's not that much of a hurry. Tomorrow or the next day will do just as well. Truth is, I don't like the look of that bruise on your temple. It might be best if Kane ran you by the hospital emergency room, just to be sure you're all right."

Regina put a hand to her forehead, wincing a little as she found the sore spot. Regardless, she wasn't some fragile Southern flower, ready to wilt at the first sign of trouble. With precision, she said, "I don't believe that's necessary."

"I insist. It's the least we can do under the circumstances." There was a note of command in the older man's voice as he glanced toward his grandson.

"By all means," Kane said promptly.

"No, really. The jewelry —"

"Tomorrow will do just as well, I promise," the older man said in calm certainty. "Let Kane drive you."

"I couldn't leave my rental car here." The excuse was valid and she seized it with gratitude, since it seemed her host really was calling a halt to the appraisal.

"Someone will deliver it to wherever you're staying, if you'll give me the keys." Kane put out his hand for them as if expecting her to obey without question, as though he thought he and his grandfather knew what was best for her. It was unmitigated male chauvinism, but about what she might have expected. Southern men were known for it after all.

"No, thank you," she said through stiff lips. Swinging away, she started toward the sitting room where she had left her handbag. The swift movement made her feel dizzy and a little sick, but she kept walking. A minor concussion could be a distant possibility, but she didn't care. She wasn't about to let Kane Benedict control another second of her time.

"You recovered quickly, I see," he called after her. "I'm glad your scare wasn't as bad as it seemed."

He was telling her he suspected she had not been as upset as she pretended. "I wasn't scared, Mr. Benedict," Regina said as she turned in the doorway, "just claustrophobic. There's a difference."

"I imagine so. You might call me Kane, so you'll recognize the name when I check on you later."

"Don't bother." The words were as close to a dismissal as she could make them.

"Oh, it's no bother," he said, his smile crooked as he met her gaze across the room. "No bother at all."

He knew she didn't want to see him, but meant to force the issue. Perhaps he thought he could shake her again, make her say something she didn't intend. Or possibly he meant to take up his questioning where he had left off. Well, she wasn't going to play his game. She had too much at stake. No matter what Kane Benedict thought, said, or did, he would get nothing from her. She would do the job she had been sent to Louisiana to accomplish, then she would be gone. She had no other choice.

Nor did she want one. Not now, not ever.

Swinging from the two men, she walked away. She didn't look back.

2

Kane watched from the parlor window as Regina Dalton marched down the drive and got into her car. She moved with swift steps and no trace whatever of sexy hip sway. She had forgotten him, had no idea he might be watching her movements. Regardless, the sight of her skirt conforming to her slender form, the flash of skin above her knee as she slid into the car seat, caused a drawing sensation in his groin. That kind of instant juvenile reaction was extremely inconvenient under the circumstances. It wasn't the right time or place and certainly not the right person. The Fates had a warped sense of humor.

"I won't belabor the question of your misconduct," Kane's grandfather said as he moved to join him at the parlor window, "but I will point out that I've been handling my affairs for some time without your interference. If — and I do mean *if* — I had been about to make a valuable gift to that attractive young lady, I would consider what you just did an act of unmitigated gall."

"I know," Kane said in moody acceptance

28

as he gazed after Regina Dalton's rental car driving away.

"Another question altogether is why you believed I'd succumb to an itch for a female young enough to be my granddaughter."

Kane sent a brief smile over his shoulder at his grandfather. "You always did like redheads."

"She does have amazing hair, doesn't she? So bright it makes a man want to touch it to see if he'll get burned. Not that either of us paid much attention."

Kane, recognizing the sly dig behind the last words, made a sound between a snort and a sigh.

"That's what I thought." The older man chuckled. "I could put her off so she stays around a while."

"Not," Kane said evenly, "on my account."

"Too bad." As a large yellow tomcat appeared from under a rattan table and glided forward to wind around his leg, the older man reached down and picked him up. Draping the animal over his arm and smoothing the fur, he went on. "You should have driven her back to her hotel."

"I think she'd had enough of me for one day."

"Very likely. Can't say I blame her, either,

considering the hand you had in her injuries."

"It was that damn cat." Kane thrust his hands into his pants pockets as he turned and leaned his backbone against the window frame.

"Samson here may have started it, but you compounded the problem. What set you off?"

Kane was silent a moment, then he said, "I came in the back way, through the kitchen. Dora told me you had someone with you. I was going to join you, but stopped a second outside the door you'd left open like a gentleman, not wanting to barge in if your business was private. Something about your guest, the way she was smiling at you, struck me as all wrong."

"Seductive, you mean?" His grandfather's eyes narrowed.

"It seemed that way at the time." Kane lifted a shoulder and let it drop. "Are you sure she's legitimate?"

"You think she might not be?" His grandfather watched him with lively interest as he stroked the huge, apparently boneless, cat.

"I don't say I'm infallible, but I have an instinct for phonies. It goes with the built-in lie detector tucked into a corner of my brain."

"Maybe the lady scrambled them both,"

Lewis Crompton suggested blandly. "The kind of charge she packs can make all sorts of things go haywire."

"Hell, Pops."

"Actually, it does me good to see you're not immune," he went on as if Kane hadn't spoken. "You used to be a rounder and a half, like your dad and all the rest of that Benedict crew out at the lake. Your grandmother, rest her soul, lay awake many a night when you were a teenager, worrying about what crazy-wild thing you'd do next. That was when she wasn't laughing over your stunts."

"Wild?"

"Wild," Pops said with finality. "Remember the time you and your cousin Luke stole the gym teacher's Frederick's of Hollywood underwear and hung it from the water tower because she dared suggest Luke's girl — April Halstead, that would have been — dressed too sexy? And what about that boat race on the lake where the loser had to cook dinner for the winners — in the nude. Your cousin Roan lost, didn't he? That was the same summer you, Luke and Roan spent on the NASCAR circuit with that killer car the three of you hot-rodded and called The Whirlwind because it was always spinning out."

"All right," Kane agreed, holding up a

hand. "You made your point."

"You grew out of it. . . ."

"With good reason."

"True. A woman can take the wildness out of most men, but especially the Benedicts. They fall hard, and none are more faithful when they decide to settle down. Your problem was choosing the wrong female. But you went too far the other way after it ended, got downright stodgy."

Kane gave him a warning look. His grandfather wasn't the only one who didn't appreciate interference in his private life.

"You can't deny Francie did a number on you before she took herself off."

"No," Kane returned. "Though what it has to do with Regina Dalton, I can't begin to guess."

"She got to you," his grandfather said simply, a gleam half-concealed in the swamp-fog gray of his eyes. "She touched off whatever imp of Satan it was that used to move you, make you act before you thought things through. Did my heart good to see it after all this time."

"That wasn't the idea."

"I know it wasn't. You judged that young woman and found her guilty between one heartbeat and the next. That's not like you at all."

Kane let that pass. "I suppose you checked her credentials before you let her waltz in here?"

"Did that," the other man agreed with a nod. "She came highly recommended, has worked with the big-name jewelers and auction houses, particularly in the past year or so. She's careful, she's thorough, known as one of the best at authenticating Victorian pieces. I feel lucky she was able to fit me into her schedule on such short notice."

"And why," Kane asked as he watched his grandfather, "was time so important? It wouldn't be because you're in a hurry to raise money?"

The older man grimaced. "I wondered when we'd get to that."

"I imagine so. Last I heard, Gran's jewelry was to be handed down."

"You're our only grandchild, in case you haven't noticed. You don't seem in any hurry to provide a wife or great-granddaughters to wear cameo earbobs, so handing them down doesn't look likely any time soon."

"Don't change the subject," Kane warned. "You're selling the collection to pay the legal fees for the suit, the fees due me."

Lewis Crompton set the cat on the sofa back nearby before he answered. "That it's your firm I owe the money to has no bearing. I take care of my obligations."

"Not like this."

"I don't think that's for you to decide."

"Not even when it's my children being robbed?"

Lewis Crompton gave him a grave stare. "Unfair, Kane. Besides, there's your partner to consider and that female paralegal you hired for this case. Not to mention the Benson girl who answers the phone for you."

"Melville and I do have other clients," Kane said shortly.

"Sure you do, but you're not chasing around all over gathering evidence for them, now are you? Or getting ready to face a barrage of high-powered New York legal eagles for their sake? I won't have you paying for my defense out of your own pocket. That's final."

Lewis Crompton was as proud and stubborn an old coot as had ever lived. Kane admired and respected him for it; the last thing he wanted was to hurt him. Still, he couldn't stand by and see him reduced to selling the family jewelry. "It's not going to bankrupt me."

"I know that, but I don't intend to be a charity case."

Their gazes caught and held, gray eyes and dark blue, boring into each other. Neither would back off. That was until Kane finally swore and curled his fingers into a fist. "If I ever get my hands on the greedy little bastard doing this to you, I'll kill him."

"Fine," his grandfather said dryly, "and I'll bury him, give him a royal send off to show him how it's done."

Kane spared a tight smile. "Serve him right, to be put six feet under in one of his own cheap tin caskets."

"At the very least. Though I'm not the only one he's pushing to the wall."

The attitude was typical of his grandfather. He was also right. The farmers and truck drivers and field workers up and down the delta were worried about the prices the big funeral service company would charge once Crompton's Funeral Home was out of business. Sam Bailey over at the feed store had mentioned it just yesterday. It was a crime, Sam said, to make people mortgage their futures to bury their loved ones. He was behind Lewis Crompton a hundred percent in the trial coming up.

Crompton's Funeral Home was a part of the community, an established tradition since 1858. It had come into being when a great-grandfather who'd run a livery stable

35

had taken a glass-sided hearse with black plumes at its four corners in trade for a used buckboard. He had soon discovered he could make a little extra by transporting the departed to their final resting places. One thing had led to another until he'd become a full-fledged undertaker.

As generation after generation of Cromptons cared for those who had gone on, the family became more intimately involved with the events that made up the lives of their friends and neighbors. To provide service, ease grief, and help conceal the deepest secrets and improprieties brought out by death became a sacred and immutable trust.

No faceless funeral conglomerate could ever hope to deliver that same degree of discretion and comfort. The organization headed by Gervis Berry had mounted a huge public relations campaign designed to convince customers of the quality of its organization, but the truth was, it was a sham. Close inspection revealed shoddy merchandise, cut-rate services, and underhanded practices as the order of the day.

Melville, Kane's partner, was particularly incensed by the practices he was turning up in the course of his investigation. Melville was African-American, and many of the more bald-faced offenses of Berry Association, Inc. seemed to be directed toward his people. Fending off the takeover bid against Crompton's Funeral Home had become a crusade for him. Not only had he accepted the firm's continuing out-of-pocket expenses without complaint, but often footed the bills himself.

That didn't make it right, of course. Not in Lewis Crompton's eyes.

"I've been thinking," the older man said, breaking the silence. "Maybe we should offer a settlement."

"Now? Just as things are getting started?" Kane couldn't keep the surprise from his voice.

"Can't think of a better time."

Kane watched him a moment. "Because of the money, I suppose?"

"Because it's dragging on too long, getting too complicated. I don't like what it's doing to you, either. You look as if you haven't slept in a week."

"And you're wondering if I'm going off the deep end, thanks to the little incident just now."

"I didn't say that," his grandfather protested. "From what I can tell, you and Melville have Gervis Berry dead to rights. I think we can win this thing. But I'm not a vindictive man, and I've better things to do with my days than spend them in court. I'd like to offer a fair settlement. You could tell Berry I'll drop my suit in return for his pledge, in writing, that he'll go away and leave us alone here in Turn-Coupe. Plus enough to reimburse you and Melville and make good the damage he's done, say a couple of million."

"I don't think he'll go for it, Pops. Berry has no idea of fairness in the sense you mean. Any offer to settle will be seen as weakness, and he'll move in for the kill."

"A big mistake."

"What do you mean?"

"I was a poker hound in my younger days, used to play cutthroat with your Granddaddy Benedict. If Berry wants to up the ante, well, I can do that. How many million do you think it would take to bankrupt Berry's corporation?"

Kane stared at his grandfather, then a slow smile curved his lips. "You old devil."

"Think we could win if we ask that much?"

"We could sure try." His smile faded. "Berry won't take it lying down, you know. Things could get nasty."

"We'll handle that when we come to it. In the meantime, you write up that offer so it's all official."

"If it's what you want."

"Good." Pops rubbed his hands together with a dry, papery sound. "Now. Are you going to see that Miss Regina gets back to her motel room all right, or are you just going to stand there?"

To that question, there was only one correct answer. Kane gave it.

A half hour later, he pulled up at the entrance of the Longleaf Motel on the south edge of town. There was no doubt about where Regina Dalton was staying, since there was only one motel in Turn-Coupe. Built in the fifties, the main office had a certain retro stylishness in its inset of glass-brick wall and its sweeping, finlike roof angles. That benefit didn't extend to the boxlike rooms behind it, though they were neat and clean. The clipped shrubbery and beds of bright annuals fronting each unit were a reminder that the owner, Betsy North, lived on the premises.

The car Regina had been driving sat outside a middle room. There were no others in evidence at this time of day, but Kane didn't care to risk disturbing a stranger. He got out of his gray Nissan and walked into the motel office.

Betsy rose from her desk behind the

counter and came to meet him. Round-faced, nicely plump, she had frosted blond hair and a comfortable manner. A third cousin of some kind on the Benedict side, she and Kane had attended high school together, known each other for years. They exchanged the usual pleasantries, then Kane asked casually, "You have a Regina Dalton registered?"

"Yep," Betsy answered, her gaze bright and not at all fooled by his offhand manner. "Checked in yesterday afternoon. From New York. Leastwise, that's what it says on her registration."

"She in her room?"

"Just drove up."

He nodded. "I suppose her car's parked in front of the right unit?"

Betsy cocked her head to one side. "I'm not supposed to tell you that, though I might be persuaded if you were to drop a hint about why you want to know."

Kane liked Betsy. Beneath her nosiness and love of being in the thick of things was a heart as wide and warm as all outdoors. She'd had a hard time these past few years, after her husband was killed while working on an offshore oil rig. She'd bought the run-down motel with his insurance settlement, cleaned it up, got rid of the trash and one-night-stand business. Now she was doing fairly well.

Neither fondness nor kinship was enough to make him satisfy her curiosity, however. The excuse he gave — delivery of a message from his grandfather — was a disappointment to her, he could tell, but she confirmed the room number for him anyway.

As he left the office, Kane knew very well that news of his visit would be all over town by daylight tomorrow. The best thing he could do to keep the gossip down would be to make his visit short and his departure as conspicuous as possible.

Outside the door with the correct number plate, he raised his hand to rap out a polite summons. While he waited, he shoved his hands into his pockets. This hadn't seemed like a good idea when Pops had suggested it and felt like an even worse one now.

He wasn't sure what had come over him back at Hallowed Ground. He'd thought he'd conquered that kind of impulse long ago. Pops's explanation for the lapse was good enough, he supposed, but the incident bothered him. Not that he regretted it, in spite of everything.

It had been a long time since a woman had stirred him that profoundly. For a few seconds, he'd lost track of where he was,

41

what he was supposed to be doing, everything except the enticing female in his arms. He wasn't sure how far he might have gone, given the slightest encouragement. That uncertainty bothered him more than anything else.

There was no answer to his knock. His second try seemed to echo for miles, and he felt as if a million eyes watched him hovering outside the motel door. He was wondering if he ought to get a passkey from Betsy to find out if Regina had passed out from her head injury when he finally heard movement inside.

"Who is it?"

He bent his head to catch the cool, precise sound of her voice through the door. Giving his name, he added, "Just checking to be sure you're okay."

"I'm perfectly fine. Good-bye."

A moment before, he'd wanted nothing more than to get away. Now, the fact that she wanted to be rid of him made him reluctant to go. "You're certain? No dizziness? No headaches?"

"Nothing whatever. If you don't mind, I was about to take a nap."

"I don't think that's a good idea. Sleepiness can be a sign of concussion. Maybe somebody should stay with you for a while."

"You, I suppose?"

A grin quirked his mouth as he heard the sharpness in her voice. There had been a time when he enjoyed feistiness in women. "I'm the only one here."

"I don't," she said with exactitude, "need your help. The last thing I require is for you to stay with me. Go away."

"Not until I see for myself there's nothing wrong."

The safety chain rattled inside, then the door was flung open. "Fine. Look, then."

She had taken off her suit and put on a chenille robe piped in satin, one faded to a color somewhere between gray and green and so soft from countless washings that it molded perfectly to her slender curves. Beneath its hem, her feet were bare. The makeup had been washed from her face, revealing the powdery paleness of her skin and bringing its dusting of freckles into prominence. Her eyes were no longer turquoise but a soft hazel color. Around their pupils were rust-gold flecks that made them sparkle with the same vibrant life as her cloud of coppery hair.

She looked fine, and perfectly dressed for a long, slow afternoon in bed with a man who could take the frost from her voice and the suspicion from her face. One word, a single come-hither gesture from the lady, and he'd volunteer for the position in one of her New York minutes. Strange, when he didn't trust her an inch.

"Satisfied?"

The inquiry was not quite so belligerent as it had been before. She put a hand to the opening of her robe, drawing it closer together.

Kane cleared his throat, erasing the obvious answer from his mind. Instead, he said the first thing that came into his head. "Why do you wear contacts? You don't need them."

"Not," she said stiffly, "unless I want to see something farther away than six feet."

She released the front of her robe and reached higher to clasp the chunk of golden amber that hung on a chain at her throat. Before her fingers closed on it, Kane saw that a winged insect, like a firefly, was caught in the jewel-like resin. Perfectly whole, exactly centered in the heavy filigree setting, it appeared almost alive in its entrapment. He said, "I mean the colored lenses you had on earlier. You have beautiful eyes. Why change them? What are you trying to hide?"

"Nothing!" she said sharply. "Though I fail to see what difference it makes to you."

She was absolutely right. It was just that the artifice bothered him in a way he couldn't explain. In an effort to hold her at the door long enough to nail it down, he nodded at her necklace. "Nice. Something you found while working?"

For an instant, it seemed she wouldn't answer. Then she said, "A gift."

"He has good taste. It suits you." Deliberately, Kane let his gaze wander from the amber to her freckles, which were the same burnished shade, then to her hair, which reflected identical highlights.

Color flooded her face and she looked away. "He wasn't — that is, he was an elderly gentleman."

"Really? A relative?" Kane felt his chest tighten. His grandfather was also an elderly gentleman.

"Yes, if you must know." She avoided his gaze, veiling her expression with gold-tipped lashes.

Her voice, the words she used, disturbed him; still he tried the effect of an understanding smile. "Family is a good thing to have. I speak from experience, being related to three-quarters of the people in Tunica Parish."

The vitality seeped from her face, leaving it grim. She stepped back to close the door.

45

"Yes, well, if you're happy now, I'll go take my nap."

"I don't think I am," he said just before the latch clicked. "I'll check back with you tomorrow."

There was no answer. Kane stood for a long moment before he turned and walked away. A frown meshed his thick brows as he crossed to his car.

He'd been right the first time. Something about Miss Regina Dalton didn't add up. The feeling nagged at him, ringing in his mind like an unanswered summons from some distant and inaccessible room.

It was, he was fairly sure, the warning bell for his internal lie detector.

3

"You got everything you need here?"

Regina looked up at the question. The blonde with the bouffant hairstyle who stood poised in front of her table wasn't her waitress. That she was addressing her was a mystery, then, nearly as much of one as why her smile was so friendly. Voice abrupt, Regina answered, "Yes. Why?"

"They're taking care of you. That's good."

She must mean the coffee-shop staff. By Regina's standards, the service was so snail-like she had a strong urge to snap her fingers, grousing, "Come on, come on." But it was a pleasant enough place in a homey, unpretentious fashion, with crisp red gingham curtains at the windows and matching geraniums on the sills. Her waitress had been kind, even motherly; the coffee was ambrosial and exactly the right temperature, and refills were frequent and free. More than that, Regina had no place to go after breakfast. She had also realized after the first half hour that it was not her waitress's fault the words "leisurely breakfast" were, in Regina's experience, a contradiction in terms.

"I'm fine," she answered, and even managed a polite smile.

"You have any problem, you just let me know. I'm Betsy North, and I own the place, for my sins. Say, didn't I see you yesterday with Sugar Kane?"

"Who?"

The woman looked quizzical. "Kane Benedict, you know. He's a great guy, isn't he?"

"Oh."

Regina lifted her coffee cup, using it as a refuge from the other woman's encroaching curiosity. Sugar Kane. She'd heard nicknames were common in the South, but couldn't quite make this one match the man she'd met.

Betsy North chuckled and she put a hand on her ample hip. "Didn't know about that, huh? You gonna ask me how he got it?"

It was the last thing Regina was inclined to do. She wasn't used to instant camaraderie with strangers. The motel owner seemed a likable enough person, but she wasn't sure how to take her. Lowering her coffee again, she began, "I really don't —"

"Guessed already, I expect." The woman laughed, a rich, bawdy sound without the least self-consciousness. "Sweet as sin —

with all the consequences, that's our Kane."

"Really," Regina commented, though it was difficult to keep the wry interest from her voice.

"Yeah, he's quite a guy. Good as gold, but you never can tell what he'll do next. Runs in the family, you might say. I should know, since I was a Benedict before I married. You wouldn't understand what that means, not being from around here. From up north, ain't you?"

"As a matter of fact —"

"New York, right? There's the accent, of course, but you got the look, like the lawyers who've been crawling all over the place on account of Crompton's Funeral Home. Say, you're not one of them, are you?"

Regina shook her head in answer. She might have brushed Betsy North off with a few well-chosen words had it not suddenly occurred to her she might learn something from her. "The look?"

"Kind of gray-faced and uptight and dressed in dark clothes, as if they don't see the sun more than once in a month of Sundays, never have any fun, and all shop at the same place." Her eyes widened, and she added hastily, "Not that you don't look nice, you do. I mean, that hair makes you a standout, no matter what you put on. But I see a resemblance."

"I wouldn't be surprised," Regina said dryly. She considered the tailored brown-knit dress she wore with a wide leather belt as sophisticated without being severe. It was possible to see, however, that it might not appear that way to a woman dressed in terra-cotta jeans, a shirt printed in desert-sunset colors, and with silver earrings set with rhodochrosite stones dangling from her earlobes. She went on innocently, "But these lawyers. What have they to do with Mr. Crompton?"

"Plenty," the woman answered with emphasis. Her lips thinned an instant before she launched into a tale of how a big Northeast funeral service conglomerate had been knocking off small funeral homes across the South, that was until they made the mistake of tackling Sugar Kane's grandfather.

"Mistake?" Regina murmured by way of encouragement.

"I'll say. Made Kane madder than hell, as you can imagine. He filed a whole blizzard of injunctions and whatnot, then topped it off with a whopping lawsuit that stopped the guy who owns this Berry Association in his tracks. Showed him there were folks in this town who didn't care for his shady business practices. The very idea — canceling the private, funeral home-owned burial policies for old ladies so they have to depend on their kids to foot the bill when they die instead of the insurance they've been paying on most of their lives. Makes me so mad I could spit, and I'm not the only one. Yes, sir, Berry found out right quick that nobody here cares two bits for his money and power, not when it comes to right and wrong."

"So it's Kane, rather than his grandfather, who is pushing the suit?"

"Oh, I don't know as I'd say that, exactly. I think Mr. Lewis looks on it as a matter of honor not to take this lying down. But Kane's the man Berry and his raft of high-powered lawyers will have to beat in district court when push shortly comes to shove."

"You think he has a chance, then?"

"You got me." Betsy North shrugged, then her lips tightened. "All I know is, I'd sure hate to see Mr. Lewis done out of what belongs to him."

"He seems like a nice man."

"One from the old school, a real gentleman. Done a lot for this town over the years — scholarships, civic stuff, donating land for things like the nondenominational church and the new middle school. Why, I could tell you — But you don't want to hear all that."

"You're related to him, too?"

The woman's rich chuckle broke out again. "You'd think so, wouldn't you? But no such thing. So, you gonna be around here long?"

Regina wasn't sure how to reply to that, even if she wanted to try. While she was making up her mind, a deep, masculine voice answered, "She'll stay as long as we can keep her."

Betsy spun toward the man approaching from the doorway behind her. "Damn you, Kane, what do you mean slipping up on me like that?"

"Not you," he said with a lazy smile, "but your customer." To Regina, he said a quiet good-morning, adding, "Mind if I join you?"

She waved briefly at the chair across the table. Perhaps he could give her some idea of when his grandfather would see her again.

A speculative look came into Betsy's eyes as she watched Kane slide into the seat. She offered to bring him coffee. When he declined, she said with wry humor, "Fine, then. I can tell when I'm not wanted. I'll check on you guys later."

As she moved away, Kane said, "So has Betsy been after your life story?"

"We hadn't got that far," Regina answered. The words were more abrupt than she intended. He was every bit as disturbing as she'd thought the day before, though casually dressed this morning in a knit shirt and pressed chinos. With his presence, the coffee shop seemed to take on new life: the sunshine through the windows was brighter, the decor livelier, the smells of coffee, bacon and maple syrup overlaid by frying onion actually becoming appetizing.

"Don't let it get to you," he recommended. "She doesn't mean anything by it."

"I'm aware of that."

A muscle tightened beside his jaw at her tone, but he let the subject drop. With a brief but intent glance at the bruise that still marked her temple, he asked, "How's the head?"

"All right." She sipped at the coffee she still held, but it was cold. She set the cup in its saucer with a clatter and pushed it aside.

"No pain or nausea?"

His polite concern made her feel a little ungracious. She unbent enough to say, "I had a headache, but took something for it when I went to bed. It was gone this morning."

He nodded. "What do you plan to do for the day, then?"

"Go back out to Hallowed Ground to talk to your grandfather, of course. I have a job to finish."

"I could drive you, maybe after lunch."

She gave him a direct look. "That won't be necessary."

"It's the least I can do. Besides, I'd feel terrible if you blacked out and ran off the road or something." He propped an elbow on the table, watching her closely.

"I won't do that, I assure you."

"I'd rather not take the chance. If something happened, I'd feel it was my fault."

She shook back her hair, her gaze cool. "Afraid I'd sue you?"

His laugh was a brief sound that made a chill slither down her spine. "Hardly. Not with the best lawyer in town ready to spring to my defense."

"Yourself?" Disdain shaded her voice.

"My partner," he corrected with a hint of steel in the words, then went on without pausing, "Why don't you want me to drive you? What are you afraid of?"

"Fear doesn't enter into it." Her dislike for such a shopworn trick was plain in her voice.

"Doesn't it? I wasn't speaking in a physical sense, you know, though I easily might, considering the way you reacted yesterday. I think you're afraid I'll find out what you're really after."

Alarm rose inside Regina, but she forced it down again. "I can see why you're a lawyer. If one argument doesn't work, you automatically look for another."

He sat back with a brooding look on his handsome features. "Why are you so defensive? I'm trying to make up for my mistake yesterday in a practical manner. Apparently, you aren't going to let me."

The obvious rejoinder, a crushing rejection, rose to her lips. She almost voiced it, but something in his level blue gaze prevented her. She felt as if she were being tested, and that made her wary. After a moment, she said, "It's nothing to do with you. I just prefer my independence."

"At the expense of safety?"

"My safety is my own affair."

He watched her a long moment, then rolled his shoulders as if shrugging off a burden. Finally, he said, "You're right. I should have told you straight out that my grandfather isn't available this morning."

With a frown, she said, "That's what all this is about?"

"Afraid so. Pops is a man of definite habits. He goes to bed every night after he watches the news and doesn't get up until after nine. He drinks two cups of black coffee and has a breakfast of hot biscuits and ham or sausage while reading the paper between nine and nine-thirty, showers and shaves between nine-thirty and ten, and instructs his cook about dinner, an important ritual, between ten and ten-fifteen. He's in his office from ten-thirty until twelve-thirty, at which time, promptly, he leaves for lunch. On Tuesday, which means today, he has a standing appointment for soup and a salad with a lady friend, Miss Elise. All this means it will be two o'clock at the earliest before he makes it back to Hallowed Ground again to meet you."

"Good grief!" she exclaimed before she could stop herself. "How does he ever get anything done?"

"You'd be surprised how much he manages to accomplish. But the point is, you can't see him this morning. Since that leaves you at loose ends, I suggest you let me show you around."

"Show me around?"

"You should see something while you're here besides the Baton Rouge airport and this motel. We'll have lunch somewhere. Afterward, I'll take you out to Pops's house."

"Your working day being every bit as re-

laxed as your grandfather's?" she
with more than a trace of skeptic

"My day being entirely at you
His smile was brief.

She should turn him down flat; that w̲
perfectly obvious. The problem was that he
made it all sound so reasonable. On top of
that, she knew the plan he'd outlined offered an excellent opportunity to find out
more about Lewis Crompton and the lawsuit. Who better to ask than the grandson
representing him in court?

She hesitated, then gave a nod. "Fine."

"You'll go?" His face mirrored his surprise at her sudden agreement.

"I said so, didn't I?"

He stood and stepped around to hold her
chair for her. "Then let's do it."

A late-model pickup, pine green and polished to a mirror gloss, waited outside the
coffee shop. Kane moved a little ahead of
her to open the passenger door. She paused,
sending him a quick, questioning glance.
He had been driving a sedan the afternoon
before.

"The roads can be pretty rough where
we're going," he said.

In some peculiar fashion, the truck
seemed to suit him better, she thought. It
had nothing to do with being a redneck.

er, the big, glossy vehicle with its latent wer was a better match for the leashed rength beneath his controlled facade as a lawyer. It was ready for anything they might come across, and so was he.

Regina climbed up to the leather bucket seat. Kane shut the door, then walked around and slid into the driver's side. With his hand on the key, he turned his head to look at her. Seconds ticked past. There was something so intent, so steadfastly appraising about his expression that she grew uncomfortable. The impulse to smile, to see if his well-formed mouth would curve in answer hovered in her mind.

"What?"

"Nothing," he muttered, looking away through the windshield. He cranked the engine, then put the truck in gear. His movements were stiff and there was a grim set to his mouth, as if whatever had crossed his mind had been less than comfortable.

They drove through town, straight down Main Street and past the old Greek Revival courthouse with its pediment-topped portico supported by columns, its wide steps, flagpole sporting a limp Stars and Stripes, and weathered bronze statue of a Civil War soldier half-hidden among the drooping limbs of a big live oak. It was a pleasant enough little town, but sleepy and a bit sad to Regina's eyes. Several stores around the courthouse square were closed, and the low-budget gift shops, beauty salons, and specialty dress boutiques that were left looked as if one customer at a time was the most they could handle.

The way out of town was lined with garages, barbecue joints, and run-down flea markets. Beyond these was a stretch of bungalows and ranch-style houses with plaster elves and pink plastic flamingos in the front yards. Washing flapped on clotheslines in the back, while children's toys littered the porches and fishing boats squatted under open carports. These gave way to fenced fields where vines twined around the posts and rose above them like nests of writhing green snakes. The black alluvial soil was striped with rows of dark green seedlings stretching arrow straight and as far as the eye could see.

The crop was cotton, Kane told her, then went on to explain the long and exacting cotton planting season. He also pointed out pin oaks and red oaks, tupelos and maples and a half-dozen other kinds of trees growing in the woods that separated the wide areas of fields and overhanging the road like enormous green canopies. The deep timbre of his voice was soothing in its lilting cadence and easy, drawling grace. Regina relaxed by such slow, lulling degrees under its influence that she almost missed his quiet attack.

"I'd rather talk about you than trees and cotton. Where did you learn so much about old jewelry? Did you have some kind of training?"

"I studied gemology with the Gemological Institute of America," she answered, sitting up straight, "but it was something of an inherited passion."

"You mean you got your start with a collection handed down in your family?"

That was what he was supposed to think, what Regina allowed most people to think, though she never said it in so many words. "Something like that."

Actually, Regina had conceived her passion for the antique pieces while hanging around a pawnshop after school. The elderly man who ran it, Abe Levine, had been the very embodiment of the word "venerable." He'd always had time for her, putting down his book or his violin with a warm smile when she came into the shop. An endless source of knowledge about all things, he seemed to enjoy taking beautiful old pieces from the cases for her to see, relating their stories, telling her about values and where stones came from, about how to tell the real from the fake. He had given her the amber pendant she always wore, her first antique. She had lied to Kane about his being a relative, but she was sure Abe wouldn't have minded. Anyway, he was the closest thing to a grandfather she'd ever known.

During the long days spent in his shop, he'd fired her imagination with tales about fortunes in portable jewels shown to him by actresses down on their luck or showgirls who had taken to heart the theory that diamonds were a girl's best friend. He knew the histories of fabulous pieces smuggled out of Russia before and after the Bolshevik revolution, or from Germany during World War II, also the tragic backgrounds of more simple pieces from those times. It was Abe who had put her in touch with the circle of buyers and sellers of old jewelry, who had helped her earn her first commission, urged her to accept her first assignment to value and sell an estate collection. Though she had also studied and learned on her own, visiting museums, reading countless books, never missing an opportunity to compare and value, she owed that gentle old man so much, including her independence.

Abe had never cared for her cousin

Gervis. The feeling was mutual; Gervis had shed no tears when Regina's mentor died.

Odd, but Lewis Crompton reminded her of Abe, now she thought of it.

"For someone who handles jewelry for a living, you don't wear a lot of it, do you?" His glance lingered an instant on her hands that were bare of jewelry of any kind.

She felt heat rise in her face, something that didn't happen too often, or hadn't until she came south. She seldom wore rings because they drew attention to her nails, which she wore extra short to keep herself from biting them. "No, not while traveling," she answered shortly. "It's too valuable to risk having it stolen."

He arched a brow. "But you must travel with other people's collections all the time."

"For which I'm bonded, of course. But I wasn't speaking of monetary value alone." She folded her arms, tucking her hands out of sight, and hoped the gesture wasn't an obvious cover-up.

"Funny," he said, his smile quizzical yet sharp. "You don't strike me as the sentimental type."

"We all have our little quirks." Turning from his probing gaze, she stared out the window. Kane, it seemed, was even more intent on getting information from her than she was on questioning him. There was grim humor in the idea, but somehow she wasn't laughing.

It was incredibly difficult, she found, not to answer his queries in full, if only to keep his attention focused on her. Something about his rich voice, the expressions that flickered in his eyes, gave the perception that he cared about what he was hearing. It was, no doubt, a valuable attribute for a lawyer.

After a time, he turned off the blacktop road they were traveling and bumped over a sandy track with potholes large enough to swallow a taxicab. Regina opened her mouth to ask where he thought he was taking her, but the truck tire fell into a pothole with a bounce that made her bite her tongue. By the time the pain subsided enough for her to talk, she caught the glint of a large body of water through the trees.

"Horseshoe Lake," Kane said as he brought the truck to a stop.

She sat for long moments, looking out over the water that sparkled under the sun as if millions of fairy lights were concealed beneath the surface. Trees hung with gray streamers of Spanish moss lined the shore and also straggled into the lake as though going wading. More edged the surrounding horizon like dark lace. The water was the color of strong tea, and cloud puffs drifting in the sky overhead were reflected on the opaque surface with a surround of blue. It was quiet, so quiet the only sounds were the wind in the trees, birdcalls, and the soft, regular slap of breeze-driven waves at the water's edge.

Regina opened the truck door and got out. Watching where she was stepping on the damp ground with its dew-laden grass, she moved toward the water's edge. Behind her, the other door slammed as Kane followed.

"It looks murky," Regina said when he came to stand at her shoulder, "like something primeval might rise up out of the depths."

"Dripping muddy slime and water lilies?" he asked, slanting a smile down at her. "You've seen too many swamp-thing movies. But there is a swamp beyond the lake, several thousand acres of marsh and snaking waterways where you can get lost and might never be found again."

"You've been there? In the swamp, I mean?"

"Played there every summer as a kid."

"Why on earth would you do that?" She barely concealed a shudder.

"The fun of it. Something to do. A cousin and I pooled our money and bought a secondhand aluminum boat and an old outboard motor. Sometimes Luke and I were gone for days at a time."

Glancing at him, she tried to feature the boyhood he described. It was so different from anything she had known that he might have been talking about life on another planet. At the same time, she didn't doubt what he'd said. In the bright daylight that exposed the strong bones of his face and crescent-shaped scar beside his mouth, he appeared rugged and capable of anything he cared to tackle. He was also rather imposing.

In an effort to regain her equilibrium, she said, "I imagine the police didn't think it much fun when they had to call out the search-and-rescue teams."

"Never happened. Luke and I always found our way home again."

"And your parents didn't mind?"

"My parents were dead, and my aunt Vivian who took care of me seemed to think knocking around in the swamp was better than a lot of things I could've been doing. Luke's folks never worried much about anything until something happened, but especially not about the backcountry — he has a real sixth sense where it's concerned. Nobody knows it better."

"Not even you?" she asked dryly.

Kane smiled without rancor. "I don't hold a candle to Luke. His ancestors have lived around the lake for centuries, even when it was still an oxbow turn in the Mississippi River. He has a Native American branch to his family tree from a long way back. Tunica and Natchez."

"Seriously?"

"It isn't that unusual around here."

Again, she had to fight that sense of being in foreign territory. The lifestyle he described and the close relationship with his cousin were unknown quantities. They were also appealing, however, perhaps because of their strangeness.

As she tried to picture it, she said, "This cousin lived nearby?"

"Just down the road. Still does, for that matter."

Surprise for her interest lurked in his dark blue gaze. Noting it, Regina felt wariness trickle down her spine. Turning back to the lake, she said, "I believe your grandfather said something yesterday about this being part of the Mississippi River at one time. Is that right?"

"Before it changed course, carved itself a

new channel," he agreed after a second. "All that was so long ago the openings to the horseshoe have silted up, forming this curving body of water, creating a lake with no access to the river. It's not an unusual phenomenon. There's another one like it above north of here called Old River, and one below known as False River, as well as others. We're a bit different because of the swamp that's caused by a creek — or actually another small river — that was blocked off from the Mississippi, so spread out into a wide area of marshland. It drains into the lake eventually, so helps keep the water fresh."

Regina nodded her understanding, though she had only the vaguest idea of what he was describing. It was so peaceful here with the warm sun dazzling her eyes, the moist breeze caressing her face and whispering in the trees overhead. The leaves, the grass, vines and low-growing shrubs, the water plants at her feet, were all such a vivid green that the light around her seemed stained with the vibrant hue. She could almost feel the tension draining from her pores, being replaced by a tenuous, almost furtive, peace.

The day seemed to slow to an easy, swaying rhythm. The impression was so insidious yet so alien that she couldn't help thinking how different everything was from the noisy, close, grime-coated streets she had left in New York, couldn't help considering how different she might have been if she had always known such natural magic.

Just then, a great blue heron that Regina had not noticed until that moment lifted from its still stance at the shadowy water's edge and sailed away with its wide wings almost skimming the water. She shaded her eyes with one hand as she followed its effortless flight.

Suddenly, her throat ached with the pressing uplift of some deep, emotional shift inside her. The day was so sublime. The huge bird was incredibly beautiful with the sun shining silver-blue on its plumage. At the same time, the heron was free, dependent on its own strength, without obligations, duties, or impossible dilemmas to cloud its mind and keep it lying sleepless, staring into the night. All it cared about was food and safety from the storms. And, possibly, comfort and security for its young.

"Had enough?"

She started, swinging around with her eyes wide and the blood rushing to her head. Amazingly, she had almost forgotten Kane was there. Forgotten, in his quiet, easy companionship, that he was watching her, judging her.

"Are you all right?" he asked, stepping closer to catch her elbow in swift support.

She gasped and gave a shaky laugh. "Oh, yes. I was just . . . a thousand miles away."

"You're sure?" His gaze touched and lingered on the bruise at her temple, half-hidden by her hair.

"I'm . . . fine. Really."

He searched her face for an instant longer before he nodded. "Time to go, then."

She agreed, and turned with him toward the truck. Still, he didn't release her, and the touch of his fingers seemed to burn, branding her flesh. His manner was protective, almost bordering on possessive.

She drew away, breaking his hold. Perhaps something was wrong with her head after all, for the gesture required a conscious effort.

It was some moments later, after they had reached the blacktop again and were barreling along past a series of big houses set back under ancient, spreading oaks, that Kane spoke again. "I need to stop by my place for a minute while we're so close, if you don't mind. I was reading a brief last night and left it on the table beside the bed. Picking it up now will save me a trip later."

The words were casual and matter-of-fact, the request perfectly polite. Regardless, Regina tensed. She had heard that kind of excuse before. She hadn't appreciated it then, did so even less now.

What on earth made Kane Benedict think she might be so gullible, much less so accommodating? It must be because she had come with him so easily, because she had not thought to let anyone know where she was going.

What was she going to do? Should she risk insulting him with her accusations, or wait and see if it really was the cheap trick she suspected? Would it be better to make her position clear in no uncertain terms, or might that only warn him that she was going to be difficult?

She felt sick. It was hard to believe Lewis Crompton's grandson would try this, in spite of the incident in the coffin yesterday. It was so isolated out here, so far away from everything she considered safe and civilized. No passersby, no telephones, no police. She had no weapon, no way, short of tooth and nail, of fighting back.

The most devastating question, then, was the one with the most doubtful answer. Was there any way on earth she could stop whatever he had in mind?

4

The truck neared an avenue of live oaks that led to a West Indies-style house with a hipped roof that overhung deep, railed porches on the front and back. A mud-splashed Jeep came down the shady drive, halting at the highway for them to pass. Regina noticed the brief movement as Kane lifted his fingers in a wave to the other driver. Instead of returning it, however, the man in the Jeep blew a quick tattoo on his horn. Kane braked to a stop, then reversed until he was at the drive again. With an expert movement, he whipped the truck off the road and in front of the sports vehicle.

A tall, dark-haired man climbed out and came toward them, walking around to the driver's-side window. "How's it going, Kane?" he said, then looked past him to Regina and touched the bill of his cap. "Ma'am."

"Can't complain," Kane answered, sitting relaxed with one strong wrist resting across the steering wheel. "Miss Dalton, my cousin, Luke Benedict. Regina's here on business, Luke."

Regina leaned across Kane to offer her hand with a conventional greeting, then added, "We were just speaking about you, I believe."

"Were you now?" Luke said, grinning as he retained her hand. "I can't imagine anything Kane could say about me that a lady like you should hear."

"Boyish exploits," she answered, responding with a smile to the unabashed admiration in Luke Benedict's eyes and sheer joy of living that radiated from him. It was easy to see the resemblance to Kane in the height, rangy build, and strong bone structure. At the same time, Luke was different, with a more blue-black shade to his hair, deeper olive coloring, and eyes of such a dark brown that the irises and pupils seemed to merge, creating laughter-bright depths like sunlight striking through dark pools.

"Even worse," Luke returned with a droll wag of his head. "But Kane can't have bad-mouthed me too much, since he must have been in it up to his neck, too. Not like now, when he's too much of a stick-in-the-mud to have fun."

"For that, you can unhand Regina," Kane said, grasping her wrist in one hand and

Luke's in the other and pulling them apart. "Why the devil did you flag us down? Make it fast. We've got places to go and things to do."

"Busy, busy." Luke winked at Regina as he spoke across his cousin. "You do know he's a driven personality? You'll have to make allowances?"

Regina hardly knew how to answer that, even if she had been paying strict attention. Her concentration was on her wrist that was still imprisoned in Kane's grasp. He seemed to have forgotten he held it, forcing her into an awkward position as she leaned across him, almost in his lap. She tugged experimentally. He didn't let go, but turned his head to stare down at her, his features so close she could see the spiky length of his lashes, the fine lines at the corners of his eyes from squinting against the intense southern sunlight. His warm breath, faintly scented with mint, ghosted over her lips. Her stomach muscles tightened with a slow, drawing sensation she felt repeated in the lower part of her body.

"I wanted to remind you about my shindig, cuz," Luke drawled, his voice a shade louder than before. "I'm firing up the usual Memorial Day extravaganza at Chemin-a-Haut and expect my friends and neighbors to gather around. Regina is more than welcome. In fact, I'll take it as an insult if you don't bring her."

"Miss Dalton," Kane said pointedly, "may not be here."

"Now that would be a shame. She doesn't know what she's missing."

"Chemin-a-Haut?" Regina repeated, her interest snagged by the unfamiliar syllables. At the same time, she snatched her arm free in an abrupt gesture fueled by annoyance and the suspicion that Kane didn't want her accepting his cousin's invitation.

"My humble abode," Luke said, jerking a thumb toward the house behind them, "French for the High Road — some also say High-handed." He grinned.

"This, er, shindig is a party?"

"An open house, sweetheart. Food and drink, music and dancing." Luke propped his elbow on the truck's side mirror. "Also fireworks, comets, shooting stars, flying saucers, heavenly artillery, fireworks to match your hair. It's expensive and wasteful and damned hard work setting everything up, but everybody loves it, including me. Say you'll come."

Voice laconic, Kane said, "It is something to see."

He was waiting for her answer, Regina

saw, as was his cousin. It gave her a strange feeling, having them both watch her so closely. For an instant, she couldn't think why, then she knew. She had their attention, their complete, courteous, almost deferential attention. Unlike most men she dealt with, they weren't waiting impatiently, tapping their fingers, for her to answer. They weren't planning what they were going to say next, or thinking of all the other things they needed to be doing, wished they were doing, elsewhere. It was disconcerting. It was also maddening.

"I'm sorry," she said abruptly as she met Luke's gaze. "I have no idea if I'll be here. It all depends on Mr. Crompton."

"Pop Lewis?" Luke asked cheerfully. "Hey, I can fix that."

"But you won't," Kane said, his voice taking on a hard note.

"Won't I?" Luke searched his cousin's face, his humor fading.

"No point," Kane said in terse explanation. "The lady will be heading back to New York before the weekend, regardless."

"She has something to do with the suit, then?" Luke glanced toward Regina. "Don't tell me you're mixed up in that mess?"

"Not at all," she answered quickly, then

compounded the lie by adding, "It's nothing to do with me."

"Good girl. You don't want to get in the way of a man's obsession."

The muscles in Kane's jaws gathered in a taut knot. "I'm not obsessed."

"You do a damned good imitation. Don't you think so, Regina?"

It sounded as if the argument was an old one. It might be foolish to comment on something between the two men that she didn't fully understand, but it was too much to resist. With a faint smile, she said, "He does seem a bit preoccupied with it."

Luke shook his head. "We should distract him for his own good. How long did you say you'll be around?"

She explained briefly about the Crompton jewelry collection and her afternoon appointment, adding that she would be leaving if everything worked out satisfactorily.

"Too bad," Luke said, and heaved a deep sigh. Then he brightened. "But if you're really here on business, I guess old Kane has no claim, right?"

"Correct," she agreed in brittle accents, though she refused to look at Kane.

"How do you feel about fried seafood? There's a great little catfish restaurant just

76

outside Turn-Coupe where they serve shrimp and oysters in a batter so light that —"

"Hold on." Kane put up a hand. "The meeting with Pops may run long. He'll expect Miss Dalton to stay for dinner. I've already alerted Dora, just in case."

"I asked her first," Luke protested.

The man beside Regina barely glanced her way before he said, "I don't think Miss Dalton wants to jeopardize a hefty commission for the sake of fried shrimp." Without waiting for an answer, he put the truck in gear and began to pull away.

Luke stepped back hastily. Raising his voice, he yelled, "You'd better come to my party anyway!"

"Don't I always!" Kane called, and stuck his hand out the window in a backward wave before he drove off.

Regina crossed her arms over her chest and stared straight ahead of her through the windshield. In chill tones, she said, "You might have let me answer for myself."

"You wanted to go to the catfish restaurant with Luke?"

She was loath to give him the satisfaction of a direct answer. "I don't need you to make my decisions for me."

"I guess you want to go back, then?" he

countered, his smile tight. "You prefer to tell Luke yourself how you really don't want to have dinner with him, but decided to turn him down in person just to show you can make up your own mind."

"Don't be ridiculous," she snapped.

"Show a little appreciation, then. I did the dirty work for you, while you came out smelling like a rose."

He really was too much. "You actually think you were helping me?"

He turned his head, watching her a moment, before he said abruptly, "Is it me you don't like, or just men in general?"

"I don't dislike anybody," she declared, shifting ground to meet this new challenge.

"You could have fooled me."

"I don't know what you're talking about." Though the words came easily enough, she couldn't hold his clear blue gaze.

"You object to my company, don't care to be touched, and can't stand being close. What else am I to think?"

The direction he had taken was not a comfortable one. She needed to distract him. She should also start taking advantage of being alone with him to do her job, before he got to his house and she was forced to do something that might alienate him for good.

"You don't have to think about me at all,"

she said as calmly as she could manage. "I'm nothing to you. Actually, I'm surprised you're wasting your time, unless this big lawsuit of yours is going so well it doesn't matter."

He stared at her a long moment through narrowed eyes. "What makes you think it's a big case?"

"How everyone speaks of it, for one thing. How angry you were when you thought I had something to do with it, for another. So what's happening? Is it dull, legal stuff or something more dramatic?"

"You don't really want to know."

The dismissive comment grated on her strained nerves. "It's something to talk about."

"I prefer other things. For instance, how come you aren't married?"

This wasn't what she had in mind, but some kind of answer was required. "Who says I'm not?"

"You aren't wearing a ring."

He had mentioned that before. She should have remembered it. Hastily, she said, "Some women don't wear rings these days, just as some women keep their maiden names."

"Is that what you're doing," he asked, "or are you avoiding a straight answer?"

A flush began at her collar and rose to her hairline. Being evasive was as natural to her as breathing, a self-protective measure with infinite uses. She only lied outright if pressured into it, but often led people into the paths she wanted them to go, coloring the truth a little here and there to make herself more interesting, more normal, or less visible, according to what was needed. Few people recognized it or cared enough to call her on it. She might have known this man would be one of the few.

"No," she said baldly, "I'm not married."

"But you implied you were."

"What does it matter?" Embarrassment and irritation made her snappish.

"It doesn't." His voice was flat as he turned his attention to the road, slowing as they approached a driveway ahead of them. "That's why it makes no sense. Never mind, forget I asked."

She would be glad to forget it. She did, too, the instant she noticed they were turning into the drive, then saw the house at the end of it.

It was a Southern dream, a Greek Revival temple, square, white, two-storied, with galleries on all four sides that were lined with rows of massive columns reaching to the roof of ancient, moss-grown slate. The columns, of a girth too wide for a man to reach around, were plaster-covered brick. The steps, which led up to the front gallery, curved in the style known as welcoming arms. There was grace and ancient peace in the majestic size of the place and also in the protective embrace of the huge live oaks that dotted the lawn. Similar scenes were familiar from a hundred magazine pictures and movies about the Old South, so Regina was forced to wonder if she only imagined its air of gracious hospitality, gracious living, or if it was real. Either way, it was still impressive.

"Come inside a moment," Kane said as he pulled up on the circular drive before the front door and started to get out. "I'm sure I can find you a cup of coffee."

She settled more firmly in her seat. Voice stiff, she said, "No, thanks."

"I'll be a few minutes, and you may as well be comfortable."

"No," she repeated more forcefully.

A faint smile tugged one corner of his mouth and he shook his head. "This isn't a seduction scene, if that's what you're thinking. It's been a long time since I threw anybody down in the middle of a hardwood floor and had my way with them."

"I'm glad to hear it," she said tartly as she

looked away from the amusement in his eyes. "But I'll still wait here."

"Suit yourself."

Regina flinched as the truck door slammed shut behind him. Then she lifted a shoulder. Let him get mad, she didn't care. She hadn't been taken in by his maneuvering, and wasn't going to be. That he'd gone striding into the house like a man who really had forgotten some papers changed nothing. She sighed, then leaned her head against the back of the seat.

The mental image his words had sketched was a potent one. She could almost see Kane drawing a woman down with him to a polished, rug-strewn floor. His shoulders would block out the light as he hovered above her. Behind his head, the celestial blue of the painted ceiling would swim with a misty swirl of clouds and cherubs and shimmering sun rays. Then he would —

A light tap came on the window beside Regina. The daydream fled and she swung with a sharp gasp to see an older woman standing beside the truck. She was slender and poised, her hair graying in a manner as natural as it was attractive. She bore a strong resemblance to Kane. Regina reached to wind down the glass.

"Good morning, my dear. I'm Vivian

Benedict, Kane's aunt. He told me you were out here. Won't you come inside for a cup of coffee, or tea? I have a nice fig cake, warm from the oven."

"Oh, I don't think —"

"Nonsense! Everybody needs a little pick-me-up this time of morning." The older woman reached for the door handle and pulled it open, rattling on in the easy manner of someone who loved to talk. "I understand you're interested in his grandmother's old jewelry. I can tell you about a great many of the pieces, where they came from, whom they belonged to — more so than Mr. Lewis can, I daresay. His wife, Miss Mary Sue, was a good friend of my mother's, and Kane's mother, Donna, and I played together as girls long before we became sisters-in-law. We were sometimes allowed to dress up in Miss Mary Sue's jewels, under strict supervision, of course. Come now, I simply won't take no for an answer."

It was impossible to resist that gently persistent urging. In any case, Regina wasn't sure she wanted to try. The house intrigued her with its aged grandeur. Kane's aunt was as charming as she was talkative. And it hardly seemed Kane would be likely to throw her down in the living room or anywhere else with the older woman on the premises.

She really had misjudged him. She hoped he didn't realize how much, but suspected he had sent his aunt because he understood her feelings only too well.

Why was he being so nice to her? she wondered. Was this the famous Southern hospitality everybody talked about, or something extra? What was he after with his kindness and questioning? What did he hope to gain when he had no idea who she was or why she was in Turn-Coupe?

At least, she hoped he had none.

She shouldn't be here, she thought as she climbed the steps to the front door and stepped into the long central hall that stretched through the house to French doors at the far end. She should be in town making as nice as possible to Lewis Crompton instead of riding around the countryside with his grandson. It had been ridiculous to let herself be distracted and more stupid still to think she was going to get anything from a lawyer.

For all she knew, the elaborate schedule Kane had given for his grandfather might have been a fabrication, and the old gentleman was wondering where she was and why she hadn't contacted him this morning.

She should insist that Kane take her straight back to the motel, then call Crompton at the funeral home. Yes, that was exactly what she should do at the first opportunity.

With that plan in mind, Regina felt better. She was even able to relax a little as she was led into the back wing of the house and seated in a bright breakfast room done in shades of fresh green and located just off an expansive country kitchen. The spicy aroma of the fig cake filled the air. The piece put on her plate was thick, moist, studded with pieces of dark and sweet preserved fruit, and glazed with a warm caramel sauce rich with pecans. The china it was served on was eggshell-thin Old Paris, the napkin beside it starched damask, and the fork she was handed ornate and heavy sterling. Against her will, Regina was impressed.

She was out of her depth.

"This is very nice," she said, "but I thought Kane was only going to be a minute."

"You like the cake? It's a recipe I'm developing for *Southern Living Magazine*."

"They pay you?"

"No, no, it's just something to keep my mind occupied, though my waistline would be in better shape if I'd pick another hobby. As for Kane, you'll have to forgive him, my

dear. He had a couple of calls to return —
he's so busy these days." The older woman
brought her own cake and coffee and seated
herself opposite Regina.

Regina watched Kane's aunt a moment.
She was a little plump maybe, but had fine
eyes and gracefully molded facial features.
Though she joked about her appearance, it
was obvious it didn't bother her; she had absolutely none of the air of an aging female
straining after her youth. Her dress of
cotton knit in a vivid teal was generously cut
and the same color as her eyes. The smile
with which she returned Regina's gaze was
open and serene. It was also a little quizzical.

"I . . . It's very kind of you to take pity on
me," Regina said, looking down at her plate
and picking up her fork to cut into her cake.

"Actually," Vivian Benedict said, "I had
an ulterior motive, or perhaps I should be
honest and admit it was vulgar curiosity. I
spoke to Mr. Lewis this morning, you see,
and he told me about the incident yesterday
with the old coffin."

"Oh." Regina's mouth was suddenly too
dry to chew the bite of warm, moist and delicious cake that she'd just taken.

"Just so," the other woman said with a wry
smile. "I didn't tell Kane I knew, of course."

Regina gave her an inquiring look.

"Why didn't I? To be honest, I wanted to see if he'd tell me. The explanation should be entertaining, or so I thought."

Regina swallowed before she said, "That might depend on your point of view."

"You don't think it's funny, then," Vivian said. "Perhaps I misunderstood the situation."

"It was just . . . embarrassing."

"Oh. Yes, I see how it might have been. Knowing Kane, I doubt he made it any easier."

Regina murmured something noncommittal, unable to correct the impression, but doubtful about agreeing.

Laughter sprang into the other woman's eyes. "I may have brought Kane up, my dear, but I have few illusions about him. He's a rascal, like both his father and his uncle, my late husband. I had my hands full with that boy, I can tell you, after his parents were killed."

"Killed?"

"Drowned, I should say, in a freak accident while deep-sea fishing off Grand Isle. Kane had stayed behind with me that weekend since he was only ten and recovering from the measles, and both our families lived here together in this monstrosity of a house. Afterward, we just kept on, my husband, Kane and I, and I feel blessed to have been allowed to do that since my John and I never had children."

"He was lucky to have you," Regina said, thinking of her own experience with being left when her parents were gone.

"Maybe, but you can see why he feels so strongly about the family he has left, particularly his grandfather. Also why he's so protective."

"I suppose," Regina said dubiously. "He was certainly suspicious of me."

Vivian Benedict pursed her lips, then sighed. "I'm afraid he has little faith in women except those who are related to him. He was engaged to a local girl a few years back, Francie, a blond beauty queen. But her mother was one of these women who live and breathe beauty contests, modeling, Hollywood gossip, and so on. She filled Francie's head with big ideas. Her junior year in college, Francie dropped out of school and went off to New Orleans for a job at some television studio. After a few weeks, she called Kane and told him she was in terrible pain with an ectopic pregnancy and needed emergency surgery that was going to cost five thousand dollars. She'd lost her job, had no insurance, she said, and her mother wouldn't help because she thought it was Kane's responsibility. Kane drove down at once with the money, which he could ill afford since he'd just started his legal practice. He wanted to stay for the surgery, but Francie said no. Her mother would be with her and was furious with Kane and would likely cause a big scene if she saw him. Later, Francie called again and said there had been complications and she needed another ten thousand." Vivian Benedict shook her head slowly as she held Regina's gaze. "I suppose you can guess where this is going?"

"It was all a lie," Regina said, her voice taut.

"Exactly. When Kane insisted on contacting the hospital, Francie wouldn't tell him where she had been, wouldn't name the doctor. It was only when Kane began to talk about legal action against whatever quack she'd seen that the truth came out. There had never been a pregnancy, ectopic or otherwise. The money was to have gone to finance a trip to Los Angeles."

"Unbelievable."

"Kane has never said much about it, but it hit him hard. He loved Francie, or thought he did. He had given her his promise and his ring and fully intended to marry her when she was ready to settle down. Family and children have always meant a lot to him. To use something so personal and intimate as the promise of a child to extort money from him — well, he was never quite the same toward women afterward."

"It seems unfair to blame all females for what one did to him."

His aunt lifted a shoulder. "Most men take that kind of thing badly."

"Even those with a nickname like Sugar Kane?"

As Regina spoke, it occurred to her that she wasn't so different from Kane. She mistrusted men because of what one had done to her, didn't she? Strange that she had never considered it in quite that light before. Commonality with Kane, however, was the last thing she needed to feel at this moment.

"You're thinking there must have been times when the shoe was on the other foot?" his aunt asked. "Oh, Kane was a little wild, and he certainly loved the ladies, but he was never heartless or careless. Even when Francie first said she was pregnant, he had doubts because he had done his best to make sure it didn't happen."

"Always in control," Regina murmured.

Vivian stared at her a moment. "I see he

has his work cut out for him with you."

"Hardly," she replied with dry humor. "I won't be here that long."

"We'll see," Kane's aunt said, and smiled.

There was no answer for that. Regina ate the last of her cake and complimented her hostess on it as she pushed her plate aside. Vivian got up to refill their cups, then sat back down again. Regina brushed away a drop of coffee that had landed on her saucer's porcelain rim before she spoke again.

"So what can you tell me about the Crompton jewelry? I'm fascinated since there are some truly exquisite pieces in the collection."

"Most are Victorian since that was Miss Mary Sue's preference. Mr. Lewis always called it his wife's collection, but he gave most of it to her, you know, over nearly forty years of marriage. They used to scour the antique shops back when the pieces were plentiful and few cared much about them. His wife adored dressing up, and she and Mr. Lewis often went down to New Orleans for the opera and the symphony. They were active on the country club and political circuits in town, too. She wore the pieces often, so they are a potent reminder of the past to Mr. Lewis."

"I wonder why he chose to sell," Regina offered carefully.

"There may be a connection with the suit, as Kane thinks, but it could also mean he's letting go because he's getting serious about his lady friend, Miss Elise, after all these years."

Seeing a chance to segue into a subject of greater interest to her, Regina said, "From all appearances, Crompton's Funeral Home has been around a long time."

"Appearances being, primarily, the age of the coffin in Mr. Lewis's parlor?" the other woman said with a quick laugh. "I'd have really loved to have seen his face when he opened the lid and saw you two. He's always saying he keeps that thing on hand in case of an emergency, but I don't think that's exactly what he had in mind."

"I should hope not," Regina returned, then added, "No longer than I've known him, I can just hear him saying something like that."

"You'd better believe it. Black humor more or less goes with the job, you know."

"I imagine it might be necessary, a form of relief."

Vivian Benedict agreed. "Human beings aren't always at their best in times of grief. The tales Mr. Lewis could tell if he just would! I've seen him shake his head a thousand times over families and how they come to blows or hair pulling over the simplest things, such as whether to have singing at the funeral, or their loved one's favorite color. And, of course, the very worst arguments are always about money. You know, who's going to pay and who will inherit."

"I'd imagine the skeletons sometimes rattle in the background, too." Regina, listening to her own voice, was amazed at its lightness.

"It can be interesting who shows up for the service," Kane's aunt agreed. "At the service for an elderly woman who died not long ago, who should walk through the chapel door except her arch enemy? They'd had words decades ago over a tree on their joint property line and had carried on a running battle about it ever since. But it seems the old dear was really broken up about the death of her adversary, that their feud was what kept her alive. At any rate, she died herself a short time later."

"People do get irate over property and money," Regina observed encouragingly as she swirled the dregs at the bottom of her coffee cup.

"That's certainly so. Another tale that went around was about the Widow Landry who had been married to an old skinflint. After the funeral, she searched high and low for the money he'd been squirreling away for years, but couldn't find it anywhere. So she had him disinterred, and there it was, sewn into the lining of his suit."

"He tried to take it with him." Regina laughed as she spoke; she couldn't help it.

"And almost succeeded, though I think, considering the state of it, I might have let him have it!"

"I should think so," Regina agreed, wrinkling her nose and shaking her head so that wisps of red hair, curling from the humidity, went flying around her face.

"You two sound positively ghoulish," Kane commented as he strolled into the room and headed for the coffeepot. His gaze lingered on her hair several seconds before he went on. "I might have expected it from you, Aunt Vivian, as one of the hazards of living with an undertaker's kin, but I'm surprised at Regina."

"She's very polite and has a well-developed sense of the ridiculous," his aunt said, her expression amused yet loving, as she held her nephew's gaze. "Unlike some I know."

He laughed. "You think I need a personality adjustment, too? I expect that's something else you and Regina can agree on."

His aunt protested, and the banter, humorous and saying next to nothing, continued until he and Regina left the house. There were no further chances for questions or probing. She might almost have thought it was deliberate if she wanted to be paranoid. But that would mean Kane had guessed she was searching out information, and that was impossible.

Wasn't it?

5

Pops was a wily old fox, Kane thought. He'd categorically refused to alter his usual schedule to see Regina that morning. Now he was making himself scarce for the rest of the day. When Kane called the funeral home office to confirm the meeting with Regina, he was told his grandfather couldn't make it. The tentative dinner afterward at Hallowed Ground was also off. Pops had received a call from a longtime friend who wanted to discuss hometown funeral arrangements for a brother who had passed away in another state. Naturally, such an appeal took precedence.

Kane didn't doubt the call had been received, but did question the necessity of his grandfather canceling the afternoon session with Regina in order to accommodate a friend. It was possible Pops felt Regina was being adequately entertained and had decided to get a sad task out of the way while it was on his mind. More likely, he was up to something.

His grandfather could be reconsidering

selling the jewelry, Kane thought, putting off the appraisal until he was more certain. He could also be matchmaking since he seemed to think Kane was working too hard and needed the distraction of female companionship, especially a certain redhead. Either way, it made Kane wary, very wary indeed.

Regina showed no inclination to take advantage of their extended time together. She was pleasant enough over the lunch they shared at a local café, but no more than that. In fact, she seemed far more interested in his legal practice and the case he was working on than she did in him as a man. When he was forced to report the postponement of her meeting with his grandfather, she opted at once to return to the motel.

Her attitude did little for his ego. He was used to women who at least pretended to enjoy his company and seemed reluctant to leave it. It felt peculiar to know the shoe was on the other foot. Not that there was anything personal about his interest; he was susceptible to Regina's brand of attraction, yes, but that didn't mean a thing except that he'd been too long without a woman. It was interesting to feel alive again in that way, though not particularly comfortable.

Luke had also been taken with Regina,

but then, his cousin just plain liked women — all ages, shapes and sizes. There was hardly a night went by when he wasn't out with some female somewhere. How he kept them straight, Kane never knew. His cousin made it look easy, however — they didn't call him Luke-de-la-Nuit for nothing. If Kane suspected Luke's wicked ways hid problems he didn't want to face, well, they never talked about it. Kane had demons enough of his own.

As far as Luke taking a serious interest in Regina, that was unlikely. At least, not without his cousin making doubly sure Kane had no claim. There might have been a time when he and Luke had competed over everything, including women, but those days were long gone. All that remained was the camaraderie of pretending. Or Kane thought that was all.

He noticed the burgundy Ford Taurus parked across the street from the motel as he returned to his own truck after seeing Regina to her room. He gave the guy behind the wheel a close inspection. There was nothing unusual about him; he was just a plain, ordinary guy reading a newspaper. Regardless, Kane caught himself frowning.

One problem was that the man was a stranger, someone who couldn't be matched with any local family resemblance. Turn-Coupe had been isolated for a long portion of its history and the resulting inter-marriages had given most people a genetic similarity that allowed them to be placed in family groups with considerable accuracy. On top of that was the fact that people seldom sat waiting in cars in Turn-Coupe except in grocery or discount store parking lots, or maybe in front of a drugstore; there was just no reason for it. If the guy was from out of town but had a clandestine appointment at the motel, then he should have been holed up in one of the rooms instead of parked in plain sight. Add the fact that he didn't seem to realize he was as conspicuous as a bump on a log, and it was easy to guess he was an outsider unused to small-town ways.

So what the hell was he doing in Turn-Coupe?

Swerving from his intended path, Kane headed toward the motel office. As he stepped inside, Betsy looked up from where she sat with her feet propped on an open desk drawer, a thick April Halstead romance novel in one hand and a juicy apple in the other. Kane jerked a thumb in the direction of the Taurus across the street. "That guy over there registered, by any chance?"

Betsy raised herself up enough to take a look out the window, then gave a derisive snort. "Not so you'd notice. He came into the coffee shop around lunchtime, bought the cheapest thing on the menu, asked a lot of questions. On his way out, he picked up a free paper left over from this morning. He's been parked over there ever since."

"What kind of questions?" Kane leaned on the registration desk as he waited for her answer.

"All kinds. What kind of town Turn-Coupe is, main industry, jobs available, beer joints, stuff like that. He also wanted to know how many guests I have and what kind of place I ran. I think he suspected it was some kind of by-the-hour dive, but I told him it was nothing that profitable." She grinned. "Then he wanted to know if I had anybody interesting, anybody different, registered."

"You tell him?"

Betsy put her book down and tossed her apple core at a trash can. "I didn't crawl out from under a cabbage leaf this morning, honey pie. No, I didn't tell him. But you know what I think?"

Kane shook his head, his gaze inquiring.

"It's my guess he's some kind of private eye."

"You sure you haven't been reading too many mysteries?"

She ignored that. "He's just got that look, you know? Could be he's after some lowlife running around on his wife, or maybe a deadbeat dad."

Kane tilted his head as he noted her dubious expression. "But you don't think so."

"There's something more interesting going on around here, now isn't there?"

"You think he has something to do with the trial?"

"Makes sense to me." She waited, her gaze expectant.

"But why would he ask after your guests? Who's he after?" Kane had his own ideas, but it couldn't hurt to hear hers.

"Your guess is as good as mine. The only people I have just now are a couple from out of town visiting their daughter, a construction crew, a cotton harvester salesman, and your Regina Dalton."

"She isn't mine," he said curtly.

"Better luck next time." Betsy grinned. "But you'll have to admit she's the kind a man might hang around to watch. Or could be your yo-yo out there is a boyfriend, maybe even a husband."

"What makes you say that?" It was an effort not to frown.

"Just guessing. Could be he's even looking out for you. Better watch yourself, Sugar Kane."

"I'll do that," he said with irony, then added as he turned to leave, "Thanks, Betsy."

"Any time." She was absorbed in her novel again before the door closed behind him.

As he drove out of the parking lot, Kane gave the man with the newspaper a closer look. He was nondescript only from a distance. Close up, he looked a lot like a possum, with ashy gray-brown hair, a straggling beard that made his face look dirty, eyes set far back in his head, and a nose as sharp as an ice pick.

Kane felt his back and neck stiffen in primordial instinct. Two to one the Taurus was a rental, but he memorized the license plate number anyway. He knew someone who could trace it in about two seconds flat.

Melville Brown was in his office when Kane poked his head inside. His law partner was on the phone, holding the receiver under his chin and taking notes at the same time. He glanced up and a grin slashed the clear, cinnamon brown of his face. Waving Kane inside, he ended his phone conversation, tossed his pen down on his neat stack of papers, then leaned back in his chair and laced his fingers across his waist. "I hear," he said in a smooth, molasses-rich voice, "that you've had yourself a busy morning. Or a busy couple of days. Now what's this about a coffin?"

"Don't start," Kane said with a grimace as he dropped into the chair in front of the desk and stretched his long legs out in front of him.

"That bad, huh?"

"I made a jackass out of myself. But I swear Regina Dalton is up to something."

"Excuses, excuses," his partner murmured.

Kane's glance was jaundiced. "You'll be talking out of the other side of your mouth when she sets us up."

The humor faded. "You're serious, aren't you?"

"As a hanging judge."

"You really think she has something to do with the case?"

There was no question which case Melville was talking about. For the two of them, there was only one these days. Kane said in brooding answer, "She's from New York."

"Lots of people are," the other man said with calm reason.

"I don't like the coincidence. Besides,

I've got this feeling."

"Oh, well, that's different. Logical, even."

"She bothers me."

Melville said nothing.

As Kane met his gaze, he could see his partner was trying not to grin. "Not like that."

"Sure. Whatever you say. Carry on, then — in a manner of speaking. In the meantime, want to hear what I dug up today?"

Melville enjoyed puns. Kane awarded this pair a long-suffering sigh as he said, "Give it to me."

"Seems Berry struck a deal with a black religious conference a while back to buy their graveyards and give thousands of black church workers jobs selling burial contracts in Berry Association, Inc. How about that?"

"Sounds good on the surface. What's the catch?"

"The contracts were only for burial. None of them included normal services such as embalming and viewing at Berry's funeral homes. Unlike similar deals struck with white church groups, which did include those things."

"Good grief."

"Exactly." Melville's smile was grim. "Berry's making several million a year off these church folks while paying them peanuts. On top of that, they can't go to his funeral homes for their services, but have to put poor old black granny in a hearse and drive miles to find a more accommodating funeral home. When they've done that, and paid extra for it, *then* they can use a Berry-owned graveyard."

"Isn't that a blatant example of discrimination for this day and age?"

"Guess he didn't expect to get caught. But I can't wait to see if his lawyers dare introduce Berry's record for creating jobs for African-Americans."

"And you think they might?" Kane said, alerted by an undertone in his partner's voice.

"It's possible. I have it on good authority they expect to pack the jury with black faces."

Kane's thoughts moved at the pace of lightning while he met his partner's expectant expression. "They intend to frame the trial along regional lines — Northern liberal versus Southern conservative."

"Your granddad will be portrayed as the hidebound Southern gentleman in his mansion, a regular Legree of the funeral industry, trying to block progress from coming to our fair community. Berry will be shown as modern, reformist, and from the Northeast, therefore naturally without prejudice."

"A flimflam show," Kane said in disgust.

Melville gave him a tight smile before segueing from his normal, cultured tones into a *Gone with the Wind* parody. "They be thinkin' they can come down here and pull the wool over the eyes of us po' sharecroppers, that we be easy led by our feelings and don't know from nothin' 'bout the *law.*"

"Are they in for a shock?" Conviction layered Kane's tone.

"We hope."

A small silence fell. After a moment, Kane said, "So did Pops's settlement offer go out today?"

Melville gave a judicious nod. "I spoke to the head legal honcho at the New York firm myself, with a follow-up in all the proper legalese by Express Mail. They'll get back to us after the offer has been presented to their client."

"Any feedback on how it might go over?"

"It was all very cover-their-asses cagey. No discussion, just thank you and good day. Frankly, I think it has about as much chance of being accepted as a poodle at a polecat convention."

"Berry doesn't have long to make up his

mind, not if jury selection begins in less than a week."

"True."

With a thoughtful frown, Kane said, "You want to handle that part?"

"Jury selection? You thinking it might play better to the media if I'm the one to object to too many black faces?"

"I'm thinking," Kane said, "that you're a good judge of character, no matter how it's packaged. I'm also thinking that African–American jurors might be a good thing if you can spring that surprise you have in mind."

"Berry's use of the black churches? You've got a point. But this will be district court, not Turn-Coupe. The black community around here knows Mr. Lewis. That won't be the case in Baton Rouge."

"Think we can take the chance?"

Melville gave a decided nod. "It'll be pure pleasure to make it work."

They exchanged a glance of easy and wordless understanding. The two of them had been roommates at LSU when both were in pre-law, then had gone on to Tulane together. There had been raised eyebrows when they set up a joint practice in a renovated mansion on the courthouse square, but they'd kept it low-key, accepting whatever came their way until people got used to the idea. They'd both worked long, hard hours, and their clientele had built slowly but surely until it was now as much as they could handle.

Kane rubbed a hand over his face, then gave a rasping sigh. "You know, I've got so used to looking for an angle behind everything, some devious purpose like this jury business, that I automatically think everybody must have an agenda. Do you think I've lost all ability to tell the difference between a scam artist and someone doing their job?"

Melville opened his eyes wide. "You talking about this bunch of New York pinstripe lawyers?"

"Wiseass," Kane said amiably. "I'm talking about Regina Dalton, and you know it."

"Yankee woman's got your thinking so screwed you're not sure how to place her, that it?"

Kane shifted a hard shoulder. "I can't believe what my instinct's telling me. Or don't want to believe it. She doesn't seem the type to con an old man."

"Sounds complicated."

"It is. She is. She says one thing, but I see something else in her eyes."

"Oh, man," Melville said with a quick shake of his head. "This one I've got to meet."

"Suit yourself. But I can handle her and I will, one way or another."

"You're sure of that, are you?"

Kane gave him a jaundiced stare.

"Right," Melville said, speculation joining the bright amusement in his eyes. "I'm dying to see how it turns out."

"So am I," Kane answered. "So am I."

Regina stood to one side of the window and carefully shifted the drape so she could see out. The car was still there, across the street from the motel.

Her chest felt tight, and her tension headache drummed behind her eyes. It had been bad enough fending off Sugar Kane Benedict's insidious questions and comments all day. She didn't need this added trouble.

For a few seconds, she played with the idea that Kane might have posted the man to watch her. Then she dismissed it. For one thing, she'd given him no reason to think it was necessary. For another, he seemed too open and aboveboard for such tactics. The best reason, however, was because he'd proven that when he wanted something, he went after it himself. As he was after her.

That was exactly what was behind his attention. She had suspected it when he first showed up this morning, but after the hours they had spent together, she was positive.

If Kane hadn't posted the man across the street, then who had? Lewis Crompton, perhaps? It seemed unlikely, but stranger things had happened. Of course, the watcher could also be after someone else entirely, such as a girlfriend sleeping around on him, a straying wife, or a drug connection.

There was one other possibility.

Swinging away from the window, she moved to the bed and sat down beside the phone on the bedside table. Drawing a deep breath, she closed her eyes and touched the pendant at her throat for luck and reassurance. Then she picked up the receiver.

The phone on the other end rang once, twice — distant, strident sounds. Then the voice of her cousin's houseman and bodyguard came on the line. "Gervis Berry residence. Who may I say is calling?"

"Regina, Michael. Let me talk to him."

"Good. He's anxious to hear from you."

The hold button clicked and strains of a Mozart concerto came on to pacify her while she waited. She listened impatiently, thinking it was just like Gervis to put something so foreign to his own personality on his phone system in pretense of a cultural background he secretly despised. At the same time, she could imagine the houseman stalking through the rooms of the spacious 72nd Street co-op, knocking on the door of the study.

She began a mental countdown from ten, betting with herself about how long it would take her cousin to answer the phone. He wouldn't pick up at ten or nine because he had to impress on her that he was a busy man. He wouldn't answer on eight or seven because he'd want to make her anxious so he'd be in control. He wouldn't get it on six or five because he enjoyed having people wait on his convenience. He wouldn't touch it on four or three because he liked thinking he could master his own urges. He would answer before one, though, because he couldn't stand to wait for what he wanted.

Five, four, three —

"Gina, baby, what's going on down there?"

Right on time.

"Not a lot," she answered, her voice carefully neutral. "I've made contact with Mr. Crompton and have an agreement to do a full appraisal of his jewelry."

"Forget the damn jewelry. I want to know

what you've found out."

"I haven't had time to —"

"Well, make time, because I don't have all year. Get your fanny in gear. Why else do you think you're down there?"

"It's crossed my mind to wonder," she said tightly. "Gervis, you didn't send someone to check up on me, did you?"

"Come again?"

"Some goon has this motel staked out. I think he may be watching me."

There was a small silence on the other end. Then her cousin spoke in pained disbelief. "Jeez, Gina, you don't think I have anything to do with it?"

"I don't know. That's why I'm asking."

"I trust you like nobody else, you know that. It's probably nothing, some reporter or something."

"All right." She dragged air into her lungs and let it out again. "I guess I'm getting a little crazy with this whole thing. You have to hear what happened." In a few succinct phrases, she told him about being locked in the coffin.

"I can't believe this stuff," Gervis said, irate for her sake. "What kind of people are they down there?"

"Intelligent ones who don't mind going a little over the edge," she answered. "They are also very careful, especially Kane Bene-dict."

"Come on, baby, you know you can run rings around this guy."

Her cousin meant he thought he could, Regina thought. He fully expected his team of lawyers to squash the competition like stepping on a poison-drugged cockroach. She had felt virtually the same way before coming to Turn-Coupe. Now she wasn't so sure.

Speaking distinctly, she said, "You may have to rethink this situation."

"What makes you say that?" His query was sharp. Gervis didn't miss much, even if he was going a little soft as he let the good life he'd made for himself get to him.

"Crompton's grandson didn't shut me up in a casket for fun, no matter what he said to pass it off that way," she replied, hearing the strain she couldn't help in her voice. "He suspects something, suspects me."

"Now why would he do that?"

"Because he isn't some Southern bumpkin without brains or imagination, a point you might remember for future refer-ence. Because I turned up at his grandfa-ther's house a bit too conveniently to suit him, and because he caught me smiling just a little more than I should while his grandfather and I were looking at the jewelry. I just don't know, Gervis. I didn't like this from the start, and now I have a bad feeling about it."

"You're shook, that's all. Take my word, it'll get easier once you get used to it."

"I don't want to get used to it!" Regina cried. "If I had known what it would be like, I'd never have agreed. I can't imagine what you were thinking to ask me."

"You have the credentials, baby. You're a natural."

"Yes, but to send me down here with so little advance preparation was criminal. You didn't tell me nearly enough about Crompton's grandson!"

"Who knew he was a maniac? Anyway, you think I wanted to send you? I care about you, kid. But there was no one else, especially no one I can trust the way I do you."

The words sounded sincere. They gave her the courage to say what she was thinking. "I'm not sure I can go through with it. I'd really like to come home."

"Don't get cold feet on me now, baby. We've got them on the run. They're offering to settle."

Relief washed over her. "You're going to accept?"

"Not on your life. They're caving. They

know they can't win. All I have to do is reach out and take it all."

"You don't understand these people, Gervis. The settlement may be like a — a peace offering because they prefer to be fair. Throw it back in their faces and you'll be sorry."

"So now you're an expert on Southern gentlemen? Just what happened in that casket, baby?"

"Listen to me, Gervis. I've met Lewis Crompton and Kane Benedict, talked to them, seen them in action. You haven't. They aren't playing games, and they won't run. You'll be fighting this battle on their turf, before a judge and jury they understand but about whom you don't have the first —"

"Yeah, yeah," her cousin interrupted. "We got that covered."

"I'm trying to tell you —"

"Well, don't, because I'm not listening. You got a job to do down there. You said you'd do it, and now I want results."

"Gervis, please."

His voice softened as he said, "You owe me, Gina. You know you owe me."

Old guilt, as predictable as it was inconvenient, rose inside her. Wincing at its sting, she said, "You've been more than generous, done more for me than I can ever repay. I know that. But this is different."

"You and me against the world, Gina. We're family. We stick together. We help each other out. That's how it's always been, how it'll always be."

The words triggered a thousand memories, each of them colored with gratitude and fleeting affection. The two of them lying on the grass in Central Park and eating cotton candy, taking in movies, staring out at the world from the top of the Empire State Building, going to ball games at Shea, riding out to the beach at Fire Island. All the rare treats of her childhood had come from Gervis. Later, he had held her hand, stayed close after the terrible time with that creep, Thomas. He'd been there at the hospital, been there for her every time. He was always there for her, as she should be for him.

A lump rose in her throat as she said, "I know, Gervis, really I do. I'm just not sure this is going to work."

"You're doing fine. Sounds to me like you've got the old man's grandson running after you because he's interested instead of suspicious. You could be thinking about how to use that, you know."

A note of impatience could be heard beneath the surface approval. He was getting ready to hang up. "It doesn't mean any-thing," she said despairingly. "He thinks I'm up to no good."

Gervis laughed, a coarse sound. "Then you'll have to change his mind, won't you? It shouldn't be hard. You can string him along as well as the old man."

"I told you —"

"I know what you told me, baby," her cousin said, his voice hardening. "I heard every single word. But I don't think you're really trying. You're holding back, Gina, and that's not good. I've got millions riding on this suit, you hear me? I don't have time for excuses, can't sit around while you wring your hands and worry about every-thing under the sun except my problems. I need you to get your job done. I need it now."

He was right, she had been thinking of herself. "I'll do my best, but it takes time to get close to people."

"I don't have time, baby. Maybe you should concentrate on Benedict since you've got him going your way. Find out what strategy he plans to use in court, what tricks he's got up his sleeve. I want every detail you can wring out of him or pick up when you're around him, right down to whether he means to wear Skivvies to the trial. I want it all, you hear me? Every last scrap. But most of all, I want the dirt on Benedict's old granddad, the secrets he'd off his own sweet mama to keep. You find out for me, or —"

"Or what, Gervis?" she asked, holding the receiver so tightly her fingers were numb.

The only answer was a dial tone.

Dudley Slater watched the light go out in the motel room. He yawned and stretched, trying to work the kink out of his back. He was getting too old for this crap. What he wouldn't give for a nice, soft bed. Especially if it had that red-haired piece in it. She'd be a handful, he figured. He wondered what color her nipples were, if they were pale pink to go with her pale skin, or more a light brown. Yeah, and if she was as red down there as she was on top. He'd give a lot to find out. Wouldn't take much. He'd opened the cheap lock on her door once already today, and nobody the wiser. Doing it again would take maybe ten whole seconds. Then it would be, "Hello there, honey pot. Drip some of it on old Dudley."

Couldn't chance it. That'd spook her, and Regina Dalton had other, more important, uses.

She was his ticket out of this crummy life:

living out of his car, nickel-and-dime scut work, taking orders from bastards like Berry. He was going to trail her right to the goods, let her sniff out the story for him. She had the cover after all, and he didn't.

Man, he was going to make it big on this one. Then he was headed for fun in sunny Florida. He'd sprawl on the beach while some hot little thing in a thong bikini brought him piña coladas and spread warm oil in all the right places. Now that was his idea of living. Hell, he might even work on that novel he'd had in the back of his head for years.

Berry was a real hard case. Holding him up for a wad of cash was going to take some doing. But Dudley Slater was no softy, either, no sir. It'd be pure pleasure to take that manipulating, egotistical little SOB, Gervis Berry, for a pile. He'd have to be careful, though, Dudley thought as he scratched his itchy beard. Had to keep it on the up-and-up. He couldn't afford any slipups, sure didn't want to be looking over his shoulder the rest of his life. Berry was mob connected, he'd bet his last pint of blood on it. If he wasn't, it was only because the *Cosa Nostra* couldn't stand the arrogant bastard, either.

Dudley shifted position again and cursed

raggedly as he let out a groan. God, but his back was in bad shape. He was going to have to make a move soon, in more ways than one. That red-haired witch had given him a once-over before she went inside; he was sure of it. He thought he'd attracted the attention of the dude in the pickup, too. That was the trouble with dinky little towns. Too hard to blend into the woodwork.

He was hungry enough to chew the steering wheel. The BLT he'd had for lunch was long gone. Steak and a baked potato, that's what he needed. Fat chance. Junk food was all he could afford, timewise. Couldn't risk missing anything.

He leaned over to paw through the litter of candy wrappers and empty chip bags, searching for something he might have missed. A bag of peanuts. It would have to do. The coffee in his thermos was lukewarm, but better than nothing.

He needed to speed things up here. Not only was he sick to death of this game, but the trial was fast heading his way. If that bitch who owned the motel was any indication, he didn't have a hope in hell of getting anything useful out of these people himself. But that was all right, because gorgeous Regina Dalton did. And she would if somebody would just light a fire under her cute little butt. He'd have to put his mind to the problem. He knew how he'd like to do it, but hey, first things first.

What if, instead, he just gave her a little hand at getting to the lawyer.

Now that was an idea. He popped a handful of salted peanuts into his mouth, then followed them with a swallow of warm coffee. Staring squint-eyed through the windshield, he chewed slowly.

He stopped.

Better yet, he could do a preemptive strike, get in ahead of her. Berry might go for that. No plaintiff, no trial, right? Right.

Yeah, that just might get it.

Yeah.

Old Dudley liked having an alternate plan. Or two. If one thing didn't work, then the other would.

6

Regina half expected to find Kane at Hallowed Ground when she reached the house next morning since he seemed to appear every time she turned around. Lewis Crompton was alone, however, having his breakfast in a sun-splashed room with a Boston fern in the bay window behind the table and his big yellow cat sprawled on the floor beside him. The air was redolent with ham, eggs, chicory-laden coffee, and the heartwarming aroma of the hot golden biscuits stacked on a platter in the middle of the table.

Mr. Lewis rose to his feet as Regina was ushered into the room by the housekeeper. Brushing aside her apologies for appearing uninvited and disturbing him at his meal, he pressed her to have breakfast with him. She wasn't hungry, but accepted a cup of coffee because it appeared he wouldn't go on with his meal otherwise. The housekeeper brought another cup from a sideboard and poured the steaming brew while her employer seated Regina. Then the woman went away, leaving them alone.

Regina cleared her throat the instant the door closed, ready to begin her carefully worded effort to discover something of use to Gervis. Mr. Lewis forestalled her.

"I believe Kane took you out to see the lake yesterday," he said, all congeniality. "What did you think of it?"

"Beautiful, so peaceful," she answered. "I've never seen anything quite like it. But what I wanted to talk to you about was —"

"You met Luke, too, I hear. You really ought to go to his open house, my dear. Nobody throws a party quite like Luke. Why, that boy has more life in him than a one-legged, one-man band. You'd have a grand time."

"I'm sure you're right. About the jewelry, Mr. Crompton?"

The man across the table waved the silver knife he held in a dismissive gesture before using it to slit a biscuit. He tucked a slice of ham inside, then put it on a bread plate and slid it toward Regina. "Vivian said she spoke to you about it. She was right taken with you, I could tell. Mentioned you had the nicest smile, raved about your hair, of course."

Regina pushed the small plate with the biscuit back toward him. In exasperation, she said, "Mr. Crompton, if you don't want to sell your wife's jewelry collection, you have only to say so."

He studied her a long moment, a judicious expression on his fine old face. Then he put down his knife and heaved a sigh. "That's just it, my dear. I don't know whether I do or not."

"Because you've decided to marry again?"

He sat back in his chair in surprise before his expression turned drolly accepting. "Now who could've told you that? Not Kane, I'd imagine. Must have been Vivian."

"Are you sure the woman you're interested in would care for it?" Regina asked, sidestepping his question. "Some people prefer to have no reminder of a former spouse."

"True, true." He sighed. "But Miss Elise isn't the problem. It's Kane."

"Kane," she repeated in resignation.

"I never dreamed he might object. Now he has, I really feel I should make certain it's not just his pride talking. I mean — suppose he has some female in mind who he'd like to marry? He deserves the opportunity to give her his grandmother's trinkets if he's so minded."

Trinkets. That was an inadequate description if she'd ever heard one. "I see what you're saying," she said as patiently as she was able, "but do you think it's a real possibility?"

"I just don't know, which is the point. Now I realize it's an imposition to ask you to hold off. You must have other things to do besides hang around, waiting for an old man to come to a decision. But I'd take it as a favor if you'd give me the time to discover what's on Kane's mind."

His suggestion was perfect, exactly what she needed. It was so perfect, in fact, that suspicion rose immediately in her mind. She searched his lined and craggy face, looking for craftiness, deceit, or at least some idea of why he might be so accommodating. There was nothing in it except warm courtesy. Which might indicate that he was absolutely aboveboard, but could also mean that he was a certified master at guile and manipulation.

Either way, she couldn't afford to refuse. She even felt a little spurt of gladness that she had an excuse to stay. That was only because it made things easier from her point of view. Naturally.

She lowered her gaze to her coffee cup. "I suppose I can do that."

"Good," he said with satisfaction. "I'm

glad we got that settled."

"On the other hand," she went on with some hesitation as she watched the steam curl across the surface of her coffee, "as I'm already here and have nothing better to do, I could look at the pieces and give you a written estimate that you could hold until you're ready. You could call me in New York with your decision, and we could take it from there."

Even as she made the suggestion, she wondered what she was doing. If Gervis knew she was throwing away the chance to stay longer in Turn-Coupe, he would have a stroke. Regardless, she was driven by an attack of fairness she didn't quite understand. She almost hoped, in a way, that Mr. Lewis would take her up on her offer so she would no longer have an excuse for trespassing on his hospitality.

"Now, now," he said, easing the bread plate and biscuit toward her again, "there's no need for such a rush. You'll give yourself ulcers, you don't watch out. Just try a bite of this, then tell me what else you and Vivian found to talk about."

Regina had no intention whatever of eating the biscuit. As she told the older man about the visit with Kane's aunt, however, she reached out idly to pick up a bit of light brown biscuit crumb with the pressure of a fingertip, then put it on her tongue. A few minutes later, she picked up another. Then she broke a little of the crisp biscuit crust and ate it with the sliver of ham that was attached. Before she realized, the whole biscuit was gone.

"Hungry and didn't know it," Mr. Lewis said, slicing another biscuit, then reaching for ham. "All you young people with your juice and granola don't know what good food is anymore. A bite here, a snack there, eat on the run, never slow down to savor the flavors or enjoy a nice, quiet conversation, and you wonder why you're tired all the time. You're not really living, just going through the motions." He shook his head as he passed over the biscuit. "Pitiful."

He had a point. Regina leaned back in her chair, sipping the perfectly brewed coffee in its fragile china cup. It was amazingly quiet in the breakfast room. No traffic noises or other hints of the mechanized world intruded on the old house on its hill. Blue jays, cardinals and mockingbirds called back and forth in the garden beyond the bay window. She could even catch the sandpaper rasp of the cat's tongue as it groomed itself.

"I just might be able to get used to your way of doing things," she said with a whimsical smile. "It's so restful."

"Not much happens to make it otherwise. Usually." He was thinking of the suit, she thought, which was a subject Regina was suddenly reluctant to explore. She asked instead, "How long have you lived here — or is that a silly question?"

"The only silly question, so they say, is one unasked. If you mean how long I, personally, have lived here, the answer's all my life. If you're talking about my family, well, my great-granddaddy came from North Carolina in the 1830s. He and his wife and a pack of children traveled in a wagon pulled by oxen, along with a caravan of six other families. They stopped for a few years in Alabama, where a couple of the older kids got married, but they left the newlyweds behind and came on. Because of that, there are Cromptons scattered all across the South."

"Were the Benedicts one of the families in the caravan?"

He shook his leonine head. "They were already here when my folks made it. Nobody really knows how long they'd been holed up out on the lake, but it's a while."

"You're talking about the Native American bloodline, as long ago as that?"

"What? Oh, only Luke's bunch have Indian ancestors, but the rest were here anyway. Story goes, there were four brothers who left England in a hurry back in the 1700s. Something to do with the death of a sister's snake-mean husband, as I understand it. They tried their hands at piracy a couple of years, but finally landed in New Orleans. Not caring particularly for the strict Spanish government in power at the time, they pushed inland and wound up here."

"Fascinating," she said, leaning forward to pick up the second ham-filled biscuit. Then she paused and tilted her head. "Unless you're pulling my leg?"

"Would I do that?" he asked, his eyes twinkling.

"In a heartbeat."

"Yes, I guess I would," he allowed genially, "but not this time."

She believed him, which seemed strange but nice. "So what happened? How did the Benedicts manage to survive and multiply?"

"The oldest brother took a Scotswoman to wife somewhere in the Caribbean, one with hair every bit as fiery as yours and a temper to match. Kane comes from that line. The next married the Indian woman who had guided them to the lake, I think. Another kidnapped a Spanish woman who wasn't too unwilling to be spirited off, and the youngest wound up wed to a French-woman he found wandering around lost in the woods."

"And they all lived happily ever after," Regina said in dry mockery directed mostly at the romantic images conjured up in her own mind.

"You might say so. At least, they had long lives and big families. Oh, they had their tragedies and mysteries, their deaths from accidents and childhood diseases and whatnot. But they endured and they prospered. Now the woods are full of Benedicts."

"So it would seem." She paused to refill her coffee cup from the carafe that sat ready, then added to Mr. Lewis's, as well. "What kind of mysteries?"

"The usual," he said, amusement lingering around his mouth for the part of what he'd said that caught her interest. "Mainly who fathered whom, how so-and-so really died, which son ran with outlaws or whose daughter was a hoyden who got men killed in duels, which child wasn't right in the head, where somebody buried their gold in the old days."

Having so little family herself, Regina was always intrigued by the stories of other people's. Added to that, her own ancestors, so far as she knew, were fairly recent immigrants from Ireland and Germany. It was hard for her to imagine a clan as diverse or long entrenched as the one to which Kane belonged. She said, "The Benedicts sound pretty colorful."

Mr. Lewis pursed his lips. "I guess they are at that. Proud as Lucifer and touchy as all Hades, most of them. They've been known to take the law into their own hands, too, living so isolated out on the lake before there was much in the way of law and order. But the Benedicts live well, love hard, and pay their bills. They're good, strong stock, no finer people in this state, I'll stake my life on it. I'm proud to be associated with them."

"Especially one of them?" she said with a teasing note in her voice.

"I'm partial to my grandson, I'll admit, but there's a lot to be partial about. Kane's put his practice more or less on hold for the suit I've got going. All his energy and brain power are being channeled into the battle. His temper may be a mite short and his manners not quite up to par, but it would be a shame if anybody let such things stand in the way of seeing the fine man he is inside."

He was making excuses for Kane. Why? Did he think she and his grandson had got off on the wrong foot, so was trying to make it right? Or was he attempting to smooth Kane's way with her because he felt his grandson might be interested? Regina wasn't sure which idea disturbed her more.

She made no answer, but allowed a small silence to fall. Then she changed the subject by asking if the china they were using was antique. Her host was involved in a comical tale of how his wife had chosen the pattern for her wedding china back before World War II when the housekeeper appeared at the door.

"Mr. Kane's coming."

"Well now, Dora, you don't say." Mr. Lewis lifted a brow as he met his house-keeper's gaze. "This is a red-letter morning. I guess you'd better heat the biscuits back up. That's if Regina and I left any."

Some communication passed between the two of them, Regina thought, a shared opinion, perhaps, on the sudden influx of company at breakfast time. Their relation-ship seemed to have the ease that comes from long years.

Dora, a tall, rawboned black woman with a Native American cast to her features, wore her hair in two braids crossed over her head and had gold earrings flashing in her ears. She seemed an integral part of the household. Regina wasn't sure what she expected, but it wasn't an arrangement that closely mirrored the same position of responsibility held by Gervis's bodyguard and houseman. Regina watched the woman as she brought another cup and saucer and plate from the sideboard, then reached for the coffee carafe. It was better than wondering why Kane couldn't go away and let her get on with her job.

He appeared in the doorway seconds later. His greeting was polite; still the temperature of the room cooled by several degrees. Regina felt the muscles of her abdomen tighten in visceral reaction. Not all of it was wariness, however. A large part was sheer female response to the sight of his broad shoulders stretching the cloth of his knit shirt and the fresh scent of just-shaved-and-showered male that he brought with him into the room. To be unsettled so easily was annoying.

"Had breakfast?" his grandfather inquired.

"I'm not hungry," Kane answered, though he pulled out the chair at the place setting where Dora had just finished pouring his coffee. He waited until she had gathered the empty plates from the table and took them away before he sat down.

"Neither was Miss Regina. Must be something going around." Mr. Lewis kept his features perfectly straight, though his eyes gleamed.

"Actually, it's Miss Regina I came to see." Kane interjected irony into that title of respect as he looked straight at her for the first time.

"Yes?" Her smile felt pasted on.

"I'm interested in hearing what your connection might be with a notorious tabloid reporter named Dudley Slater."

Her reaction to the accusation she heard in his voice was instant and instinctive. "I don't know what you mean."

"No? You've never heard of him?"

"Afraid not. What makes you think I might have?"

"He's camped outside your door, for one thing."

Kane was talking about the man in the car across the street from the motel. She shook back her hair. "Really?"

He took a couple of folded pages from his shirt pocket and unfolded them, then tossed them over in front of her. "That's what he looks like, and also his rap sheet."

She glanced at the fax page, which showed a blurred photograph of a man with a thin face, sharp nose, and narrow, haggard eyes. After a moment, she looked up at Kane again. His gaze bored into hers. She blinked quickly in reflex action, though she recognized that was a mistake. With as much composure as she could manage, she said, "I saw this man across from the motel, I think, but he could be interested in anyone."

"He could, but I don't think he is." Kane's words were grim, though his attention seemed to wander an instant to where sunlight shafting through the window was warming the top of her head.

"Are you suggesting he's there because of me?"

His eyes narrowed at the amusement in her voice. "It crossed my mind."

Lewis Crompton cleared his throat with a loud rasp, a warning, apparently, for the accusation in his grandson's tone. He asked, "How did you find out about this reporter?"

"I noticed him yesterday and had Roan run a make on the rental car. The Taurus was picked up at the airport in Baton Rouge. Slater has a record a mile long for harassment, assault, breaking and entering, not to mention enough parking tickets to paper several rooms."

Breaking and entering. Regina turned those words over in her mind in dismay. At the same time, she watched the two men with care. If either of them had set this Dudley Slater to watch her, then the other didn't know about it. But she didn't think they were involved. No one could be that good at faking either the concern of Mr. Lewis or the grim effort to get to the bottom of the business that was plain in Kane's face. It was not a pleasant discovery.

"Who," she asked in clipped tones, "might Roan be, and just what is his part in this?"

"Sheriff Roan Benedict," Mr. Lewis answered in polite explanation. "He's the law here in Tunica Parish." Turning back to Kane, he went on, "Why would this Slater bother with Miss Regina? Why isn't he after me? Or you, for that matter?"

Kane looked at Regina, his gaze unyielding. "That's what I'm trying to find out."

"Maybe he thinks I'm a star witness," she quipped with more bravado than she felt.

"Could be," Kane allowed with a curt nod. "The only question is whether for the plaintiff or the defendant."

She frowned as anger for his unending suspicion flowed through her. "Why would you even think such a thing?"

"I don't know what to think. I'm listening

if you'd like to tell me anything."

The force of his will was like a powerful magnet. The impulse to tell him whatever he wanted to know shivered along her nerves. It was compounded, she thought, of fear that he could see through her and an insistent need to gain his approval, to see him smile at her as he did at others. If this was what it was like to face him from the witness stand, then she pitied anyone who wound up there.

Moistening her lips, she said, "You'll have to excuse me. I can't help you."

He didn't believe her; she could see it in his face. There was nothing she could do to prevent that. She didn't need this, couldn't stand it just now. More than that, she had a strong urge to get back to the motel, check her room and the things she had left there.

"Thank you for the breakfast," she said, summoning a smile for her host as she rose to her feet. "I'm sure you two have business to discuss, so I'll leave you to it. Perhaps you'll give me a call when you've made your decision?"

"I'll do that," Mr. Lewis said genially, rising to his feet and taking the hand she offered. "This has been a very great pleasure."

She was warmed by his words even as she wondered if they were mere politeness.

"For me, also," she said, and meant it. She turned to Kane who was standing, as well. She felt like striding off without a word to him, but that would be too pointed after her cordial farewell to his grandfather.

Before she could speak, he said, "I'll see you to your car."

She could hardly object without adding to his suspicion. "If you like."

He indicated that she should precede him, then followed her from the room. She was acutely aware of him behind her, so much so that it was difficult to walk naturally. As she stepped past him onto the front porch, he said, "You aren't carrying jewel cases, so I'm assuming you still don't have the collection."

"Your grandfather decided to give you another chance at it."

"Did he now?" There was an intrigued note in his voice. Closing the door behind him, he walked beside her across the porch and down the steps.

"That was my impression. I expect he'll get around to talking to you about it soon, since he asked me to stay on a couple of days."

"Crafty old devil," he muttered, staring straight ahead.

"What?" She flung a glance at his set face.

"Never mind. It looks as if you'll be on hand for Luke's open house this weekend after all."

"I suppose." Her tone was not encouraging.

"I'll drive you, if you care to go. Before you say no, let me add that my only motive is hospitality. You're kicking your heels here because of Pops. The least we can do is provide a little entertainment."

"That would certainly be considerate," she said, "if I believed it."

He stopped. "Are you calling me a liar?"

"Lawyers aren't exactly known for their ethics. Isn't bending the truth the name of the game?"

"Not for any I choose to play."

She gave him a sardonic glance. "Of course not."

"I mean it. I prefer the truth as a weapon."

"And I'm supposed to accept that while you doubt every word that comes out of my mouth?"

"There's a difference," he said, his eyes as hard as his voice was soft.

She stared at him. He meant he made a habit of stating facts, but knew she did not. Heat rose in her face as she exclaimed, "Of all the —"

"I guess this means you won't be going

with me to Luke's after all?"

"I can find my own way, thank you very much." With a scathing glance, she started again toward her car on the drive.

"Suit yourself."

In a childish need to have the last word, she said over her shoulder, "I intend to."

He returned no answer for long seconds. Then, just as she opened her car door, he said, "Regina?"

She stopped and looked back at him, caught by an undercurrent of concern in his voice.

"Watch out for Slater. He doesn't play by the rules."

She had suspected as much. That didn't make his continued assumption that she had some connection to such a sleazy character any less irritating. Her gaze as lethal as she could make it, she said, "But you do, right?"

"Always."

Strangely enough, she almost believed him. She looked away, then stepped into her car and slammed the door. The loud noise was satisfying. Still, she knew the last word hadn't been hers after all.

Regina's thoughts were chaotic as she drove back to the motel. Fine tremors ran through her hands. She didn't know why she let Kane Benedict get to her. Her defenses were many and well perfected against most people. She was a grown woman, not a teenager overwhelmed by hormones and a romantic imagination. She had seen handsome men before and had brushed off her share of those who assumed red hair equaled a passionate nature or who saw her disinterest as a challenge. They got nowhere against the barricade of her indifference.

She wasn't indifferent to Kane. He had pushed through her defenses at their first meeting, closing in before she was prepared. She felt exposed, emotionally vulnerable in a way she hadn't in years. It was disturbing on some level she preferred not to explore. It was also nerve-racking.

Back at the motel, everything in her room was exactly as she had left it. Nothing was gone, nothing out of order. If Slater had been there, he was very good at what he did.

Not that there was anything for him, or anyone else, to find; she had seen to that. Regardless, she was outraged at the possibility of intrusion. Her personal privacy was important to her, and the thought of having it breached for no good reason was far too much like a violation to be tolerated.

What bothered her more than anything else, however, was the possibility that her cousin had not been aboveboard with her. She intended to get to the bottom of it.

Gervis should have been at his office since it was the middle of the morning. He wasn't, according to his secretary. Instead, he was at the apartment. That worried her even before he answered the phone.

"Gina, baby," he said, his voice hard, "I hope you're calling with good news because I could sure use it."

"I'm calling to find out what you think you're doing."

"Me? I'm doing something? Hell, I'm not doing anything because I'm too busy fighting a lawsuit. Which you're supposed to be helping me with. If you've got nothing to report, why are you wasting my time?"

She would not let his irascible mood throw her. "I want to know why you lied to me about Dudley Slater."

"Baby, baby, what do you take me for?"

"I'd be hard put to say right this minute," she said as his abrupt change to a caressing tone rang alarm bells. "You told me you had nothing to do with the man watching me, this Slater, yet you knew he was a reporter. Why is that?"

"Must have been a lucky guess. Gina, listen —"

"No, you listen. I've heard you talk about

142

doing this to other people, but never dreamed you'd try it on me. Why? That's all I want to know, just why?"

He said nothing for a minute, then he asked, "They really made Slater as a reporter? Somebody down there is on to him?"

"You could say that," she returned with irony.

His only answer was several short and pithy comments on the reporter's mentality and antecedents. They struck her as incredibly vulgar, not to mention lacking in imagination, when they would hardly have registered not so long ago. The change, she thought, was a direct result of not hearing such phrases in her presence over the past few days, something she'd hardly noticed until now.

"What is this all about, Gervis?" she demanded, cutting him short. "Don't you trust me?"

"It's not that, sweetheart. It's just that you're not exactly a pro, you know? I thought you needed backup."

"A cheap reporter with a face like a weasel and a record to match is supposed to help? Give me a break!"

"All right, so I wasn't sure you had the guts for the deal, okay? You're great with people, they like you right off, whereas with me — but never mind that. You said yourself you were on shaky ground. You think you're tough, you talk tough, but you don't know how to take care of yourself. I got a right to worry about you, now don't I?"

"If you were really worried about me," she said with sudden pain in her chest, "I wouldn't be here. I want you to call off Slater."

He gave a long-suffering sigh. "I can't do that."

"Can't or won't?" She held her voice steady with a valiant effort.

"I don't have the man on a leash. He's a newshound and he smells a story."

"He's a cut below a paparazzo, a certifiable creep!"

"Be that as it may, he's arranged his own deal with his magazine, one that's got nothing to do with me and what I sent him to find out."

She hesitated, thinking hard. "Are you saying . . . ?"

"What, baby?"

She didn't answer. Abruptly, she couldn't speak at all as her concentration focused on something else entirely, a sound that she had been hearing all along. In the background, from the living room beyond the study, a television program was going. She recognized it without any trouble since it was the soundtrack of a cartoon movie she had heard a thousand times before.

Her cousin hated cartoons.

"Gervis," she said, her voice taut, "who do you have there with you?"

"Now, Gina. It was supposed to be a surprise."

"Is Stephan there?"

"It's just for a few days."

"You took him out of school?" Her voice was rising, but she couldn't help it.

"Now, Gina, don't get all upset."

The sharper her own words, the more soothing, almost oily, her cousin's became. On the edge of panic, she demanded, "What are you doing with him?"

"He was missing his mama, so I brought him for a visit. Take it easy."

"How can I take it easy? He has to have his medicine and have it on time. He shouldn't be upset, and you know he doesn't like Michael, won't take his medicine from him or from you."

"It's fine. I've taken care of it, hired a nurse and everything."

"Why?" she demanded with panic fluttering in her chest. "Why are you doing this?"

"For you, for Stephan. What else?"

"Let me talk to him."

"I don't think that's a good idea. You'll upset him for nothing. Maybe next time, when you've got something to report."

She didn't like what she heard in his voice, didn't like it at all. "What do you want from me?"

"Now, baby," her cousin complained, "you know what I want."

"Don't call me baby!" she yelled into the phone. "I want you to take my son back where he belongs."

"Sure, sure, I promise. When you're done with the job down there."

She breathed in quick gasps, trying to think. "I'm no miracle worker, Gervis. I can't find out secrets that aren't there or manufacture crooked deals where there aren't any."

"You can do something, damn it! How you coming with Benedict? Are you close enough to work on him?"

"Work on him how?"

"Talk to him, come on to him, screw his brains out. Hell, Gina, you're a female. Figure it out for yourself."

Horror shafted through her. "I can't do that!"

"You'd better try. I turned down the old

man's offer and now they're upping the ante, hinting about millions in damages. They win, I'll be bankrupt. I want the goods, and I don't care what you have to do to get them."

"But you know how I feel. You know why." He was the only one who did, the single person who had stood behind her during that terrible time. She couldn't believe what he was asking of her now.

"I know you've been hiding behind that for years. It's time you got over it."

"But what if —"

"Don't 'what if' me, Gina. I'm doing you a favor here, making you face this, if you want the truth. Lots of people have bad things happen. They don't let it get to them, but pick themselves up and go on. You get in there and do whatever it takes. Use your imagination, your feminine wiles, your tits and ass. Hell, I don't care. We got a week, give or take, to get something and figure out how to use it. Either you do this for me or you can expect to be sorry."

"You wouldn't hurt Stephan, you couldn't."

"I won't have to if you come through for me, now will I? But all I got to do anyway is tell him what a bastard his old man was. Tell him how his mama nearly died having him.

We could have a nice discussion about what a terrible thing it is, the way the law forces girls who are children themselves to carry babies that come from rape. Especially babies with problems. You think that'll make him feel good, huh, Gina?"

"How can you do this? How can you even think of it?" she cried, her voice thick with unshed tears. "He's like your own. We're family!"

"Families stick with each other, Gina. I've been begging for your help here, and you keep making excuses."

"I told you I'm trying," she said thickly.

"And I'm telling you I'm a desperate man. Maybe you'll believe me now. Maybe you'll be desperate, too, so you'll get something done. What do you think, Gina? Think you can find out what I need to know now?"

Before she could answer, the phone was slammed down on the other end. She sat motionless, staring at nothing, until the automatic request to hang up came on the line. Then she dropped her own receiver into its cradle and put her hands to her face. She pressed hard against the facial bones as a shudder ran over her. Tears seeped from her eyes, trickling through her fingers.

Stephan was the most important thing in

life to her, her whole world. He was so young, so sweet and defenseless. How could anyone hurt him? The very thought made her feel as if her heart were being squeezed in a vise.

Surely Gervis didn't mean what he threatened? Her cousin was only trying to frighten her. He had been so good to Stephan from the time he was born, had brought in a nanny when he was a baby and, later, paid the bills for expert evaluation, a special school. She would never have made it without Gervis.

She owed him so much, had wanted to do something in return for so long. Coming to Turn-Coupe was the first major thing he had ever asked. If not for her gratitude and sense of obligation, she wouldn't be here.

Still, Gervis had changed in the past few months. She hardly knew him. It was worry over business that caused it, she thought. Now the fear that he might lose everything he had worked so hard to gain had pushed him over the edge. That was it, it had to be.

He had started with nothing, a welfare kid from the back streets of Brooklyn. His father had died shortly after he was born, and his mother, left alone, could never quite cope. She had depended on wine and fashion magazines to get her through the days. She'd lived on dreams of striking it rich, winning the lottery or some sweepstakes, too involved in the fantasy and her depression to be much of a parent. Taking in Regina after her mother died had been an act with more heart than practicality, even if she had been Regina's mother's best friend. It hadn't lasted all that long in any case. Gervis's mother had died of a prescription drug overdose barely five years later, when Regina was fifteen.

After that, it had been just her and Gervis. As he was reminding her now. He needed her, and she couldn't afford to fail him.

If he harmed Stephan, she would never forgive him. Nor could Gervis ever live with himself. Or so she would have thought just a few days ago.

It was possible she was wrong.

She had never dreamed he would ask her to spy for him, either. And the last thing she expected was that he would demand she sleep with his worst enemy.

7

Regina felt as if a thousand people were watching her as she climbed the steps of Chemin-a-Haut on Saturday evening. There were guests everywhere, wandering under the trees in the lingering light of dusk, chatting in groups on the wide front veranda, or gallery, of the West Indies-style house, or clustered in the open parlor that stretched across its width with double French doors both front and rear. They were all age groups, it seemed, from youngsters who ran and played on the lawn, reminding her achingly of Stephan, to teens clustered on the stairs and older couples gathered near a bank of rocking chairs. They were all enjoying the relative coolness of the early summer twilight caused by gathering clouds, the music played by a Cajun band set up on the back gallery, the food and drink spread in abundance, and each other.

She was forced to acknowledge after a few minutes that the supposed spotlight was in her own mind. She attracted a friendly nod or two and quite a few smiles, but there was nothing focused about it. If speculation crossed the faces of those around her, it was perhaps not unusual since she was a stranger and obviously out of place.

She was an interloper, but that was nothing new. She had always been that, or so it seemed, always on the outside, with no real place of her own. It didn't matter. She wasn't here to become a part of the community or this family.

That rationalization made no difference; she was still on edge. She had to breathe in a deep and slow rhythm to prevent herself from turning tail and running like a rabbit. She couldn't do this, she just couldn't. What Gervis wanted of her was impossible.

She had never set out deliberately to attract a man, had not even tried it in high school. The very idea made her feel awkward and embarrassed. It seemed everybody who glanced at her should be able to tell what she had in mind.

Not that she decked herself out as a femme fatale. Her wardrobe didn't run to low-cut silk or satin even at home in New York; she certainly hadn't tossed any garment remotely seductive into her suitcase for this trip. A straight black suit skirt with a knit shell of cream silk and a wide belt pulled a notch tighter than usual was the best she'd been able to do. Her main effort had been to leave her hair down on her shoulders instead of clipping it back out of the way.

She'd also substituted plain contact lenses for her colored ones at the last moment. She felt naked and oddly vulnerable without the turquoise shading between her and the world. Still, they were an experiment that had become a habit. She hadn't been hiding behind them as Kane suggested. If he preferred her without them, however, then why not? He was the person she had to please, one way or another.

She saw Luke at once. He was moving here and there on the front gallery, playing host while looking rakish and engaging in a pair of close-fitting black jeans and a white dress shirt. Clinging to his arm was a giggling girl with her blond hair cut in a style that made her head look like a shaggy chrysanthemum blossom. He seemed to be teasing her just to hear her giggle.

Kane's grandfather was on the back gallery talking to an African-American in a pin-striped suit who she thought might be Kane's partner. She almost went to join them, but decided against it when she saw other friends approach the pair. She didn't want to look as though in search of a safe haven.

If Mr. Lewis was on hand, however, it seemed likely Kane had arrived, as well. She searched the crowd more diligently, locating him seconds later.

He was talking to a willowy-looking woman with a spill of long brown hair that glinted with golden highlights. They appeared absorbed in each other, there in their parlor corner, oblivious to anything else going on around them.

Kane was casual perfection in jeans and a blue chambray shirt as he leaned one elbow on the wall above his companion. The woman had her back pressed to the wall and her hands behind her while she looked up in serious consideration at the man next to her. Kane almost smoldered with the intensity of his concentration. The woman, wearing plum-colored silk that draped and flowed around her, appeared graceful and more elegant in a purely Southern manner than anyone Regina had ever seen.

She felt outclassed. It wasn't a promising start for the evening.

Just then, Kane glanced in her direction. His gaze, midnight blue with consideration, held hers for long seconds before he nodded with a lifted brow, as if surprised to see her. A flush rose to her face and she lifted her chin. She hadn't said she wouldn't attend the party, just that she didn't need him as escort.

He seemed so sure of himself and his place in the world as he stood there. Tall, wide shouldered, good-looking with his shining dark hair, the high slashes of his cheekbones, and determined chin, he was a man at ease with his own body. He was also surrounded by his family and friends, protected by their connection to him as she had never been protected in her life. He looked to be solid establishment, yet had a reputation for being unpredictable, not quite tame. Like his cousin, he seemed something of a throwback to his rugged, freebooter ancestors. How was she ever supposed to get close to him when he needed nothing and no one? Where was she to start?

Most of all, what was she going to do if she succeeded?

She had no clue whether she was capable of the cold-blooded approach to physical intimacy suggested by Gervis. The very thought filled her with dread. Regardless, she was aware of a heated, flooding sensation as she looked at Kane Benedict. The memory of the way he had kissed her as they lay in the coffin made her lips tingle. The feel of his arms around her, his long-fingered hands upon her, lingered in her mind with an odd sensation that was almost like longing. There had been such strength and security in his arms, even as she shrank from the threat he represented.

The humid breeze filtering through the open doors at the back of the house swirled a little more strongly, flapping the edges of a tablecloth, making dishes on a sideboard rattle together with a bell-like chime. Its coolness felt good on Regina's warm face.

Was Gervis right? Was she capable of overcoming her aversion to the touch of a man? She didn't know, she really didn't. She had lain awake most of the night before, thinking of Kane and trying to picture how it might be between them. The idea was paralyzing, but there was also fascination in it. He affected her as no man ever had. If the situation were normal, if she could get to know him in a simple, pleasant manner with no time constraints, then perhaps it might work.

Time for that was not available. The guilt and fear of discovery she felt, added to the urgent need for seduction, made it unlikely she could ever relax enough to have a normal relationship.

She had to try. If she reached the point where making love with Kane was unavoidable, maybe she could fake it. Or else close her eyes and think of something else, perhaps the pieces of shining jewelry worn by Victorian ladies who had been no more excited by sex than she was. Antique jewelry had always had that ability to soothe her and take her out of herself, away from all that was disturbing or disagreeable.

"So you did come. I was afraid you wouldn't."

The deep, masculine voice laced with humor and appreciation came from behind her, right beside her ear. She whirled on a sharp gasp, facing Luke with her eyes wide and her heart pounding in her throat.

"Whoa, slow down, beautiful lady. I didn't mean to startle you." He put a firm hand on her arm in a calming gesture.

She managed a smile even as she wondered if she looked as furtive as she felt. "I guess I'm a little jumpy."

"No need to be. You're among friends," he said easily, then shifted to encircle her waist with a light and casual grasp. "Come along with me and I'll introduce you around. We'll have you feeling at home in no time."

That had a lovely sound, almost too lovely. Luke tried, too; Regina had to give him that.

A natural host, he moved from group to

group, clasping hands and making jokes with the men, showering endearments, compliments and quick hugs on the ladies. Regina was included with a careless few words that made her presence seem normal and even inevitable. When the queries and glances of speculation seemed to warrant it, he slipped in a quick explanation of her business in town. It was all fairly painless, especially with the help of the wine he snagged from a bar of polished cypress set up on the back gallery and pushed into her hand.

Regina smiled, nodded, and made the usual remarks about the food and the weather. Still, there was no hope that she would ever be a real part of the gathering, and she accepted the depressing certainty after the first few minutes. She was set apart by her accent, her clothes and her attitudes, but most of all by what she was and why she was there. She might be accepted for a few hours, but no longer. Never longer.

She and Luke were standing alone for a brief moment. Glancing down at her, he said, "I noticed you didn't come with Kane. Why is that?"

"We barely know each other. There was no reason for him to bother."

"No?" Laughter glinted in his dark eyes.

"Looks to me like he may have gone and got himself in trouble with you."

"I don't know that I'd put it that way," she said carefully. The rising wind sweeping through the open doors made her fingers feel chilled against her cold, condensation-wet wine flute. If she listened closely, she thought she could hear an occasional low rumble in the distance that might be thunder.

"A few days ago, he was like a dog with a favorite bone, and tonight he's keeping his distance. Something must have caused it."

"Maybe I'm the one in trouble," she quipped, shielding her gaze as she sipped from her glass.

"Well now, we can't have that," he said with a quick shake of his head that loosened an errant black curl so it fell forward onto his forehead. In a sudden movement, he swung with her toward where Kane and his lady friend still stood.

"No, wait," Regina exclaimed, pulling against his hold, but it was too late. Luke was already waving the other pair forward, closing the gap between them.

"You and Kane know each other, of course," he said easily. "This gorgeous creature with him, Regina, is April Halstead, our resident writer here on the lake. She gives advice to the lovelorn on the side, being a romance author. That is, she advises everybody but me."

"It's the last thing you need," April returned, her voice carrying a slight edge in spite of its musical quality, before she greeted Regina.

"You'd be surprised," he answered laconically.

There was an undercurrent of some kind between the two, Regina thought, as she watched April put her hand on Luke's arm and draw him aside to ask a low-voiced question. The impression was wiped from her mind when Kane spoke.

"So you decided to come after all."

"I never said I wouldn't." She met the dark appraisal in his eyes with valiant effort. She was supposed to come on to this man. Incredible.

"How does it strike you?"

For an instant, it seemed he might have read her mind, then she realized he was talking about the party. "Lovely. It's literally an open house, isn't it with every door and window thrown wide?"

"A week later, and it would have been too hot without air-conditioning, but it's turned out fine so far," he replied, watching her over the rim of his glass as he drank.

"I thought I heard thunder a few minutes ago. Do you think it might rain?" It was trite to fall back on the weather for conversation, but she could come up with nothing else.

"A shower maybe, though it shouldn't last long this time of year. One of the many advantages of living in the Deep South."

"Is that where I am? I've more or less lost my bearings since I flew in."

"Much deeper and you'd wind up in the Gulf of Mexico."

His voice was polite, as was hers. They might never have met before, she thought with despair. This wasn't going to work. But what was she supposed to do? He'd suspect something, surely, if she suddenly began to act as though she was panting to go to bed with him.

She couldn't do this, she really couldn't. Some women, she knew, had only to see a handsome man to immediately begin planning how they would seduce him. They enjoyed taking the initiative, began shucking their clothes at the first possible moment. She wasn't made that way, and couldn't be sure, now, whether she was glad or sorry for it.

Glancing around, she said, "Are you and Luke really related to all these people?"

"Most of them. Not that I claim kinship with the more suspicious ones, like the guy behind you."

She turned as he spoke, alerted by the humor surfacing in his eyes as he gazed past her shoulder. Nor did she need to be told that the new arrival to their group was another cousin. The resemblance was too plain for doubt, in spite of the sun-bleached lightness of his hair. In addition, he wore a tan and brown uniform with a Western-cut jacket that had a discreet silver star pinned to the pocket. Regina's nerves tightened another notch as her gaze brushed over that symbol of office. Extending her hand, she said, "Sheriff Benedict, I presume."

"Call me Roan, ma'am, and I'll excuse the terrible company you're keeping," he said with a swift grin at Kane and Luke. He nodded and smiled at April as he swept off his Stetson, then took Regina's hand. His gaze lingered on her hair an instant. "You'll be the lady who's been visiting with Mr. Lewis, I expect."

"I suppose you could say that." She liked his deep and easy drawl, slightly more pronounced than Kane's, and also the steady look in his gray eyes. He would be a person people could depend on, she thought, which should make him an excellent law officer. However, there was a firm set to his jaw that suggested he would not be a good man to cross. She hoped devoutly that she need never put the idea to the test.

"You have any trouble with that reporter hanging around?" he asked as he released her.

"No, not so far," she said with a quick glance at Kane.

"What's this?" Luke asked. "Something I should know about?"

"Later," Kane answered.

Roan Benedict ignored them both, keeping his gaze on Regina. "You have a problem, let me know. Any time."

"I'll do that," she said, and felt warmed by his concern.

The sheriff smiled, then directed a keen gaze toward Luke. "I hate to take you and Kane away from such fine company, but could you spare a few minutes?"

"No problem." Their host glanced around for a table on which to set his glass down, then raised a brow at Kane, who indicated his readiness. "Excuse us, ladies?"

Regina murmured something appropriate, though depression settled over her. Now she would have to manufacture some other way to get near Kane again.

"Men," April Halstead said with a shake of

her head as she watched the three walk away.

Regina could only agree with the terse comment on the mysterious departure. At the same time, she couldn't help watching the three of them. They made a striking picture with their broad shoulders, lean hips, and free-swinging strides. An odd feeling settled in the pit of her stomach. Strange, but it felt almost like a warning.

Voice compressed, she said, "I don't suppose you have any idea what's up?"

April laughed. "I'd say they're going to set up the fireworks for later."

"You really think so?" She wanted to believe it since she'd been half afraid the conference had something to do with her.

"Luke makes a big deal out of it. Nothing is too much trouble. The other two are more adult about it, but of course they have to help."

"But since Roan is the sheriff —"

"That just means he feels responsible for making sure nobody gets hurt. The amount of firepower Luke shoots off every year could start a small war. One year, he even shot tracer bullets."

"You mean with a gun?"

"A rifle. You know how Southern men are about their firearms. Everybody has one or two, or a dozen."

"Not with them?" Regina glanced around uneasily.

"No, no," the other woman answered on a laugh. "At least, no one except Roan, and he's allowed. You know, now I think about it, I expect the guys are going to get everything in place for the main event before it starts raining. Wouldn't do for the firepower to fizzle out, now would it?"

April's manner was free and easy, her inner warmth plain in her voice. She had grace and charisma and a soft-edged beauty that was restful and nonthreatening. There was also an intelligent light in her golden brown eyes that weighed but did not judge. Regina could not help liking her, in spite of herself.

"I take it you're not a Benedict?" she commented.

April's smile widened. "No, thank goodness. I committed the unpardonable sin of invading Benedict territory when I bought an old plantation house out here on the lake."

"Thank goodness?"

"I'd never be able to get any writing done if I was a part of that clan. One person's problem is everybody's, and everybody's problems are one's own — which has its advantages, I'll admit, since you never have to fight a battle alone — but it means endless discussions and family councils over things large and small, never being alone in anything."

It sounded lovely, so lovely that Regina felt an odd, desolate ache in her chest. "You've lived here quite a while, then, to know them so well?"

"I was born in Turn-Coupe, but moved away for a few years. I've been out here on the lake for a while now."

The vague answer might mean something or nothing at all, Regina thought. Certainly, it didn't suggest any conversational leads. Trying valiantly to keep something going, she said, "How did you get started writing romance novels?"

"I loved reading romantic fantasies, so why not write them? My start was with historical romance, and I still do one now and again when the spirit moves me, but I concentrate on contemporary women's fiction."

"Which is?"

"Stories about male-female relationships today, women in jeopardy, women who must make major decisions that will affect the direction of their lives and of others around them. Actually, it means any story that has validity for the lives of women."

"You write modern stories, but live in an old house?"

April laughed. "It's the romantic in me, I guess. I like to think I must have lived in another time, when candlelight and long dresses were standard fare."

"Past lives?"

"It's fascinating to think about, don't you agree?"

It was another evasion, polite, not at all confrontational, but effective. Regina thought she should be taking lessons. Or better yet, she ought to be delving for information Gervis could use instead of exercising her own curiosity. "I suppose people come to you with all sorts of stories, all kinds of family legends and secrets?"

"Sometimes." April's clear, golden brown gaze was a little too knowing for comfort.

"Do you ever use any of them?"

"Hardly ever. Truth is supposed to be stranger than fiction, but fiction is a great deal safer in these litigious times."

Regina couldn't help smiling at the droll expression on her face. "I expect so."

April was still studying her. In curious tones, she said, "You had something in mind?"

"Not really. I guess I was just thinking of

this business with Kane's grandfather. The suit is one thing, of course, but with his family having the funeral home for so long, it seems lots of interesting things must have occurred there in the past."

"If they did, no one will ever know. Mr. Lewis likes to tell stories about the old days, but would never think of gossiping about his friends and neighbors."

"I'm sure you're right," Regina said reflectively.

"And yet you wonder, yes? Well, so do I. Actually, I seem to have heard something about a woman who died a suicide, but when they removed her wedding band, the initials inside were not her husband's. Now that kind of thing might make a story if I dared use it."

"Why wouldn't you?"

April tilted her head so her long, sun-streaked brown hair fell over one shoulder in a shimmering slide. "Kane wouldn't like it."

"Kane? What would he have to say about it?"

A rich chuckle broke from April. "A great deal, I imagine, and all of it lethal. He's very protective of his grandfather, you know. Especially now."

"Yes, I suppose," Regina agreed. "It's

very caring of him, really, very —"

"Sweet? That's Sugar Kane." The look in the other woman's eyes was soft.

"You're the second person who's called him that," Regina said dryly, since the words were not exactly what she'd had in mind.

"Actually, I was the first. I gave him the moniker back in high school."

"Did you?" She let her tone carry the appeal for more.

April lifted a silk-clad shoulder in a resigned gesture. "Kane was something else when we were kids. He and his uncle worked their old place out here on the lake, raising soybeans, cotton, and enough sugarcane to make syrup every fall. All that farm labor gave him muscles and a tan that were a sight to behold, not that he ever gave it a thought. He and Luke were a pair, always up to some outrageous prank and dragging Roan into it half the time. That was before they all discovered girls — or the girls discovered them. They turned into rebels then, totally cool in a laid-back kind of way. They were the most popular guys in town, had every female for miles around ready to swoon."

Regina could imagine it. Too well, in fact. As April paused, she said, "Go on."

"They were special, the three of them. Never took advantage of a girl, but seldom refused what was offered — and you couldn't pry a word out of them about it afterward. They never said a word they didn't mean or promised what they couldn't deliver. Kane, especially, had a Galahad streak a mile wide. He was always the first to offer a pretty girl his coat in cold weather, the first to tell a boy who got out of line to back off or put an end to teasing that got too raw. He's the kind who would have ridden off to the Crusades in another era."

"Somehow," Regina said dryly, "the knights of the Crusades never struck me as sweet."

"You've got me there," April agreed, "though I'm sure some of them must have been. What I'm thinking of is that image of chivalry and daring. Anyway. Where was I?"

"The nickname?"

"Right. In our senior class was a banker's daughter, a poor girl almost six feet tall, plagued by buckteeth and hair like a Brillo pad. She never had a date, never had a boyfriend. Her father tried to help her by hiring the son of a family friend to take her to the senior dance. He took her all right, but left her sitting against the wall while he had himself a good time. Everybody knew, of course, and some were laughing about it. The girl was near tears. Then Kane stepped up and led her out onto the floor. He slow danced with her through the most romantic piece of the evening, like Prince Charming with Cinderella. She was absolutely dazzled."

"What about his date?" Regina asked with an arched brow.

April laughed, a warm, easy sound. "That was me, and I didn't mind at all, mainly because I was dancing with Luke at the time. But I couldn't help watching Kane and the banker's daughter. When Luke noticed, I said to him, 'Isn't that the nicest thing for Kane to do? He's sweet as sugar, don't you think?' Of course, Luke being Luke, that was all it took."

"He thought it was funny?" Regina couldn't keep the censure from her tone. She rather liked the idea of Kane rescuing the contemporary equivalent of a damsel in distress. Perhaps because the few times she had needed a Galahad there had been none available.

"He thought it was priceless," the romance author corrected with a reminiscent smile. "He also thought it was wonderfully descriptive, completely appropriate — and guaranteed to get Kane's goat. Which it did.

Still does, for that matter. You'd have to know Luke to understand. He's every bit as complex as Kane, in his own way."

"You seem to think a lot of them both." Regina swirled what was left of her wine, watching it with exaggerated attention.

"That's one way to put it. We all grew up together, dated together, ran around all over the country together."

A choked feeling that might almost have been jealousy moved through Regina. What must it have been like to be part of such a close-knit group, to have enjoyed the kind of uncontrolled freedom that the woman beside her seemed to be suggesting. In careful mildness, she said, "But you didn't wind up married to either of them."

April gave a rueful shake of her head that made her hair sway down her back. "Francie came along and took Kane out of the game. Then something happened to Luke, a terrible accident. As for me, well, I was stupid. But it's all done now, and there's no use worrying about it."

"By Kane being out of the game, you mean . . . ?"

"Engaged. To Francie. She was something else, that girl, a hellion on heels." April stared at Regina an instant, her gaze intent. "I probably shouldn't mention it, but you're the first woman Kane has shown any interest in since."

"I think you may have the wrong idea. We hardly know each other." She could have kicked herself the instant the words left her mouth. What was the matter with her that integrity kept getting in her way. Unless it was the examples around her?

"That's not how I heard it from Vivian Benedict." The sparkle in April's eyes was a strong indication she'd heard the tale of the coffin. The last thing Regina wanted was to explain the details. She said hastily, "Vivian also mentioned Francie and what she did to Kane."

"Did she now? That's interesting," April said. "I must not be the only one grateful that Kane's waking up and dragging himself away from the law books. So you know all about the fake pregnancy scheme?"

"Apparently, there was every possibility his fiancée could have been pregnant."

"Well, yes. But to tell a man he is going to lose his child in one breath and demand money in the other — particularly a man like Kane who places such value on family — doesn't that strike you as cruel?"

Regina put a hand to the amber pendant at her throat. "Yes, certainly, and also incredibly stupid. She should have known he wouldn't leave it at that, that he would be concerned enough to follow through and discover if everything turned out all right."

"See there!" April exclaimed in triumph. "I knew you had to be special. You only just met Kane, but you see and understand the kind of caring, responsible person he is far better than Francie who had known him most of his life."

"What I see," Regina said with a wry twist of her lips, "is his tenacity, the iron-hard determination to see things to their bitter end."

April frowned, but made no answer, for they were joined by a would-be writer who wanted to speak to her. Left temporarily to her own devices, Regina glanced around her, noticed Lewis Crompton still holding court out on the back gallery. Since she felt a bit in the way and enough time had passed that it wouldn't look quite as if she was reaching for a lifeline, she moved purposefully in that direction.

Kane's grandfather saw her coming. With a wide gesture of one arm, he welcomed her into the circle that had formed around him, a bit of courtesy for which she was supremely grateful.

There was an older woman standing at his side, one with a lithe and upright figure, magnolia-like skin, and silvery hair brushed back from her face in gentle waves. She was introduced as Elise Pickhart, and Regina realized this was the lady who occupied Mr. Lewis's lunch hour every Tuesday.

It was fascinating to see the older couple together. They interacted with each other in a seamless duet of small touches and smiles to direct attention or make a point. Miss Elise finished Mr. Lewis's sentences for him and supplied missing words, while he deferred to her opinions and introduced topics on which he seemed to know she would shine. It was as if they had long been married, Regina thought, and wondered why they were not.

Not that it was any of her business. Wondering about the people of Turn-Coupe and the lake was counterproductive. The last thing she needed was to get involved.

Still, as she stood there, watching the play of warmth and affection across Lewis Crompton's face, seeing the esteem in which he appeared to be held by the people around him, she was swamped with guilt. To all appearances, he was a genuinely good man, one she liked very much. He had been everything that was kind and helpful to her. In return, she was going to betray him, to search out the scandals and secrets of his life and expose them for all to see.

She hated it, she really did.

The only thing she hated worse was the growing fear that he would prove to have no shame or disgrace in his blameless life, no secrets she could expose. What in the name of heaven was she going to do then?

8

Kane, returning from setting up the fire-works beside the lake, watched the emotions that chased themselves across Regina's expressive face and wondered what she was thinking. Something had disturbed her, he thought, for she had been smiling with every sign of pleasure just moments before. There was no cause that he could see. She was with his grandfather, and Pops could be depended on to keep the conversation running in smooth and well-worn channels, with only pleasant surprises along the way.

She was holding her own among his friends and relatives, he'd give her that much. She and April had seemed to be getting along with amazing ease just moments ago, talking ninety-to-nothing with their heads together in the secretive way women had that could drive men to drink. He'd give a lot to know what they'd been discussing.

Regina sent a quick look his way, then glanced away again. In that brief instant, he thought he saw active fear in her eyes.

He whispered a curse. In spite of her attempts to be forthright and brassy, she was always anxious when around him. That she was not that way toward other people, other men, made his hackles rise. He wasn't used to feeling like some kind of fiend who frightened women.

So he had held her, had used his superior strength to force her to remain beside him, had kissed her in a coffin. He'd goaded her, subjected her to interrogation, yes, but all in a good cause. It had been a stupid miscalculation, but hardly criminal. He hadn't hurt her or anything near it. Besides, he'd apologized, hadn't he? And she had seemed none the worse.

Why, then, did he still feel so bad about it?

Yes, and why did he keep wondering if it was the coffin or the kiss that had upset her that first day? So much so that he could think of nothing except trying the second part of it again just to see.

It was also possible that was a self-serving excuse of gigantic proportions. He couldn't get the luscious softness of her mouth out of his mind, or its sweet, delicate flavor. Just looking at the coral curves of her lips, like some rare and succulent fruit, made him feel reckless with repressed need.

He wondered if she had any idea of what

she was doing to him. And if she was being so elusive just to keep him off balance.

On the other hand, it seemed she might be a little more approachable tonight. He wished he knew why, as well as just how far it went. The urge to find out was irresistible. Before he could have second thoughts, he moved toward her.

"How are you making out?" he asked, leaning close enough to inhale her soft, feminine scent. "Had about enough of the Clan Benedict?"

"I'm not sure what you mean," she answered, shifting to put a small space between them, not looking at him.

"We can be a little overpowering in large doses, or so I'm told." The racket and family habit of talking back and forth across each other in several different conversations at once sometimes got to him, if the truth was known.

"I'm fine. I rather like watching everybody, especially the children."

Kane thought she meant it, which surprised him. Benedict brats were fairly well behaved as far as manners went, but were always exhaustingly healthy, which meant they had more energy than they knew what to do with. Everyone would suspect they were sick if they weren't chasing each other up and down the galleries or hanging by their heels from the stair railing.

"I expect you could use a break anyway," he suggested. "Have you seen the house and grounds? If not, I could give you the grand tour."

"I haven't, no." She looked up finally to meet his gaze.

"You're not wearing your contacts." He spoke without thinking, startled out of his normal prudence. It was as if she had removed protective shields, twin layers of hard, sea green plastic that had prevented anyone from seeing what she was inside. The change was startling, much more so than he'd imagined from his brief glimpse before. It also affected him more drastically than he would have dreamed.

"They made my eyes uncomfortable," she said. "Something to do with the extra humidity, possibly."

"I like it," he said simply.

Her slow smile was a sight to behold. It was also the first time she had directed such unshadowed warmth in his direction. He needed no other encouragement, which was a good thing, he thought, since it was all he was likely to get.

Kane made their excuses, not that anyone noticed. Then he took the wine Regina had hardly touched from her and set it aside. Tucking her fingers into the crook of his arm, he led her from the room.

The house was old and historical and it looked it. The draperies in the living room were heavy, faded silk and original to the house though astonishingly well preserved due to decades of good care and an outdoor kitchen that prevented the deterioration caused by cooking fumes. The floors had been cut from heart pine in random-width planks, the walls carried the original plaster in most rooms, and most of the furnishings were original, if ramshackle, antiques.

Outside, the hand pump was still in place in the cistern house, the summerhouse-type structure built above the underground cistern. The covered "whistler's walk" between the dining room and old outdoor kitchen, so-called because footmen who carried the food from the kitchen in the old days were required to whistle to make certain they didn't sample it on the way, was still usable, one of the few left in the state. An oyster-shell path led down to the lake where a gazebo covered by the rampant vines of wisteria provided a cool place to sit during the day and a hidden trysting spot at night.

Kane felt a couple of drops of fine rain as

they paused outside the gazebo. He stepped inside, pulling Regina with him. She came readily enough, but stopped near the door.

Night had fallen with semitropic suddenness. The music from the house, a slow blues piece, made a rich, lulling background for the other evening noises: the sweeping sigh of the wind in the trees, the whirring of insects, and the insistent calls of frogs anxious for spawning time promised by the rain. The house lights penetrated the lattice of the gazebo and the mass of vines overhead in errant gleams. A windblown leaf rustled across the cypress floor, while the ripple and slap of waves and forlorn call of a waterbird could be heard from the direction of the lake.

Kane stood a moment, letting the thundery coolness of the night seep into him. If he breathed deep enough, he discovered, he could catch the faint perfume caught in the shining, copper-bright hair of the woman beside him, brought out by the dampness. He should fight the enticement, he knew. He didn't want to, lacked the fortitude, right this minute, even to try.

"Dance?" he said, and stepped closer, offering his arms. She watched him a single instant, there in the moist darkness, then she put out her hand and let him draw her close.

Perfect.

They fitted together like yin and yang, nut and bolt, plug and socket. For a single, stunned instant, Kane was beyond thought or intention, certainly beyond judgment. The darkness deepened around them. The mist from the rain that sifted down stronger now beyond their cover was warm.

Regina swallowed, an audible sound in the stillness. Voice stilted, she said, "It's a lovely party."

"It is," he agreed in deep tones, torn between sympathy and amusement for her obvious nervousness. Inhaling as he collected his own scattered thoughts, he said, "You seem to hit it off with April."

"She's easy to talk to, a nice person, very real. But then, everyone is so open and friendly that I'm . . . overwhelmed."

"Somebody been asking too many personal questions?" he queried in dry humor.

"Oh, it isn't that. I just keep wondering why they aren't more self-protective, why they aren't afraid people will take advantage of them."

There was a note in her voice that intrigued him. "Who would do that?"

"I don't know. Somebody, anybody."

"You think they're naive, is that it?"

"Maybe," she agreed hesitantly, "a little."

"You're wrong. They know very well there are people in this world with hidden agendas. They only prefer to believe everyone is aboveboard until they prove otherwise. But once a person trespasses, there are few second chances."

She put a little space between them as they swayed to the music. "Is that your philosophy, too?"

"You could say so, up to a point."

"The point being that you aren't half so trusting as most? Or half as forgiving?"

He was silent a moment, turning her words over in his mind. Was she right? It was possible. Still, the lawyer in him automatically took the offensive. "I thought that was your role."

"Mine?" she asked, her expression suspended there in the dimness. "What makes you say that?"

"You're still holding a grudge over the coffin."

"Not at all."

"No?" he queried, the word husky as he stepped close and caught her against him. "Then I suppose you didn't mind this, either?"

She shivered as he lowered his lips to hers,

for he felt it. Whether it was from pleasure or disgust was impossible to say. Then he ceased to care as he was lost in the warm honey taste of her, the satin-smooth surfaces of her mouth, and the startling magic of her skin against his own. It was a homecoming, a physical fusing of hollows and planes so exact, so consummate, that his mind reeled with the need for more.

He delved deeper, growing feverish with the tantalizing textures and sleek abrasion of his tongue against hers. Intent vanished, leaving only pure sensation that spiraled into impure instinct. His grasp tightened and he pressed closer. He couldn't get near enough, not with layers of clothing and civilization between them. He would never be near enough until they were alone somewhere and he was inside her, matching his hard urgency to her hot, wet softness, his strength to her willing welcome.

She moaned in distress. That low sound struck him like a bucket of cold water. He dragged air into his lungs, then released her and stepped back in a single sharp movement designed to keep himself from clinging. He came up against the opposite side of the doorway. Setting his backbone against it, he clenched his hands into fists, then slowly, carefully, relaxed.

Voice hoarse, he said, "You did mind."

"I was just surprised."

He tested the breathless quality of her voice and its quiver, then shook his head. "No, or at least that's not all of it. What I want to know is why did you come out here with me if my company is so repulsive?"

"It's not. You don't understand." She swung away, hugging her arms across her chest.

It was barely possible, he conceded. There had been a few seconds when he felt her response. It was, just possibly, what had driven him over the edge. But he also remembered her shudder.

"I don't believe you," he said with deliberation.

"You wouldn't, of course. Everything is cut-and-dried with you, yes or no, right or wrong, isn't it? You were born to such comfort and privilege that you have no idea of the complications of other people's lives or the things that move them in ways you can't begin to understand."

"So what moved you just now?" he said in trenchant willingness to be convinced.

She turned her head to stare at him. Before she could speak, however, there came a small explosion from down beside the lake. Suddenly, the night sky burst into

186

brilliant light. It spread, exploding into colors of red and blue and gold that went off with rocket blasts, then sprinkled down in shooting stars falling toward their own reflections in the rain-dimpled surface of the lake beyond the open doorway. It was Roan setting off Luke's fireworks before the rain made them useless. In their glow, he saw pain darkening Regina's eyes, and limitless despair.

He whispered her name, stepping toward her in alarm.

"No!" she cried with the tightness of tears in her voice. She whirled from him then, running through the falling raindrops and sprinkling stars of fireworks, back toward the house.

Kane took a step after her, then stopped, afraid he would only make things worse. At least he knew now that it had not been the coffin alone that she had hated. He swung around, bracing himself stiff-armed against the gazebo column as he muttered a heartfelt curse.

"Lost your touch, Counselor?"

Luke followed his question out of the darkness. Stopping near the gazebo entrance, he followed the burst of another rocket overhead before turning to look at Kane.

"Who says I ever had one?" Kane asked in rough tones.

"You used to have finesse. At least enough not to scare off your women."

Kane heard the undercurrent of censure in the other man's voice. He didn't much care for it. "You don't know anything about it."

"I know women are fine company if you don't treat them as if they're on the witness stand and you're the prosecution, judge and jury in a neat wad."

"That wasn't the problem," he answered shortly. "Regina was fine as long as we were fighting tooth and nail."

Luke was silent a moment. When he spoke again, there was repressed amusement in his voice. "She wasn't thrilled with the cease-fire? Dixieland delight didn't go over too well?"

"Something like that." Kane rolled a moody shoulder.

"A fine old custom, making out in the gazebo, but you must be rusty."

"Apparently."

Luke tilted his head back, a shadowy movement as he followed yet another rocket barrage whistling heavenward to blossom into red and yellow. "She's getting under your skin, isn't she?"

Kane gave him a hard stare. "Don't you

have better things to do than meddle in my business? Like minding your fireworks?"

"It's under control," Luke said with off-hand confidence. "You know, I could give you some competition."

"This isn't a sporting event." It was a warning.

Luke shook his head. "Sure it is, Kane, the oldest on record. You just lost heart a while back and dropped out. But that doesn't mean no one else is on the field or keeping score."

"I mean it," he insisted. "Regina isn't . . ."

"What?" His cousin waited for him to go on.

"I don't know." Kane closed his hand into a fist as he tried to find words for a situation he didn't quite understand himself. "There's something about her, something that needs time."

"Time and a slow hand? I happen to have both."

Kane felt the hair on the back of his neck rising to a bristle. Through clenched teeth, he said, "Leave her alone, Luke. I mean it."

"Listen to yourself, man. You sure your interest is business?"

"I know what mine is. I'm just wondering about yours."

"Pure devilment. What else?" Dry humor

had returned to his cousin's voice.

Kane shook his head even as he forced down the possessive urge to stake a claim. "You've got a point. What is it?"

"Maybe I'm worried about you," Luke answered as he turned and ambled back toward the house, sublimely careless of the misting rain.

"You sure it's not Regina on your mind?" The question Kane called after him was blunt.

"Might be. Might not."

Kane let him go since it was pointless to do anything else. Luke was like a force of nature, hard to second-guess, impossible to stop once he got an idea into his head. The only good thing was that his instincts were excellent.

The things he had said turned in Kane's mind as he watched the explosions of bottle rockets and boom blasters light up the raindrop-fogged sky. Some of the phrases he rejected, some he filed for future reference, but a few he sifted word by word for hidden meaning. It did no good. As the last bright fire blossom faded into nothing, he was no closer to the truth than he had been when the evening began.

He returned to the party, but it was already winding down, dampened by the rain. Pops and Miss Elise were among the first to leave. He saw them to their car with a doorman's big umbrella, then went back inside with Roan and Luke and a couple of other guys to have a beer and talk about ice hockey in the Superdome and who would be starting quarterback for the New Orleans Saints in preseason. They were working on their third long neck and second bowl of peanuts when Roan's beeper went off. The sheriff heaved his long frame to a standing position and stepped out onto the gallery, taking out his flip phone from a shirt pocket as he went. The discussion, such as it was, went on without him.

A moment later, Roan stalked back inside. Kane glanced up, saw the set look of officialdom on his cousin's face, and felt his gut tighten in immediate reaction. He was already on his feet when Roan jerked his head in a beckoning gesture. Kane set his beer on a side table and went to join him.

"Sorry," his blond cousin said, putting a big hand on his shoulder. "It's Pops. There's been an accident."

Kane felt his heart jerk in his chest. "Is he . . . ?"

"He's alive, but that's all I know. Come on, we'll go in my squad car. I'll have you there in five minutes."

"I might need my own wheels. You clear a

path and I'll keep up with you."

"You got it."

When Kane and Roan pulled up at the site of the wreck, it was only a blur of glaring lights, flashing blue and white in the rain-drenched darkness. They had beaten the ambulance. Pops was lying on the wet ground with his head in Elise's lap while she held a pathetic, half-crushed umbrella over him with one hand and smoothed his cheek with the other. Roan stopped to speak to the patrolman in charge, but Kane strode straight to his grandfather and went down on one knee beside him.

"Pops," he said tightly, "I'm here."

Lewis Crompton opened his eyes, his gaze bewildered yet angry. His voice was querulous and frighteningly weak as he spoke. "Damn fool ran me off the road."

A strong mixture of relief, grief and anger tightened Kane's throat. Roan had said Pops was alive, but Kane had needed to see for himself before he believed it. He didn't like the looks of the dark red blood that matted his grandfather's mane of white hair, or the flaccid immobility of his arm that lay across his chest. Still, he would be taken care of soon. The wailing of an ambulance siren could be heard in the distance.

Kane cleared his throat of its sudden obstruction. "Who was it, Pops? Who did this?"

"Don't know." His grandfather grimaced and pressed a hand to his ribs. "All happened so fast."

Elise broke in then, as if to spare him the effort. "The car came up from behind us and started to pass. We mostly saw headlights. I think it was dark colored and a fairly late model, but I don't know one kind from another these days. I'd like to be more helpful, but . . ." She gave a tired shake of her head.

"You're all right?" Kane asked, his gaze assessing as he turned his attention to his grandfather's lady friend.

She nodded. "Lewis swung the car so it struck the trees on the driver's side. He saved me."

Kane's grandfather gave a dissenting grunt. "She's the one who saved me. Reminded me to put on my seat belt."

"No such thing," Miss Elise said.

Lewis Crompton reached up to take her hand. "I know better."

That they could argue over it said a lot for their condition, Kane thought, feeling his concern ease a fraction more. They were both banged up and would feel their scrapes and bruises for some time, but it could have been worse. Much worse.

The ambulance came tearing up and shrieked to a halt. The driver and the EMT piled out and hustled toward them. Short minutes later, Pops and Elise were speeding on their way to the hospital. Kane followed behind Roan at a faster clip than he'd driven since his racing days.

The next three hours passed in a surreal time warp, moving with both excruciating slowness and incredible speed. At the end of that time, the report was fairly decent. Pops had a broken arm and cracked ribs, plus multiple contusions and abrasions. They wanted to keep him a couple of days but, barring some unforeseen problem, he would be fine.

Miss Elise was fixed up with a couple of butterfly bandages before being released to go home. She wanted to stay with Lewis, but he wouldn't hear of it. Kane thought she finally agreed to leave only because she didn't want to upset his grandfather by going against his wishes.

Kane drove her home. At her house on the edge of town, he opened his car door to get out and see her inside. She reached over to touch his arm. Voice tremulous, she said, "Wait."

"What is it?" Something about the way

she searched his face with her faded gaze, in the greenish light from the control panel, made his heart kick into a faster rhythm.

"There's something I need to tell you. I know I should've mentioned it to Roan for his report, but I just wasn't sure. . . ."

"Something about the accident?" he asked to help her get whatever she wanted to say out in the open.

She dipped her head with its soft silver wings of hair. "Everything was muddled. I couldn't think straight until I knew Lewis was going to be all right." She stopped, pressing her lips together until they were white.

He put his hand over her cold, frail fingers that still clutched his arm. "Just tell me. I'll sort it out."

She took a fortifying breath. "The first time that car crowded us was at the old bar pit. You know where I mean?"

Kane nodded in grim acknowledgment. The bar pit was a deep slough left behind after sand and gravel were excavated for roadwork. Any hole in the ground in Louisiana inevitably filled with water. The bar pit was a death trap nearly thirty feet deep that had claimed more than one victim. If Pops and Miss Elise had gone off into it, their chances of surviving the plunge would have been slim to nonexistent.

"Lewis swerved, or we would have gone through the guardrail. The next time, he — he couldn't stay on the road. And then . . ." She put the fingers of her free hand to her mouth, staring straight ahead with her eyes wide.

"What? Tell me."

"I was so shaky, trying to get out of the seat belt to see to Lewis. Then there was the rain. The man driving the other car stopped down the road from where he ran us off, then he reversed and stopped on the road above us. At first, I thought he meant to help. He got out and started back toward us. I thought . . . but it was dark except for his taillights and I wasn't seeing or thinking too clearly. I was so worried about Lewis, too, because he was unconscious for three or four minutes right after we hit."

"Miss Elise, please." Urgency made Kane's voice husky.

She turned her hand in his and clasped it tight. "He had a gun, dear. I'm sure of it. For a minute, I just knew he meant to —"

"Don't think about it. Just tell me what happened."

She gasped, shook her head as if to banish a bad dream. "Then a truck came over the rise, a big eighteen-wheeler. The man ran back to his car and tore off like hell's hounds were after him."

"Did you get a look at him?"

"I don't know. It was so dark."

"Was he short, tall, fat, skinny, white or black, wearing a hat or not?" Kane asked in grim concentration. "Can you remember anything? Anything at all?"

She blinked as she met his gaze. Then she said, "Not short or tall, but sort of medium and skinny. I don't think he was black, but I might be mistaken. He had on one of those ski caps, and something over his face like — I think it may have been a stocking."

"That's great, Miss Elise," he said, smiling as he warmed her cold hand in both of his own. "You did fine."

"Oh, I'm so glad I told you," she said on a long, relieved sigh. "Now maybe I can sleep."

Kane hoped she could because he wasn't sure he would be able to, not for some time. The man she described sounded familiar. He sounded, in fact, a lot like Dudley Slater.

There was one person who might know for sure. That person was Regina Dalton.

He could ask nicely, but that might not do the trick. In which case he'd have to force the truth from her. He had a good idea of what method to use. It might not be particularly noble, but it was sure to be effective. All he had to do was get her alone someplace where there was no possibility of her running away from him again.

He knew just the spot.

The only trouble was, there would be no escape for him, either, and he wasn't sure how far he could trust himself with her. How long he could remember all the cold, hard reasons for what he was doing.

What he had in mind was explosive. There was no doubt about it. One wrong move and it could blow up in his face.

Why, then, did he have such a reckless urge to see just how short he could cut the fuse?

9

Regina slept late. It was hardly surprising since she had tossed and turned for hours before dropping off. The sound of sirens tearing in and out of town from the direction of the lake had disturbed her, so she lay worrying about the wet weather and all the people who had been at Luke's party. The main reason, however, was the turmoil in her mind. Even after she woke, she didn't get up, but lay staring at the plaster ceiling above the bed with its flecks of starlike glitter and trying to make sense of the night before.

She had not been repelled by Kane's kiss. The hard heat of him against her and the strength of his arms had ignited impulses she had felt only in dreams. His firm, smooth lips and tender exploration were revelations. The taste of him had sizzled through her veins like champagne until she felt euphoric and careless of the sweet, sinful consequences of making love to Sugar Kane. Or perhaps even eager for them.

Then his hold had tightened until it seemed there was no escape. She had suddenly become too aware of what she was doing. The familiar, panicky need to get away surged up inside her and she acted on it in blind, conditioned response.

Yet the instant he released her, she had felt so alone and desolate with the need to be in his arms again. Even now, she would like to be lying with him. Not in passion, no, but in simple security, with the kind of protective affection she had sensed between him and the members of his family, the people he loved.

Impossible. There could be no security for her anywhere near Kane Benedict.

Even if she could overcome her distrust of physical intimacy, even if she and Lewis Crompton's grandson fell into a mad, delirious affair, there would never be anything in it for her except heartache. The instant he learned of her connection to Gervis Berry he would despise her. It would be over. And if by some remote chance she discovered information to help defeat his grandfather, then he would never forgive the betrayal. Never. He was far too upright and law-abiding to understand the gratitude and loyalty that made deceit not only possible but necessary.

She had hurt Kane with her rejection, for she had seen it in his eyes. The injury was only to his male pride; still she regretted it. She had also angered him and that was another problem altogether. What in the world was she going to do to get back on the intimate footing that Gervis demanded? Even if she could manage it, how was she to prevent the same situation from coming up again?

She shouldn't, according to Gervis.

What would it be like to release all the doubt and fear she kept hidden and trust a man? Could she do that for Gervis and Stephan? Would she ever be able to trust Kane that far? If she did, could she bear it when he turned on her as he would, inevitably, when the truth came out?

He had been betrayed by a woman once. What would it do to him to have it happen again? Did she really want to know?

The sound of footsteps along the walkway outside her room caught her attention. Hard on them came the quick tattoo of a knock on the motel door. Regina shoved herself upright in the bed. Her immediate thought was that it had to be Kane. She wasn't ready to face him again, had no idea what to say to him.

The knock came again. She threw back the covers and reached for her robe, dragging it around her. At the door, she peeped through the fish-eye viewer.

Betsy North. Regina closed her eyes, let out the breath she had been holding, then reached for the knob.

"Sorry to disturb you, hon," the motel owner said, setting a hand on her ample hip clad in purple cotton knit. "I know you're probably working or something, cooped up in here, but I thought you should know about Mr. Lewis."

Betsy was obviously bursting with news she couldn't wait to impart. Still, there was a grim cast to her features that sent alarm along Regina's nerves. "What's wrong?"

"Mr. Lewis and Miss Elise had a wreck last night, coming from the lake. Somebody ran them off the road."

"Oh, no." Regina put her hand to her amber pendant, holding tight. She could feel its warmth against the sudden chill of her fingers.

"Son of a gun didn't bother to stop. It wouldn't surprise me if it was deliberate." Betsy's lips thinned with her angry disgust.

"Are they . . . ?" Regina couldn't finish the question, couldn't bring herself to say that final, so final, word.

"They're okay, no thanks to whatever low-down skunk — well, never mind. They released Miss Elise, but Mr. Lewis is still at the hospital." Betsy went on to recite his injuries.

Regina was so glad Mr. Lewis was alive that she felt weak. She couldn't stand the thought of anything happening to him. It was a special horror to think he might have been killed because of her and what she was doing.

She said hesitantly, "You don't truly believe there's a connection between the accident and the trial?"

"Looks that way to me."

"Couldn't it have been a coincidence, somebody who had too much to drink, or who couldn't see for the rain?"

The other woman wagged her head in a negative. "Mr. Lewis is a good driver in spite of getting on in years, and he don't scare easy. If he says the man was after him, that he meant to run him off the road, well, I'm inclined to believe him. Besides, it's too much of a coincidence."

"Meaning?" Regina was sure she knew, but needed to hear Betsy's reasoning.

"The suit against this Berry Association, Inc. was filed by Mr. Lewis. He's not only the plaintiff, but the star witness against the big funeral company. Nobody knows the background of the charges, or the business itself, the way he does. If there was no Mr.

Lewis, there'd be no suit. You figure it out."

"But you said the other day that Kane is the force behind the legal action. Surely he would go ahead if anything happened to his grandfather?"

"Maybe, maybe not, depending on what else he's dug up against this Berry. But I wonder if that scum-bag didn't figure putting Mr. Lewis out of commission was worth the risk."

"It sounds like something out of a television movie," Regina protested.

"Yeah, well, maybe that's where he got the idea," Betsy said darkly.

Regina did her best to conceal the shiver that rippled over her skin. In an attempt at a more normal reaction, she said, "You've been to see Mr. Lewis?"

"Not yet. I'll go this evening, after my night manager comes on duty. I did call the hospital and talk to the nurse on his station. She gave me the lowdown because she's —"

"A Benedict?" Regina supplied before Betsy could finish.

"Married to one," the other woman answered with a fleeting grin before she launched into a complete description of the accident as culled from the nurse who had gotten it from one of the patrolmen.

Regina listened while stifling a strong

urge to drive straight to the hospital to see for herself that everything was really all right. She might have given in to it except for a distinct feeling that it would be hypocritical. She was far from eager to face Kane just now, too. Nor was she sure he would welcome having a near stranger around during the family crisis. At the same time, she turned the details of the accident over in her mind, searching for something, anything, to make her feel more easy about it.

As Betsy paused again, she said, "They haven't identified the other driver?"

"No, and Kane is mighty upset about it. There'll be hell to pay if he ever discovers who it was."

"I would expect so."

"He'll keep searching, don't you ever doubt it. I hope he finds him because it's only God's mercy that both Mr. Lewis and Miss Elise weren't killed. Why, I could strangle the man with my bare hands myself."

Regina made noises of agreement. At the same time, she glanced beyond Betsy to where Dudley Slater's car had been sitting for two days. It was gone, just as it had been gone the night before when she got back to the motel.

Following her gaze, Betsy asked, "You

looking for the guy who's been over there? I wondered myself what became of him. Won't hurt to mention to Kane that he took off."

Regina gave the motel owner a quick look. "I imagine Kane noticed."

"Could be. Not much he misses."

"I'm beginning to realize that." The words were grim.

"Well, I'll let you get on with your rat killing." Betsy turned away. "Just wanted to let you know Mr. Lewis won't be available for a day or two, in case you needed to change your plans."

"Yes, thank you," Regina replied, and added a few more words of appreciation before closing the door. She thought that the other woman was disappointed that she had not had more to say about the incident. Regina couldn't help it. She was in no mood for meaningless chatter.

She paced up and down the room, squeezing her hands together in front of her while her thoughts ricocheted in her head like the metal spheres inside a pinball machine.

Had Slater forced Mr. Lewis off the road? If so, whose idea had it been? Could Gervis have engineered it? Would he go that far?

She had always known there were certain

business matters he never discussed. Though she helped him with his private computer records kept at the apartment and often served as a sounding board for him, she didn't push it out of respect for his privacy. Still, that didn't keep her from wondering or putting certain facts and figures together until she had a far firmer grasp on how Gervis ran his operation than he realized.

She wished now that she'd paid even more attention. It had suddenly become extremely important to guess how far he would go. If he would order the death of an elderly man who happened to be his opponent in a civil suit, then saying hurtful things to a small boy might mean nothing at all.

No, no, it wasn't possible. She couldn't accept such a thing. To do that would be to acknowledge everything she had thought and felt for years was a lie.

Regardless, Gervis's threat toward Stephan, whether he meant it or not, had left her shaken. It struck at the foundations of her world back in New York. Without Gervis, what would she do? She would be alone, she and Stephan. They would have no one in the world who cared what became of them.

Regina was so disturbed in her mind that she could settle down to nothing. She took a shower, dressed in a T-shirt and slacks. With a great show of industry, she made a few phone calls about an estate sale and two or three antique jewelry exhibitions she was due to attend over the next couple of months. She read an auction catalog that she had brought with her, making notes on the values of pieces for future reference. The room turned stuffy and overwarm as the sun brought out the mugginess left by the rain. She turned on the air conditioner and stood in front of it for long moments with her eyes closed. After a quick lunch for which she had no appetite, she tried to watch an old Fred Astaire musical on television. The plot was contrived and silly and even the music couldn't hold her; she clicked it off again.

When she could stand it no longer, she placed a call to the hospital. They would tell her next to nothing about Mr. Lewis, perhaps because of harassing calls from the press or the defense lawyers. When the operator offered to put the call through to his room, Regina, suddenly nervous that Kane might answer, hung up at once.

Mr. Lewis's housekeeper, Dora, might tell her something if she rang Hallowed

Ground, she thought, then again, perhaps not. The best bet was probably Luke. He wasn't close to Mr. Lewis, but she was fairly sure he would know what was going on.

The phone at Chemin-a-Haut rang endlessly with no answer, nor was it picked up by anything so recklessly modern as an answering machine. She would try again later in the evening.

It was almost sundown when she decided to go in search of something to read, a couple of magazines or maybe one of April's books if she could find it. She brushed her hair, smoothed on a little lip gloss, then picked up her keys and headed out the door. It was then she saw the car.

Slater was back, parked in the same place across the street. She hadn't noticed, hadn't heard him, for the pulled draperies in the motel unit and the roar of the air conditioner.

Her lips tightened and a frown pleated the skin between her eyes. The need to do something, to have concrete answers, congealed inside her. Without stopping to think, she stalked toward the car.

The evening was suffocatingly humid. Damp heat rose around her ankles from the pavement, coating her skin in a light glaze of perspiration. The odor of exhaust fumes caught in her nose, mingling with the smell of frying chicken from the motel restaurant and honeysuckle fragrance drifting from where a mass of vines climbed a roadside utility pole. Somewhere a dog barked, then was quiet.

The man in the car watched her approach. He spat out the window, a warning shot that brought her to a stop a couple of steps away.

"What are you doing here?" she demanded without preamble.

His lips curled in his sharp face. "Don't know what you're talking about. I'm just sitting. No law against it, is there?"

"I know exactly who and what you are, or pretend to be." As she spoke, she stepped back a pace. The sour miasma of old sweat, beer breath, and stale cigarette smoke from inside the car was nauseating.

"Yeah? You read my stuff?"

"Not if I can help it. If you were any kind of reporter, you'd be at the hospital, wouldn't you?"

"You've got a smart mouth, you know that?"

"I'm well aware Gervis Berry is calling the shots here for you. What I want to know is how much of what you're doing is on his orders and how much on your own hook."

"The setup is real simple, sweetheart," he drawled. "I stick around here, do what I'm told, and I get a story, a big story. If I stumble onto the same thing you're looking for, then I get a bonus that'll set me up for life."

"What I'm looking for?"

"The secret, the key, the skinny, the info that's going to blow the case these hick lawyers are putting together to-hell-and-gone."

"Is that where you were last night, looking for this information?" She allowed suspicion to filter into her voice.

His eyes narrowed. "Where else?"

A couple of cars passed on the street just behind her, flapping her shirt with the wind of their passage. When she was sure she could be heard, she said, "Out toward the lake, improving the odds for Gervis?"

"Now where'd you get that idea?"

"And today you were staying clear until you found out whether Lewis Crompton was going to recover."

The reporter studied her for a second, then raised his brows in pained innocence. "You got it all wrong."

"I don't think so. So did Gervis tell you to do it?"

"I swear I don't know what you're talking about."

"I think you do," she corrected grimly. "There's no one else it could be."

He squinted at her as he reached to extract a cigarette from his shirt pocket along with a cheap plastic lighter. As he flicked the lighter into flame, the glow turned his skin yellow and exposed the feral enmity in his eyes. Then the light went out.

"Maybe you'd better take it up with Berry," Slater said, deliberately blowing smoke in her direction. "While you're at it, ask him if he's happy with my little solution to his problem."

She had been right. Cold horror slithered down her back. It increased, spreading, as she recognized one thing more: Though she knew Slater was behind the attack on Kane's grandfather, there was nothing she could do about it.

She backed away an instinctive step as she asked tightly, "Gervis doesn't know? Did he tell you to go after Mr. Lewis?"

"Didn't tell me not to."

"Maybe what I should ask, then, is how he's going to like your getting him involved with attempted murder."

"You think it'll bother him?"

The words were rasping in their dryness. Regina felt her scalp crawl. It was all too possible he was right and Gervis wouldn't mind. Her cousin, like some mob boss, might well be capable of sending a hireling to take care of the situation, then protesting his innocence if the man blocking his way wound up dead.

Voice tight, she said, "It could bother you both if Kane Benedict figures it out. I wouldn't underestimate him if I were you. Or his cousin who's the sheriff."

Slater gave another hacking laugh, then hawked and spat before he said with heavy irony, "I'll keep the warning in mind when I report to the boss man. He just might be interested in how thick you're getting with the law, too."

"No doubt you'll enjoy telling him," she said bitterly. She had suspected that Slater was reporting her movements; he'd just confirmed that, as well.

"I was sent to do a job. I'm doing it the best I know how."

"Where do you stop, tell me that? How much further will you go?"

"I stop when it's done, go as far as it takes," he answered with a snort. "But you got no right to come over all high-and-mighty. The way I see it, you're not a damned bit better."

He was right. It was sickening, but she couldn't deny it. Her voice compressed, she said, "I have my reasons."

"Don't we all."

"Anyway, it's none of your business." She squared her shoulders, exhaling in an effort to rid herself of the noxious recognition of blame. "You're not needed here. I can take care of things just fine on my own."

"You mean with Kane Benedict? Question there is, are you taking care of him? Or is he taking care of you?"

Heat rose in her face as she heard the innuendo in his voice. "What do you mean?"

"Just what you think," he countered, his lips wet with spittle. "He's good-looking, rich, and has the hots for you. You weren't exactly turning him off there for a while last night, now were you?"

"How do you know?"

"Never noticed me sneaking around, did you? Maybe I make a better undercover man than you thought."

She ignored both the jeer and her own quiver of distaste. "Why? What reason would you have to follow me?"

"Figured it might be interesting, and damned if I wasn't right. Just like a picture show, it was, seeing you make up to Benedict. But I did wonder about it for a second there. Seems to me somebody needs to watch out that you don't go over to the enemy."

"That's ridiculous!"

"Berry might not think so."

"He knows me, knows I would never do anything against him. Besides —" She stopped abruptly, unwilling to give this revolting little man anything else to use against her.

"There's the boy to keep you in line, isn't there?"

She said nothing, only lifted her chin.

"Surprised, huh? I make it my business to find out whatever there is to know."

There was another car coming. She turned her back on it. "My son," she said distinctly, "has nothing to do with this."

"Maybe, maybe not. I think I'll keep my eye on you anyway, for the charge if nothing else."

Disgust curled her lips. "I can imagine."

"You got me all wrong," he protested. "Watching's okay, but I got me a yen for some of what you were passing out. You want to work together on this, it'll be fine by me."

The look in his eyes made her feel as if she needed a bath. Her answer was instinctive and instant. "Never."

"Fine," he growled. "Then don't mess with me again. I'm after the dirt, the shit that's gonna help that bastard Berry get what he wants, because that's how I'll wind up with what I need. Get in my way and I'll stomp you flat."

"Will you now?" she said, holding his gaze.

"You better believe it." His features were animalistic as he stared at her from the car's cavelike interior.

Regina swung away, putting her back to him as she checked out the traffic, then started across the road. She could feel his gaze burrowing into her. It was a relief when she reached her room and let herself inside. She put the chain on and turned the dead bolt, then slumped against the door and closed her eyes. She breathed in and out in deep gasps, as if she had been running for miles.

It had been a mistake, perhaps, to throw his suggestion back in his face with so little tact. Injured pride could make him a dangerous enemy. She couldn't help it; even pretending to cooperate with him was beyond her.

Something had to be done, but what? What?

She could call Gervis, but to what purpose? He'd said before that he had no control over Slater. Assuming, of course, that he wanted to control him.

The next best thing might be to call Kane and throw herself on his mercy. She well might, except there was no guarantee he would be merciful, much less willing to understand her involvement.

Going to Roan Benedict was no better option. If she did that, it would all come out. There was no possible way to explain what she knew or make anyone believe it without implicating Gervis. If that happened, her cousin would go crazy. There was no telling what he might do.

And Stephan would be there alone with him.

Stephan, her son.

No, bringing the sheriff or authority of any kind into this was clearly impossible. That left only one thing. She had to find something Gervis could use against Mr. Lewis in court. She had to find it fast, before Slater took matters into his own hands again. If she managed that feat, then there would be no reason for any more threats, any more danger.

Kane was the key after all, though it had nothing to do with mercy. She was going to have to go through him to get what she needed.

She put her hand to her pendant, holding it in a death grip. Squeezing her eyes shut so tight that she could feel her lashes pricking the skin around them, she listened to the hard, frantic pounding of her heart.

Could she do it? Did she have the nerve, not to mention the sex appeal or the pure, unmitigated gall? Could she manage it while Kane was so concerned for his grandfather? She didn't know, but she was going to have to find out.

She had to follow Gervis's orders. She had to do it as soon as she was able, tomorrow, the next day, whenever she could find the glimmer of an excuse.

There were so many ugly phrases for what she needed to do, so many crass, contemptuous, vulgar words to describe an act that was both simple and profound, a joining of the flesh that could not be accomplished without some degree of mental bonding. There were also a few with gentle, even resplendent, meanings.

She needed to make love to Kane in order to get close to him, to become intimate with him so she could discover what he knew.

The last was far preferable. It was what she would choose, if she must.

Or if she dared.

10

It was Betsy who first mentioned the welcome-home reception for Mr. Lewis two days later. To call Luke on the pretext of discovering the progress of the patient, then work the reception into the conversation, required more nerve than it did guile. She hated deceiving Kane's cousin, but the resulting invitation to go with him was important. It represented the first step in her plan of attack.

Not that the gathering was a formal occasion in any way. It was just a few friends and neighbors showing up when Mr. Lewis was brought home from the hospital. According to Luke, no one wanted to tire Kane's grandfather or make him feel he had to entertain them when he might not feel up to it. They would stick around long enough to show how glad they were that he was okay and have a little cake and coffee, then they would go.

The gathering would be out at Kane's house, The Haven. Mr. Lewis was to stay there a few days under his grandson's eye and Vivian Benedict's care. They were afraid he would try to get out of bed too soon or do too much otherwise.

Regina and Luke reached The Haven before Kane arrived from the hospital with Mr. Lewis. They joined the others clustered in the shade of the long, column-lined front gallery. The rumble of voices was steady, punctuated now and then by a ripple of laughter, but spirits were subdued. The general feeling seemed to be that they had come close to losing Mr. Lewis, and that was not something to be taken lightly.

A great deal of attention was paid to Miss Elise, who sat pale and composed in a rattan peacock chair someone had brought out from the sunroom. She seemed to be enjoying herself in a quiet way, though she tried more than once to get up to help with the refreshments. All such efforts were kindly but firmly refused by Kane's aunt, who seemed in her element as hostess. Bustling here and there, talking ninety-to-nothing, Aunt Vivian supervised the arrangement of the cakes and pies brought in by different women to be added to the bounty she had baked herself. The only person she allowed to do anything was Dora from Hallowed Ground, and then only because the housekeeper came armed with a silver cake knife and pie server and ignored all efforts to prevent her from wielding them.

April Halstead was also on hand, looking graceful and put-together in a simple dress of sunny yellow cotton knit worn with citrine earrings. Betsy arrived a few minutes after Regina and was fairly muted, for her, both in the shirt and pants she wore and the volume of her comments.

Regina recognized one or two others from the open house at Chemin-a-Haut, though she couldn't recall their names. She did know Roan Benedict, however, and would have even if he hadn't been wearing his badge. Thankfully, there was no time to do more than smile and nod a nervous greeting before someone announced that Kane was arriving with Mr. Lewis.

Everyone crowded toward the wide front steps, congregating there and on the brick walkway below. Regina hung back. She had no real place among the group and was reluctant to claim any. Added to that was her uncertainty over how Kane might feel about seeing her there.

He homed in on her presence with laser-beam accuracy, singling her out among the other well-wishers. Even while helping his grandfather negotiate the brick steps up to the gallery, his dark blue gaze meshed with her hazel one. For long seconds, there was nothing except trenchant speculation in his expression. Then his firm mouth relaxed into a smile.

That lack of hostility felt like a benediction. She caught her breath in soundless pleasure. As she felt the glow of it, she realized how tense she had been, bow fearful that she had lost all chance of gaining his attention. Her heart lifted with hope that she knew was reflected in the tentative curving of her lips in return.

Mr. Lewis was hugged and had his uninjured left hand clasped a dozen times over on his way up the steps. He nodded, smiled, exchanged quips and jokes about his driving, the hospital nurses, and how anxious he was to get to Miss Elise. She met him with a kiss at the wide front door, and they made their way into the house together.

Wine and coffee were served along with the various desserts. When the glasses and cups and plates had been passed around, Luke proposed a toast, and all drank to the honoree's health and good fortune in avoiding more serious injury.

Mr. Lewis raised both his cast-encased right arm and his glass to indicate that he wanted to reply. "To my good friends, my great neighbors, and all my favorite relatives by blood and by marriage, I thank you. This is certainly something worth living for, I promise you." His eyes crinkled at the corners in whimsical amusement. "I wouldn't have missed it for anything, particularly a longer rest in that wooden box I keep in my parlor."

There was a general laugh, for which he waited before he went on. "Since you're all here, this seems as good a time as any to make a little announcement, one some of you have been expecting for quite a while. Miss Elise was more shook-up than she let on by what happened the other night because she's not letting me drive her home anymore. She's put her foot down, decided she's going to live at my house."

"Now, Lewis . . ." the white-haired lady protested, blushing.

"That's not the way it is?" he asked, his eyes twinkling as he put his arm around her, cast and all.

"You know very well it's not," she scolded, though her gaze was more than a little flirtatious.

"Oh, yes," he said, pretending sudden understanding before he looked up, beaming, at the rest of the gathering. "The two of us are going to get married first."

The round of chuckles and chorus of congratulations lightened the atmosphere. Conversation became a general buzz. The food and drink disappeared at an astonishing rate. Then, before Mr. Lewis began noticeably to flag, people started to find excuses for going. There were more hugs and handshakes, then a general exodus.

Miss Elise was among the last to depart. She gave her new fiancé a gentle kiss, then accepted the arm that Roan extended in support, since he had offered to see her home. Because she looked a little teary, the sheriff teased and flirted with her, exerting such outrageous charm and gallantry that he had her smiling again by the time they reached the front steps.

Soon there was no one left with Mr. Lewis, Kane and his aunt except Regina and Luke, who had been asked to help get the patient up the stairs to his bedroom. As the others eased the older man from his chair and helped him toward the upstairs bedroom, Regina busied herself picking up cups, glasses and dessert plates.

"Don't bother with that, dear," Aunt Vivian said over her shoulder. "I'll do it later."

Kane, three steps up the staircase with his grandfather, paused to glance back down at

Regina. "But don't go just yet, will you?"

"I can't," she said, awkwardly balancing fragile cups and saucers, "not until Luke is ready."

"I brought her," Luke put in from where he stood lending his arm to support the invalid.

Kane met his cousin's dark gaze for a flicker of time far too short to guess what he was thinking beyond the fact that he was not pleased. Then to Regina, he said, "I'll be back in a second."

It sounded vaguely like a threat, but she refused to let it get to her. Her resolve was bolstered by Mr. Lewis, who gave her a jaunty wave and a wink before continuing slowly upward with his escort.

It was Aunt Vivian who returned first. With a warm smile that erased years from her face, she said, "I thought I'd leave Mr. Lewis to the boys. He'll be more comfortable that way, I imagine. Would you care for more coffee?"

Regina declined the offer. "You think he's really going to be all right?"

"Oh, yes. A few more days of bed rest and he'll be his old self — except for the arm, of course, which will take a while to heal. It was a lucky escape."

"Yes." Regina was glad Kane's aunt had

no idea how lucky.

"He's a tough old buzzard, tougher than us all, I sometimes think." The other woman gave a low laugh as she waved Regina toward a seat on the couch, then dropped down beside her with a sigh. "He draws strength from the good he does for others and his pleasure in helping them through trying times. His greatest problem with the accident is that Miss Elise might have been harmed."

"He seems a remarkable man." The words were spoken with all sincerity.

"I certainly think so. You wouldn't believe some of the things he's done. He likes to talk about how wild Kane used to be, but I can tell you the tendency didn't all come from the Benedict side of the family."

Regina felt uncomfortable taking advantage of the other woman's natural gregariousness, heightened as it seemed to be by the excitement of the homecoming. At the same time, she didn't dare pass up the opportunity. "I find that hard to believe," she said encouragingly. "He looks like such a perfect gentleman."

"I'll admit it's hard to picture him doing anything the least bit out of line. Regardless, he was quite a ladies' man in the days of slouch hats and hair tonic, before he married Mary Sue. There's even a tale that he and his father helped cover up a killing back in the early thirties."

"It's common knowledge?" Regina asked, startled.

"No, no, I only heard about it because my husband's family was involved."

"The Benedicts." Regina supplied the name to be certain she got the story straight.

"Exactly. I don't know all the details, but it seems there was a lowlife pestering one of the Benedict women. She'd have nothing to do with the man, which drove him wild. One night, this creep caught her alone. When they found her, she was bruised and covered with blood, scarcely half-alive. The Benedict men went after the attacker — it was the kind of thing they did back then. He opened fire when he saw them coming. Shots were exchanged, and the lowlife wound up dead. Next day, so the story goes, Crompton's Funeral Home buried two caskets in the same plot at old Granny Murphy's funeral, one on top of the other. If the Murphys should ever exhume the dear soul, they'll be shocked to discover who Granny has been sleeping with all these years."

Regina couldn't help smiling at the droll expression on the other woman's face. As tragic as the incident might have been, it had taken place long ago, so had the feel of some distant legend. If the story she'd just heard had been about Mr. Lewis instead of his father, it might have been useful for Gervis's purpose. Unfortunately, it wasn't.

"I suppose," she said carefully, "that there are . . . certain advantages to the funeral business. You often know, literally, where the body is buried."

"There are responsibilities, too," Aunt Vivian commented. "People ask for the strangest things."

"Oh?"

"Some want to be buried with their jewelry or photographs. One widow wanted to be buried with a plaster cast of her husband's face. Then there was the man with the pharaoh complex who asked to take his pet cat with him into the afterworld. Of course, someone would have had to destroy it, and Mr. Lewis wasn't about to be the executioner, being fond of cats himself. That was one request he sort of let slide until it was too late."

"I would imagine so."

"But he did honor a last request that touched his heart. A woman from Turn-Coupe quarreled with her sweetheart, then flounced off and married the wrong man. She spent her whole life being a good wife, then discovered she had cancer. When she knew she was dying, she asked Mr. Lewis to bury her next to the man she had never stopped loving, her sweetheart who had died the year before. When the time came, Mr. Lewis swore she had requested a closed-casket ceremony, then buried an empty coffin in the designated place and laid the woman to rest for eternity beside her soul mate."

"And the family never discovered it?" Regina asked with close interest. The story was intriguing, even if it wasn't damaging enough to be useful to her. Or was it? Might there not be a twist Gervis could put on it to make a case for some kind of fraud?

"Not to my knowledge, and I feel sure there would have been repercussions if it had come out. But you see what kind of man we're dealing with, don't you?" Vivian tilted her head to give Regina a glance from the corner of her eye.

Regina did indeed. Mr. Lewis was far too kindhearted and accommodating for his own good. She hated, really hated, that she was being forced to inform against him. She hated still more that his grandson, who was too much like him, was going to be caught in the fallout. Supposing, of course, that this secret she'd just discovered would be sufficient for her cousin's purposes. She wouldn't bet on it.

Kane came quietly down the stairs behind them. To his aunt, he said, "Luke is going to sit with Pops until he falls asleep, which shouldn't be long. I know you're worn out, too. Why don't you lie down while Regina and I take a little walk down to the lake?"

Vivian Benedict searched her nephew's face. Apparently, she saw something there that Regina couldn't detect, for she didn't argue. With her easy, natural grace, she thanked Regina for coming and said she would see her on her next visit. As she left them, Kane indicated the hallway that led toward the double French doors at the back of the house, then fell into step beside Regina as she moved in that direction.

Her arm brushed against his shirtfront when he held the back door for her. She was so tense that her nerves leaped, tingling at the touch, and it was all she could do not to pull away. Under the circumstances, it was impossible for her to refuse his request to speak to her alone. She was even grateful that she needn't find some way of arranging it herself. Still, she was distinctly edgy about discovering what he wanted.

"So you're on the lake, too?" she said in an effort to ease the strain.

"Not like at Luke's, if that's what you mean. My great-granddad who built The Haven preferred to be closer to the road, saving the bottomland for sugar-cane."

"Someone, April, I think it was, told me you worked in the cane fields as a teenager."

"I expect that's not all she told you."

"No," she admitted with a quick glance. "There was something about a nickname."

He made a sound of disgust and shoved his hands into his back pockets.

Studying his closed expression as they moved down the steps, she said, "I take it you're none too happy about it?"

"If April would stop telling people about how she gave it to me, it might die a natural death."

"I think it's interesting, even cool," Regina said.

"Cool," he repeated in pained tones.

"Very descriptive," she added, controlling a smile.

"How would you know?" As they reached a gravel pathway meandering past a series of outbuildings and toward the distant glimmer of water through the trees, he gestured to indicate they should turn that way.

"Just guessing." Her glimpse of his set face was fleeting as she passed him, then went on ahead.

"You couldn't," he said with deliberation, "be more wrong."

Her stomach muscles clenched in a spasm. She sought a response and found none. They walked several more yards, passing beyond outbuildings that he described as an old smokehouse, a tractor shed and a barn. As they reached a wooded area and moved on through the cooler, lengthening shadows under the trees, she said finally, "Is there a point to this?"

"Actually, there is," he said.

"And that would be?"

"Exercise, relaxation, companionship? Take your pick."

She didn't believe it, not for a second. Something in his voice snagged her attention, a shading very like regret. Uneasiness shifted inside her, and she opened her mouth to demand an explanation.

It was then that she heard a vehicle start up back at the house. She halted. "Isn't that Luke's Jeep?"

"Don't panic," he said, his gaze steady as he came even with her. "I told him I'd run you back to the motel."

"Did you now? That was nice of you, nice and high-handed."

"Wasn't it?" he agreed, not at all perturbed.

"You might have asked."

His gaze held humor as well as purpose before he moved on beneath the trees. Over his shoulder, he said, "And risk your refusing? Not a chance."

"Of all the —" In her irritation, she couldn't think of a phrase strong enough to satisfy her without being profane.

"Of all the chauvinistic, ill-mannered, downright redneck dumb tricks?" he supplied.

"Something like that."

"That's all right. Don't spare my feelings."

She stared after him. Her first impulse was to refuse to go another step, but what would she gain by it?

"I don't intend to spare anything," she declared as she closed the distance with fast, hard steps. "What is it with you? The women you know may be impressed by a take-charge attitude, but I don't care for it. I'd just as soon go back to the motel, if you don't mind."

"But I do mind."

He stopped as they came to the shore that was much the same as the water's edge where she had watched the flight of the blue heron the first time he'd brought her to the lake. The main difference was the sturdy, covered boat dock built out over the water like a house on pilings and the fishing boats with motors, two of heavy fiberglass, two of lighter aluminum, which lay tied up in its slips. His eyes were a deep, vibrant blue in the summer sunlight as he turned to face her.

Annoyance combined with a half-formed fear that her attempt to reestablish a relationship between them might have worked too well roused her combative spirit. "I said I'm ready to go. If you won't take me, I'll find my own way."

"I don't think so."

"Watch." She spun on her heel, heading back toward the house.

He moved so silently she didn't hear him, so fast her brain had no time to issue a warning. One moment, she was walking off; the next, she was caught and lifted against his chest in hard, enclosing arms. He swung her in a dizzying circle and stalked back toward the boat dock.

Disbelief held her rigid for long seconds. Then she strained against his hold, trying to shove away from him. He didn't even slacken his pace. The warped boards of the dock rattled under his fast, hard strides. Face grim, mouth set, he marched to the slips where the boats floated above their wavering reflections and stopped at the very edge.

Regina went still, casting a quick look below her as she felt herself suspended above nothing but water. His hold loosened slightly, becoming less constricting. In quick reflex, she clutched his shirt collar.

"I'm not going to throw you in, no matter how tempting the idea may be, but we are going in the boat," he said in grim warning. "Be careful how you fight if you don't want to get wet."

"What are you doing?" The question was embarrassingly husky. A strong shudder shook her, chased by one stronger still. She kept her gaze on the water, afraid to look at him.

He was silent an instant. Then he said in curt reply, "You'll see."

Swinging toward the nearest boat slip, he shifted his hold and released her knees to lower her feet to the dock. With one strong arm, he clamped her to his side, then stepped down into the larger fiberglass fishing boat and swung her into one of its center seats. The low craft rocked with the sudden motion, and she grabbed for the side. In that precarious moment, he cast off and shoved out of the slip, away from the dock. Reaching the driver's seat beside her in a couple of long strides, he cranked the motor. It caught with a dull, spluttering rumble. Then they were off, skimming over the water, threading through the encroaching cypress trees into the main channel of the lake.

Regina briefly considered screaming, but that would be a waste of breath since there was no one near enough to hear. She could jump overboard and swim for shore, though the distance was widening every second and she wasn't the strongest of swimmers. More than that, the water was dangerously full of stumps and cypress knees, plus there was no guarantee that Kane wouldn't overtake her and haul her back. A mad urge to leap up and try to shove him overboard tugged at her, but she suspected strongly that she'd also wind up in the lake. She sat still, then, and tried to tell herself that he had threatened no bodily harm beyond a dunking. For all she knew, he might be taking her for a quick ride to prove some macho point.

Of one thing, however, she was absolutely sure. Kane Benedict was not nearly so upstanding and gentlemanly as his grandfather after all.

"Where are you taking me?" She pressed her palms flat against the cushioned boat seat on either side of her to keep her hands from shaking.

"You'll see." His attention was on a

channel ahead that gave access to the open water. He sent the boat gliding through it.

"Don't you think I have a right to know?"

He met her gaze, his own opaque. "And spoil the surprise?"

The dispassionate sound of his voice should have been a relief, but wasn't. Instead, its deep timbre sent dread rushing along her nerves. "I don't like surprises," she said in tight control.

"Don't you?" His gaze narrowed before he looked away. "I thought you did."

What did he mean? And was there really a surprise to be seen, or did he intend something else altogether? She hovered on the edge of her seat as she tried to decide. It didn't seem possible he meant her harm, but there was the incident with the coffin to consider. Besides, she had been wrong before, years ago.

She had not fought against being taken where she didn't want to go that other time because she didn't want to appear naive and foolish. Now she didn't want to look like an alarmist. Funny, how little she had changed.

The lake was smooth except for an occasional glittering wind shiver or the arrow-shaped ripple of a swimming waterbird. Its dark color, caused by the endless drip of tannin-loaded tree sap and a mud bottom, made a perfect mirror for the evening sky so that swathes of indigo, violet and crimson lay across its surface like painted streaks of watercolor. The stately cypress trees around the edges lifted their flat branches toward the clouds in open, pleading gestures. Regina stared around her, taking deep breaths, trying to stay calm. It didn't help.

They were totally alone on the lake. She spotted three or four fishermen in boats along the shoreline, easing slowly along under the power of trolling motors as they cast for bass. A speedboat with a rooster tail of spume zipped toward them, then past them in the wide channel, and another bass boat crossed their bow and buzzed away for parts unknown.

She lifted her hand in a halfhearted signal to the man in the bass boat, but he only gave a brief wave and looked away, as if embarrassed to be caught staring at another man's woman. It would have been infuriating if it wasn't so discouraging.

Kane wove the boat deeper into the lake, taking one branching channel after the other. At first, Regina tried to remember the different turns, but soon lost track since they all looked the same. The boat ride became an endless blur of trees and water, of marsh grass and floating duckweed and mats of water hyacinths tucked into swampy inlets that smelled of mud and fish. Then the trees grew thicker again. Kane never hesitated, only twisted this way and that among them as if following a well-worn path. Several times, they passed small structures on stilts, too small for human habitation, too large for use by birds or animals. She thought they must be duck blinds since she'd heard a snatch of conversation at the open house about duck hunting.

Minutes after they had seen the first blind, Kane headed toward one that was somewhat larger than the others. He pulled the boat in under its tall, stiltlike pilings and cut the engine. In a quick, expert movement, he tied up beneath a ladder leading to what appeared to be a trapdoor above their heads. He stood and pushed the door open on its hinges, then laid it back on the floor inside.

"This is it," he said, moving aside out of the way. "Climb up while I hold the boat steady."

Her first instinct was to refuse, but that had gotten her exactly nowhere earlier. She tightened her lips, then stood gingerly and mounted the first rung. As she moved upward, Kane swung onto the ladder close behind her, too close. She climbed more quickly. When she gained the upper floor and got to her feet, he pulled himself inside with a lithe movement. Swinging around, he dropped the trapdoor shut with a solid thud. Then he straightened and turned to face her, his features masklike in the shadowed interior of the blind.

They were shut up together.

For a suffocating instant, Regina felt her old terror return. She was alone in this boxlike contraption with a man who had the promise of danger in his voice and empty eyes. The dim reaches of this swamp area on the edge of the lake spread around them, a buffer zone of watery silence. The day was waning and evening closing in. She was caught, isolated, weaponless against a menace she had brought on herself.

A cry of panic crowded her throat, but she swallowed it down. Desperately, she concentrated on the feel of the rough texture of the walls behind her and smell of damp cypress wood, the shifting air currents that touched her face, the lap of the water against the pilings and the boat under the blind. She dragged air into her lungs and let it out in slow control.

Focusing more carefully, she noticed the space was not as small as it first appeared, but was at least eight feet square and seven in height. A metal chest sat in one corner, along with a contraption that looked as if it might be a gas heater. Three of the side walls appeared to be hinged to allow them to swing down, probably for hunters to take aim on incoming ducks from various directions. Best of all, the roof was open to the sky halfway across its width, though the other half had a flat roof to provide rain protection.

She met Kane's gaze while searching the last depths of her soul for bravado to use in place of her vanished courage. With the huskiness of cramped vocal cords, she said, "This is the surprise?"

"In a manner of speaking."

"I've seen it. We can go." She took a step toward the entrance behind him.

He blocked her way, his shoulders looming twice as wide as normal, his feet planted directly above the only exit. "Not yet."

She stopped, unwilling to come too close to him, to touch him. The implacable hardness of his voice made her heart kick into a faster rhythm. She moistened her lips. "There's more?"

"You could say that." He put his hands on his hips, his stance rock solid.

"Well?"

"Now we talk."

"I may be wrong, but I thought we'd been talking."

"This time," he said deliberately, "I choose the subject."

She stepped back to the opposite wall where she put her shoulders to it and crossed her arms over her chest. Praying her voice wouldn't quiver, she said, "This should be interesting."

"So it should. Let's start with what you were discussing with Slater in front of the motel three days ago."

It took her a split second too long to form an answer, but she tried anyway. "I don't know what you mean."

"I think you do. You were seen in broad daylight."

"Whoever said so was mistaken." The last rays of sunset through the cypress trees still had heat, she thought. She could feel droplets of perspiration dampening her hairline.

"Not likely."

Betsy. It had to be. Regina felt her spirits sink. She should have realized someone that interested in people would be watching, might have remembered if she'd been less upset. In rapid recovery, she said, "If you must know, I got a little tired of being spied upon and decided to find out why."

"And did you?"

The skeptical look in his eyes was intensely annoying, but she could hardly explain that Slater considered her his competition. "I think I convinced him that watching me wasn't worth his time."

"You're lying," he said evenly.

"No, I —"

"I think you are." He took a slow step toward her, and then another. "I think you have been all along. But I know how to get at the truth, right here and now, once and for all."

He was closing in too much, getting too near. She started to sidestep, but he shot out his hand to catch her arm, holding her against the wall while he moved in until his chest brushed the tips of her breasts and his thighs cradled hers. She turned her head, straining away from him, but he pressed his palms to the wall on either side of her head and leaned so near that his cheek brushed hers and his warm breath fluttered across her lips.

"Don't!"

"Don't what?" he whispered, his warm breath feathering along her neck. "Don't touch you? Don't hold you? Or just don't expect to get what I want from you?"

His nearness was compelling yet frightening, both a powerful attraction and a profound disturbance. She wanted to be unmoved, but it didn't work. At the same time, she was struck by the terrible irony of her position. She had meant to use sex to discover what she needed to know from Kane. Now it seemed he intended to use the same weapon against her. The worst of it was that he was far more expert at it than she'd ever dreamed of being.

There was a difference, however, or so she thought. It was not her susceptibility to his lovemaking that he expected to use as a lever, but rather her fear of it, her horror at intimacy in a confined space, which he had discovered in the antique coffin. That put an entirely different twist on it.

He eased closer still, brushing his warm lips along her cheek, inhaling as if he would take the essence of her into his body. The heat and power of him engulfed her, swamping her senses, sending her reactions and instincts tumbling in confusion. Then she felt the brief press of firm male heat against her abdomen.

She jerked her arms up, slamming her elbows into his ribs. As he gave way a fraction, she shoved hard and launched herself away from the wall. He stumbled back a step, unprepared. She lunged for the trapdoor. He caught her from behind as she bent to grab the handle. She staggered, tripped, went down. A sharp cry left her as she landed on one knee.

Then he was on her, his weight flattening her, knocking the air from her lungs. Before she could draw breath, she was rolled to her back. He flung himself across her upper body and pinned her legs with one knee. Snatching her wrists, one in each hand, he held them on either side of her face.

She lay still, eyes closed tight as she concentrated on breathing. She could feel her heart trying to burst out of her chest, feel his thudding against her also in a fast, pounding echo. Tremors ran along her nerves; she jerked again and again beneath his weight. In her mind was nothing except a red-black haze of dread.

Then Kane lowered his head until his lips were warm against hers, until he drank her harsh gasps. "Now," he said in relentless calm, "where were we?"

11

"Don't," she whispered.

"Tell me why I shouldn't," he murmured, his lips brushing hers with each syllable like tiny electrical charges.

"Decency?" It was a desperate chance. She could have sworn he had that in him.

He hesitated, for she felt it. Then he shook his head. "There are things I want to know, and I can think of no other way to get the truth from you. Try again."

"You don't know . . . what you're doing to me."

His laugh had a winded sound. "If it's anything like what you're doing to me, then I expect it to be highly effective."

Her stomach muscles clenched as the deep resonance of his voice vibrated in places already sensitized by the heated heaviness of him against her. The words strangled, she cried, "I don't know any-thing!"

"Somehow I have trouble believing that."

She tried to control the shudders building inside her, the darkness that threatened to overwhelm her, but knew ahead of time it would be impossible. "Let me go. We can . . . talk standing up."

"I tried that already and it didn't work. Now I prefer lying down."

The words were feathered with hoarse suggestion in her ears. "I don't! Please . . . you've got to —"

"The faster you answer me, the sooner I let you go. If I let you go. You can start by telling me what you're really doing in Turn-Coupe."

"You know why I'm here."

He shook his head, a slow movement that teased her mouth. "I know what you say is the reason," he replied before dipping his head to taste her lips, then running his tongue along the sensitive inner edges. "What I don't know is who sent you."

"No one," she answered with a catch in her voice as she twisted her head away. "It was a referral. To look at your grandfather's jewelry."

"You'll have to do better than that." This time, he took her mouth more firmly, pressed deeper.

She shivered with the distress inside her. Her lips tingled and burned, and the sweet taste of him seemed to spread through her bloodstream like some potent, debilitating liqueur. At the same time, a dim and intuitive recognition of how she might counter what he was doing to her hovered at the edge of her mind. It grew, blossoming into an idea so simple it shocked her into stillness, made her drag air into her lungs in abrupt reaction.

She had thought she needed to be close to Kane Benedict to get what her cousin needed from him. Surely it was impossible to be much nearer than she was at this moment.

Self-control, that was what she required. She must conquer the old fears, stop the automatic reactions. This man was not the one who had betrayed and hurt her. Though he was holding her confined in his arms, Kane wasn't harming her, hadn't caused her pain. If she could only forget the past, let go and think of this clash as mental combat, a battle of wills and imaginations, then she might gain something from it.

With a supreme effort, she stopped avoiding his kiss, allowed her lips to soften, to conform to the pressure of his mouth. Desperately, she concentrated on the warm, smooth contours, the friction of his tongue over hers, and the intimation of desire that mixed with the taste of him in her mouth. And slowly she felt, creeping in upon her like a fog, a vast and pleasurable lethargy that seemed as if it might banish the fear that hovered still behind her resolve.

He murmured in wordless surprise. Releasing her wrists, he gathered her close and captured her mouth once more with honeyed, drugging sweetness. The tender abrasion of his tongue invited her exploration in return, incited her to join in the sinuous play. She accepted, testing with wonder his satin smoothness, and also the firm promise of another, more intimate, invasion.

Abruptly, his muscles went taut. He raised his head. In razor-edged contempt that might have been for his own impulses as well as hers, he demanded, "What are you to Gervis Berry? And how does it feel to almost kill a man who never harmed a living soul?"

"Nothing! I didn't," she cried, shocked and bereft at his unexpected change from tenderness to terrifying accusation. Tears sprang into her eyes, forced upward by the painful tightening of her chest and throat. They ran backward across her temples, tracking into her hair.

"You did," he said in harsh answer. "You fingered Pops for Slater, didn't you? You pointed him out so he could follow him home, run him off the road."

His face was a blur above her, the words he spoke a dull roaring in her ears as the old horror returned. Her senses swam in sickening waves. She hardly knew what she was saying as she turned her head from side to side, moaning, "No, no, no."

"Yes," he insisted, brushing his hand across her breast, then cupping it. "You knew, and did it anyway. Why? *Tell me why.*"

His touch on the sensitive peak of her breast was like a lightning strike. It ripped through her, bringing the surge of panicky, white-hot rage. She bucked under him, twisting in insane strength to break his grasp. He was flung backward, catching himself on his elbow. She rolled, pushing free, scuttling away from him to the nearest corner where she turned at bay. Teeth clenched and eyes blazing, she waited for him to attack.

He surged to his knees, whipped around. He met her gaze, his own hot with fury. His muscles tensed to lunge.

He stopped.

For long moments, neither of them moved. Then Kane sank back on his heels. He wiped splayed fingers over his face, then plunged them through his hair and down the back of his neck. He shut his eyes so tight the lashes looked like rows of tiny spikes. When he opened them again, the rage and determination had vanished from their blue depths. His gaze held only tired self-disgust.

"Don't," he said softly. "Don't look at me like that."

She lifted her chin, not taking her eyes from him for a second. It was impossible to loosen her clamped jaws enough to speak.

"What happened to you?" he went on in low concern as he dropped his hand to his knee. "Who did it, and when? And why in the name of heaven hasn't someone helped you get over it?"

"It's no business of yours." She hadn't meant to answer him; the words seemed to come by themselves.

"I think it is, since it almost caused me to do something we'd both regret."

"It was you," she said with a sharp, negative gesture. "Your own idea."

"But it would never have crossed my mind, except you obviously objected to being —"

"Except you saw it as a weakness to be exploited." She dragged air deeper into her lungs and felt her fear loosen its grip.

Tipping his head so the light moved across the blue-black waves of his hair, he

251

avoided her gaze as he said, "I thought I could, and would, do anything to help Pops. I was wrong."

It was both an apology and explanation, if she wanted to accept them. Did she? She wasn't sure, though she might be forced to it if she was to stay in Turn-Coupe. At least she had been right in her feeling that he was too inherently decent for such a ploy. Which didn't mean she had to make this easier for him. She remained silent.

In that moment of stillness, a hollow thump came from beneath the blind, vibrating through its timbers. The noise would not have been familiar an hour ago, but now Regina recognized it at once. It was the sound of a boat knocking against one of the duck blind's pilings. That was followed by quiet, rhythmic splashes as someone paddled away. They were not alone here in the swampy back area of the lake.

Hard on that realization came the racketing roar of a motor being cranked into life, then changing as it was put into gear. Whoever had been under the blind was leaving. And he was in a hurry.

Kane sprang to his feet. Reaching the nearest wall in a single stride, he flipped the latches that held the hinged portion, then let it down. Bracing his hands on the rough-cut edges, he leaned out to search the water around them with his hard gaze. He swore in fluent virulence.

"What is it?" Regina put a hand to the wall behind her and dragged herself to her feet.

He didn't answer. Instead, he whipped around toward the trap door, lifted it, and laid it back. Swinging into the opening, he disappeared down the ladder. She followed him to the square hole, saw him clinging to the wooden ladder while he stared around in all directions.

Regina dropped to her knees and leaned forward to search the empty expanse of water that surrounded the duck blind. As Kane looked up, she met his gaze. In stunned understanding, she said, "The boat. It's —"

"Gone. And it didn't come untied by itself."

"Someone took it?" The other boat and motor they'd heard hadn't meant company or even rescue, as she had half imagined. "Who would do that?"

"You tell me."

He started back up the ladder. As she moved out of his way, she retorted sharply, "How should I know? This is your territory, remember?"

"But you're the one with the strange

friends." He regained the floor level, then seated himself on the ledge, letting his feet and legs dangle in the trapdoor opening.

"Your friends know how to get here. And your relatives."

Something flickered in his eyes and was gone. "They wouldn't, not on their own. And I have no reason whatever for arranging to be left here with you."

"You think I want to be with you? That I've got somebody following me around making sure of convenient encounters? If you believe that, then you're more of a dumb redneck than I thought!"

He stared at her a moment, then a grim smile tugged one corner of his mouth. "At least you got your feistiness back."

"For what good it does me," she muttered, looking away. To cover a comment that might be more revealing than intended, she added, "So what do we do now?"

"What do you suggest?"

"I don't know!" she shot back in exasperation. "Something besides just sit here and wait for dark to fall."

He watched her with interest but no great concern. "It's a long swim back, but if that's what you want, be my guest."

"That's your only suggestion?"

"Unless you can walk on water."

She was about to blast him for that chestnut when she noted the amused twitch of his lips, the speculation that lay behind his bland expression. "You're enjoying this, aren't you?" she said, clenching her hands in her lap. "You planned it. It's your way of turning the screws."

"No," he said in positive rejection as his amusement vanished. "I wouldn't go that far."

"Come on, why should I believe that?"

"Because I said so," he answered, his gaze lethally straight.

She held his eyes as long as she could, until her own burned from the strain. Then she lowered her lashes. "So what happens now?"

"We wait."

Her attention snapped upward again. "For what? Doomsday?"

"For Luke, probably. He's our best bet since nobody knows the lake and swamp better. Or is more likely to guess where I might be."

"You mean," she said in incredulous comprehension, "that no one really knows where we are? Not your aunt or your grandfather? Not Luke? No one?"

"It isn't the sort of expedition you advertise."

She could see that all too well. They were stranded, then. It was unbelievable. In this day of cellular phones, pagers, modems, satellite communication around the globe and even from outer space, they were stuck in the middle of nowhere with no means to get back and no way to let anyone know where to find them.

"There must be something we can do!"

"We can make ourselves comfortable."

"Comfortable." Frustration and suspicion freighted the word.

He sent her a brief, sardonic look, then sprang to his feet with easy grace and closed the trapdoor. Turning toward the metal chest in the corner, he knelt before it to lift the lid, took out a wool army blanket and tossed it toward her. That was followed by a couple of small cans of sausages, a can of beans, soft drinks in plastic bottles, and a plastic cracker box. The last thing he set out appeared to be a camping lantern.

"Always prepared," she said with laconic lack of appreciation.

"Were you a Girl Scout?" He waited for her reply with a grin hovering at one corner of his mouth.

"Hardly. But I imagine you were a Boy Scout."

"Matter of fact, I was. But I learned about

anticipating emergencies the hard way, from experience."

"In the swamps, or while slaughtering migratory birds?"

"I hunt," he said. "This isn't my blind, though. It belongs to Pops."

"Which you use as the mood strikes you, I suppose? I'm surprised there's no gun in there. You could bag us a duck for dinner."

"Wrong season." He gave her a brief glance over his shoulder. "Anyway, it's too damp here on the water. Metal rusts overnight. That's if I wanted to risk having a firearm stolen."

"We couldn't have that, now could we?" she asked sweetly.

He closed the lid of the metal chest and swung around on one knee. "Are you always this cranky when things don't go your way?"

She held his gaze an instant, then looked at a place just past his left shoulder. "Not always."

"If you're afraid of me, don't be. I wouldn't touch you now with a ten-foot pole."

"What a gentleman," she said acidly.

He watched her a moment. "I don't think I ever pretended to be that, and a good thing under the circumstances."

He felt guilty. It was a startling revelation.

More startling still was the fact that she felt little grudge against him. Holding his gaze, she said abruptly, "Don't be so hard on yourself. Some men wouldn't have stopped at all."

"And you know, or knew, one of them?"

She didn't confirm his guess, but neither did she deny it.

His eyes narrowed slightly. "Don't worry. As I said, you're safe from me."

That should have been comforting, but wasn't. The reason was because he saw entirely too much of what she was trying to conceal, what she had kept hidden for too long.

Kane Benedict was a dangerous man, though not only by virtue of being daring or unpredictable or even extremely watchful. It was, instead, because of his intelligence. Added to that was the fact that he made her regret, for a brief, amazing instant, that she would have no further opportunity to practice her self-control against his caresses. As hard as it was to believe, she could not deny a fleeting inclination to discover whether she could endure being held by him in a less isolated, less dangerous situation.

She must be losing her mind. She'd never been even slightly ambivalent about physical contact with a man before. Now was a fine time to start, a fine time indeed.

Kane seemed to hesitate a moment, then he turned to the lamp and began to inspect it. It seemed a sensible precaution, making sure it was in working order before night fell. Regina followed his movement for a moment, then she crawled over to sit with her back against the wall near where he worked. Drawing her legs up, she smoothed her long, full knit skirt down to cover her feet, then clasped her arms around her bent knees.

The silence grew strained. After a moment, she glanced at Kane again and cleared her throat. "How long do you think it may be before anyone finds us?"

"A while," he answered without looking up. "Aunt Vivian's used to me coming and going when I get ready. I'll be surprised if she realizes there's a problem before midnight or later. That's if she and Pops manage to wake up before then. They were both pretty worn-out."

"You don't think she'll call the police, maybe send out a search party, when she does suspect something?" The ripple and stretch of the muscles in his back and shoulders caught her attention, and she followed them intently.

"She's never been the type to jump at every phone call or police siren. It could be hours before she gives up expecting me to show up and decides to call Luke. She might be more concerned if she knew you were with me, but I suspect she thinks Luke saw you home."

"You suspect?" she asked, adding as he glanced her way, "Don't you mean you know she does?"

He was silent, his gaze holding the same motionless depths as the lake. It was as close as he was going to come to an admission, she thought. Releasing a hissing sigh of frustration through her teeth, she looked away again.

"Relax," he said. "If you can't overcome it, you might as well enjoy it."

"Enjoy being trapped here? You must be joking."

He looked around at the opalescent light of the gathering sunset through the trees, the pastel glow of the vast arch of sky directly overhead. "No, not at all."

It was peaceful in its way, she had to agree. So quiet. The only sounds were the gentle lap of water, the sigh of a breeze, and calls of birds and frogs. If she closed her eyes, she could almost sense a strangely peaceful mood indigo that might, if she let it, segue into acceptance.

She couldn't afford that, not with Kane so near.

Or could she? His presence was more re-assuring than disturbing now. He was quiet and purposeful in his movements, not given to inane comments just to fill the silence. He was self-sufficient, secure within his own body and persona, without the need for approval or applause from other people and minus the compulsion to prove anything to anyone, even himself. She might have appreciated these things in him given different circumstances.

"Are you hungry?" he asked, directing an inquiring glance her way. "Or would you rather eat later?"

She had eaten a late breakfast, and though she'd had no lunch, she'd indulged in a filling piece of pound cake with her coffee earlier. "It doesn't matter."

"I vote for now, while we have daylight to see what we're doing."

Reaching for a sausage can, he opened it and handed it to her, then passed over the plastic box of crackers. Regina got to her feet and drained the liquid from the meat into the lake before fishing out a sausage, putting it on a cracker, then turning to hand it to him.

He had started to open a can for himself. Seeing it, Regina felt foolish with her of-fering of food. She didn't quite know why she had done it; the last thing she should be thinking of was feeding the man who had kidnapped her. Still, he had been so polite in serving her first that it had seemed natural to return the favor.

Heat rose in her face. With a small shrug, she began to pull her hand back.

Quickly, he reached for the sausage and cracker with his free hand. His fingers brushed hers, and the tingling contact was so unexpected she almost bungled the transfer of food. She stepped away, regaining her seat. They sat in silence, solemnly consuming their scanty meal. After a short time, Kane opened a bottle of warm soft drink and passed it over. She accepted it, but drank sparingly since she had a feeling bathroom facilities would be as Spartan as everything else.

By the time they had finished and cleared away the trash, the sun had disappeared and dusk was drawing in, becoming night. The water seemed to hold the light longer than on land, reflecting it back into the darkening sky. The last pink glow of evening shone on Kane's face for a few short minutes, then it faded away.

With the darkness, Regina became intensely aware of the rich, earthy scent of the cypress wood used to build the blind, the cries of night creatures, the freshness of the wind with its taint of dampness and decaying vegetation. A mosquito sang around her, then sailed away. A moment later, Kane slapped at his arm, then rubbed his hand on his shirtsleeve. That was, in her opinion at that particular moment, a far more worthy service than slaying a mere dragon.

She was becoming fanciful, she thought, sitting there with nothing to do. Shifting restlessly on the hard floor, she tried for at least the hundredth time to think of some way out of their dilemma.

Kane turned his head, watching her across the increasing darkness. She couldn't quite see his face, however, certainly couldn't read his expression or his intent. When he spoke, his voice was deep and deliberate as it came out of the dusk that lay between them.

"You want to tell me about it?"

"About what?" She knew, but had to ask anyway, in case she might be wrong.

"What happened to you to turn you off men. Who hurt you so much you can't bear the thought of letting anyone touch you again."

"What makes you think —"

"Cut the pretense, okay? You don't have

to prove to me how tough or independent you are."

She swallowed the rest of what she meant to say, blurting out instead, "I'm not tough, and you know it better than anybody, especially any other —"

"Any other man? Why?"

"You're the only one who's managed to get close enough in a long, long time."

The soft sound he made, as if he'd been punched, was perfectly audible. With irony, he said, "You certainly know how to make a guy feel better."

"It wasn't my intention to make you feel anything."

"I know, and that makes it worse. But I asked you a question."

His intense interest was seductive, his manner compelling. It was as if what she said mattered to him on a personal level that had little to do with her connection to his grandfather. She wondered if this was the secret behind the myth of the Southern gentleman, or a trait peculiar to Kane alone. If so, it worked, for it seemed that he knew so much already, it should be no great thing to tell him the rest. In any case, it was better than sitting there in twitching silence, waiting and wondering.

Once started, she held back nothing. Not

the silly, precocious teenager that she had been, her bad judgment in developing an infatuation with a Harvard accent and a fast car, the sickening taste of cheap wine laced with some so-called date-rape drug, or the pain and degradation of waking up and discovering that she had been assaulted while unconscious. The only trouble with telling him these things in such detail was that she also could not spare herself.

"This Harvard guy was prosecuted?" he asked when she was done.

"His father was a big shot with a whole stable of lawyers. Besides, no proof existed other than superficial bruises and a trace of the drug in my blood. I would have tested positive for having had sex and being a recent virgin, but there was nothing to show I was forced. It would have been his word against mine, and amnesia is a side effect of the drug. I couldn't remember what happened, couldn't say where we went, when I had the wine, who else was there, nothing concrete. But I must not have been quite out of it toward the end because I have this sense, almost like a dream, of being held down, in the dark, unable to move, while —"

"Don't," he said in low command. "I get the picture."

She stopped, as much because her throat

was suddenly too tight to produce sound as at his request. She sat staring into the darkness with burning eyes while somewhere inside there was a dissolving feeling, as if a barrier long and closely held had begun to disintegrate.

"So the man who did it got off scot-free," he said after a moment. "He got away with his version of scalp collecting. What was your family thinking of?"

"I have no family. At least . . ." She stopped as she realized she couldn't tell him about Gervis. "My father left when I was a baby. My mother died when I was ten. Nobody wanted to help me fight a battle I couldn't win, one that might cause more scars than it could heal."

He turned his head to watch her. "There was no one to help you, then? No one to take you to counseling or recommend therapy to help deal with the emotional baggage?"

"I dealt with it," she said, raising her chin, staring at the stars beginning to show one by one in the night sky above them. There was wetness under her eyes, but she didn't wipe it away for fear of drawing attention to it.

"Did you? Looks to me as if it's still hanging around."

"Nothing that's important, not so long as

I still have . . ." She stopped, warned by some lingering remnant of self-preservation.

"What?"

She looked at his dark shape that rested nearby. The words thick with tears, she said, "My son. Stephan."

Stephan of the bright smile and crooked teeth and warm, loving baby kisses. Stephan, who adored her, depended on her. Stephan, who must never know how he had been conceived or what manner of spineless, reckless, criminally selfish man his father had been. Stephan, who loved her with all his tender young heart because she was his mother and the only real anchor in his small, unstable world.

Stephan, for whom she would do anything. Anything at all.

"Don't, Regina," Kane said, his voice gruff with concern as he stared at her through the darkness. "Don't cry. I didn't mean to bring it all back."

"No," she said on a hiccuping breath. "I know."

She did, too. She knew that for all his anger and forcefulness, he would never intentionally cause her real pain. It simply wasn't in him.

The knowledge gave her courage, offered hope. It also made it plain that the time had come to finally do the job she had been sent to accomplish.

Decision time. No better opportunity was ever going to present itself.

It had to be done. For Gervis, because she must. For Stephan, because he mattered most. And maybe, just maybe, for herself, for reasons that had nothing to do with either of them.

Now or never.

The words scarcely more than a whisper, she said, "If I asked you . . . ?"

"What?" He turned his head attentively as she paused.

"Would . . . would you hold me for a minute, Kane? Just hold me, and nothing more?"

12

"Do you have any idea what you're asking?"

There was a peculiar note in Kane's voice as it came to Regina across the darkness. She wished she could see his face clearly to judge if he was incredulous or trying to warn her of something. It sounded as if it could easily be both. Not that it made any difference.

Swallowing hard, she said, "I know you said you wouldn't touch me, but I took that to mean you wouldn't, that is, that you didn't want —"

"Exactly." The edge on the word was honed to fillet-knife sharpness.

"Well, neither do I. But I've sometimes thought that if someone would just hold me, it might be all right. Not forever, but for a little while. Do you understand what I'm saying?"

"I think so, but what about me?"

"I don't know what you mean."

"You don't know much about men, do you?"

She moistened her lips. "I haven't had a lot of experience. What should I know?"

"Never mind," he said, exhaling with a tired sound. "I guess I owe you something. Come on, then."

He was reaching out to her. She had asked for this and couldn't back out now. Setting her teeth so firmly that her jaw creaked, she shifted closer. He circled her waist with his arm. Instantly, she went stiff. Then, as he made no move to tighten his grasp, she forced herself to relax again by slow degrees.

"You all right?" he asked.

"I think so, yes." It was true, at least for the moment. Regardless, a shiver rippled over her.

"If you're okay, what was that?"

She couldn't believe he'd noticed since she had barely been aware of it herself. He was much more attuned to her reactions than she might have imagined. Voice husky, she answered, "I can feel how warm you are. I suppose it made me realize how cool it's turning now the sun is gone."

"You're chilly? Here." He reached for the blanket that lay near the chest and dropped it into her lap.

"Not really. It's actually pleasant." Regina unfolded the heavy stadium blanket halfway and spread it over the floor next to them, then eased over to use its thickness as a cushion. As she reached toward Kane to invite him to join her, the tips of her fingers brushed his thigh. She immediately pulled back, but not before she felt the muscle across the top of his leg tighten in an involuntary spasm. He drew a swift breath, becoming as immobile as a stone wall.

Doubt drew her brows together as she settled back again. "If you'd rather not do this after all, I'll understand."

"Don't worry. I'll survive."

"I don't want to put you through more than —"

"Believe me, I can stand it." The words were taut. With stiff movements, he shifted closer to hold her again.

She twisted to look up at him, trying once more to see his face. It didn't help; his features were perfectly blank. She leaned back again.

In her concern, she had settled nearer than before, she discovered, resting more against his chest and shoulder. It didn't seem a good idea to move again and, in any case, it didn't appear to matter. She slowly relaxed once more, giving against him until she could feel his muscle-sheathed rib cage, the sculpting of his pectorals, the firm biceps of his arm. His warmth surrounded her, stealing into her. His scent drifted to her, an elusive mixture of clean cotton, wood-and-moss aftershave, and something more that was his own masculine essence. She breathed deeply, aware at the same time of an odd, comfortable feeling she couldn't quite place.

Then she had it. Security — that was what she felt. She had a deep sense of safety as she sat there in Kane Benedict's arms. It was such a foreign reaction she'd almost failed to recognize it.

Did it come from him or was it something inside herself that caused it? Was it a fluke or some natural phenomenon of the male-female relationship? She didn't know, but it was a staggering discovery when not long ago she had been desperate to break away from him.

His arm, ridged with firm muscle and corded tendons, was behind her back, his hand resting lightly at her waist. She knew exactly where every fingertip touched, could discern the latent power of his grasp. He had long, aristocratic fingers. Before, his hand at her breast had thrown her into a panic. She wondered if it would be the same if she was expecting it, anticipating it.

He wouldn't make a move now, or so he had sworn. Any approach of that sort would have to come from her. Did she dare? If she found the nerve, could she bear the consequences?

She was going to have to find out. Time was passing. A few brief hours, a few short minutes even, and the chance would be gone. Once vanished, it might never come again.

She reached up and ran her fingers through her hair, then lifted the long swath that was caught between them and let it fall back behind her, draping across his shoulder on which she leaned. As she lowered her arm again, she let her fingers come to rest on his hand at her waist. She paused a long moment, then began to trace his knuckles with an absent touch, to smooth the pad of her thumb idly across the square, well-formed back as if her mind was anywhere else except on what she was doing.

She discovered a scar on the side of his index finger. As she followed its path around to his palm, he obligingly turned his hand over to permit access. Voice light, she asked, "What happened here?"

"Accident with a cane knife. I was cutting a stalk of it for someone and she decided to tickle me."

"Tickle you?"

"Just playing. Some women are like that, or some girls, I should say, since it was a long time ago."

A small shaft of something that might almost have been envy, or even jealousy, cut through her. "You must have been furious."

"Why? She didn't mean it to happen." He tilted his head to look down at her in the dimness.

"She still hurt you."

"I hurt myself. It wouldn't have happened if I'd been more careful. We were both clowning around."

"Who was it?"

"The girl? April Halstead."

She'd expected him to say Francie and wasn't sure whether she was glad or sorry that he hadn't. She said quietly, "I wish I could have had that kind of relationship."

"What do you mean?"

"Impulsive. Friendly. Where taking liberties and horseplay are normal and forgiveness comes easy."

His voice as he answered sounded deeper than before. "One based on trust, you mean."

"I suppose."

"You don't know what you missed," he said simply.

She looked up at him, made bold by the darkness, as she said, "I'm beginning to realize that."

He stared down at her, his eyes catching

faint, dark gleams. His lashes flickered, then his attention drifted lower, to the curves of her lips. She sat entranced as she waited to see what he would do. For the briefest of instants, he dipped his head. Then he drew back.

He was keeping his word. He didn't intend to touch her beyond what she'd asked, wasn't going to help her over this impasse between them. It was inconvenient, yet strangely enough she was glad. It felt good to be able to trust, if only for this moment.

Glancing away, she stared into the thickening darkness inside the blind, thinking, remembering. After a long moment, she said in almost inaudible tones, "I missed a lot of other things, too. Holding hands, for instance. Or the kind of innocent kisses boys and girls exchange in grammar school. My mother was sick a lot. I had to stay in with her, so I never had time for that. Afterward, the woman who took me in was so strict and suspicious that she never allowed anything of that kind. Of course, I got in trouble not all that long after she died." As she spoke, she smoothed her fingers along his upturned hand until their palms matched, then twined her fingers with his.

"Regina . . ." he began, then stopped.

"You don't mind, do you? It's so dark now. I don't know when I've ever seen such darkness, without a light anywhere, no streetlamps, car headlights or building lights." It wasn't a lie, even if seeing was the least of her concerns.

"I should crank up the lantern."

His voice sounded strained, she thought. Perhaps he was not as calm as he seemed. She would like to think so, for her own pulse was something less than even.

"I'm not complaining," she offered. "I think I might even like it, once I get used to it. We should have a good view of the stars."

He looked up, tilting his head so it rested against the wall behind them. On a pained chuckle, he repeated, "Stars."

"You can hardly see them at all where I come from." She turned her head, her gaze on the shadowy outline of his face, his mouth. "Kane?"

"What now?"

"Would it bother you very much if I just . . ." She paused, undecided about how to put it.

He closed his eyes, for she saw a flicker of movement. "You want to kiss me, is that it?"

"How did you know?"

"A lucky guess."

"It would only be an experiment. If you wouldn't mind?"

"Why in hell should I mind?" he muttered. "Be my guest."

She loosened her grasp on his hand. "You do mind."

"Not being kissed," he said as he tightened his own fingers to retain her hold. "What I mind is not being able to cooperate. But I'll get over it."

"You're sure?"

"Positive. I can take any torture you can dish out."

She drew back a little. "If you feel that way, let it go."

He gave a slow shake of his head. "Forget I said anything, will you? Just get on with it."

She was no longer certain this was such a good idea. It seemed possible Kane might understand what she was after better than she thought. What would she do if he turned the tables on her? Where would she be then?

In the same situation very likely, she answered herself with honesty. That being so, what difference did it make?

She sat up straight, turned more toward him, then hesitated. The only way she was going to be able to reach his lips was if she sat in his lap, and she wasn't quite ready for that. She moistened her dry lips before she said, "Could you just . . . help a little?"

He slid down the wall, stretching out to lie full length, half on, half off the blanket. Raising his arms above his head, he used his knit fingers for a pillow. "Better?"

It was and it wasn't. She eyed him, wondering if he was amusing himself at her expense. Anything was possible, she was coming to believe, with Kane Benedict.

She eased down a bit and braced herself on one elbow before leaning over him. Her hair fell forward across her cheek, and she reached up to draw it back out of the way. Eyes wide, wary of any sudden movement, she bent her head and brushed her lips across the warm curves of his mouth. She drew back hastily, watching him.

He didn't move, gave no sign he had felt the contact that sizzled on her own lips. The tension inside her ebbed. In a sudden excess of relief, she pressed a kiss to the cleft of his chin, then tasted it with her tongue, feeling the prickly beard stubble with a sense of amazement. He remained immobile, almost as if comatose. Lowering her lashes, she blazed a path of tiny kisses from his chin to his lips once more. She explored their tucked corners, their ridged edges, left a moist path along the edges of their joining.

His chest was rising and falling at a quicker pace and the muscle of his arm was rock hard where she leaned against it, yet he kept his eyes closed, held his hands-off position. Greatly daring, she released the hair she held and used her fingertips to test the heat of his mouth, its smooth yet firm texture. She eased a bit higher to graze his eyelids with her mouth, taste the salt at the base of his lashes. Then with a soft sound in her throat, she swooped back down to his mouth and settled her lips against his, matching contours and edges with precision before she swept the firm line between with her tongue, gathering the unique, sweet flavor of him, enjoying the texture of the smooth flesh. For long seconds, that satisfied her. Then almost as if compelled, she sought, delicately, to see if he would permit her inside.

He allowed it, encouraged it with slow refinement by opening no farther than she required. She was enthralled by the freedom of being the instigator, the explorer. That he was deliberately placing that power in her hands brought a surge of some emotion that she didn't quite recognize, but thought might be gratitude.

Her heart jarred her ribs. The blood that

raced in her veins felt hot. She wanted more of him, needed more in a way she had never felt before. Languor welled inside her so she melted bonelessly against him, allowing the rounded contour of her breast to mold to the hard plane of his chest. She felt like a seductress, more wanton than she'd ever dreamed. There was a purpose to this, she knew, but the compulsion that had driven her in the beginning seemed distant and unimportant compared to the things she was discovering. About Kane, yes, but also about herself.

His tongue was a swirl of warm velvet, a satiny enticement. His taste was fresh and wholesome yet heady, like the rum made from the sugarcane for which he was named. She set the pace, but was pushed to stay ahead of him, to sweep the edges of his teeth without letting her tongue be captured, to flick the quilted lining of his lower lip and not be caught by his forays past her own defenses.

She lifted her head. Breathlessly, she said, "You aren't supposed to join in."

"I don't remember that being mentioned," he returned, his voice sleepily sensual, his eyelids half-closed. "I only promised not to touch you. Besides, isn't it better when you have help?"

"How should I know? You've been helping at least a little all along."

"Try it and see."

Confidence and challenge were plain in his voice. It was annoying enough to make her disregard her instinctive distrust. Placing her free hand in the middle of his chest to brace herself, she leaned over him once more.

This time, he let his lips remain lax and still. There was no response when she laved the grainy surface of his tongue with hers or flicked across the clean edges of his teeth. Regardless, she could feel his heart throbbing under his sternum with hard power that shuddered up her arm. She drew back.

"I was right, wasn't I?" he asked, his voice slumberous.

"You were right," she said quietly.

"The rest of it works the same way."

"The rest? Oh, you mean —"

"I mean making love," he agreed, and waited.

She shook back her hair. "I'm supposed to trust you on that after what you tried to do before?"

"That's your choice," he said. "I'm only making a point."

It was one she wasn't ready to face. The best way to avoid it, she thought, might be to kiss him.

This time, his cooperation was total, a concentration so complete that her senses were flooded with the force of it, with the infinite variety of tastes, textures and incitements. She made a soft sound deep in her throat as she abandoned reason to follow where instinct led, let down her guard and accepted his tender invasion.

The duck blind and its hard floor ceased to exist. She was lost in the slow expansion of her senses, in the magic of touch and heat, scent and flavor, and the burgeoning wonder of merging bodies.

Abruptly, he broke away. He brought his hand up to clamp her wrist and lift it away from his chest. In a voice like a rake dragging through gravel, he demanded, "Are you sure you know what you're doing?"

The hand he was holding had been pressed against bare skin and a soft mat of chest hair. Somehow she had pushed her fingers between the buttons of his shirt, pulling them loose. What she regretted most, however, was the loss of warm, human contact, the feel of taut muscle under her palm.

She moistened her lips. "I didn't know," she whispered, "but I do now."

He was still for the space of a heartbeat. The night air swirled between them. Then with infinite care, he placed her hand back where it had been before. "As long as you know who's responsible," he said. Releasing her, he relaxed once more.

She could stop or she could go on. It was her choice.

Or was it? Was it, really, when love and loyalty pushed at her from all directions, or when her own needs and fears clamored in her mind? The love of her son and loyalty to her cousin, the need to feel the ultimate closeness to another person, and the fear that if she drew back now this chance might never come again. Yet how much easier it would have been if she had only controlled her automatic rejection earlier and let Kane force the decision.

But would he have carried through with it? She didn't think so. He had stopped when he realized exactly what he was doing to her, had let her go because he didn't like the method he was using to gain what he wanted.

Had he abandoned that desire now, or was his consideration and momentary quiescence only another way of getting to her? Exactly who was seducing whom here?

She was thinking too much, which was a good way to lose her courage. What did motives matter anyway, when she was alone with Kane in the damp stillness of the night?

What need was there for justification when there was no one to see, no one to know or care, except the two of them?

Her palm against his bare chest felt hot. She smoothed it in small circles, opening his shirt wider as she enjoyed the friction and also the contrast between his firm skin and the springing softness of the hair that grew in a ragged V from his breastbone to his waist. Discovering the nub of a nipple in the crisp growth, she concentrated her attention on it. That it reacted much like her own was amazing. She lowered her head and wet the tight bud with her tongue, tasting the salt seasoning of it, and was secretly gratified at his swift-drawn breath of reaction.

The hollow of his throat, the strong turn of his neck where his jugular pulsed, the angle of his jaw — each caught her attention in turn. Her exploration was thorough, unhurried. Nor did he seem inclined to rush her. There were times, she conceded in silent appreciation, when the Southern penchant for taking one's own sweet time could have advantages.

Kane shifted slightly, and she felt his touch at her waist. He ran his hand lightly up and down her side, then along her back. There was no confinement in the caress, however, no hint of coercion. It might have been meant to encourage or, perhaps, to beguile. It served its purpose, for she did not object as he threaded his fingers through her hair, gently massaged the back of her neck, then guided her mouth to his once more.

This kiss was deeper, stronger, longer. Somewhere in the midst of it, he took the initiative, though it was done with such care that she could not be certain when she relinquished it to him.

With heated lips, he nuzzled the tender skin of her cheek, inhaling its fragrance, before making a delicate foray down her throat. She felt his hot breath through the thickness of her knit shirt as it feathered over the curves of her breasts. Her nipples contracted immediately. He brushed his cheek across one, with his beard stubble catching on the cloth covering, a gentle grazing. Yet he encroached no farther, only teasing through her clothing, blowing warm air against her, enjoying her softness while never quite touching the ultrasensitive points of her nipples. She pushed his shirt from his shoulders, clasping and releasing the hard musculature in spasmodic, unfocused yearning.

Then and only then, he skimmed the peak of one breast and hovered as if waiting for permission. She gave it by offering what he wanted, then shivered with pleasure as he closed his lips on the turgid nipple.

With iron strength, he caught her waist and rolled with her, carrying her with him so she felt the floor beneath her back. As he rose above her, she sensed the rise of the old terror, the freezing paralysis. She closed her fingers on his shirt between his shoulder blades, squeezing tight.

She must not succumb to the dark distress, had to fight it, push past it, conquer it. She would; there was no other choice.

Then he picked up a strand of her hair that spread around her. Releasing it again, he let it drift down, catching the starlight in red-gold shimmers. "God, you're beautiful," he whispered, "so beautiful."

Beautiful. Not gorgeous, pretty, cute, or any of the other substitutes for that one perfect word. Beautiful. It might not be true, but suddenly she felt beautiful for once in her life. Beautiful, and desired.

Like finding and pulling the loose end of a tightly knitted piece of cloth, she felt the knotted skein of her old fears unravel. Bemused wonder took its place. The freedom of it was heady, euphoric. At the same time, she felt daring and seductive. She wanted more — more sensations, more revelations, more tastes and textures and closeness.

More of the man who held her.

Perhaps he saw that need in the dark recesses of her eyes, for he slid his hand under her shirt that had worked its way out of her skirt. Slowly, gently, giving her time to object, he cupped her breast. She only lay still and expectant. He bent his head then, to tend her desire with moist suction, cautious nibbles, and unhurried discovery.

A quiver of vivid rapture caught her unaware. Pure distraction, it reached her as nothing else could. She welcomed it, absorbed it. Sliding her fingers through the thick silk of his hair, she held him to her.

Imagination, that was the key to the magic they built between them as the moments passed. Imagination in technique, yes, but also of the mental kind known as empathy, which gave the ability to enter into the reeling senses of the other person, to feel what they felt, then extend further to guess what they longed to experience. The imagination to know that more was required than mere lust and the headlong rush toward completion. To set aside cool calculation and reach for the outer realms of instinct. And, finally, to offer, with open hands, the ultimate expression of generosity, which was to give themselves without reservation.

How had they come to be so attuned when so much was wrong between them? Regina could not begin to guess. She only accepted it as she accepted the miracle of her vanquished fears. Accepted it and reveled in it.

She stripped away his shirt and dropped it to one side, the better to feel his power and his heat. He dragged off her shirt, unsnapped her bra, and disposed of both without either of them noticing where they went. Her skirt, his pants, were obstacles to be overcome, and were discarded along with their shoes and the other civilized bits that satisfied modesty or convenience. Body to body, they came together on the blanket, doing their best to merge through their bare skin by osmosis.

He left a hot, wet path down her abdomen on the way to teach her a new joy. She marveled at the silken length and heft of him in her hand. He pulled her above him, holding the soft mounds of her hips. She suckled his nipple as he had hers, while clasping his tumescent heat between her thighs.

When they came together, it was a gradual and scrupulous penetration against her tightness. Yet it was also a liquid slide, a benediction and divine disclosure. Tears squeezed from her eyes and tracked down her face. She held him tightly against her, while her heart filled with something so near love that she knew she would never forget this man or the moment, no matter what happened.

Then the turbulence took them, and the glory. They strove with it while their lungs strained and burned, their skins reflected star shine, their blood raced in hot splendor through their veins, and the world moved far, far away. The night gathered around them, shining in their eyes. They sounded its wonder, searched its last corner for ecstasy. And they finally found, in mutual gratitude and mercy, its brightest promise.

For a long time, they lay still, limbs intertwined, skin cooling. Regina's pulse slowed to normal. Kane reached to draw the blanket over their lower bodies. They separated, easing apart, though Kane stopped her when she tried to remove her head from the pillow of his shoulder. Still, they didn't speak, but lay staring at nothing, lost in the slow surfacing of questions and doubts.

It was the buzzing of a mosquito that roused them from the trance that held them. Kane let it land on his shoulder, then killed it. But afterward, he searched out their clothes and pushed Regina's into her hands. Dressing quickly then, he rose and picked up the lantern, found the matches. A moment later, light flared that seemed far too white and glaring. Too revealing.

Caught with her bra on but her shirt in her hands, she hesitated, then quickly slipped the soft knit over her head. Only then did she feel able to look to where Kane knelt, watching her. His features in the glare of lamplight were stern, his lips compressed. His eyes were darkly blue, and in their depths was stark self-contempt. And also a lingering shadow of desolation.

13

"I'd have found you sooner if you'd fired up the damned lantern as soon as it was dark."

Kane weighed the words of greeting from his cousin as he held the trapdoor open. His gaze was pensive before he answered briefly, "I know."

What else could he say? It was true enough, and he'd known it all along. Besides, he and Regina were both a little too rumpled, their faces a little too pale and lips too puffy, for him to play it any way except straight.

Luke gave him a sharp look as he stood in his heavy fishing boat that rocked gently against the bottom of the ladder. Then Kane's cousin lifted a brow and a slow grin spread across his face there in the subdued glow of lantern light shining down on him. When he got no response, his appreciative grin widened while wicked enjoyment danced in his eyes.

Kane gave him a hard look of warning. Luke's expression sobered as discretion won out over humor, or possibly he realized

291

anything he said would embarrass Regina more than its target.

"So what happened?" he asked as he wrapped a line around the bottom rung of the blind's ladder. "You forget to tie up?"

Kane told him how the boat had got loose in a single laconic sentence. He wasn't proud of the fact that he'd been caught off guard like some randy teenager with his girl.

"Who? How?"

"Your guess is as good as mine." Kane had his suspicions, but didn't feel like voicing them just now, couldn't see how it would serve any purpose to let Regina know that he'd been too intent on his business with her to notice they were followed from The Haven.

"You thought I did it," Luke said, still grinning.

"It crossed my mind."

"I might have, if I'd seen the chance."

"I know. And enjoyed the joke, too, until I caught up with you."

Luke didn't find that quite so funny, which was just as well. Kane thought he might have had his cousin's head on a platter, or sure tried, if he cracked any more jokes. He definitely wasn't in the mood.

All the same, Kane was glad it was Luke who had found them. His cousin might carry him high about the incident for the next month, but Kane knew he could be counted on not to breathe a whisper of it to anyone else.

The rescue got under way in record time, since none of them was inclined to linger. He and Regina stowed the gear they had used, picked up their trash, and lowered themselves into the rescue boat. Luke took off.

The ride back toward the house was fast, but damp and cool. It felt good to Kane, but Regina sat huddled in her padded chair with her arms wrapped around her upper body as if cold inside. He would have offered to hold her, to protect and warm her if that was what she needed, but wasn't sure she'd let him.

God, what had gotten into him? He couldn't begin to understand. He'd certainly never meant to take things so far. The last thing he needed was this complication in the middle of everything else.

But she had been so soft and delicious, and he had thought — Hell, what had he thought? She needed him? That she was trapped by her terrible inhibitions like the damned prehistoric fly was trapped in the amber? That he was the one man to perceive and resolve her fears, the only one who could set her free?

Saint Kane with his trusty sword. So to speak.

What an idiot.

He'd been seduced. The combination of desire and vulnerability, fear and bravado that she had used was lethal and tailor-made for someone like him. He'd been so entranced by the performance that he hadn't seen what was coming at him until it was too late.

Of course, he might not have noticed because he was too busy concentrating on his own agenda. He had set himself up and had no right to complain. So why did he feel as if he'd been blindsided?

She'd got to him, she really had. Somehow he had identified with her, had felt her rootless, unattached state when she was left without family, as he had been left in much the same limbo when his own parents were killed. It had seemed, too, that the intimate betrayal she had been through was on a par with the ugly breach of faith Francie had used in her attempt to extort money from him. They had both trusted the wrong people, both been hurt when their intrinsic need for love and connection was used against them.

Was there really any kind of correlation, or was it all in his head?

Even if there was one, the questions remained: Why him? Why now? How much of Regina's lovely surrender was from sincere emotion, and how much due to shivering calculation?

The answers had begun to haunt him the minute she was out of his arms. They would continue until he had the truth.

The reluctance she'd shown in the beginning wasn't counterfeit; he'd stake his life on that. He hadn't been taken in to that extent. What bothered him most was the thought she might have faked the rest, the need, the pleasure, the release — the whole nine yards. Had any of that been real, or was she only a very good actor, the consummate liar?

Kane turned his face into the wind created by the boat's swift flight and inhaled long and deep. He hated the idea that the love they had made might have left her cold while he still burned with the aftermath. While he wrestled with the need to do it again.

She had used his emotions against him, and he had let her. How had that happened when he had been all set to use hers to get at the truth? He had no idea. She had made him lose sight of his goal, and he didn't like it. Even less did he like realizing she made him feel guilty, as if he'd taken advantage of her. She baffled him, and he liked that least of all.

Still, it had been an experience he wouldn't have missed, no matter the cost. The feel of her in his arms had been so right. Perfect, in fact. He could spend hours discovering the many faces of her, and all the tender, delicate places he had not yet touched. He'd like to devote days to teaching her all the things she needed to know about making love while reveling in the shape and taste and hot, satin depths of her.

It wasn't over by any means. If she thought once was enough to put him off her trail, she'd soon discover her mistake. No, he and Regina Dalton had seduced each other. Fine. Now they'd see who wound up on top.

He'd also find out who had made off with his boat, setting up the whole infernal sequence of events. It was vaguely possible that it was an accident, that someone had noticed them entering the blind and decided it would be funny to strand him with the new lady in town. But he didn't think it happened that way, any more than he thought Luke was to blame.

He probably should have been more

careful about throwing accusations at his cousin. Still, the lake and back swamp were Luke's bailiwicks, and he was more than capable of creating a problem to make a point. He'd shown a certain protective interest in Regina, as well, and might have decided his cousin needed a lesson in the dangers of browbeating women if he'd overheard any portion of the exchange between him and Regina. And Luke could also have figured out that Kane had a less than noble reason for getting rid of him so he could be alone with Regina.

Second thoughts convinced Kane to abandon that notion. Any reaction from Luke to the confrontation between him and Regina taking place during the boat theft would've been expressed with considerably more force. He'd have been far more likely to hand out a swift punch in the nose than let matters continue by removing their transportation.

That left Dudley Slater. Kane was disgusted to think of the little creep following him and Regina, but it could have been done by making use of one of the other boats from The Haven's dock. What his motives might be was the main problem with that idea. Assuming he was on Berry's payroll, it was hard to see what kind of trouble stranding him and Regina together was supposed to accomplish.

Or was it? It might make sense if Slater was in Regina's confidence, if he knew she would welcome the isolation. Kane gave a grim shake of his head as that thought struck him. Was it really possible, or was he headed off the deep end on this thing?

Time would tell, and a good thing, too, since he wasn't thinking too clearly himself. He needed to back off and regroup while he worked things out. It wouldn't surprise him to know Regina felt the same way. The best thing he could do would be to see her back to the motel. They could both sleep on it. In separate beds.

It was the right decision; he knew it. Why, then, did it feel so wrong?

The following morning, Kane met Melville in Baton Rouge. They came together on the steps of the courthouse where the preliminary maneuvering for the case was being played out in district court. Louisiana law required the case be heard in a higher court because it involved compensation and damages in excess of twenty thousand dollars. A local venue would have been more convenient for Pops and the witnesses who would be called from Turn-Coupe, but made little difference to Kane. Trying cases before a district judge was business as usual.

He had driven straight to the state capital from home since he was running late. Unable to sleep the night before for thinking of the way Regina had been and how she had looked lying on the floor of the duck blind, he got up at 2:00 A.M. to check on Pops, then worked for a couple of hours. When he felt sleepy, he fell back in bed for a quick catnap, but his hospital vigil and the long hours he'd put in during the past few weeks had caught up. He hadn't roused again until half past seven, and the district courthouse was a good hour from Turn-Coupe.

"How's your granddad?" Melville asked as the two of them mounted the wide steps of the courthouse building, their footsteps grating on the worn surfaces that were hollowed in spots by countless other steps.

"Grouchy," Kane answered. "Ready to go home and sleep in his own bed."

"Giving your aunt a hard time, is he?"

"So she says, though she gets a kick out of having someone to talk to besides me." The smile curving Kane's mouth faded as he noticed the thin, scraggly-looking man leaning against one of the portico columns with a cigarette in his hand. Tipping his head in that direction, he went on, "Looks like the buzzards are circling."

Melville gave a nod. "Can't keep them away, though I don't know what that one expects to gain. I've seen him here, there, and everywhere around Turn-Coupe in the past day or two."

"He bothers me. I just don't like it."

"I expect he's no worse than the rest. You want a problem to worry about, I've got a real one for you." Without breaking stride, he flipped open the top of his soft-sided briefcase and extracted a file folder, which he handed over.

"What's this?"

"Dossier on the lady who's been hanging around your granddad."

Kane felt his heart clench in his chest. He met Melville's dark brown gaze for a long moment. Since they were close enough to Slater to be overheard, he chose his words carefully. "You put a chaser on that problem?"

"Seemed like a good idea."

It was. One he should have thought of himself, Kane realized. No doubt he would have if he'd been tending to business instead of getting involved up to his neck. Or if he hadn't been so determined to handle Regina his own way.

Voice tight, he asked, "And?"

"Read it for yourself."

He would. He'd have to, though from Melville's attitude, he could tell he wasn't going to be happy with the results. The look he gave Slater, as he passed the scrawny reporter, was murderous, easily twice as hostile as it might have been a minute earlier.

Catching the tail end of it, Melville frowned. As he got the heavy entrance door, then followed Kane inside, he said, "You didn't want me to check out the lady?"

"Yeah, sure. I'm just not wild about having to investigate every person who comes within spitting distance of this case."

"That scruples talking, or you got something going there?"

Kane checked himself. "What gave you that idea?"

"You've been seen coming and going a lot at the motel. Word gets around. You were with her at Luke's bash, then out at The Haven yesterday. It adds up."

"My own brand of investigation." He spoke over his shoulder as he walked on.

Melville caught up with him in a few steps. "So did you get anything?"

"Nothing informative." That wasn't the truth, but it was all Kane felt like saying. He just didn't want to talk about it. Any of it.

Melville got the message, apparently, for he said no more.

It was after court recessed for lunch that Kane forced himself to open the folder. The facts were worse than he'd suspected. Regina Dalton resided at the same address as Gervis Berry. They claimed to be related, but there was no actual blood tie. That added up to only one thing.

Staring at that damning data, Kane was engulfed in sick rage. How could she and Berry suppose they wouldn't be found out? They must think they were dealing with backward good old boys who had grits in their heads as well as in their voices. Berry, sitting in his New York office, was bad enough, but Regina was on the spot. She should have known better.

He'd like to get his hands on her. He'd have the truth out of her one way or another. For two cents, he'd turn the legal maneuvering over to Melville right now while he went to have it out with darling Regina.

No, that would be too easy, too final. He'd much rather catch her in her lies and deceit and throw them back in her beautiful face. There were other, more personal, ways to make her regret what she was doing and he knew every one.

So would she before he was through. So

would she.

The interminable court proceedings ground their way through the afternoon. When they were finally over, Kane and Melville drove back to the Turn-Coupe office to discuss the developments. It was late when Kane finally called it a day and headed out for The Haven. As he passed the funeral home, he noticed the car his aunt usually drove parked near the side entrance.

Aunt Vivian might be attending to some chore for his grandfather, but he didn't want to bet on it. What was far more likely was that Pops had sprung himself from confinement as an invalid and borrowed transportation to come to town. With a soft curse, Kane hit the brake and wheeled into a parking space.

The first thing he heard as he walked into the reception area was a slow, familiar drawl holding forth somewhere in the back. He lifted an inquiring brow at the receptionist on duty.

Miss Renfrew, a termagant who wore her gray hair in the same bun she'd sported for decades and knew more about the business than anyone except Mr. Lewis himself, gave a grim nod. "You're hearing right. Himself is in the back. I told him he ought to be home in bed, but he said he was tired of being mollycoddled."

As she finished speaking, Kane heard a different, more feminine voice issuing from the back in counterpoint to Pops's deep tones. "He brought Miss Elise with him?"

Miss Renfrew shook her head. "The young woman who came about the jewelry. Apparently, he had an appointment with her. They're back in the casket room if you want to join them."

It sounded like an excellent idea.

Kane could hear them laughing before he reached them, an easy sound of shared rapport that set his teeth on edge. The pair was standing among the caskets that sat along the walls with the lids open like so many giant bassinets lined with pink and blue, cream and white. They turned as he entered. The smile that lit up Regina's face would have been enough to tie his insides in knots if he hadn't been positive it was an act.

To play it cool went against the grain, but seemed best for the moment. He didn't want Pops upset, nor did he want him taking sides.

Returning Regina's smile, he walked up between them and put his arm around both, though taking care not to bump his grandfather's cast. With a mock stern look at the older man, he asked, "What are you doing out and about?"

"Man's got to do what a man's got to do," Pops answered with a glinting smile in Regina's direction, which suggested supreme ease between them.

It was all Kane could do to keep from grinding his teeth. "At least you have pleasant company."

"Don't I though? I was showing her around the joint, and she was telling me about your adventure yesterday evening."

Kane met Regina's soft hazel gaze, his own a bit jaundiced as he realized how effectively she had raised his grandfather's spirits. "She doesn't look any the worse for wear."

"I'm fine," she answered for herself.

He'd just bet she was. "Not too many mosquito bites?"

"Nothing to speak of," she said with a twitch of her lips. Watching that movement distracted him for a second, doing odd things to his insides.

"I was just telling her she ought to come out to The Haven for dinner," Pops said. "When I left, Vivian had her *Southern Living Cookbook* out and was doing interesting things to a roast the size of a football. Elise is coming over, but it might help save us from the leftovers if Regina joined us, too."

"I've been trying to convince him that

your aunt might not want a stranger dropping in on her again," she explained, her hazel gaze soft with doubt.

"I'm sure it'll be no problem," Kane said. The agreement was perfunctory. He much preferred a more private setting when he saw Regina again.

"That it won't," Pops agreed. "Vivian likes feeding people."

"And does a wonderful job," Regina said, "but I don't know."

Taking advantage of her hesitation, Kane inserted smoothly, "On the other hand, I think something was said about a pizza party tonight, wasn't there?"

She met his gaze, her own questioning. He made his expression as warmly significant as he could manage under the circumstances. Color rose at once under her pale skin, and he watched its spread with both satisfaction and a strange, aching regret.

Before she could answer, one of the men who worked with his grandfather stuck his head into the room. "Phone, Mr. Crompton."

"Be right there," Pops called over his shoulder. To Kane, he said, "You'll take care of Miss Regina while I'm gone, won't you?"

"I'd like nothing better," he answered,

and meant every word.

He waited until the two men were gone, their footsteps retreating toward the front of the funeral home. Then he reached for Regina, swinging her into his arms and clamping her close against him. When she turned her startled gaze up to his, he swooped down and pressed his lips to hers.

He had meant it to be a hard, fast reminder of what had happened between them the night before. It was that, but also a refresher course, a spiraling clamor of the senses that threatened to get out of control. She was so soft and sweet and cooperative that it was perilously easy to forget what he was doing and think only of what he'd like to do. Now. In this room or anywhere else that might be handy.

He raised his head, loosened his hold. Her lips were moist and pink, the pupils of her eyes dark and open. With her hands resting on his chest, over his heart that slammed against his breastbone, she said, "Is something wrong?"

The urge to tell her exactly what was bothering him and ask for some explanation he could believe was so strong it burned like acid in his brain. The only thing that prevented him was the certain knowledge that she would concoct some tale to throw him off the track. He didn't want to hear it, couldn't stand that just now.

Reaching for a careless smile, he said, "Should there be?"

"You just seem — different."

"I've spent all day in court wrestling with the hydra-headed monster otherwise known as the Berry Association legal team."

"Hydra-headed?"

"Cut off one objection or exception and it sprouts twice as many just like it."

Her smile of commiseration came right on cue. Rubbing a fingertip up and down the silk of his tie, she said, "They have you outnumbered, is that it?"

"About four to one. There must be at least eight of them, all wearing the same Brooks Brothers suit and wing tips. I think they're clones."

"I didn't realize you were already involved in court with the case."

"Didn't Pops tell you? It's advance stuff, mostly tap dancing around each other to figure out how the script is going to shape up and who'll get to play the lead. It'll be a few more days before the show gets on the road."

"I see," she said, actually sounding relieved.

"So which is it going to be? Aunt Vivian's

home cooking, or pizza for two delivered to the motel?" The last word was husky and slightly suggestive whether he wanted it to sound that way or not.

"Whatever you prefer." She shielded her eyes with a downward sweep of her lashes, but he still caught the soft, gray-green promise behind the gold-tipped fans.

It was unfair, but he was the one who felt the charge of her reply, felt it squarely in an uncomfortable part of his anatomy. "I'll see you around 7:30, then," he said, and let her go before things got away from him. Before he succumbed to a wild urge to put her in one of the caskets surrounding them and take up where they'd left off the day they met.

That same need, made up of equal parts of anger, sexual hunger and beguilement, still simmered inside him when he reached the motel two hours later. He'd shaved, showered and changed to remove the traces of a strenuous day and in anticipation of an evening ending in bed. If he was right about Regina, there was little chance it would turn out otherwise.

Still, it felt cold-blooded and overly cynical, going about things this way. Using the kind of fireworks that ignited between them to gain the upper hand was far from his idea of a perfect relationship. It was possible he had more romantic illusions left than he thought.

When Regina opened the door to his knock, he inhaled the heady smells of oregano and basil, hot tomato and mozzarella cheese and yeasty bread, and also an elusive perfume redolent of gardenias. The pizza, he saw, was laid out on the table under the room's single window.

Regina had already ordered and paid for everything, which didn't sit well with him at all. Other people might think it was fine, but in his part of the world there was an unwritten law that said a man paid for the food, especially when a couple was on intimate terms. Not that there was a quid pro quo involved; it was simply the natural order of things, like any male animal providing food for his mate. Any other arrangement made him extremely uncomfortable. If that made him a chauvinist, then so be it.

Kane walked into the room, put down the ceramic dish holding the dessert provided by his aunt, then took out his wallet and began to count money onto the console table that held the TV. He dropped enough bills for a large pizza with all the trimmings and the fat tip it had probably taken for the special delivery.

"What are you doing?" Regina inquired in tight distress from where she stood with her hand still on the doorknob.

"Paying you for —" he began.

"Out!" she said, swinging the door wide again. "Get out."

He was genuinely puzzled for a split second, then he saw the look on her face. "Now wait a minute!"

"For what? You to get naked? No, thank you. Take your money and go."

He put away his wallet with deliberate movement. Voice toneless, he said, "Selling yourself a little cheap, aren't you?"

Her eyes narrowed. "I'm not selling myself at all, you sorry —"

"Well, that's just fine," he cut across her tirade, "because I'm not buying. Anything except pizza, that is." He picked up the bills, fanned them, and held them out to her so she could see it was not nearly enough for what she obviously thought was taking place.

Silence descended. He saw the color recede from her face until her freckles stood out against the powdery fineness of her skin like flecks of gold and he was afraid she might faint. The words husky with strain, she repeated, "You're paying for the pizza."

"That's the idea."

311

She closed the door, then leaned her head against the frame a second with her eyes closed before she turned back to him. "I don't know what to say. I thought —"

"I know what you thought. Sorry to disappoint you, but, believe it or not, I've paid for sex exactly as often as you've sold it." He met her clouded gaze, willing her to accept his word, offering her his own belief in her integrity.

Quiet hovered between them. She searched his face, her own shaded with lingering doubt. "That first day, at Hallowed Ground, you seemed to think I was some kind of call girl."

She was right. "I discovered my mistake."

"Yes, you did," she agreed darkly.

"I didn't mean it that way." He wanted to move closer, to take her in his arms, but was too wary of the implication she might put on that urge to move.

"No," she said on a deep breath as she linked her fingers at her waist. "I don't suppose you did. I may be a little touchy on the subject."

It was a definite understatement, but Kane was sure she had her reasons. What surprised him was how much he wanted to know what they might be. He was also puzzled as he recognized that he bore her no grudge, but respected her stand.

A crooked smile tugged at his mouth as he asked after a second, "Would you really have thrown me out?"

"I'd have tried." She shook back the bright curtain of her hair as if daring him to laugh at the idea.

"Good. I like a woman who knows what she wants." It was the exact truth, though he had never expected to say it to Regina Dalton. Especially not tonight.

She watched him a long moment, her expression still shadowed. "Fine," she said at last. "What I want now is food."

It was not the start that he'd planned for the evening. The question was, could he salvage the end he had in mind? All he could do was try.

They ate their pizza in an atmosphere of subdued politeness punctuated only by scant comments about the food. They might as well have been eating cardboard, however, for all that Kane knew or cared. It was only as he disposed of the scraps and she opened the container holding the dessert he'd brought that things began to loosen up.

"Strawberries," she said in awe as she saw the big, ripe berries inside, then leaned over to inhale the sweet, fresh-picked fragrance that rose from them. "Did you get them at a farmer's market?"

"From Aunt Vivian's garden. She's as good at growing fruits and vegetables as she is at cooking them."

"And this is a sauce?" She set the ceramic bowl with its center depression holding coconut cream on the table between them, then sat down across from him once more.

"A dip. Something decadent my aunt whips up out of cream of coconut, cream cheese, powdered sugar and vanilla. You dunk the berries in it like this." He demonstrated, holding the strawberry by the hull and stem that had been left when the berries were rinsed clean. With the thick, rich cream dripping from the dark red strawberry, he offered it to her.

"Ummm," she said as she opened her lips and bit off half the berry, then reached for the rest. "That's wonderful. I do love strawberries."

Kane agreed, while ignoring the drawing sensation in the lower part of his body caused by the sight of her lips enclosing the round, tender fruit. Reaching for a berry for himself, he said, "You realize that, all things considered, we know very little about each other, our likes and dislikes, what we enjoy and don't, or even things more important.

For instance, you've mentioned very little about your life in New York, other than the fact that you live with a cousin and have a son."

"There's nothing much to tell. I buy and sell jewelry, travel for auctions and appraisals. When I'm home, I help my cousin with his paperwork." She shrugged without looking at him as she swirled a second strawberry in the dip.

"No other family? No grandparents, for instance?"

"None on my mother's side. She always said that she was an orphan, though I think her family may have washed their hands of her when she ran away from home in Kansas to marry my father. As for his parents, they may still be alive somewhere, but I never knew them."

No family, or at least none who cared about her. She had apparently taught herself not to mind, but it had affected her, Kane thought as he watched the flicker of emotions that crossed her face. Sympathy was not going to help him, however.

He said, "So who was it took care of you after your mother died?"

"An aunt."

"But I thought you had no contact with either your mother's or your father's families." His tone was carefully neutral, though he watched her closely.

"Actually, she wasn't related, but only a friend of my mother's, a woman she met soon after she came to New York," she answered, her gaze wary, as if she suspected what he was doing. "She decided we should tell people she was my aunt to avoid trouble with the child-service people. She was afraid they wouldn't let me stay with her if there was no blood tie, though I doubt they cared. Anyway, it became such a habit that it almost seemed true."

"I think you said before that this woman died?"

She dropped the hull of the strawberry she had just eaten onto her plate and didn't reach for another. In toneless agreement, she said, "Five, almost six years after I went to live with her."

"What then? You must have still been fairly young since you were only — what? Ten, wasn't it — when your mother died?"

"The woman had a son who was like a brother to me. I stayed on with him."

"So the two of you made a family of sorts."

"Of sorts," she echoed, her gaze on the strawberry hull she nudged around the edge of her plate with the tip of one finger.

"Except he isn't really a cousin." Kane wanted to accept that the situation was as she said. The surprise was how much he wanted to believe it.

"You've no idea what a hassle finding an apartment can be in New York. I keep meaning to move out on my own, but somehow, with the traveling and everything else, I've never gotten around to it." She abandoned the strawberry hull. "I suppose it must seem strange to you, considering the size of your family."

"It's a bit hard to imagine."

"Having so few people close to you makes you cling to those who are there," she said, lifting her gaze finally and holding it level.

Kane refused to be affected by the undercurrent of stress in her voice. "Especially your son, I imagine," he added quietly. "Who takes care of him when you're out on the road like this?"

"He's in a special boarding school because of a learning disability. It makes him frustrated and hyperactive, and . . . resistant to discipline or control of any kind, which is dangerous in a place like New York where he might dart into traffic or wander away from the apartment and be found by anyone, any kind of creep. He takes medication, but still needs constant supervision."

She made a helpless gesture as she trailed into silence. The sheen in her eyes had the look of unshed tears before she glanced away toward the strawberry bowl. She reached for another berry and took a bite, though he didn't think she wanted it.

"Is the boy the reason you never married, never started a real family of your own?"

She swallowed and licked some sugary dip from a finger before reaching for a napkin. "Part of it. I suppose," she answered, "though you know the rest." She looked up, her face changed, hardened. "What is this interrogation? If you're going to keep asking questions, maybe I should call in another lawyer."

"Only if you have something to hide," he said, and waited with a suspended feeling in his chest for her answer.

She hesitated a millisecond and her eyelids flickered, then she gave a low laugh tinged with irony. "I don't suppose I have any more secrets than the average person. You, for instance."

She was good, he thought. So far, she had told enough of the truth to be plausible while still concealing the facts by omission. Yes, she was very good, but so was he.

"The only thing I'm hiding," he said, smiling ruefully as he propped an elbow on the table and rested his chin on his palm, "is a strong urge to see how you taste with Aunt Vivian's dip on your mouth."

"Like coconut and strawberries, I'd imagine," she said, her voice suddenly uneven.

"Two of my favorite flavors."

She licked her lips. "Are they?"

It was all the encouragement he needed. He got to his feet and moved to her side of the table. Taking her hand, he pressed the palm to his lips, then placed it at his waist as he bent over her. With a knuckle under her chin, he tilted her mouth and settled his lips on hers.

The luscious mixture of tastes, including her own nectar, melted on his tongue, spread through him with the power of some mystical elixir. It made him yearn for more, even as he knew it would never be enough. Bemused by the magic, he lifted his head and saw the same glazed wonder in her face.

Why? Why did it have to be so good? Why couldn't he have found this amazing physical affinity with some simple, loving female who believed in all the things he believed in, who understood his values, hopes and dreams? Why did he have such bad luck with women? Were there no honorable ones, or was he simply, inevitably, attracted to the wrong kind because of some inner flaw?

It was a useless question, one that vanished from his mind the instant he took her mouth again. His senses expanded as he realized there was no shrinking, no denial in her touch. She was all giving grace and accommodation. She allowed him entrance, followed his lead, swayed a little and caught his arm for balance with a touch that seemed to burn through his skin to the bone.

His heart was on fire, and his lower body, as well. He needed her as he had never needed another person in all the accumulated days and minutes of his life. Against all common sense, he wanted to lavish her with love.

Impossible. But he could do the next best thing. He could show her a different kind of loving, teach her the intense communication of selfless physical passion.

He went down on one knee, at the same time placing a drift of small kisses along the point of her chin to the pulse in the long sweep of her neck, down to the hollow of her throat. She wore a rust silk blouse that glided open beneath his questing fingers. To pull it free of her skirt took less than a second.

Her breasts were milk white and blue veined under a covering of peach lace, gentle globes that fitted his hands as if molded for them. Their warmth and delicate fragrance mounted to his head with narcotic force. His senses reeling with it, he pressed his hot lips to the valley between them while he slid her bra straps down her arms.

It had been too dark to see the night before. Now the beauty of her nipples, like tight and tender rosebuds, moved him beyond words. To touch them, it seemed, was to risk damaging them, yet his mouth tingled with the need to capture their perfection. Unable to help himself, he bent his head and wet first one, then the other, with his tongue. That glistening moisture was the ideal enhancement. A faint smile curved his mouth before he tasted them again.

But there was another variation lying like a gem in his mind. Moving with slow care, he reached to scoop his finger into the bowl of coconut-flavored dip. Applying it to the nearest nipple, he spread it in a slow circle.

"What are you — doing?" she asked with a catch in her voice.

"Anointing you," he said distractedly.

"Why?"

"For this," he said, then began to lick the

lovely treat he had created. She brought her hand up to run her fingers through his hair, but didn't interfere. Nor did she object again.

How he moved her from the chair to the table was a mystery. It was also an improvement. By then, it seemed, her doubts had faded away. With a glance from under the veiling of her lashes that was as daring as it was wary, she dipped her fingers into the milky coconut concoction, too. Dabbing it in interesting spots on his chest, she chased the drips with her small pink tongue, catching the errant drops with maddeningly efficient flicks.

He loved it, loved her delicacy and shy participation, and encouraged both with his hands on the firm curves of her hips. Nudging her thighs open with his own, he pressed against her feminine heat, trying to assuage the ache in his groin. And the feeling that rose inside him was both earthy and sublime, a desire to possess in fast, hard coupling and the need to lose himself in her, a passion to take and a need to cherish.

Minutes ago, or perhaps it was vast eons of time past, he had held a motive in his mind for this particular form of seduction. It was gone. Long gone. Caught in her sensual spell, he didn't care what she was doing to him or why so long as she didn't stop.

Hot, he was so hot, and so on fire with need and pleasure that he lost all trace of finesse, abandoned the last vestige of mental deliberation. All that was left was instinct and power, hard muscles and moist, yielding flesh, rising passion and inventive explorations seasoned with coconut and exhaustive self-control.

Until he was tested too far. Then he pressed into her and set a rhythm that taxed his muscles and shivered his soul — a slow, endless testing of her silken depths, her arching acceptance, her achingly gallant response. He wanted to go on and on, connected, fused in a mutual bonding of heart and mind that was sealed with body heat and desperate intentions.

Mindless, disregarding time and place, he was lost in the wonder. Absorbed in the blood pounding in his veins and the wet, hot contact, he knew only the blessed striving that made them one for a single explosive instant.

But it couldn't last, that oneness. Wouldn't. Didn't. And its passing left him as empty and lost as he had been before. Left him weary and disgusted by his search for truth and glory where none was to be found.

14

The shrilling of the phone woke Regina. She lay in the semidarkness as her brain roused from the deepest, most complete sleep she had known in a long time. It was a strange feeling. Stranger still was the realization that she was naked under the blanket that covered her, and that Kane, whom she was using as a warm and embracing pillow, was in the same condition.

The phone rang again. Alarm struck through her like the blade of a knife. There was only one person who would call her here.

Gervis.

Kane was awake; she could sense the alertness in his nerves, feel the muscles under her cheek shift as he lifted his head. He stretched a long arm toward the phone that was on the opposite side of the bed from where she lay.

She sprang up in panic. Flinging herself across his body, she caught the receiver a split second before he touched it. Her voice was breathlessly tight as she spoke into it.

"What the hell's going on down there, Gina? Why am I not hearing from you?"

"Sorry," she said in swift answer, "but you have the wrong room."

"Now that's a stupid —" The man on the other end of the line halted. "Got somebody with you, that it? How about that, this time of night. Call me ASAP, baby, because you've got some explaining to do."

"No problem," she said in dismissive tones. As the line went dead, she reached to hang up again. She held the position a second, feeling her heart banging against her ribs and thanking God for experience with hotel nuisance calls that had given her an excuse for this one. Then she glanced back to Kane.

He was watching her. For an instant, she thought she saw accusation in the dark pools of his eyes. It must have been no more than the reflection of her own guilt, for she blinked and it was gone.

She started to squirm backward off him, but he clamped a hard hand on her backside. The sound she made was somewhere between a yelp and a gulp. In protest, she said, "I'm squashing you."

"That's not how I'd describe what you're doing." He began to massage the curve he held, smoothing his warm hand in slow circles, creating strange sensations in the pit of her stomach.

What was happening to him was not exactly a mystery if the heated hardness under her abdomen was any indication. "Let me up."

"I don't think so." The scar beside his mouth, the scar she had traced with her tongue a short time before, stood out as a small half-moon.

"Turn me loose."

His grasp tightened. "You're driving me crazy, do you know that?"

"It's all in your mind." She wriggled, trying to move, but he was holding her down.

"I know. That's the worst thing about it."

There was a note in his voice that she didn't like. She stilled, spoke with more determination. "Let me go. Right now."

He rose up in bed with a sudden wrenching of muscles, using his momentum and leverage to flip her onto her back. In a coiling glide, he followed her, landing on top of her with his body pinning her to the bed though he rested his weight on his elbows. She lay staring up at the dark shape of his face, stunned yet entranced by the nudge of something very purposeful against the softness between her thighs.

"Am I bothering you?" he asked, his voice dulcet, but carrying an undercurrent of steel.

Was he? She hardly knew for the race of excitement and anticipation in her veins. To hide it, however, seemed pure mother knowledge. "No. No, you're not bothering me. Exactly."

"You don't feel the least bit of an inclination to go into panic mode and pound me between the eyes?"

She saw what he was getting at and couldn't believe he'd needed to make the point so plainly before she remembered. In some irritation, she said, "We aren't shut up in a coffin together."

"No, but we're certainly in the dark, with me holding you confined and with even less between us and final jeopardy than there was that day." He pressed inside her a teasing inch to show her exactly what he meant. "Maybe you weren't bothered then, either. Maybe it was an excuse to get away from me."

"Or maybe," she countered with a pugnacious jut of her chin, "it's just that you're not a threat anymore."

"Wrong," he said, and slid into her with a strong twist of the hips that took him to the hilt. "Wrong," he repeated as he withdrew, then mimicked the same motion. Then again. And again. Endlessly, until the refrain echoed in Regina's brain with the rising tide of perilous pleasure and she thought she might hear it in her dreams.

Kane was gone when she roused again an hour later. It was the closing of the door behind him that caused her to surface through layers of darkness this time. She lay still with her eyes closed, listening to the sound of his truck as the engine roared into life and he drove off.

It had been courteous of him to try to let her sleep, but she would rather have had a chance to say goodbye. She would also have preferred a chance to look him in the face before he left her.

There was something about the evening she had just spent with Kane that made her restless, uneasy. Something had been going on beneath its surface, she was sure of it. As she thought back, it seemed every word, every movement, carried some disturbing message if she could only see it. At the same time, she didn't really want to think about it, didn't want to investigate Kane's behavior or her own too closely. Fear of what she might find was too real and threatening.

She sat up and pushed the hair back from her face with a tired gesture, then reached for the travel clock on the bedside table. After twelve. It would be past one in New York. Replacing the clock, she leaned back against the headboard and closed her eyes.

She should call Gervis. He would be awake, waiting to hear from her. Her cousin was a night owl who liked to stay up until the wee hours, then sleep in. That had been one of the things that had bothered him most about having a child in the house after Stephan was born — that he had to change his sleeping habits to accommodate a small human being who rose at dawn.

The nagging worry about Stephan caught at her. She hoped he was all right with Gervis. She'd never left her son alone with him before. Gervis was fond of him in his way, but Stephan made him tense. He seemed to resent the amount of time and attention he took. At the same time, it was almost as if Gervis was afraid of him, afraid of not doing what was right around him.

A sudden longing swept over her to hold Stephan, to snuggle his warm, bony little body against her and feel his quick, hard hug. To hear him say he loved her. She had taught herself not to think about such things ever since he'd been in his hospital-like boarding school, but it was hard, so hard. She had let Gervis talk her into the arrangement, had listened to the expert he'd insisted on bringing in to examine Stephan and who said it was necessary for him to attend the special school. She wanted her child to have what was needed, wanted what was best for him. Still, she missed him so much. And in her mother's heart she wasn't sure such intense therapy was necessary for Stephan. Like the evening just past, it felt all wrong.

Everything seemed wrong, really: being separated from Stephan, coming to Turn-Coupe under false pretenses, conning Lewis Crompton, becoming involved with Kane for what she could learn from him. It was also a mistake to allow herself to feel much too much for a man who was going to hate her when he found out who she was and what she had done.

She couldn't stand it, she really couldn't. It was time she stopped, time she told Gervis she wouldn't do it anymore.

Did she dare?

Gervis wasn't reasonable these days. Whatever friendship and family feeling he might have had for her after years of treating her like a younger sister seemed submerged in his need to win this suit at all costs. Sometimes, though, she wondered exactly what he felt, whether he considered her a convenient hostess or just a responsibility inherited from his mother, an accepted part of his life, or a habit from which he could find no way to break free.

If Gervis deserted her, she would be alone. Could she stand that solitude, the loneliness of having no one to depend on except herself, no one to help with the difficult decisions that cropped up in her life? She thought she could, for herself, but wasn't sure she could give her son the care he needed. She had to be sure for Stephan's sake since he was the one who mattered most.

It always came back to that in the end — what was best for her son. Always. Sighing with resignation, she reached for the phone.

Gervis answered on the second ring. As he heard her voice, he growled, "About damned time. I was getting ready to send Slater in there to find out if you were okay."

"You wouldn't."

"Don't bet on it."

"If you had any idea what he's like, it would be the last thing to cross your mind."

"Yeah, yeah. So what gives down there?"

"Nothing. Everything's the same. Is Stephan asleep?"

"What? You think at this time of night, he should be waiting up for his mommy to call him?"

"Gervis, don't," she said as evenly as she could manage. "Don't be like this."

"Why not? I hear you're getting it on with the hick lawyer."

"It's what you suggested, isn't it?"

"So are you finding out anything or just having a good time?"

The anger stirring inside her came to a sudden boil. "If this is the way you're going to be," she said with precision, "then I'm hanging up."

"Don't you do it!" The command was fast, but much more moderate. She could hear him breathing in short, heavy pants through his nose, as if conquering rage he didn't intend to show. He was pacing with the remote phone clamped to his ear, she thought, for she could hear brief waves of static and the slap of the leather soles of his handmade Italian house shoes on the hardwood of the penthouse hallway.

"Tell me about Stephan," she said. "Does he like the nurse you hired? Is he all right being away from the school? You haven't talked to him about anything, have you?"

"The kid's fine. He'll be even better when his mother gets her job done and gets herself back here to him."

"I'm trying. But I wish you'd let Stephan go back to school where he belongs. He's bound to pick up on what's going on if he's around very long. My son is hyperactive, not stupid."

"He's also useful, Gina, honey. I need him to keep you in line."

The meaning behind the words wasn't subtle, nor was it meant to be. "You don't, Gervis, I promise, and I'd rather he was where he belongs. I can't do what I'm supposed to with this threat hanging over my head."

"You'll have to, baby, because that's the way it is."

"Why? You know you can trust me." She hated the sound of her voice, could hardly force the pleading words from her throat.

"That so? I hear you got yourself marooned with Benedict out on some lake, spent hours alone with the guy. But did I hear about it from you? No, not a peep. I had to get it from Slater. I'm thinking maybe I should turn this whole job over to him."

"He'd love that. In fact, I expect it's what he's after."

"You don't like him much, do you?"

"He's the worst kind of scum. In fact, I think he may have —"

"Get the job done and he'll be out of your hair," her cousin cut her off with sarcasm layering his voice. "Speaking of which, you sure you got nothing for me?"

The suspicion in the question sent what she was about to say out of her head. Should she tell him about the switched caskets and the lovers buried together? If she thought it would satisfy him, she might, but she didn't think it would. He would hound her for more details, more dirt, would make something corrupt out of a generous and compassionate response to a woman who had made a mistake. "No," she said, her voice as firm as she could make it. "I told you, there's nothing to tell."

She had hesitated too long. He was silent for an explosive second, then he cursed. "You're lying, baby. You got something. You're just too much of a bleeding heart to lay it on the line. Slater's right. You're not cut out for this job. You've let that bunch of rebels down there get to you. I don't watch out, you'll be doing me more harm than good."

"What do you mean by that?" she asked, holding the phone so tight her fingers ached.

"I mean you'll blab everything you know about me to Crompton and that grandson of his. You'll set me up."

"For heaven's sake, Gervis, what kind of

person do you think I am?"

"You're a woman. No telling what a woman will do."

That was a far more blatantly sexist remark than anything Kane had come close to making, even if he felt it, which she wasn't sure he did. There was, she realized, consideration and protectiveness underlying most of Kane's more chauvinistic impulses. "Look," she said, "I'm doing the best I can."

"I don't think so. You're waffling, playing both ends against the middle and trying to keep your hands clean. It ain't gonna work, I see that now. I think it's time I pulled the plug. I want you out of there."

"Leave? Just like that?" Distress vibrated in her voice.

"This second, babe. Get yourself a seat on the first plane out of that rinky-dink place. I want you back here as soon as you can make it."

"But I can't just drop everything."

"Don't give me any crap, Gina. Do it now. Don't tell anybody you're going. Don't stop to say good-bye. Be on that plane, or I'm warning you, you won't like what happens."

The order was followed by the click of the remote phone being punched off. Regina lowered the receiver to her lap. She sat staring at nothing while his words slammed around inside her head.

Leave. Now. Leave Kane when she had just begun to know him. Leave Mr. Lewis and Elise, Luke and Vivian, even Betsy. The thought of it made her feel empty and sick. She had only been here a matter of days, but there was something about the place and the people that drew her to them, made her feel warm inside. She didn't want to leave.

Yet how could she stay? There was no future in her relationship with Kane or any of the rest of them. They were going to despise her when they learned the truth. All her half-formed dreams of acceptance and belonging were just that: dreams. Useless, silly visions of the impossible.

Stephan needed her just as she needed him. He was her center, her refuge, her very life. He had been from the moment he was born and would be always. She must let no harm come to him because of her. She couldn't stand it if it did.

He was her family.

Kane had his, and she had hers. His was large while hers was small. Only two people, really. Yet the loyalties and love that bound them were the same. Her tie to Gervis might not be of blood, but it was of long standing.

He had protected her, sheltered her, sent her to school. He had been there for her on the terrible night Stephan was conceived, and afterward, when her son was born. She owed Gervis so much, and he had a right to expect loyalty from her in return. It would be unforgivable of her not to give it, even if she didn't agree with what he was doing.

Yes, but why did it have to be so hard? So very hard.

Regina closed her eyes and squeezed them tight. Tears beaded along the bases of her lashes. She wiped them away, smearing them across her cheeks. Then she shook back her hair and turned on the lamp. The phone book was tucked into the drawer of the bedside table. She turned to the yellow pages, found the listings for airlines. Picking up the phone again, she started to dial.

Regina was gone.

Kane couldn't believe it. Gone, just like that, without a word of explanation. Without good-bye, so long, see you around. Nothing.

He'd have expected better of her if he'd had any idea she'd leave at all.

Somehow he had thought the love they shared had meant more to her. He still felt that way. There were only two reasons that he could see, then, for why she might have left. One was that she had found out he was on to her. The other was that someone had forced her to go.

Of course, there could be a third reason if he wanted to reach for it. She could have gone because she needed to get away from him. Because she had faked her pleasure in making love to him and could pretend no longer.

He had to know which it was or else, couldn't stand not knowing.

Betsy had told him that Regina had checked out in too big a hurry to have much to say to the night manager, then had driven off in her rental car. Betsy also said that Dudley Slater had asked for a room the day before, but spent more time away from it than he did in it. The newspaper reporter wasn't there when Kane knocked on the unit's door, but he was in the coffee shop. Kane headed straight for the booth where he sat and slid into the cracked plastic seat across from him.

"Make yourself at home, why don't you?" Slater said in sour greeting as he looked up from his morning paper. With elaborate care, he folded the newsprint to a different section and began to read again.

"Thanks, I intend to." Kane plucked the

paper out of the man's hand and placed it on the seat beside him. "Now that we've got the preliminaries out of the way, how about a little meaningful discussion? Such as what happened to Regina?"

Slater studied him. The resentment in his skeletal features turned slowly to sterile humor. "Your honey pot's gone, huh?"

The insinuation in the man's voice grated on Kane's nerves, but he let it go for the moment. "Something like that. Know anything about it?"

"Nothing I'd tell you."

"I suggest," Kane said in slicing warning, "that you reconsider."

"What you gonna do? You and the sheriff so tight you can have my ass thrown in jail? Big deal. I been in better lockups in better towns than this."

"It still might be worth it for the satisfaction."

"Hard-nosed, aren't you? As if I give a shit."

"You might care a lot," Kane said evenly, "if I decide to break your neck."

"Lay a hand on me and I'll write you up as a mad-dog attorney, all brawn and no brains, outclassed and outmaneuvered by the most prestigious law firm in the Northeast. You'll be a laughingstock."

"And I'll slap a suit for slander and defamation on you and your paper before the next issue hits the streets," Kane countered without raising his voice. "Now, would you like to give me a straight answer?"

They stared at each other for long moments. Then Slater gave an elaborate shrug.

"You want to know where Regina Dalton went? Hell, Benedict, where do you think? She went back to New York where a classy broad like her belongs."

It was not what Kane wanted to hear. "Why?"

"How the hell should I know? I guess she got what she came for. Or maybe her cousin decided he'd rather have her warming his bed than out boffing the competition."

"Be very careful," Kane said, narrowing his eyes, "or you may wind up with more to write about than you expect."

"You asked a question and I answered." Slater licked his lips, his gaze avid. "Tell me one thing, Benedict. Was she good?"

Kane shot out his arm and grabbed the front of Slater's shirt. There was no decision, no plan, just suddenly he had a wad of grimy cotton clutched so tightly in his fist it shut off the little man's wind. And he didn't care who saw him or when he let go.

"Hey," Slater rasped. "God."

"I asked a civil question," Kane said, the words distinct, evenly spaced. "I'll have a civil answer or you don't get to breathe."

"Berry called. She went. What else you need to know?" Slater plucked at Kane's fist while his face turned a sickly purple.

"Why did he call? Why now?"

Malevolence glittered in the reporter's bulging eyes as he rasped, "Why you think? Berry found out what was going on, decided his woman was having too much fun on the job."

"How is it you know what he decided?" Kane released the man and sat back in his seat, suppressing an urge to wipe his hand as if he'd touched something dirty.

"It's my job to know." Slater rubbed his throat as he stretched it, trying to swallow. As Kane leaned forward again, he added hastily, "For Christ's sake, he said so when I reported to him."

"Reported what?"

"The two of you getting so cozy. What else?"

"Why should that bother Berry if she's like some kind of adopted cousin?" Kane thought the repellent scumbag was proud of his information-gathering abilities. Let him display them, then.

"Who says she is?"

"The lady herself."

"Yeah, sure. All I can say is Berry's name's on her kid's birth certificate."

Kane sucked in air as if he'd been kicked in the stomach. For an instant, his vision was red around the edges.

It had all been a lie — Regina's aversion to sex, the tragic tale of date rape. More than likely, she wasn't an orphan, either, had never been taken in by Berry's mother as a young girl.

The betrayal hurt. It hurt more than he had ever dreamed it could, far more than the con Francie had pulled. More than he might be able to stand if he let himself think about it.

He wouldn't. Couldn't. Not now.

"Didn't know that, did you?" Slater asked, his voice oozing gratification. "Never crossed your mind to find out. Now me, I make it my business to dig up that kind of dirt. There's more than one angle to a story, more than one way to make a buck off a case. People will pay big to know about Berry's love life once this case gets rolling."

Kane snorted in disgust "You'd go against the man paying you?"

"Call it insurance. I got to protect myself in case he don't come through."

"It would be more accurate to call it

blackmail, wouldn't it?"

"So it's blackmail, fine. I'm no high and mighty Benedict, just a poor schmuck trying to make a living the best I know how."

"What else," Kane said with deliberation, "do you know about Berry?"

Slater stared at him a long moment. Then he smiled. "How bad do you want to know? How rich are you Benedicts?"

If he flashed enough cash, Kane knew, he could have everything he needed to know to put Berry Association, Inc. six feet under. It would take about two seconds to run the case through the court and pull down a verdict in his grandfather's favor. Two seconds to remove all threat to Pops.

He couldn't do it.

It stuck in his craw to win by trafficking with such scum. More than that, Lewis Crompton would rather lose than stoop that low.

Kane got to his feet. "Sorry," he said in quiet disgust, "I don't work that way."

"Too good, that it?"

Kane made no answer. Turning, he walked away with unhurried treads. He didn't look back.

Slater began to curse in a virulent undertone. He was still at it when Kane passed out of hearing.

15

New Yorkers, Regina thought from her new, Southern-tinged perspective, could be friendly enough when they wanted. For the most part, however, they hurried along both oblivious to each other and suspicious at the same time. Encased behind their self-protective mental barriers, they made no eye contact, but focused on their own problems to such an extent that all they wanted was for everyone else to get out of their way. They talked too fast and with little consideration for how what they said might affect someone else or what others might want to say in return. Nor did they notice or care that their habits made them appear distant and self-centered.

It seemed peculiar that she had never noticed, more peculiar still that she had been that way herself before she went to Turn-Coupe. But the sad part was that she would probably be exactly the same again after a few days back in the city.

In the meantime, she found herself having to make a conscious effort not to smile too much or speak too familiarly to the cabdriver who loaded her bag in his taxi at the airport, the doorman who let her into the apartment building, or the man who held the elevator for her as she approached it. She had no such problem, however, when she unlocked the door of the penthouse apartment and saw Gervis waiting for her.

"Well, it's about time," he said with heavy sarcasm from where he stood in the study doorway, filling the opening with his burly body.

"There was no flight out until this morning, then nothing without a layover."

"Why didn't you call?"

"Don't tell me you were worried about me?" she said in dry disdain.

"I expected you hours ago."

"Did you? I'd have flapped my arms harder if I'd known." So much for her polite consideration for other people. It hadn't lasted a day.

"Don't give me any lip," Gervis warned.

"Fine." Swinging from him, she wheeled her suitcase away down the hall toward her bedroom and set it inside out of the way, then freed herself from the strap of her shoulder bag that she'd automatically crossed over her chest as she deplaned.

"I'm not through talking to you," Gervis growled, following her as far as the bedroom doorway.

She didn't bother to answer. Throwing the shoulder bag on the bed, she walked back to the door, put a hand on his barrel chest, and pushed him aside. It was surprise that made Gervis give way, she thought, but the reason didn't matter. She'd have walked through him if necessary. Stepping farther along the hall, she opened the door of the adjoining room.

The small boy sitting on the bed looked up from the book spread over his lap. The afternoon sunlight streaming into the room caught glints of red in his brown hair and made his small, pale face look as fragile as fine china. His gaze was lackluster, his eyes heavy lidded. Then a slow, beatific smile spread across his face.

"Mama," he cried, and began to push clumsily out of the bed.

Regina crossed the room in a flash and scooped him close as she dropped down onto the mattress. Rocking back and forth in a glorious excess of maternal love and pleasure for the familiar scent and feel of his thin young body, she murmured against his hair, "Stephan, my honey, my tiger, I missed you."

"I missed you, too," he said, his voice thick.

"Now that we've settled that," Gervis said from the hallway in sneering impatience, "could we talk here, Gina?"

She ignored him. Loosening her hold on her son, she ran her gaze over his small face, searching for reassurance. "How have you been, sweetheart? Has everyone been treating you okay?"

"I guess," Stephan said, sending a quick look toward Gervis before giving a nervous shrug and lowering his gaze.

Her stomach muscles tightened, but she didn't press the question. "What about school? Is it all right? Have you been doing fun things?"

"Well . . ."

"What is it?"

"I'd rather be here with you."

Heart aching, she caught him close again. "I wish you could be, honey. I wish you could so much."

"C'mon, c'mon," Gervis said, snapping his fingers in harsh impatience.

Regina gave him a quelling look. To her son, she said, "Where's your nurse?"

"She's lying down," he said slowly, as if it was difficult to remember. "I'm supposed to be taking a nap, too."

"A nap? But you're too old for that." He

was nine years old and usually had too active a mind for that kind of thing.

"She doesn't think so. Michael doesn't, either."

Michael was the houseman who served as Gervis's bodyguard on occasion. Regina couldn't help wondering if Stephan's nurse had been using the hulking ex-football player to frighten her son.

"We can talk here if that's the way you want it," Gervis said, shoving into the room and planting himself in the middle of the floor. "Matter of fact, it might be best."

She looked up at him, her face set. "I don't think so."

"I'm tired of you avoiding this, baby. I want to know exactly what went on down there in Louisiana. I want to know how come you turned on me."

"Considering whom you heard that from, I'd think you'd be embarrassed to believe a word."

"You saying it's not true?"

"There was never a chance." Which was the exact truth, though not, perhaps, in the way she hoped he would take it.

He grunted. "So why was I getting zilch in the way of news out of you?"

"Did it ever occur to you there might be nothing to be had?"

"You saying that bunch is so squeaky clean I should give it up? Never in a million years. Either you weren't trying hard enough, or you're holding out on me. Which is it?"

"Neither —" she began.

"Oh, yeah. Slater says you were getting it on pretty good with Benedict. So why wasn't I told? Why didn't I get a report on what you asked him and what he said? Or were you too busy to say anything?"

"Please," she said with a meaningful glance at Stephan who was watching them both with wide, frightened eyes.

"Don't sweat it. I think maybe it's time the kid found out what kind of mama he's got. I think maybe you been holding out on me for years, Gina. I think you fabricated that little tale about being forced against your will, there, years ago."

She stared at him with a frown meshing her brows. "That's crazy and you know it."

"Is it? Seems to me you got over being against sex mighty fast. You been holding out on me about that, too, haven't you? We could have been real cozy all this time if you'd been straight with me."

"I don't know what you mean," she protested. "We're like brother and sister."

He grunted a coarse laugh. "I think you do."

"You think we should have —" She stopped, not wanting to say the words in front of Stephan.

"Why not? You don't think I noticed you that way? I could have gone for you, might even have married you. But a cold fish for a wife didn't exactly turn me on, and besides, I figured I owed you after the Harvard man."

Regina had grown attuned to nuances of expression in the past few days. Something she saw in Gervis's face tripped a sensor in her mind. "You owed me?"

"Yeah, well." He lifted a shoulder and diverted his gaze to a spot above her head. "The guy asked me to set him up with you. He'd seen you, liked the way you looked. It was part of a package deal, business between me and his old man, you know?"

"No, I don't know, Gervis," she said slowly, "though I remember you arranged the date. Was the date-rape drug part of this deal?"

"That's a hell of a question!"

"Isn't it." The agreement was without inflection.

Red splotches of color appeared on his jowls. He opened his mouth, then closed it and shrugged.

"What did you think?" she asked in low

amazement. "That I wouldn't care? That it wouldn't matter?"

"I didn't know, okay?" he said, flinging up his hands. "The guys he ran around with bragged about slipping dope to women so they could put it to them while they were out, but hell, it could have been just talk. Anyway, you weren't supposed to remember. How was I to know he'd screw it up, get in too big a hurry. Or that he'd knock you up?"

She couldn't speak, could only stare at him, this man she'd thought she knew. Regardless, there was a sense of completion about it, as if some long-missing piece of a puzzle had been found. The suspicion must have been hovering at the edge of her consciousness since the beginning. She'd pushed it aside all those years ago because it would have meant she had no one, nothing to cling to while she waited for Stephan to be born.

Gervis waved a dismissive shrug, then stepped closer. His voice hardening, he said, "That's not the problem right now. I want a full report on what went on between you and Benedict. No more excuses, no getting around it. You owe me, Gina. I put clothes on your back for years, shelled out for schools, hospitals, and a thousand other things. You've got by without a payback till now because I was suckered. That's over. You'll give me what I want or I'll take it out of your hide."

"You're not going to hurt my mama," Stephan said, his lower lip thrust out and his small fists tight as he struggled from the confinement of her arms.

Gervis barely glanced at him. "Not if she's smart."

"I can't believe you're doing this," Regina said, catching her son to her again and holding tight.

"What, I'm supposed to tiptoe around you forever? I always knew you lived in a dream world, someplace like where that old jewelry came from, with ladies and gentlemen and hand kissing. I just never figured you were soft in the head."

"I'm an idiot because I don't think like you, is that it?" she asked in disgust as she got to her feet. "You're the one talking in circles. You owe me, you say, but only until you want something, then suddenly I owe you. Well, not anymore. We're even, starting now. You'd better go talk to that rat you hired."

Gervis shifted to block her way to the door while his fleshy lips thinned. "I can see I'm talking to the wrong person here, all right, but I think I can still get some answers." He lowered his hard gaze to Stephan. "Tell me something, boy. You got any idea where you came from?"

"Don't," she exclaimed, setting her feet in a fighting stance in spite of the trembling in her knees.

"I told you how it was going to be, but you don't seem to get it. Guess maybe it's time I showed you." He jerked his head in Stephan's direction. "Well, kid?"

"It won't work. He's not likely to know the words you'd use."

"He can understand, can't you, Stevie? You can understand real good. For instance, you know you don't have a real daddy, don't you now?"

Stephan blinked hard, frowning. He meshed his fingers, twisting them together. "A lot of the kids at school don't have a daddy. It's all right."

"He's a bright little bugger, see?" Gervis gave her a hard grin. "I think he'll get the point just fine. You sure you don't have something to tell me before I get into the really interesting parts of what the Harvard man did to his mama?"

"This is sick," she threw at him as she tightened her protective hold. "You're insane."

An ugly look came over Gervis's face. Holding her gaze, he said to Stephan, "You know how babies are made, boy?"

"They grow in the mama's stomach." Her son looked up at her for corroboration and Regina gave him a strained smile. She had to think, had to find something to give Gervis to pacify him for at least a little while. But what?

"That's right, son. And do you have any idea how —"

"Wait!" Regina took a step forward, pulling Stephan with her at the same time. "Please, wait. Don't you know what you're doing? He won't know it doesn't matter anymore. He won't —"

"Hey, I can't help it, Regina. It's your doing. But he'll understand just fine, I promise you, because you're exactly right about his brain power. There's not a damn thing wrong with it."

"The emotional damage could be terrible if he thinks —"

"Are you dense or something? I'm telling you the kid is perfectly normal."

She stared at Gervis, not quite comprehending, yet afraid she understood too well. Her hands were trembling with a combination of horror and hovering anger. "What do you mean, normal? The doctor said — I

354

was told over and over that there were definite learning and behavior problems."

"The doctor said," Gervis repeated with a sneer. "Find the right one, name the right price, and he'll tell you whatever you want to hear."

"You're saying Stephan was misdiagnosed?"

"I'm saying I paid off the experts to tell you the kid had to have special schooling. I was tired of his noise and mess, and it was the only way you'd agree to let him go. Besides, you were taking up too much time with him. Between that and work, you weren't carrying your part of the load around here. You never had time to talk when I needed to bounce ideas around . . ."

She said with care, because she had to be very sure, "You put my son into an institution *for your own convenience?*"

"Now you got it, and about time, too." Gervis smoothed his thinning hair. "No need to pull some outraged-motherhood act about it, either. It's a boarding school, for crying out loud. People send kids there all the time."

"It's not just a school! He's been sedated for a solid year because of your experts!" Hearing the pain in her voice, Stephan turned and flung his arms around her, burying his face against her side.

"So what? It hasn't hurt him," Gervis said, the words exasperated.

She had been separated from her son for no reason other than the man in front of her had wanted it that way. He had taken Stephan from her and left him in the care of strangers. All her protests that her son was normal had been turned aside with jargon and statistics and condescending assurances that a mother never wanted to believe her child was flawed. And, finally, she had betrayed Stephan by listening, by letting herself believe she was doing what was right for him. He had been kept like a small, pale zombie for nothing. *Nothing.*

Rage such as she had never known swept through Regina, rage that fired her brain while leaving her heart cold. Sheer, unadulterated rage that made her want to kill.

Her voice a harsh rasp in her throat, she said, "Get your backpack, Stephan. Put everything in it that you truly need, everything you don't want to leave behind."

Gervis put his hands on his hips. "If you think you're going somewhere, you can think again."

"We're leaving. For good." She watched with grim anticipation as Stephan ran to his closet and jerked out his backpack, shoved jeans and a couple of shirts inside, then turned to scramble among the toys on his special shelf.

"I don't think so," Gervis said, spite glittering in his eyes. "Not with the boy."

"I won't let my son remain here."

"Your son? Aren't you forgetting a couple of things?"

"I don't think so."

"Number one," he said, counting off points on his stubby fingers, "you'll have to get by Michael. Number two, the boy belongs to me."

She opened her mouth to deny it. Then she remembered.

Gervis was listed on the birth certificate as Stephan's father. She had done that herself because the hospital nurse who'd filled out the papers had insisted the space couldn't be left blank. She'd known Gervis wouldn't object and wanted no possibility that the real father could ever have a claim.

Moistening lips that were suddenly dry, she said, "You can't mean to hold on to him?"

"Want to bet?"

What she wanted was to smash the gloating satisfaction that shone on his face. She wanted it so badly she felt sick with it. "I'll fight you."

"Do that, if you think you can win."

If you think you can win . . .

Did she? Could she? Was it possible?

Gervis had wealth, access to excellent lawyers, and the kind of vindictive drive that made coming out on top the only thing that mattered. If Stephan was hurt in the process, Gervis would blame her, not himself. He'd say she should have done what he asked, given him what he wanted.

Maybe, just maybe, he was right.

No. She couldn't win.

A laugh, a low sound of intolerable pain, left her. She had to laugh or she would scream. Stephan knew what it meant, she thought, for he turned to look at her. Then he slowly put the space toy he had selected back onto the shelf, dropped his backpack to the floor.

He really was a bright child.

She reached out to her son, waiting until he was safe in the circle of her arms again before she said, "What is it exactly that you want to know?"

"Now that's more like it," Gervis said with a twist of his lips. "Give it to me, every little whisper you heard about Crompton. I want it all, including how often he goes to the toilet. That will do for a start."

She searched her mind, trying to dredge

up something, anything, that might satisfy Gervis. "Well, to start with, he keeps a coffin in the parlor of his old house."

"Good, good, we can hint the old guy's batty, thinks he's some kind of vampire or something. What else you got? C'mon, give."

"He has a lady friend he's been seeing for some time, but he's only recently decided to remarry. I think he may have still been hung up in some way over his first wife."

"She's dead, right? He spend much time in cemeteries, got a yen for corpses? Nah, that won't work. What else? C'mon." He furrowed his brow, looking for angles, even as he snapped his fingers, motioning impatiently for her to speak faster.

"His grandson, Kane, is the most important person in his life, and the two of them make a formidable team. They will pursue the suit to their last breath and can hold out indefinitely because the law firm is in the family."

As the words left her mouth, Regina felt the stirring of an idea. Gervis wasn't the only person with access to an excellent lawyer. She knew one with a crusader instinct, one who might help her if only she could talk to him, make him see how important it was.

"Benedict & Brown are small potatoes," Gervis said with a sneer. "My guys will mop the floor with them."

"I wouldn't be too sure."

He gave a coarse laugh. "Hell, Gina, you think Benedict's a miracle worker?"

Did she? It was possible. He had helped her before and might again with the right incentive. The only question was what it would cost her.

What was the going rate for a first-class miracle? What would Kane want from her in return for what she intended to ask?

She had no idea. But whatever he wanted, she would have to pay.

16

The hardest part of getting away from the New York apartment and Gervis again was leaving Stephan behind. She hated having to do it, cursed Gervis for the necessity, but could find no way around it. She was free to come and go. Her son was under guard.

No doubt Gervis thought she would never leave without Stephan or, if she did, could always be forced to come crawling back. He was partially right.

It was nearly noon the following morning, after Gervis had left for his office at the Berry Association building, that she told Stephan she was going. The look on his face as he realized she was leaving him behind almost broke her heart.

"Don't go," he whispered. "I don't like it when you're not here."

For a single instant, she wavered, almost ready to remain for his sake, accepting whatever conditions Gervis imposed. It wouldn't work. He would expect Stephan to return to his school, and she couldn't bear that. She'd also have to live in constant fear of what else Gervis might do to him.

She dropped to her knees in front of her son, putting her hands on his shoulders as she searched his small face for understanding. "I'll be back soon," she said, her voice breaking. "I'll be back to get you, then we'll go someplace far away where we can always be together."

"But I want to go now," he insisted, his eyes huge and liquid with need.

The fervent urge to snatch up her son and make a run for it clutched at her heart. She forced it down. The houseman, Michael, was in the kitchen making brunch for the nurse, a busty blonde who cooed over Stephan when either Gervis or Regina was around, but spent the rest of the time coming on to Gervis's hired goon. The houseman was definitely interested there, but that didn't keep him from checking out every move Stephan or Regina made. He would be sure to either block her escape or chase her down. Gervis would then be put on his guard. She would be jeopardizing her chance of gaining total custody.

"I'd take you if I could, sweetness. Really, I would. But I just can't this time." The instinctive endearment she'd used was a vivid reminder of Kane. Sugar Kane, her only hope.

"Will you be gone long?"

Her son's voice was so small she could barely hear it. It triggered memories of all the weeks and months he had been left at his school, all the times she had walked away from him with tears streaming down her face while telling herself she was doing what was best for him. As she was now.

"It won't be long at all," she said thickly. "Not a single second longer than it absolutely has to be, I promise."

He looked at her, his hazel green gaze earnest, painfully accepting, agonizingly trusting. "Cross your heart and hope to die?"

"Cross my heart," she whispered, making the quick mark on her chest. "Oh, cross my heart."

She caught him close, holding tight, aching with love for the feel of his small arms around her neck as she rocked him against her, imprinting it on her memory. Then she released him and went quickly from the room and the apartment while she was still able.

Back in Turn-Coupe, Regina checked into the motel and asked for the same room she'd had before. Betsy seemed a little cool as she handed over the registration card to be signed. She stood for a moment watching Regina fill out the blanks before she said, "Kane was fit to be tied when he found out you were gone."

"Oh?" It was the best Regina could do. She didn't look up, but her every sense was alert for anything more Betsy might tell her.

"He was about ready to call the police, tell them you'd been kidnapped, until I told him you'd checked out. I still had to let him in to see for himself. Even then, I don't think he got the message, not until he found out you were on a plane to New York."

"He called the airline?" She hadn't thought he would go so far.

Betsy took the registration and Regina's credit card as they were pushed toward her, then processed them with quick, practiced motions. "I did it for him while he stood right there where you're standing. He wasn't happy with what he heard. Can't say I'd want to be in your shoes when he finds out you're back."

"He was angry?"

"Livid, honey. How come you took off like that without telling him where you were going?"

"I — didn't think he'd notice since it was for hardly more than twenty-four hours." That was untrue. She'd thought she wouldn't be coming back. She'd expected that, when the trial started if not before, Kane would discover her connection to Gervis. Then it wouldn't matter to him where she went.

"Lord, have you got a lot to learn about Southern men," Betsy said in dry warning. "You want I should give him a call, let him know you're here?"

The very idea made the hair rise on the back of Regina's neck, though she could see Betsy was dying to give Kane the news. Hastily, she said, "I'll ring him myself when I get to my room."

She didn't make the call. For one thing, she needed time to think about what Betsy had told her and decide what she was going to say to Kane. Asking an angry man to help her gain custody of her son the minute she saw him didn't sound like a workable plan. Most of all, she needed to gather the courage to make her appeal. It had to be right since it was so important that Kane listen to her, help her. She didn't know what she was going to do if he refused.

When the knock came less than an hour after she checked in, the first thing that went through her mind was that Betsy had called Kane anyway. Apparently, he'd lost no time in getting to the motel. More disturbed than she cared to admit, she walked to the door and threw it open.

It was Slater who stood outside. He was a little cleaner than when she'd seen him last, but not by much. His pants were rumpled and his shirt looked as if he'd rinsed it out by hand and put it back on still damp. His smile was loose lipped and cynical.

"Well now," he said as he slouched in the doorway with his hands shoved into his pockets. "Look who's back."

"What do you want?" Even as she spoke, she silently berated herself for not using the peephole before she opened the door.

"Berry wanted to know when you showed up. I'm checking for him."

"Lovely," she said in brittle disdain. "Now you can relieve his mind." She started to shut the door.

Slater stuck out his foot to stop her. "Hold on there. I trotted over for Berry, but I'm staying for me."

Something in his expression sent alarm zinging along Regina's nerves. In quick reflex, she rammed her shoulder into the door and shoved. Slater cursed and leaped to thrust his arm into the opening, using the leverage to throw her backward. She stumbled, almost falling. He whipped inside and kicked the door shut.

"What do you want?" she demanded as she regained her balance and backed away.

His lips formed a grin of snide triumph as he let his hot gaze slide over her, from her hair that was drawn back on either side of her face with gold-and-tortoiseshell barrettes to the curves of her body under a cotton shirt and matching skirt in old gold. "Thought I'd tell you you're wasting your time here. I already found out all there is to know."

"That couldn't be much," she said, acutely wary. Keep him talking, she thought. That was what all the self-defense manuals preached, wasn't it?

"Enough. Seems the old man's been burying people in the wrong place. On purpose. Now we can't have that, can we?"

"How did you . . . ?" She clamped her lips together, angry with herself for letting him know she had also come across that information.

"You'd be surprised what buying a few beers for the right guy will do, such as one of the old codgers who works down at the funeral home."

"Gossip," she said with scorn. "Gervis will want something that can be documented. I'll be surprised if he pays off."

"You got his number, don't you? He offered less than half what he said at first."

So Gervis already had the information. She'd refused to give it to him, had held her tongue in spite of everything. It had given her distinct pleasure to think she had thwarted him. All for nothing. "Whatever you found out isn't likely to damage Lewis Crompton."

"Yeah, that's what Berry thought, though he was less polite about it. But he's going to twist it around into something he can use, so I don't see what right he's got to hold out on me. That's where you come in." He licked his lips, a slow movement of his coated tongue, as his gaze rested on the firm curves of her breasts.

She crossed her arms over her chest. "I can't imagine what you expect me to do about it."

"Berry's got too many connections for me to touch him. But you're his main woman, his safety piece, the one he keeps stashed in his apartment — or were up to now. Did he put you onto Benedict, or was that your idea?"

"None of your business."

"Your mistake, honey. I been keeping my eye on you because of Gervis, but I like what I see. I think we'd be a good team — you with the looks, me with the know-how."

"What you've got is gall."

"You saying you won't go for it?"

"Exactly." Every ounce of the repugnance she felt was in her voice.

"You don't want a partner on the deal, then maybe you'll ante up the difference Berry owes me."

She looked him up and down. "Why on earth should I do that?"

"Why not?" he countered. "Didn't I help you out there the other night so's you could get it on with Benedict? That oughta be worth something."

"I knew it had to be you. Though I can't imagine why you bothered."

"Had to do something, it being too dangerous to go after old man Crompton again. Figured you might be grateful to have it fixed so you finally got something out of Benedict, might even see we'd make a team. I should've known better."

"What makes you think he told me anything?"

He lifted a bony shoulder. "Stands to reason, the way you took off out of here."

"Then why would I come back?"

"You and Berry had a falling out over what you been doing. Leastwise, it seemed that way to me, reading between the lines. Which is why I thought you might like to join forces."

"Forget it. I'm not joining you in anything."

"That so? Guess I'll have to settle for my payoff, then."

He moved toward her. She stepped back at the same time. "I don't have any money, only plastic."

"That kind of pay," he said with a lewd grin, "ain't what I had in mind. I've had me a real itch for a redhead several days now. Don't see why I shouldn't scratch it since old Berry seems done with you."

"No." The refusal was as forceful as she could make it. At the same time, she wondered if Gervis had really given up on her since he had what he wanted. Not that it mattered. Invoking his protection was the last thing on her mind; she had no intention of ever being obligated to him again.

"Oh, yeah," he whispered, advancing.

"Stay away from me."

Sickness boiled inside her as she retreated. Why any man would think he could use a woman without her cooperation was a mystery. That this scrawny excuse for humanity dared threaten her with it was an insult.

"I don't think so."

He was between her and the door. If she led him deeper into the room, she might be able to fake him out, make a break for it. She didn't know what else to try. There was no weapon anywhere in the sparsely furnished unit.

What was it about her that made both Gervis and Slater view her as easy prey? Not long ago, she would have thought she looked like a victim, as if she had the word stamped across her forehead in big letters. Now she wondered if her newfound initiative wasn't a challenge they couldn't resist trying to knock down.

Even as these ideas flickered through her mind, she recoiled from Slater's cocky advance. Glancing over her shoulder, she saw the door of the motel's tiny bathroom standing open like an invitation. Abruptly, she whirled and dove inside.

Slater was after her in a flash. As she swung the door shut, he hurled himself against it, driving her back a pace. She braced her feet against the tub, grunting as she put her shoulder to the door, jamming it closed while she snapped the lock with quick fingers. Then she released it and jumped back.

The door shuddered and rattled in its frame as Slater thumped it with his fist, then slammed into it with his shoulder once, twice, a third time. Plaster crumbled from around its hinges. The wood creaked and groaned. As he hit it yet again, the hollow-core construction began to splinter and break apart. Beneath the noise, she could hear the newsman cursing, ranting, telling her exactly what he was going to do to her when he got to her.

Regina put a hand to her amber pendant as she swung around, searching for something, anything, to use to defend herself. The only thing she saw was the toilet tank lid. She grabbed it with both hands. The porcelain rectangle grated with a nerve-shattering screech as she jerked it off, but it felt comfortingly heavy. She lifted it high and stood ready.

The doorjamb ripped loose, but the lock held for an instant. Slater thrust his arm through, feeling for the knob with its push-button catch. Regina took a deep breath and smashed the tank lid down on his wrist.

He howled and jerked his arm back. Quiet fell for a split second.

Then Slater attacked the door in a frenzy, cursing and yelling as he pounded into it with his shoulder again and again. Wood screeched. Plaster flew. She glimpsed the snarl on his face through the ragged opening. The door was going to give way. Regina backed up, wedging herself between the lavatory and the toilet.

Suddenly, somewhere in the background, a different, more muffled crash sounded, followed by a deep voice in exclamation. Slater barked out a startled oath. A second later, he vanished from behind the mangled door. Then the only sound was a labored, asthmatic wheezing.

"Regina?"

Kane. It was Kane.

Relief flooded her so suddenly that it forced a strangled gasp from her throat. Her hands shook as she put the toilet tank lid on the floor. She fumbled with what remained of the bathroom door, dragged it open a small space, then pushed her way past the broken frame.

Kane had Slater against the wall, holding him there with a hard forearm across his throat while the reporter made choking noises and scrabbled for purchase with his dangling toes. There was black fury in Kane's eyes and a dangerous set to his mouth.

Stepping quickly to his side, she put her hand on the corded muscle of his arm. "I'm all right," she said. "Let him go."

Kane turned his head, meeting her gaze for a long, searching instant. Then he released the newsman with an abrupt, open-handed gesture of contempt. Slater fell back against the wall and grabbed his throat with one hand, while the other flopped at an odd angle in front of him. All the fight and threat seemed to have gone out of him.

Kane touched her arm, turning her to face the light coming from the open entrance door. He lifted his hand to brush her disheveled hair back from her face, then let his fingers linger on the curve of her cheek. "You're sure you're okay? He didn't hurt you?"

She nodded wordlessly, shielding her gaze with her lashes, afraid to answer for fear her voice would break. His concern triggered a strong need to burst into tears and throw herself into his arms. Another time, she might have succumbed, but there had been something dark and severe in the first glance he'd thrown her, which suggested it might not be a good idea. The effort to control the impulse left her rigid and breathless.

"I ain't all right," Slater croaked. "She's broke my damn arm."

"You're lucky I didn't break your neck," Kane said, swinging on him with such menace that the reporter shrank back. "What the hell did you think you were doing?"

Slater threw Regina a quick look of terror as he sidled a few steps farther along the wall. "Nothing, nothing. Just a misunderstanding."

"Is that right?" Kane looked toward Regina again.

She could agree, try to pass the whole thing off, but she didn't think Kane would accept it. Nor could she afford it. For one thing, Slater might try again because he thought she didn't dare accuse him. But the main reason was because she so desperately needed Kane's help. To have even a small chance of getting it, she had to level with him.

The time to start was now.

Swallowing hard, she said, "It was a misunderstanding all right. Slater seemed to think that I should pay him off since Gervis Berry won't."

"And what," Kane asked, "do you have to do with Berry?"

"He's my . . ." She stopped with a frown drawing her brows together as she realized what she was about to say. Speaking quickly, before she could change her mind, she said, "I live with him. Or I did."

Alertness but no surprise sounded in Kane's voice. "You don't anymore?"

"We've parted company."

"Why?" It was a word without compromise.

"Ethical differences." She searched his face to see if he understood at all, but there was nothing to give her a clue.

"Now see here —" Slater began.

"Shut up." Kane slung the words at the reporter in quiet ferocity. To Regina, he went on, "Do you want to press charges?"

"Hey!" Slater protested. "She's the one broke my goddamned —"

Kane silenced him with a single look. The reporter's mouth snapped closed so quickly his teeth made an audible click.

Regina answered Kane's question with a shake of her head. "All I want is to have him gone and never have to see him again."

Kane watched her a moment, his gaze dark blue with cogent thought, then he gave a slow nod. Over his shoulder, he said to Slater, "You heard the lady."

"Fine by me," Slater growled as he sidled past them, supporting his limp arm as he headed for the door. "I'd as soon shake the dust of this stinking town off my shoes. As for seeing this bitch —"

The gaze Kane turned on him sent the reporter scuttling for the door. He plunged through and slammed it behind him. A moment later, a car roared into life in front of a nearby unit, then tore away with tires screaming.

"You're going to just let him go?" she said uncertainly.

"He won't get far. Roan has a few questions he wants to ask him about Pops's accident."

The implacable sound of his words robbed Regina of any reply. The stillness that settled in the room was as thick and oppressive as the plaster dust in the air. She could feel its weight pressing on her shoulders. Staring in blank concentration at the wall beyond Kane's left shoulder, she thought of how he had just connected Slater to the attempt on the life of Mr. Lewis, about his lack of any real response to what she had told him and the possible reasons behind that impassivity. There was only one conclusion. As she came to it, slow, poisonous despair seeped through her. When it seemed she would be crushed by it and the quiet around them, she stirred at last and turned her gaze toward him.

"You knew," she said in stark acceptance.

"Days ago."

She closed her eyes as pain and regret burgeoned inside her, cutting off air from her lungs, impaling her heart, mangling hope. The words a thread of sound, she said, "I'm sorry, so very sorry. For everything."

For long seconds, he made no answer. When he finally spoke, it was as if he had not heard her at all. Voice even, without emotion, he said, "That you've left Berry is news. When did it happen?"

"This morning." Her throat ached as if each syllable was embedded with spikes, but she followed his lead by going on to relate what had happened in New York.

Kane gave a short laugh of contempt when she finished. "Some relationship you and your so-called cousin had."

"It wasn't so bad once," she said tiredly. Reaction from the excitement seemed to be catching up with her. Suddenly too exhausted to stand, she turned from him and walked to the bed where she dropped to the mattress.

"So the change of heart is because of the boy," he said from where he stood.

She knit her fingers together, clasping them so tightly the fingertips were white. "And also because I don't like the things Gervis is doing or wants me to do. Because I can't stand hurting people. But yes, it's mostly for Stephan. Gervis has him and he's going to keep him from me unless I . . . cooperate."

"And I'm supposed to believe this heart-rending tale?"

She looked up in dismay. "You have to. It's the truth."

"Is it? You and the facts don't have too close an acquaintance. Why am I supposed to take your word now?"

He had a point. "I told you I was sorry, and I am. Sorry for all the things I said in the past that weren't exactly so, sorry for approaching your grandfather under false pretenses, sorry for getting involved with you for all the wrong reasons. If there had been a different way to go about it, I'd have taken it."

"That much I can believe."

She looked away, unnerved by the steel in his voice. "I know it wasn't right or fair, but sometimes a person has to do things they don't want because — because there's more at stake than they can stand to lose. Anyway, I had the idea you weren't exactly seeing me for the fun of it."

An arrested look appeared on his face. In reluctant tones, he said, "You may be right." A moment later, he went on, "But since you left without even a decent good-bye, I doubt you came back because of anything between us. Would you like to satisfy my curiosity by telling me why?"

With tears rising to rim her lashes, she said, "Because I need you. I need you to help rescue my son."

"Rescue?"

"I told you Gervis has him. He thinks I'll do whatever he wants as long as he's got him drugged and shut up with someone to watch him." Her voice failed her as she choked out the last word. She looked away, at the floor, the walls, anywhere except the condemnation in his eyes.

"And will you?"

She lifted her shoulders in a hopeless gesture that could be taken for assent. "I have little way to fight him. He has grounds for claiming legal custody."

"I know about that."

"Do you?" Surprise brought her head up.

"He's the father."

"No, he's not!" she exclaimed in revulsion. As his brows snapped together in a frown, she explained in a few hurried sentences. Regardless, there was no relenting in his features.

"So I'm supposed to supply some legal razzle-dazzle — injunctions, temporary custody, DNA testing to disprove fatherhood — whatever it takes to prevent Berry from claiming the boy. Is that it?"

That had been the obvious solution, the

one she had thought of first. On the plane somewhere over the mountains of Tennessee, she had come to a different conclusion. Now she wiped distractedly at her eyes as she shook her head. "It would take too long, and in the meantime, Gervis might ship Stephan off somewhere, to a different institution or some foreign school where I could never find him. What I want — would like — is for you to help me take him away from Gervis."

"Take him away? You mean you want to abduct him?"

His grim disbelief was not encouraging; still she nodded. "I know it's against the law and all the black-and-white, right-and-wrong things you believe in, but I can't think what else to do. Stephan is all I have, the only thing that's ever meant anything in my life. I can't lose him, I just can't! And he's only a little boy, so little. I failed him before, when I believed Gervis and let him send Stephan away, keep him drugged when it wasn't needed. But I can't this time. Please, Kane, you're his only chance!"

"Am I?"

"I don't know where else to turn. There's no one else to ask who might be able to do it."

"Such touching faith," he said softly. "I

don't know how I'm supposed to answer. Unless I should go down on one knee, hand on heart, and declare I'm yours to command?"

Wariness gripped her. Her voice thick, she answered, "No, not at all."

"No?" He tilted his head, his gaze assessing. "Then maybe I should ask, in language you'll no doubt understand, just what's in it for me if I agree to this rescue."

Hope stirred inside her. She licked her lips. "If it's money you want, I — I don't have any. But I could sell —"

"I thought," he said with a taut smile, "that we had dispensed with the idea of passing money between us the last time we were together like this." He moved to stand over her as he spoke.

Slow color mounted to her face as her gaze was caught and held by the dark intensity of his eyes. "You mean . . ."

"I do. In spades."

The breath caught in her throat. She could not have spoken if all eternity depended on it.

"Don't look so shocked. Isn't that how it's done where you come from?"

"No!" she cried, recovering with a strangled gasp. "No, it isn't, not for me. I never thought that you, of all men, would ever —"

"Stoop so low? I'll admit it's a change."

Baldly, she said, "But it makes you no different from Slater."

"Because he meant to take what you weren't interested in giving? It's not the same at all, because we both have something the other wants. You use me. I use you. It's a mutual exchange. What do the methods matter so long as we're both satisfied in the end?"

She hesitated, but the need to know was too strong. "You want me?"

"That should be pretty obvious."

Her gaze brushed downward from his face to the long, firm outline under his zipper that she had failed to notice until this moment. She looked away at once, her gaze landing on the mirror over the console table that held the TV. The two of them were reflected there in a frozen tableau, male and female discussing an age-old surrender. How many times had it happened in this very room, on this very bed? And how many of those, she wondered in anguish, had been driven by desperation on one side and revenge on the other?

Lowering her head, she reached for the buttons of her blouse with trembling fingers. He made no move to stop her, said not a word, but watched with hooded eyes and a flexed muscle standing out in his jaw. Still, her skin felt scorched by the heat of his gaze, and the blood that raced in her veins was near boiling point. She felt as if she were moving in slow motion. At the same time, it seemed her clothing melted away too fast, her skirt falling to the floor as she stood to release it, her shoes and thigh-high stockings almost sliding off by themselves.

Kane swallowed, an audible sound, when she peeled away her bra and let it fall. Wearing only her panties of coral lace, she stepped closer to him. His chest was warm beneath the silky-smooth oxford cloth of his shirt as she placed her hands on the hard planes. Then with trembling fingers, she began to slip the buttons free. As she pushed the shirt from his shoulders and arms, she saw his muscles were rigid and his hands clenched into fists.

She didn't pause, but moved as if controlled by something outside herself, perhaps by his unbending will or even her own regret combined with her pleasure in touching him, in sensing his all too human warmth. Her nipples crinkled into pale pink nubs as her breasts brushed his arm when she reached for his belt buckle. Her senses swam with giddy disorientation and her breathing grew uneven.

Kane wasn't as unmoved as he pretended, she thought. Her knuckles skimming the taut surface of his abdomen brought an instant rash of goose bumps to his shoulders and arms. As she reached for his zipper, she thought she heard him grind his teeth together.

Sliding the zipper downward grew difficult as she reached his tumescence. He pushed her hands aside and attended to it himself, then pulled off his pants and briefs with efficient impatience. As he straightened again, he caught her behind the knees and toppled her back onto the bed. Following her down, he settled between her spread thighs.

His weight confined her, held her immobile. The silken swirls of hair on his chest teased the curves of her breasts, her upper abdomen. Then he entered in fast, relentless invasion, probing the warm, moist vulnerability at the center of her being with the satin-sheathed steel length of his maleness. She gave a gasping cry, writhing against him with the sudden filling, then she was absolutely still.

He hovered above her, unmoving. Slowly, she lifted her lashes. For endless moments, his eyes held hers, his own dark with bitter triumph. She sustained that regard with defiance. Regardless, she could not prevent the slow, acid seep of tears. They pooled in her eyes and overflowed, collecting in the hollows beneath her lashes, running backward in wet tracks into her hair. At the same time, her muscles, her nerves, her mind, began an inevitable rejection.

A long shudder, like a tidal wave of the blood, ran over her. She tried to stop it, breathing rapidly so her chest rose and fell against him, clenching her muscles, her jaws, fists, and even the internal ring that encompassed him. That only made it worse, for she was that much more aware of him inside her, of his intimate possession, his dominance.

Abruptly, his face changed. The glaze of anger fled from his eyes, leaving them strained and liquid with remorse. "Don't," he whispered. "Please don't. Dear God, Regina, I'm so sorry. I don't know what — I'm just so sorry."

He released her, cupping her face with one palm. She clasped his broad shoulders, meaning to push him away. He started to rise, to disengage, but that movement made her feel panicky. She sensed long years of fear stretching before her. And an incipient loneliness more desolate even than the wound to the heart he had given her.

Abruptly, she wrapped her legs and arms around him, gripping tight, holding him to her in sudden, convulsive need. "Help me," she whispered, her voice shaking. "Please help me."

His lashes flickered in a hesitation so slight it might have passed unnoticed if she hadn't been so aware of his every breath, his every pulsing heartbeat. Then he bent his head and brushed her soft lips with his own in mute apology. In a quick experiment, he slipped his tongue lightly along the sensitive line where they joined before raising his head with a question in his eyes.

"Yes," she whispered. "Oh, yes."

He eased inside her once more, his gaze still resting on her face to gauge her reaction. Her tension faded. She drew a slow breath, felt herself relax still more. But she didn't want to be watched or tested. She wanted forgetfulness, erasure, mindless ease for the ache in her heart and the dread of being forever fearful of love that hovered so close around her. She smoothed her hand along the strong slope of his shoulder to his neck, then pressed him deeper inside her once more.

He followed her lead while kissing her brow, her eyes and cheekbones, the tender skin below her ear. Against the turn of her neck, he murmured, "I told you once I was not nearly so noble as you thought. I didn't intend to prove it."

"I never meant to give you cause," she answered, a breath of sound.

He sighed. "Tell me what you want and it's yours."

"Love me," she said, and turned her head in a quick, compulsive movement to put her lips to the hard molding of his jaw. Or she thought she said the words, though she may have spoken them only in her mind. Either way, the results were the same.

He gathered her close and made amends of slow, thorough caresses and long kisses that were as deliberate, hot and deep as a Southern summer. He melted her bones and molded her to him, setting aside all anger, all fear. Drawing out her desire, he tended it, stoked it, drove it higher until she clung, moist and panting, hovering on the edge of conflagration. Then he caught her hips and took them both up in flames, driving out her terror for good, giving her the healing strength of his power and the gift of utter transcendence. Afterward, courteous and protective, he smoothed the tangled strands of hair from her face, cradled her against him, and soothed her until she slept in his arms.

But he made no promises.

17

What in the name of heaven was he doing?

Kane couldn't quite remember agreeing to this child abduction scheme, yet here he was, winging his way toward New York with Regina like some brain-damaged commando on a secret mission. Pops had often told him his temper would get him in trouble one day. He should have listened. Out of rage and righteousness, he'd made a fatal mistake, one that left him hot with shame every time he thought about it. Which was too often for any kind of comfort.

What had got into him? The trigger, he thought, had been hearing that he meant nothing to Regina Dalton, had no place in her life. To her, he was the hick Louisiana lawyer she'd conned into thinking she was a sexual neophyte, someone she could use any way she had in mind. She'd made a fool of him, it seemed, and thought she could do it again with her pitiful tale about her son. He'd intended to show her it wasn't going to happen, had meant to force her to offer her body in exchange for what she claimed to want, then walk away without taking her up on it.

He'd gone too far.

In his stupid, stubborn pride and trust in his own infallibility, he'd declined to consider that she might be telling the truth, or what desperation might force her to do. He'd also failed to allow for her effect on him. Her sweet, naked vulnerability had gone to his head. One touch, and what he'd been thinking with was no longer his brain.

He'd lost control. Lost sight of everything except the need to have her in the most basic, primitive way possible since she could never belong to him in any other.

It was amazing she hadn't called the cops and had him arrested. She might well have talked Roan into it. His cousin the sheriff was as much a stickler for the letter of the law as Kane was himself, and a pushover for a wronged female.

Wronged. By him, Kane Benedict. No matter how often he winced away from the idea.

It was the tears that had gotten to him finally. Even for the few seconds when he'd been certain they were blackmail of the worst kind, they'd still clutched at his heart. It almost killed him when he realized they were real. Nothing had mattered then, except his desperate need to make the mistake up to her.

She had let him. She'd reached out to him, asking him silently to soothe the pain he'd caused, give her back the trust he'd taken away. The tenderness of that surrender caught at his heart with a stabbing ache. The passion she'd summoned to match his need was something he would remember all his days.

He had tried to take her self-respect and wound up losing his own. She had abandoned her pride for the sake of her need, and in the process returned his self-respect to him.

He'd said something about allowing himself to be used, doing whatever she wanted. That must have been where his agreement to this wild conspiracy had come from. That was all right, then. He was obligated to her. And the Benedicts never shirked a debt.

If he was going to go through with this, he'd make a damned good job of it. No half measures, no mercy. He almost wished Berry was going to be on hand when they took the boy, wished he'd try to stop them. In the mood he was in, Kane thought, it would be a great pleasure to mend his manners for him.

Luke, in the pilot's seat beside him, took his gaze from the controls of the plane that was winging through the late evening and studied him a moment. With wry amusement in his dark eyes, he said, "Don't look so grim, son. If they catch us, the charge will only be kidnapping with maybe assault and battery thrown in for good measure. The worst that can happen is they'll clap you behind bars and throw away the key."

"A regular bundle of cheer, aren't you?" Kane answered. "I knew I brought you along for something."

"You brought me along because it's downright awkward to pull off a decent kidnapping with public transport."

"There is that." The fact that his cousin could make anything from a Learjet to a crop duster behave as if an angel was at the controls, plus had friends who didn't mind lending their company planes, also played a part. More than that, Luke was a good man to have at your back.

"That you needed a referee was only an afterthought, I suppose," Luke added, his expression bland.

"Now why would you think that?"

Luke gave him a brief look. "I can read the signs. You're in deep manure, buddy, with no way out except to paddle like hell.

Only what you can't see is that fertilizer makes the roses bloom."

"Meaning?"

"Stop paddling, fool."

"An expert, are you? That mean you and April are all straightened out?" The jeer was a low blow, but better than dignifying the rest of his cousin's observation with an answer. He'd been forced to tell Luke the whole story before he'd agree to be a part of this rescue effort. Could be he'd told him too much.

"Yeah, well, we all screw up from time to time," Luke said as hard lines formed around his mouth. "You're just doing it on purpose."

"You don't know what you're talking about."

"I know you're making Regina pay for what Francie put you through. That strikes me as more than a tad unfair."

"Mind your own damned business."

Irritation flashed in Luke's eyes. "A fine argument, Counselor, so profound, so articulate, so logical. You should wow a jury with it sometime."

For a moment, anger burned in the pit of Kane's stomach. Then it faded as he realized Luke was right. Not that he had any intention of admitting it. Turning his head to stare out at the faraway glow of a town on the dark horizon, he said, "I won't have to worry since this is going to get me disbarred for life."

"No problem. Melville can take over the whole trial instead of just jury selection."

Kane gave a morose nod. Trial strategy was one of the things he'd discussed with Luke and Roan the night of the open house. "He's all set to kick things off anyway, when we get started on Monday."

"You're all right, then. He's a good man."

It was, in the lexicon of Turn-Coupe, fulsome praise. Kane agreed, and they let the subject drop. After a few minutes, he turned in his seat to glance toward where Regina sat in the main cabin. She was leaning back with her eyes closed.

Luke, noticing where his attention had wandered, spoke on a quieter note beneath the engine roar. "So have you thought about what you're going to do with Regina and the boy afterward?"

"Why would I do anything? They're not my responsibility."

"Fat chance she'll have of staying ahead of Berry if he's bent on getting the boy back, then, but I guess that's not important. You'll have kept your part of the bargain, now won't you?"

"Exactly," Kane said.

Luke muttered something he didn't quite catch, but it seemed best not to ask him to repeat it.

It was some time later that Kane got to his feet and moved back to where Regina was sitting. She hadn't stirred in so long that he figured she was asleep, and he was right. Taking a light blanket from a side bin, he shook it out and draped it over her. As he tucked a fold behind her to hold it in place, his fingers brushed her hair. The silken touch scorched his nerve endings as if he'd brushed against a live wire. He straightened abruptly, but didn't move away.

She looked so fragile lying there. Shadows of exhaustion lay like purple bruises under her eyes, and her freckles stood out against the paleness of her skin. Her mouth was tender and moist, her lips slightly parted as she breathed in the even cadence of sleep. She was so defenseless yet delectable that he was torn by a strong urge to sit down and pull her into his lap. The only trouble was, he couldn't be sure whether his impulse after that would be to protect her from all comers or ravish her himself.

God, what was he coming to that he could even think of such a thing? She was driving him crazy, stirring up dark corners of his soul that he'd thought decently mastered in adolescence. The fierce ache of need she roused in him was like an addiction. The more he had of her, the more he wanted, and the more he wanted her, the more it seemed who or what she was, or where she was leading him, made no difference compared to the need to hold her in his arms.

He didn't like it. It was galling. It was also scary. The sooner she was out of his life, the sooner he could repossess his common sense and be himself again.

Bringing her on this trip was a bad idea. He and Luke needed to move fast and by instinct if they were to have any chance of success. The last thing they needed was a woman slowing them down.

She'd refused to stay behind. Short of locking her up, there had been no way they could prevent her from coming with them. She could get them into Berry's apartment without their having to circumvent normal security, she'd said, and the boy would also be easier to manage. Both things were probably true. Still, he wished she was back in Turn-Coupe. She was an extra person to be safeguarded, another soft, warm body that could be harmed if they made a misstep. It was bad enough being responsible for her son, a child who might get in harm's way if there was trouble; keeping an eye on Regina, as well, was one worry too many.

At the same time, he had a grudging respect for her refusal to stay behind. She obviously distrusted Berry every bit as much as she adored her son. She was terrified the kid would be hurt if she wasn't there to protect him. As if she could protect a gnat.

Still, she hadn't yelled or screamed or begged. She'd just set her jaw and looked at him and Luke as if they were Neanderthals without a set of finer feelings between them. Who knew? Maybe she was right.

He admired a great many things about her. She might have her faults, but she also had a rare kind of strength. She did what she had to do and didn't count the cost. She fought her demons instead of letting them conquer her. She stared defeat in the face and didn't flinch. Not many could say the same.

He didn't like admitting that, either.

When the trial was over, she would be out of his life. She would go away somewhere with her son and that would be the end of it. No doubt it would be for the best.

He reached out once more, taking a fine strand of her hair between his fingers again, feeling its tingling warmth. He had wondered, with Pops that first day, if it would burn. It did, it had, and he would carry the scars his whole life long.

The landing in New York was uneventful. The paperwork for the return trip was a major pain, but something that had to be done. It took time, however, so it was late when they reached the apartment. That was fine because everyone should be asleep. With any luck, they could be in and have the situation under control before the body-guard and nurse knew what was happening.

Berry was not supposed to be in residence, which was one reason they had chosen tonight. A check with his law firm had revealed that he was scheduled to arrive in Baton Rouge this evening for the start of the trial on Monday. That was one complication out of the way.

They breezed past the doorman, who greeted Regina and asked about her trip with such smiling, single-minded attention he hardly seemed to notice she had two strangers behind her. Once they were upstairs, Kane used Regina's key, then pushed the apartment door open and let it swing back on silent hinges. He glanced toward the spot where he had positioned her down the hall, making sure she was out of the way. She gave him a small wave, her face reassuringly calm.

Taking out the handgun that nestled under his belt at the small of his back and holding it ready, Kane nodded at Luke, who was also armed. In tandem, they slid inside and whipped away from the door, pressing their shoulders to the near wall. They waited in strained silence while searching in the dimness for movement, listening intently for sound.

Nothing.

It was clear. They moved forward.

Regina had described the layout of the apartment in detail, including the sleeping arrangements. Her room should be the first on the right of the long hall that opened from the living room. The nurse ought to be in the one at the far end on the same side, with the boy's bedroom sandwiched between the two. Berry's master suite lay across the hall, while the bodyguard had a smaller room next to it.

With Luke behind him, Kane skirted overstuffed leather furniture and heavy tables while blessing the sound deadening effects of Berber carpet. The two of them were helped, more than expected, by the lambent glow of millions of city lights that filtered through the expanse of uncovered glass in the penthouse walls. It penetrated everywhere, turning the interior into a milky, brownish gray underworld.

The door of the bodyguard's bedroom was closed. Kane and Luke stationed themselves on either side of it. At Kane's nod, Luke reached out one hand to turn the knob. They sprang inside and rushed the bed.

There were two people under the covers. The bodyguard was just heaving himself up, reaching for a handgun that lay on the bedside table. Kane lashed out with a hard kick that made the man grunt with pain as he crashed into his bed companion. Then Kane lunged to jerk the man in the bed over and chop a hard forearm across his throat. Shoving the muzzle of his weapon under the bodyguard's chin, he said in hard warning, "Freeze, if you like breathing."

The woman in the bed, an overblown blonde whose raccoon circles from smudged eye makeup were visible even in the uncertain light, uttered muffled curses as she fought free of the covers. Seeing Kane hovering over her lover, she dragged in her breath to scream. Luke, skirting the bed, placed the muzzle of his handgun gently between her pendulous and very naked breasts. She changed her mind.

Within seconds, the bodyguard, sleep stupid and with laughably tiny black briefs covering his crotch beneath his beer belly, was securely tied and gagged. So was the nurse. They made swearing, protesting noises as Kane and Luke left them roped together in the middle of the bed, but were ignored without a qualm.

Kane started toward the living room to summon Regina. It wasn't necessary; she was already inside. She emerged from Berry's study, tucking a small, square object into her shoulder bag as she walked. Kane wondered briefly what she'd found to repossess besides her son before annoyance banished the question from his mind.

Voice rough, he said, "I thought I told you to wait for the all clear."

"The fighting stopped. That's clear enough for me."

"But you might —"

"I might what?" she asked, pausing as she came even with him in the dim room.

He made no answer, couldn't have if his life had depended on it. What he had been about to say was that she might have been hurt. The mere idea of her catching a stray bullet or getting in the way of a cretin like the bodyguard made him feel sick to his stomach. He'd known he hated the possibility, just not how much.

"Nothing," he muttered, and motioned

for her to go ahead of him back down the hall to her son's room.

Nevertheless, he reached out to halt her at the bedroom door while he checked to be sure there was no other guard. The only thing he could see in the pastel green glow of a night-light was a small mound in the single bed pushed against one wall. A very small mound.

At his signal, Regina went straight to the sleeping boy and pulled back the covers. She sat down on the bed and rolled him toward her. She made a hissing sound of mingled anger and pain.

The boy was limp, pale, totally unresponsive. Kane felt as if a giant fist had slammed into his gut. He stepped forward, put his hand on the small, thin neck, felt for a pulse. A second later, he let out his breath in sharp relief. The boy's skin was warm. A light but regular pulse beat beneath it.

In quiet tones, Kane asked, "Is he always such a heavy sleeper?"

She shook her head in an emphatic negative. "I tried to tell you how it would be."

So she had. The boy was drugged. It had seemed a minor point when she had mentioned it earlier. As he saw the effects, it was minor no longer.

For a tense instant, Regina's eyes, limitless pools luminous with unshed tears, met his in the gloom. Then her gaze slid away as if she refused to let him see, much less share, her anguish. He wanted to share it, he discovered, needed to join her in it because it was a part of her, needed desperately to take it from her in any way possible. Stunned by the insight, he stood watching her.

She spun away from him. Moving with quick competence, she found jeans, a sweatshirt, socks, sneakers, then stuffed them into a kid's bright-colored backpack. She handed these things to Kane, who swung the short strap over one shoulder. Then she rolled the boy in the bedspread that covered him and hefted him into her arms.

It went against the grain with Kane to let her carry the sleeping child, but he needed to run interference until they were in the clear. He checked the hall, got a high sign from Luke at its far end, then motioned Regina forward. They moved toward the living room. Luke ghosted over to join them there. Seconds later, they were at the front entrance. Kane transferred his weapon to his left hand, then reached out to open the door. At the same time, he instinctively reverted to courtesy, stepping to one side so that Regina, a woman with a burden, could go ahead of him.

The door swung open under his hand, would have crashed into him if he hadn't leaped back. Light flared in blue-white brilliance as the living room chandelier came on. In that first second of blindness, Kane moved without thinking, dropping the backpack he held to leave his hand free, putting himself between Regina and the source of danger. Half-crouched, shoulder to shoulder with Luke, he faced the door.

The man who stood there was Gervis Berry. Kane had seen enough pictures of the square, burly funeral services executive to recognize him at a glance. If that wasn't enough, the small pistol in the man's fist, pointed straight at his belly, represented convincing evidence.

"Look what we have here," Berry said with snide jocularity. "If it isn't somebody making off with my boy."

"Regina's son, the way I heard it," Kane answered as he straightened slowly, preparing for a less physical form of combat.

"You think maybe it was a virgin birth?" The other man chuckled at his own mordant wit.

"I know you had nothing to do with it."

Berry's expression turned ugly. "She told

you that, did she? I guess it means she's gone over to your side, then. You being Benedict?"

"That's right." Kane's voice was curt, his gaze watchful.

"Thought so. Wonder how this method of influencing a witness will set with a jury."

"Witness?"

Berry gestured toward Regina with a careless wave of the weapon in his hand. "I figure she's traded what she knows for your help here. But maybe that's not all she's trading. Maybe she's still swapping personal service, the kind she put out on my account."

"Gervis!"

That angry yet unsurprised exclamation from Regina would have condemned her even if she hadn't as good as admitted the charge already. Even as he recognized that, he saw something else. She had stepped from behind him, was deliberately moving forward with the boy in her arms to draw the attention of the man with the gun. She must figure Berry wouldn't fire at her. Kane wasn't so sure. His stomach knotted as he saw the pistol barrel swing toward her.

"Don't sound so shocked," Berry sneered, watching her. "You think I shouldn't talk like that because we're family? Well, I thought so, too, and now look what you're doing, siding against me, going behind my back. What kind of relative does things like that?"

"The same kind who used my son to make me do what you want, which is no kind," she answered in low virulence. "We're not family, never have been, never will be. And I'm glad, do you hear me? I didn't like what you wanted me to do when all this started, and now I hate you for it."

Berry jerked as if she had hit him. "Bullshit. You don't mean it."

"I do mean it," she declared, her eyes flashing green sparks. "Do anything more to harm my son or take him from me, and I'll kill you."

"You're not fooling anybody, baby," he said on a nasty laugh. "This isn't about any kid. What happened? Benedict here better at taking care of you than me, especially in bed?"

"No!"

Kane hardly knew what got to him more, the accusation or the denial. He moved forward a quick step, intent on drawing Berry's fire toward himself again. "Could be she's sick of both of us and looking out for herself for a change. You thought of that?"

"Yeah, sure, like a cheap whore," Berry

said as he wheeled in Kane's direction.

Kane lunged the instant the pistol's aim cleared Regina. His fist connected in a hard right to the chin with every ounce of his outrage and power behind it.

Berry fell backward into the hall. He hit the floor on his backside. A sharp report rang out and the gun in his hand spat a red streak.

Something tugged at Kane's waistline, spun him around. Then Luke was hurtling past him, flinging himself on Berry. Luke ripped the weapon from the other man's fist and laid it alongside his head in a short, hard rap. Berry went still. Crouching over him, Luke looked up at Kane with his face set in taut concern.

Kane knew what his cousin was asking. He was hit; he could feel a numb spot along his side and the creep of warm wetness at his waistline above the belt. Berry's handgun must have been small caliber, however, for he didn't think the damage was major. Anyway, there was no time to think about it, much less discuss it. The sound of the shot could bring more company down on them than they wanted or needed.

He stooped to pick up the backpack with the boy's clothes that he'd dropped, then clamped it against his side to help conceal and control the bleeding. Grabbing Regina's elbow to make sure she kept close, he jerked his head at Luke. "Let's get out of here."

The trip to the airport seemed to take forever, the preflight checks and preparation longer still. Finally, they were airborne, climbing high into the night sky. They rose through a fluffy cotton mattress of clouds, then banked in a sweeping curve that would take them on a southern course. At last, they leveled off. Kane leaned back in the copilot's seat and closed his eyes.

His side hurt like hell, now that the feeling was returning. At the same time, he felt out of it, as if he could drift off into something like bone-deep sleep if he let go. It seemed like a fine idea.

No. Mustn't. He had to stay awake and help Luke. Had to get Regina home. He had to find out if the boy — what was his name? Stephan. Yes — had to find out if Stephan was all right.

Hands touched him, shaking him. A competent palm was pressed to his forehead as if searching for fever. When was the last time anyone had done that for him? He couldn't remember, but he thought it must have been when he was thirteen and had the flu.

"Kane? Kane, wake up!"

It was Regina, her hands, her voice. Both were cool yet urgent. He liked that. He pried his eyes open and was vaguely surprised at the effort it took.

She was leaning over him, trying to unfasten his seat belt. He searched her face that was so close, willing her to meet his eyes. When she did, he found he preferred staring into their intriguing hazel depths instead of speaking.

"You're bleeding," she said as if he were committing a terrible crime.

"I know."

"Why didn't you say something, for heaven's sake? What were you doing being such a macho martyr?"

"It's nothing."

"Oh, sure. Just a scratch, I suppose. Who do you think you are, Eastwood and Stallone rolled into one?"

He grinned, couldn't help it. "Why are you so mad? I'm the one who got shot."

"Because you've got blood all over Stephan's clothes, you jerk," she answered, dragging the sodden backpack away from his side, refusing to meet his gaze again. "Come on, get up and let's go to the back so I can do something about whatever hole you've got in you."

Luke, frowning as he glanced away from

the plane's controls, said to her, "First-aid kit's in one of the bins. Should be some sizable bandages in it."

She nodded her thanks, then leaned down to remove Kane's seat belt. "Come on, get up," she insisted as she lifted his arm and put it around her neck. "I can't move you by myself, though I'll help all I can."

He let her take a part of his weight, not because he couldn't make it by himself, but because it was irresistible. He wanted to see how far her care would go. He was also curious to know what drove it, whether gratitude or guilt, simple human kindness or something that he could give no name.

Her hands were gentle as she helped him out of his light jacket. She frowned and sank her teeth into her bottom lip as she saw the gory sight he presented under it, but reached at once for the buttons of his shirt. Briefly, he was reminded of the night before, when he had forced her to undress him. It almost seemed that this repeat under far different circumstances was a suitable punishment for that crime.

"Why didn't you tell someone about this before we took off?" she asked in a strained undertone. "You need more than a bandage. You need a good doctor."

"We could have wound up spending the

rest of the night in an emergency room and all day tomorrow at a police station after the doctor filed his gunshot-wound report. No thanks."

"You'd rather bleed to death first?"

"I'd rather you stopped fussing as if I were no older than Stephan and just fixed me up."

She gave him an incensed look. "I'm trying!"

She was, though he saw her shiver and turn pale as she looked closely at the bloody mess of his wound. Still, she didn't balk at tending him, only swallowed hard, then set to work. But her hair that brushed his arm set him on fire, and the clean, fresh scent of her had an effect on his senses like twelve-year-old bourbon. His side ached and he felt dizzy, yet all he could think of was pulling her down on his lap in the female superior position and seeing how much of him she would take, how deep inside her he could get, before he passed out.

He was losing it. Moistening his lips that seemed far too dry, he said, "I don't suppose there's any orange juice or cold drinks on board?"

"Orange juice?"

"I need the sugar for glucose, to counter blood loss."

She gave him a swift, appraising glance, then pushed abruptly to her feet. "I'll see."

The juice was sweet and cold and hit his system like a blood transfusion. He downed the whole can and asked for another. Afterward, he was able to stay awake while she peeled his sticky wet shirt away from the wound. She wouldn't try cleaning it, she said, because the long gouge had almost stopped bleeding and she didn't want to start it again.

Kane was just as happy. His family doctor, a man as old as Pops and twice as discreet, would see to him when he got home. He told her so, and it seemed to satisfy her. She strapped him up in a couple of gauze pads, two whole rolls of bandaging, and a few metal hooks. When she was through, he felt as if he was wearing a corset that barely allowed him to breathe, but had conquered both his queasiness and peculiar sexual impulses.

Regina disappeared into the rest room, presumably to wash his blood from her hands. When she came back, she draped a blanket around his shoulders, then sat down in the seat beside him. Folding her hands like a prim child, she looked at him for long moments with pained regret in her eyes. Finally, she said, "I'm so sorry you were hurt because of what I asked you to do. I'd never have asked you if I'd known this would happen."

"You weren't the one who took it for granted Berry wouldn't be around just because his lawyers said so." He kept the words light, hoping she'd let it drop.

"I could have told you he carried a pocket pistol."

Kane lay with his head resting on the back of the seat, observing in fascination the shift of color under her pale skin. "It might have been nice to know, but it wouldn't have changed a thing."

"Maybe, but I still feel terrible." She looked down at her hands and her voice was compressed as she went on, "I can't thank you enough for what you did, getting Stephan out of there for me. You had your reasons, I know. Still, I'm more grateful than I can say. If there's any way I can repay you, you have only to ask."

Weariness hit him like a hard right to the heart. He didn't know why the few words she'd spoken should affect him that way, but they did. Maybe he was weaker than he knew. His voice toneless, he asked, "What are you suggesting, Regina?"

"Whatever you like." She gave a small, helpless shrug. "I owe you so much that —"

"You owe me nothing." The fans of her

lashes were like rust-and-gold moths, shadow fine against her skin. He wanted to touch them, to run the edge of his tongue along them, more than he'd wanted anything in a long time.

"But I do. Without you, I would never have seen Stephan again, at least not without knuckling under to Gervis and doing exactly as he wanted. You were hurt, might even have been killed, because of me." She looked up with rose color flaring across her cheekbones. "There's nothing I wouldn't do to make it up to you."

"No." It was the hardest word he'd ever spoken, but also the most necessary.

"No?" Her glance was shadowed, hesitant. "But you said the other night that you expected it. You seemed to want —"

"No. Not now, not ever again. I didn't go after your son for the sake of having you in my bed. I went to make up to you for what I did to you, for what I took from you."

Speaking so softly he had to strain to hear, she said, "You didn't take anything I wasn't ready to give."

He stopped breathing, almost forgot to start again. He wondered how much it had cost her to make that simple statement and exactly what it meant. Asking didn't seem like a good idea, however; he preferred to keep a few illusions. "Good try," he said in wry salute, "but I know differently."

She lifted her chin as she stared at him. He held her gaze, wondering if his own was as hard to read. He thought it must be, for it felt stiff and unnatural, like a mask to hide his doubt and pain.

"I'd still like to do something, somehow, to repay you," she said after a long moment.

He closed his eyes, resisting the urge to squeeze them tight. "Forget it. I don't have much use for sacrificial lambs."

The plane vibrated, cushioned on air and nothing else, as it held its course in the dark, star-spangled night. The engines made a deep, steady roar. After a long, long time, she replied in toneless understanding, "No, I don't suppose you do."

18

Sacrificial lamb.

The phrase came back to Regina again and again in the hours that followed. It was with her as the plane finally landed at the airstrip outside Turn-Coupe. She couldn't get it out of her mind as she lost an argument with Kane over whether she and Stephan were going to the motel or continuing on with him and Luke to let the doctor look at Stephan at Hallowed Ground. It echoed in her thoughts while they all, including Mr. Lewis, waited for the doctor to arrive.

Was that really how Kane saw her? Did he think she had endured the love they'd made with gritted teeth? She had meant to, had thought it would be necessary at first. It hadn't turned out that way.

Kane had freed her from her crippling fears and taught her the sweet, untrammeled pleasure of loving. She would never forget that. At the same time, she never expected to find another man she could ever trust in the same way, never expected to love again.

She loved him.

She loved him, and it wasn't about sex or gratitude for what he had done, or even because he had risked so much for her sake and been hurt in the process. She loved him for all the things he was, for his strength and sense of right, for his bone-deep honor and his attachment to the place he lived, for the way he protected his grandfather and stood steadfast with his family and his friends against the things that threatened them. She loved the way he smiled and the way he frowned, the way he touched her and held her, and even the way he didn't do it when he felt it wasn't right. And more, so much more.

How had it happened with all that lay between them? She didn't know. It was simply there, a bedrock certainty in the hidden center of her heart.

It seemed impossible that he couldn't see. She had been so afraid that he would. If he thought it had been a sacrifice for her to he with him, however, then he could have no idea.

The urge to tell him the truth hovered inside her. She didn't dare risk it. That would be to presume it mattered. It could also force him to tell her that he didn't care for her at all. She didn't think she could stand that just now, wasn't sure she could ever face that particular truth.

Stephan, curled up in an overstuffed chair, began to stir as he tried to wake. He whimpered, and she went to him at once and gathered him in her arms. He opened his eyes, stared into her face for long seconds, then his sweet, joyful smile spread over his face.

"Mama."

The amazed happiness in the single word shredded her heart and filled her eyes with tears of love and grief for all he had been through and anguish that she had let it happen. Beneath them burned a fierce resolve that nothing and no one would ever touch him again. "I'm here," she whispered against the silk of his hair. "I'm here, and I'll never, ever leave you."

Kane, lying on the sofa across from her, turned his head toward where she sat. His movement drew her attention and she met his dark gaze over her son's head. There was a suspended look on Kane's face, as if he was struggling with some conclusion that didn't sit particularly well with him. He glanced at Luke, who lounged, face impassive and long legs stretched out before him, in an armchair between them. For an irrational moment, she thought he seemed impatient, as if he wished they were alone.

"Regina —" he began.

The chiming of the doorbell interrupted him. Mr. Lewis, who had been waiting in the long entrance hall for the doctor, ushered his friend into the room. The moment passed.

The elderly physician was introduced as Dr. Tom Watkins. He grumbled from the moment he set foot in the house, a rumbling and irascible undertone that carried as much caring as it did complaint. After a cursory examination, he informed Kane that he'd have to give him something for pain while he explored the wound and cleaned it thoroughly, then stitched it closed. The surgery would be better performed under sterile conditions, but since Kane had been dumb enough to get himself shot, then he'd have to risk the infection. Seeing as how he, Dr. Watkins, was about ready to retire, he was more than willing to "forget" to inform the authorities that he'd treated a gunshot wound, but there was no way to keep the thing secret if they went through the hospital. And he'd thank Kane to follow his grandpa's example and heal quick as he was able, not go fretting himself into a high fever that required some danged young emergency room intern to ruin all his good work.

Kane insisted that Stephan be looked after before the doctor set to work on him. Regina's son was pronounced healthy except for the lingering effect of some potent tranquilizer. There should be no lasting harm, Doc Watkins said, ruffling the boy's soft hair. Fluids, food, and a watchful eye until the drug wore off were the only recommendations. If Stephan seemed inclined to fall asleep again, it would likely be the result of long-term stress as much as the drug. In that case, they weren't to fret, but just let the boy be, let him rest.

Turning to Kane then, the elderly physician ordered him to find a bed to use for the necessary procedures and get in it. Mr. Lewis offered his own downstairs bedroom, and Luke gave the patient a shoulder to lean on as he headed in that direction. Regina offered to help, but was refused with gruff kindness and then barred from the makeshift surgical center by a firmly closed door.

She concentrated instead on Stephan, who roused from his tranquilized stupor by rapid degrees. He claimed to be hungry and followed Dora into the kitchen to watch with intent interest while she stirred up a batch of pancakes and put them on the table. He also had a million questions to ask, as if he had bottled up the need to talk for months and was now letting it all pour out. Eyes bright with curiosity, waving a fork on which he had speared a huge bite of pancake dripping with butter and syrup, he fired off salvo after salvo as fast as he could get them out. He not only demanded to know exactly where they were and how they got there, but seemed determined to extract every particle of information anyone could give him about the wonders of Hallowed Ground. Exhausting Regina's scanty knowledge in short order, he turned to Dora. He soon had the dour housekeeper laughing, telling him stories, and promising to take him to see the new litter of kittens in the old carriage house by the back garden, kittens sired by Mr. Lewis's cat, Samson.

Stephan rushed through the rest of his meal, then turned to Regina and asked to be excused in the careful way that he'd been taught. When she agreed, he swung to Dora, his expression expectant yet doubtful as he asked, "May I see the kittens now, please?"

The housekeeper raised an inquiring brow in Regina's direction. She nodded at once, but couldn't control the grief that rose inside her as she realized how restricted, how endlessly corrected and controlled, her son had been to make him so terribly polite or doubtful about such a simple pleasure.

The housekeeper's gaze held compassion as she met Regina's eyes. "Don't you worry, honey," she said as she took off her chef's apron and tossed it over the back of a chair. "I'll take good care of him."

"I know," Regina said over the lump in her throat. The housekeeper had carefully avoided mentioning the fact that she'd had to wash the bloodstains from Stephan's clothes before he could wear them. They both knew it was a detail from which he needed to be protected.

"It'll be all right, you'll see," Dora said. "This boy stays around here, we'll have him running and ripping in no time."

It was all Regina could do to retain her smile as the housekeeper handed her son a napkin to wipe his milk mustache, then took his hand and led him away. Stephan would not be staying long enough for the running and ripping. There was nothing for either of them at Hallowed Ground or in Turn-Coupe.

She heard the front door close a short time later. Thinking it might be the doctor leaving, she rose from the table and went in search of Mr. Lewis to find out if everything had gone all right with Kane. As she passed through the parlor, she saw the older man still outside on the front drive where he was seeing off his friend and physician. Regina watched the two a second, but made no move to join them. She had already thanked Doc Watkins for looking at Stephan and could think of nothing to add to her fervent expression of gratitude.

Whatever was under discussion out there seemed to be taking a while. Turning away from the window, Regina moved down the hall to the bedroom where the doctor had been working over Kane.

The door was shut tight. She hesitated, then turned the knob and stepped inside.

Kane was alone and apparently asleep. He lay perfectly still except for the steady rise and fall of his chest. The white bandaging around his torso made a stark contrast with his sun-darkened skin as he lay naked to the waist, his arms on top of the sheet. His color was much better now that the frightening pallor he'd acquired during the long flight had receded. His jaw was firm beneath its obscuring stubble of beard, and his hair was crisp and black against the monogrammed cream linen of the pillowcase.

He wasn't, and never would be, an easy person to know, Regina thought as she sat down carefully on the edge of the bed. He appeared so vital and self-contained, even in sleep. No one could get behind his guard unless he allowed it, and that seemed unlikely to happen. He was formidable in his certainty about truth and justice. Unyielding. It was doubtful he could ever understand, much less forgive, the conflicting needs and beliefs that had brought her to this place.

Regardless, she wouldn't have him any other way. Too many people allowed far too much in the way of excuses these days, it seemed. They spoke disparagingly of hard-and-fast judgments while taking advantage of the multiplying shades of gray. Such sophistry was no substitute for what was right and true. Absolutes had their place, as did drawn lines and firm stands. They were the necessary bedrock of civilization. She applauded the fact that Kane believed in them, even if it meant they could never agree, never be together.

She had to go. She couldn't stay here at Hallowed Ground, couldn't continue to accept the hospitality of these people she had tried to harm. She had no right to expect special consideration or to take advantage of the fact that it was offered in spite of her transgressions.

She would love to stay, would love to sink

into the comfort and caring, to become a part of the vast encompassing warmth of Kane's family. Not just his Pops, of course, though she liked him so much, but all the others, as well: Luke and Betsy and Miss Elise, and the endless circle of Benedicts who knew and respected each other, depended on and looked out for each other. She longed to be one of them, both for herself and for her son, needed it in some way she couldn't begin to explain, with a yearning too deep for words, almost beyond imagining.

It wasn't going to happen. She was alone, and it was time she realized it, accepted it. She might as well start now.

Still, she couldn't quite force herself to move, not yet. So she watched the man on the bed, thinking of all he had done. His protection, his caring, his courtesy. The gift of loving he had given her, and the gift of getting her son back.

The need to touch him one last time was so powerful, so necessary, that she reached out to place her fingers on his hand. It was not enough. She smoothed her hand along his arm, carefully avoiding his bandage, then up his shoulder. Pressing her palm to the steady beat of his heart, she closed her eyes an instant, then opened them again to trail the backs of her fingers upward over the strong curve of his neck and his beard-rough chin. His lips were incredibly smooth and warm. She brushed the firm contours with her fingertips.

He didn't stir. There was no change in his breathing. Holding her breath, she leaned down and molded her mouth gently to his.

For an instant, she was swamped in re-membered sensations. In bittersweet memories flavored with regret.

Gone. Never again. A single tear seeped from under her lashes, fell on his cheek. She lifted her head, used the soft stroke of one finger to brush away the salty track. Then she eased herself to her feet and turned away.

Lewis Crompton stood watching her from the open doorway. Worry grooved his face, but there was compassion in his eyes.

"I was just . . . checking on him," Regina said as the heat of a flush surged to her hairline.

"Yes." Kane's grandfather cleared his throat with a rasp. "He'll be all right, you know. Tom — that is, Doc Watkins — says all he needs is rest. Kane won't let this get him down. He's got things to do and he'll be ready to get after them as soon as he wakes up."

"I'm sure you're right." Before he could say anything more, she went on, "You must be tired, especially after your accident. I could watch Kane if you'd like to go back to bed yourself."

"No, no, I'm fine. Never did have much use for lying around. Anyway, I don't think Kane will need much watching now except for checking to be sure he doesn't run a fever."

She agreed without looking at him. Pops was looking after Kane as Kane had looked after his Pops. It seemed right. To fill the awkward silence that threatened, she said, "Where's Luke?"

"He went on home soon as he was satisfied Kane would be okay."

"I should probably go, too," she said, adding awkwardly, "I — expect you think I have a nerve, coming back here anyway, especially to this house."

"Why would I think that?"

"After all that I've done," she amplified with heat riding her cheekbones.

"I'm afraid," he said gravely, "that I don't know much about it. My grandson and I are close, but his confidence doesn't extend to keeping me informed about his personal life. Or vice versa."

Her gaze returned to his face. "You mean

he hasn't told you about me?"

"Apparently not."

She wished she hadn't mentioned it, but since she had, there was nothing for it but to go on. "I . . . came here under false pretenses."

"You're not a jewelry appraiser?" He lifted his thick white brows, though a faint smile came and went on his face.

"Well, yes, I am."

"You never intended to bid on my wife's jewelry or arrange for me to sell it?"

"Of course I did, but —"

"Then what's false about it?"

She gave a helpless shake of her head as she answered, "Everything else. I'm so ashamed of imposing on you, for lying to you, for all of it."

Long seconds ticked past before he answered. His penetrating gaze searched her face. Then he said, "You did come back last night, or actually early this morning, when you didn't have to. Why is that?"

"I couldn't leave Kane," she said, frowning. "I mean, he'd been shot because of me, had lost so much blood. The least I could do was make sure he was all right."

"In other words, you care about him just like the rest of us."

She looked past his shoulder, at the

pocket of his shirt, anywhere except his face. "I suppose I do. I really hate it that he was hurt, couldn't stand it if what I've done, what I asked of him, had been — fatal." She gave him a strained smile before she went on. "Not that it matters what I feel. It's best that I just go. If you're sure there's nothing I can do to help, then Stephan and I will be leaving. That's if someone could drive us to the motel?"

"I'm not too sure Kane would appreciate finding you gone when he wakes up." The older man's expression was judicious.

"Or he might be just as glad to have us off his hands. I've foisted myself on him, and you, long enough."

"I haven't heard him complaining." That ghost of a smile was back in his eyes. "Certainly, I'm not."

"You're a kind man," she said with difficulty, "but really, I have to go."

"I won't try to keep you if you're hell-bent on leaving, but I'll say this much. Could be Kane needs someone like you. If I was a mite more superstitious, I'd say the powers-that-be sent you along for him, to keep him from being so all-fired sure he knows what's what. They have a tendency to do that now and again."

Regina couldn't quite see what he meant,

but it didn't matter. "Kane has high standards, and I don't think I measure up. Stephan and I will be better on our own, honestly. Besides, I need to rent a car, do some shopping. Stephan has only one set of clothes and nothing else, not even a toothbrush, since we came away in such a hurry. Actually, I left my own things behind, as well, so you can see . . ."

He gave a slow nod. "Well now, I can take care of at least part of your problems. Let me get my car keys."

It wasn't easy persuading Mr. Lewis that he should leave her and Stephan at the motel when the shopping expedition was done. By the time she had managed that and put away the things she had bought, she was exhausted. Stephan also seemed to have run out of energy. They ate a sketchy lunch from the collection of canned and packaged snacks that she had bought, then lay down together in the bed for a quick nap.

It was late evening when Regina opened her eyes again. She lay for a long time simply holding her son and staring at nothing. She knew there were things she should be doing, but couldn't think what they were, couldn't make herself move. Depression was a dark weight in her mind. Everything seemed too much trouble.

She wondered if Kane was awake by now and if he was still okay, but couldn't bring herself to pick up the phone to see. In any case, it seemed that the less contact she had with him, the better it would be in the long run.

She might never speak to Kane again, never hear his voice or watch the quick flash of what he thought and felt mirrored in his eyes. Never match wits and tempers with him, feel his arms around her, or sense the slow rise of passion that only he could produce inside her.

She wouldn't think about that. She couldn't.

This mood wouldn't last; she knew that. She still had Stephan. They were a family of two, and she had to take care of them somehow, on her own. She needed to think about where she was going to go from here, also what she was going to do when she got there, how she was going to spend the interminable rest of her life.

There was something else troubling her, too. She wasn't sure where it came from exactly, but had the nagging feeling there was something left undone. There was something she should consider or be a part of before she could close the door on this episode and go on to the next. The only trouble was, she couldn't quite catch hold of what it might be.

It came to her later, after she and Stephan had shared a pizza for their dinner. After they had watched a Disney movie on television, then checked out the late news. After she had watched Stephan brush his teeth, told him a bedtime story, given him a hug, and turned out the light.

There had been a piece on the news about the suit, one that included an interview with Melville Brown, Kane's law partner. The television reporter had thrust a microphone in the lawyer's face and demanded to know his views on the rumors that the case was being tried as a racial issue; an old-fashioned funeral home with an owner steeped in all the ancient Southern traditions and prejudices against a progressive Northeastern firm that gave preferential treatment to blacks.

The black lawyer had answered with easy competence, saying he and his client, Mr. Crompton, had no interest in perpetuating stereotypes, but were planning on winning their case on its own merits. The issue, he declared, was the financial health and well-being of the consumer of funeral services. When it was presented in those terms, he was sure the jury would disregard any attempts by the defendant to confuse matters and would vote according to their common sense and their consciences. The reporter, in his closing remarks, seemed to cast doubt on that idea, signing off with a shot of Crompton's Funeral Home in the background and the comment that the whole country would be watching Baton Rouge and the little town of Turn-Coupe to see the outcome of this landmark case.

Regina lay awake thinking about the report. Somehow it had never occurred to her that the case would be of national importance. That fact made it that much more necessary for Kane and his partner to win.

She couldn't stand the idea of Gervis triumphing over a man like Lewis Crompton, hated the thought of him coming into Turn-Coupe and building some modern monstrosity of a funeral services building, then charging the farmers and other hardworking people she'd met at Luke's house three times the normal burial rate in order to line his pockets.

Something had to be done to stop it.

Someone who knew all the dirty tricks and underhanded deals Gervis had pulled over the long years needed to come forward with what they knew. Someone like her.

She had thought she would have to offer

the knowledge she held of Gervis Berry's organization to Kane in exchange for his help in freeing Stephan. It hadn't been necessary. Now she'd do it for no reason except that it was right.

Or perhaps there was one other reason. She owed something to Kane and his grandfather, to Luke and all the others. They had done so much for her, and now it was time to repay them.

The Benedicts weren't the only ones who paid their debts.

19

A dull droning, like a swarm of flies, hung over the courtroom. Every seat was filled and more people milled around in the hall outside, a situation unchanged since the trial got underway a week ago. From the comments Regina had overheard around her, she thought Mr. Lewis's friends and neighbors, black and white, were united in supporting him against the big corporation that was trying to run him out of business. They also seemed to have an Us-versus-Them feeling about the proceedings, as if the Northeastern funeral home syndicate had become the symbol of another Yankee invasion. It was mentioned with chuckles and sidelong glances, but the aura of partisanship was strong.

More than a few of those attending today were either Benedicts or family connections who had made the drive to Baton Rouge. Luke and Miss Elise, as usual, had commandeered places directly behind the plaintiff's table where Melville sat with Mr. Lewis. April Halstead and Dora were seated a few rows back, while Dr. Watkins was on the center aisle not far away, where he could stretch his legs. Those around Regina, who were more distantly related, craned their heads and stared and murmured among themselves, with the names of the participants, especially Kane's, mentioned again and again in one context or another. She listened closely as she had all along, grateful for both the distraction and the information that she could tuck away to complete the picture of the man who had come to mean so much. At the same time, she enjoyed the endless other bits about family marriages, divorces, births, deaths, school accomplishments, job prospects, and the comparative health of different members. It allowed her to pretend, at least for the moment, that she was a part of it all.

She was helped in the last by Betsy North, who sat with her on the back bench she had chosen, there on the other side of Stephan. Kane's cousin provided a running commentary on anyone under discussion. She also introduced Regina to lots of people, giving her name in an easy, offhand fashion which suggested there was nothing in the least unusual about her being in court. She could almost believe that herself since no one seemed to connect her with Gervis Berry.

That was before she caught a brief glance from the corner of one woman's eye as she turned away from her. It was avid yet resentful, and showed plainly that Regina had been targeted as being from the enemy camp. Whether from something Slater had said, a stray memo or fax, or some casual remark by a New York lawyer, the news of her association with Gervis was apparently out at last. In a way, it was a relief since it meant she could stop dreading the revelation.

Gervis, when he appeared, seemed totally unaware of the undercurrents. He marched into the room with his usual swagger, surrounded by a phalanx of lawyers like a living barrier between him and the onlookers. With his Armani suit, two-hundred-dollar tie, and irritable attitude, he looked as if he felt the whole thing was a waste of his valuable time, something he was impatient to have over and done with as soon as possible.

Moments later, Betsy sat forward in her seat. "Oh, look, Kane's here today," she said, almost falling off the bench in her excitement. "You sure can't tell by looking at him that he's got a hole in his side."

Regina followed Betsy's gaze. Kane was just threading his way through the crowd, shaking hands, smiling, nodding, tossing off quips as he went. He looked tanned, fit, at ease on his home ground, with no strain whatever showing in his face or his movements.

Somewhere inside, she felt the ebb of tension she had not known she was holding. This was the first time Kane had appeared in the courtroom since the trial began. All the reports on his condition had said he was fine, but she hadn't been able to accept them until now.

"That's him, that's the man who came to get me?" Stephan asked in awe. He slid off the seat and stood up, staring at Kane.

Regina's voice was husky as she confirmed it. Her son had made a hero of the paragon who had been able to take him away from his nurse and Michael. The fault was as much Betsy's as it was hers, since the motel owner had taken a shine to Stephan and fired his imagination with all sorts of tales about Kane. Still, Regina had done nothing to stop it. Her son seemed to need a man to look up to just now, and she could think of none better.

"Maybe I could tell him thank-you." Stephan looked at her with anticipation shining in his eyes.

"Oh, I don't know about that," Regina said in quick concern as she reached to smooth his hair back from his forehead. "He's a very busy man."

Betsy gave her a puzzled glance above Stephan's head. "Not so busy he won't have time for a kid. Honestly, you ought to know Kane better than that."

"Well, yes, but now isn't a good time," she answered evasively. It wasn't that she thought Kane would slight Stephan. Rather, she didn't feel up to facing him herself any time soon and certainly not in so public a place.

As if attracted by their focus on him, Kane turned his head in their direction. His gaze was intent but unreadable. Regina swallowed hard and looked away. She didn't risk another glance until after the judge mounted the bench and the formalities began.

She didn't know a great deal about lawyers and courtrooms, had never had occasion to find out. There was a certain fascination about it now, since it was Kane's element, though it still looked like some kind of complicated game with more rules than strictly necessary. She had been following events, watching as Melville Brown helped seat the jury, then took a parade of witnesses through different business practices, good and bad, in the funeral industry.

Most of this background was familiar to her, but it was fascinating to watch the details become public knowledge.

Melville was easygoing in his manner, but highly competent. Under his prodding, the testimony had unfolded with logic, down-to-earth clarity and a series of minor revelations that, in accumulation, were slowly building an impressive case against Berry Association, Inc. Still, it seemed that something was missing. It was almost as if everything was going too smoothly.

Melville assumed the lead today, also. The first witness on the stand was a custodian for a funeral home in Mississippi. His testimony illustrated the fact that Gervis's company didn't always provide the services, or even the same casket or vault, that appeared on the invoices submitted to customers. This had been a hotly debated issue the day before and was no different now. The legal debate and procedures over it came to an end, however, and the witness stepped down.

The next person called was Lewis Crompton.

Melville took Mr. Lewis through a short history of his family's ownership of Crompton's Funeral Home, then went over a few questions to portray his commitment to quality service at reasonable prices. Kane's grandfather sat on the stand relaxed and at ease, looking every inch the distinguished gentleman. His voice was a deep, rich baritone. He was neither aggressive nor defensive, but stated his case with calm certainty.

"Mr. Crompton," Melville said, "will you tell the court and members of the jury just why you saw fit to bring suit against Berry Association, Inc.?"

Mr. Lewis inclined his white head. "I filed suit for one reason. Because they were trying to run me out of business."

"What led you to that conclusion?"

"I had evidence that they were deliberately lowering prices in unfair competition."

"And how were they able to do that?" Melville studied his case notes while he waited for the answer.

"By volume purchasing. A consolidated funeral operation like Berry's, with several hundred homes, is able to buy caskets and other merchandise at lower prices, just like the discount chains."

"Isn't this their right, to buy cheap, then lower prices?"

"Oh, absolutely," Mr. Lewis agreed, *"if* what they're doing is giving people a break by passing along the savings to the consumer. But that's not what's happening. The Berry homes, and others like them, cut prices long enough to get rid of the competition until family-owned homes like mine are forced out. They concentrate their attention on a single region at a time, so they wind up with a cluster of funeral homes in that particular area. After they gain a monopoly, then they suddenly jack up prices. When it's all over, the cost of a funeral is as much as fifty percent more than it was before, and there's not a thing anybody can do about it."

"Just how would you characterize this method of doing business."

"Sheer chicanery followed by price gouging. That's the best I can say about it in present company."

Laughter rippled over the courtroom. Melville waited until it subsided before he spoke again. "And is this taking place only in Louisiana?"

"No, sir, not by a long shot," Mr. Lewis said with an emphatic shake of his leonine head. "It's everywhere. Consolidation is just getting heated up. Less than twenty percent of the country's funeral homes are involved right now, but more are being sucked into the conglomerates every day.

Service and personal concern with a community's grief are out the window when the corporations come into it. What becomes important is profits, the almighty bottom line. Some so-called 'Death Care' chains like Berry's are such big business they're traded on the New York Stock Exchange."

"So your concern in this is to protect your customers?" Melville smiled as he spoke, his brown eyes lighting with warmth.

Mr. Lewis looked rueful. "I'd like to claim that, and it was certainly on my mind in the beginning. I'll have to admit, though, that it's become a bit more personal. In fact, you could say it's come down to a private war between Berry and me."

The rumble of laughter was louder this time, and the judge frowned it into silence. When Melville could be heard again, he said, "Why has it become so personal?"

"I don't much care for the way he fights." The glance Mr. Lewis threw at Gervis was tinged with challenge.

"Have you encountered personal danger?"

"I have, along with the lady I was with at the time. There have been other threats, other injuries, as well." The glance of the older man touched Kane, then reached to the back row to where Regina sat with her son beside her.

The defense objected to that remark, and the judge ruled in their favor. Melville seemed satisfied to abandon that line of questioning. After a few more minor points, Mr. Lewis was turned over to the opposition.

"Well now, Mr. Crompton," the head of Gervis's entourage of lawyers said with a patronizing smile, "I understand you've been taking care of the funeral needs for the people of Tunica Parish for many years. Is that correct?"

"It is." Mr. Lewis watched the other man, his manner alert but confident.

"In this capacity, you've been privy to any number of family secrets. Would that be a fair statement?"

"I suppose it might."

"Yes or no, please."

"Yes."

"You consider that you are a safe repository of these secrets?"

"Yes, I hope so."

"In fact, you've been known to honor certain rather irregular requests from time to time. Is this not true?" The New York lawyer turned his back and walked away as he spoke.

Mr. Lewis frowned, but answered in the affirmative.

"On one occasion, you falsified the birth date of a lady to prevent it from being known that she'd lied about her age for years. Is that correct?"

Mr. Lewis sat with his lips tightly pressed together. The lawyer turned to face him, waiting in what appeared to be a game of wills, a test to see who would break the silence. It soon became plain that it would not be the man on the stand.

"I must insist on an answer!" the lawyer snapped, his face red at being forced from his position of strength. "Did you, or did you not, falsify records to keep the woman's true age from her friends, neighbors, and even her husband, who was younger by several years?"

Mr. Lewis's voice seemed to thicken and his speech to slow as he said deliberately, "I've been known to omit the truth in order to protect the honor of a lady."

"In other words, yes."

The man on the stand agreed with a sigh.

"You have a soft spot for the ladies, don't you?"

Melville entered an objection to that question, and it was sustained. The lawyer pursed his lips, then rephrased the question, saying, "Would you agree it's justified to say that the fair sex has, on occasion, imposed on your good nature and natural respect for their kind when it comes to requests for favors?"

"I haven't the least idea what you're trying to say," Mr. Lewis returned.

"Let me put it plainly, then, Mr. Crompton," the lawyer said with a thin smile. "Have you ever buried someone in the wrong place at a woman's request?"

The buzz of comment that swept through the room had a titillated edge. It seemed obvious, from what Regina could hear, that it wasn't so much Mr. Lewis granting such a request that interested the onlookers, but rather for whom he had done the favor.

Mr. Lewis tilted his head and waited while the judge pounded his gavel for order. When the courtroom quieted again, he said with dubious frankness, "I guess maybe it all depends on what you mean by the wrong place."

"Did you, or did you not, bury an empty casket at the monument bought and paid for by the woman's lawful husband, then, in the dead of night, bury the woman herself at the side of another man?"

"Oh, that's what you're driving at," Mr. Lewis said in his most countrified Southern manner. Smiling genially, he leaned back in his chair and clasped his hands across his midsection. "In that case, I guess I'll have to answer with a yes."

The muttering in the courtroom grew louder. Regina, who had come to know Mr. Lewis fairly well, gave him a wary stare. The defense lawyer apparently had no such misgiving, for he pounced on the admission of guilt.

"You don't consider that as heinous conduct, a direct violation of your much vaunted ethics?"

"Can't say as I do," Mr. Lewis said after earnest reflection. "I didn't take payment for it, you know. And since it wasn't public knowledge until this minute, I don't see that it hurt a soul."

"You don't see it as a gross betrayal of the husband who paid for the interment, a man who had expected to sleep for all eternity beside his lawfully wedded wife?"

"Well," Mr. Lewis said, lifting a finger to rub the side of his nose, "that's just it."

The lawyer sighed. "What is?"

"She wasn't."

"She wasn't what?"

"His wife." Mr. Lewis's smile was patient, earnest.

"That is patently ridiculous. We have already established the fact the woman who died was married to the man in question."

"Well, yes," Kane's grandfather allowed, then turned to look up at the judge. "Perhaps I could tell a little story about that, Your Honor, so everybody will be sure to understand?"

"That won't be necessary," Gervis's lawyer said with some stringency. "What we want to know is why you failed to bury the client in the correct plot."

"I'm trying to tell you she wasn't just a client," Mr. Lewis complained. Rearing back in his chair and turning toward the bench, he said in appeal, "Judge?"

"Proceed," the judge answered with a casual wave of one hand.

The lawyer swung around in outrage. "This is highly irregular, Your Honor. I must insist the witness be instructed to answer the questions in the prescribed manner."

The judge leveled a narrow look through his bifocals at the man before him. "The prescribed manner," he drawled, "is whatever I decide it is at any given time. Right now, it's a story." He turned away. "Mr. Crompton?"

Mr. Lewis nodded his appreciation, but refrained from any show of triumph. "Well, it all started back during the last year of the Great Depression. A local girl ran off with

448

the town bad boy. Her folks chased after them and caught up with the pair in Arkansas. The girl's father and her two brothers were upset over the incident, and they took it out on the boy, left him lying half-alive on the side of the road while they brought the girl back home. After a while, a hobo came along — there was a lot of that kind back then. He found the boy, patched him up, took care of him, dragged him on a train when one came along. When the boy woke up and came to himself, it was weeks later and he was in California. The boy wrote to his girl right off, but she didn't answer."

"If this touching tale is going somewhere," the lawyer said through tight lips, "I would appreciate it if you'd get to that point."

Mr. Lewis inclined his head. "Just hold your horses, I'm getting there. So the boy and the hobo just kept going then, riding the rails, working a little here, a little there — until along came the big war, World War II. The boy joined up. He was trying to outrun his sorrow over losing the only girl he'd ever love, see, didn't care whether he lived or died, so he became a hero, decorated and everything. After the fighting was over, he went to work in the oil fields. He worked so hard, took such chances, he became a millionaire by the time he was forty. That was fine, but he couldn't forget the girl, so he came back to Turn-Coupe with all his money. But the girl had become a woman, had married another man, and had a beautiful daughter who was almost a teenager by that time. Turned out she'd been told our hero died in Arkansas. She had grieved for him, then gone on with her life."

Mr. Lewis paused, glancing over the courtroom with a faraway look in his eyes. The crowd was quiet, waiting. After a moment, he went on again.

"Now this bad boy turned millionaire had himself a secret. He knew that he and the woman had been married, and this marriage had never been legally dissolved. That made the woman a bigamist and her child illegitimate. He could cause a stink and ruin the lives of the woman, her husband and her daughter, or he could keep quiet. He wrestled with himself over the decision, but finally decided to hold his peace. He never married, wound up dying of a heart attack after a few years. You don't hear much about men dying of broken hearts, but I can tell you that some do, some do."

"Mr. Crompton," the counselor for the defense said wearily, "if you could just give us some idea of what this has to do with the burial?"

"I'm about to do that," Mr. Lewis said, lifting an aristocratic hand. "Now this woman the millionaire loved knew, of course, how things were, how they'd been. She'd been tempted to run off with the man who came after her, but she was a fine, honorable woman. She kept the wedding vows she'd made in error, loved the man she married the second time around the best she was able. Still, there was always an emptiness in her life. When she found out she was dying of cancer, she came to me, asked me to bury her beside the man who was her real husband. Seemed like a good thing to me, so I did it. And if that's wrong, then I'm sorry, but I'd do the same again."

"You're asking the court to believe you falsified official records and risked your business reputation out of mere sympathy?"

"You could put it that way." Mr. Lewis's expression turned grim. "What's more, I don't take kindly to you bringing it up in public court so all the sacrifice those two people made while trying to do the right thing was for nothing."

"A noble attitude," the defense lawyer said with a jeer in his voice. "But if you expect us to believe this fantastic tale, I think you'll have to give us the name of this female paragon whose dying wish you're supposed to have granted."

Lewis Crompton said nothing. Sitting like a statue with his lips pressed together, he only stared straight ahead. The spectators' voices rose to a loud hum.

"Come now, Mr. Crompton, we're waiting. What was the woman's name?"

The defense lawyer's tone was unbearably pompous. It was plain to see he thought he had won, either because he figured the man on the stand couldn't name the woman whose story he had told, or else because he would refuse to do it. Whichever it turned out made no difference, it seemed, as long as victory was in his grasp.

Then Lewis Crompton sighed. His lips moved in an apparent answer, but the words were little more than a whisper.

"Louder, please, so the court can hear. Who was this woman?"

Kane's grandfather looked up at the lawyer then, his gaze clear and direct. When he spoke, the words were precise and perfectly audible, though edged with pain.

"The lady," he said, "was my wife."

Pandemonium broke out. Much of it came from amazed conjecture, but the majority expressed anger with the defense for forcing Mr. Lewis to expose his family secrets. The people of Turn-Coupe who had driven to Baton Rouge to follow the trial were angered by the condescending attitude of the lawyer and callous trading in their private scandals.

Regina ached for the ignominy Mr. Lewis had been forced to endure, would have done anything to prevent it, even as she admired the way he had turned the tables on the defense by making a triumph out of what was supposed to be his breach of conduct. For this was obviously, allowing for the distortions of gossip, the same story Vivian Benedict had told her, the one Slater had come across and passed on.

Gervis, caught in the fallout from his muckraking tactics, was whispering in vicious fury to his team of expensive lawyers. That his underhanded trick had backfired on him gave Regina a rich sense of rightness and jubilation. This was what justice felt like, then. She'd never have guessed.

Order was restored shortly. The defense, in temporary disarray or perhaps fear of further revelations, allowed that they were finished with Mr. Lewis. He stepped down and walked with dignity to resume his place at the plaintiff's table.

There was a brief consultation between

Mr. Lewis, Kane and Melville. Then Kane rose to his feet. He glanced toward where Regina sat, then turned and faced the bench. Though the room had already begun to settle down, it grew quieter still. Kane waited until it was perfectly silent, then he spoke into it with grim and intimidating authority.

"At this time," he said, "the plaintiff calls Miss Regina Dalton to the stand."

20

This was not supposed to happen. Regina had not agreed to testify. She had told Melville everything she knew about Gervis's nefarious business operations and turned over the computer disk taken from his study, which held accounting information, private letters and memos to back up what she said. That was supposed to be the end of it. There were other witnesses who, under Melville's guidance, could tie up the loose ends of the case as well as she could.

Surprise for the abrupt change of plans held her in paralyzed stillness. It was only as Betsy poked her in the ribs and nodded toward the witness stand that she forced herself to move.

Her knees trembled as she walked to the front of the courtroom. Her heart pounded so hard against her breastbone that she thought her blouse front was fluttering because of it. As she passed the table where Gervis sat, she met his malevolent stare. Strangely, her nerves settled a fraction. His venomous resentment filled her with bitter certainty that what she was being asked to do was right.

At the witness stand, she mounted to the chair inside the railed box. She took the oath, then seated herself and waited tensely for Melville to begin his questioning.

But it was Kane who rounded the end of the plaintiff's table and walked toward her. Kane who placed his hands on the railing of the witness stand, leaning toward her, regarding her with dispassionate consideration. Kane was the man who had deliberately called her today when her guard was down.

Kane was the lawyer for the plaintiff who faced her as if he'd never kissed her, never held her, never fitted his body into hers as if providing the key piece to an intricate, interlocking puzzle. It was Kane who glanced toward the jury, then looked back at her with the chill gaze of an executioner.

"You are Miss Regina Dalton, resident of New York?"

"Yes." Her voice was almost nonexistent and she cleared her throat, reaching up at the same time to clasp the amber oval at her throat. It offered no comfort. She released it.

"Until recently, you resided with the defendant, Gervis Berry, at the following location?" He reeled off the address of the 72nd Street apartment.

"That's correct."

"Did anyone else live there with you on a regular basis?"

She gave a stiff nod and supplied Michael's name and occupation as houseman before adding, "There was also my son, when he wasn't at school."

"Your son. Is he in court with you today?"

"He is."

"Point him out to us, if you will."

Regina did as she was requested, though her hand trembled. Stephan, she saw, didn't care for public notice any more than his mother. He slumped in his seat, staring white-faced at his feet while Betsy circled him with a plump and protective arm.

"You say that your son was in school when he was not with you. Can you tell us the name of this school?"

Regina gave it, though her head swam as she tried to figure out what Stephan had to do with the case at hand. Apparently, Gervis's lawyers felt the same doubt, for they demanded to know where the testimony was headed. After a brief consultation before the bench, however, the judge ruled that Kane could continue.

"You call this a school," he said when he

stood before her once more, "but I don't believe that's quite correct. In fact, it's an institution for problem children, isn't that so?"

"My son isn't a problem child. It was all a mistake."

"I must ask you to confine your answers to the questions at hand. Was this, or was this not, an institution?"

She replied that it was, staring at him with active dislike. If he felt it, he seemed able to ignore it. Mr. Lewis was not quite so sanguine. He motioned for Kane to approach him at the table and the two of them exchanged brief comments accompanied by mirroring frowns.

That consultation made no difference. Seconds after it was over, Kane returned to the attack.

"Was it your idea, Miss Dalton, to have your son live apart from you?"

"No, never," she answered, searching his face for some idea of what he was doing. The only thing she saw was that the small scar beside his mouth was white.

"Then the initiative for that came from someone else. Would you tell the court who arranged for your son to be institutionalized?"

She told him, then answered a number of

questions intended to establish her exact relationship to Gervis.

"So this man is not now, nor has he ever been, a blood relative. More than that, he has no blood relationship to your son. Is that correct?" Kane paced in front of her as he formulated his questions.

"That's right."

"Yet he took it upon himself to consign your son to what amounts to a permanent hospital."

She agreed.

"Tell the court, if you will, how that was done."

She complied as briefly as possible since her voice wasn't too reliable.

"Gervis Berry manipulated you into allowing your son to be removed from your care," Kane said in summary. Swinging toward her, he added, "Is that the reason you decided to betray him?"

She opened her mouth to speak, but nothing came out. It seemed she was damned as a traitor no matter which way she answered.

"Remember, please," Kane warned with exacting grimness, "that you're under oath to tell the exact truth."

She looked at him and felt as if she were drowning in the intense sea blue of his gaze.

He wanted something from her, she thought in momentary distraction, but she couldn't tell what it might be, couldn't quite understand the significance of the caution he had given her. What did it matter anyway? It was all over — her stay in Turn-Coupe, her brief part in its affairs, her even more brief relationship with Sugar Kane. There was no point in holding anything back, no need to conceal a thing.

She moistened her lips before she said, "I don't consider what I did a betrayal. Gervis forfeited all right to loyalty when he sent my son away to suit his convenience. Or if not then, when he sent me here to spy for him."

"You spied for him?" The question came with such promptness she was certain her answer was exactly what he expected.

"Yes," she admitted with a twisted smile. "At least, I tried. I wasn't very good at it."

"That's debatable, I believe. You arrived in Turn-Coupe with no advance preparation, nothing except an introduction, and wormed your way into a lot of places, a lot of . . . hearts." With the briefest of pauses, he demanded, "Were you in any way responsible for the accident that injured Mr. Crompton?"

"No! I would never do such a thing!" She stared at him, aghast that he would even suggest it. Was this what he was after? Was she to be pilloried for everything that had happened, including the attempt to injure his grandfather?

"Then who was responsible?" The question rang like the crack of doom.

"That was Slater. Dudley Slater. He admitted —"

"Who is this Slater?"

"A man employed by Gervis."

"Explain the exact nature of their working arrangement as you know it."

She tried, though it wasn't easy. Kane was relentless in his pursuit of details, firing questions at her one after the other so quickly that she had little time to think, no room for doubts or half-truths. The opposing lawyers, in evident disarray over the introduction of this new line of questioning, talked with their heads together. They emerged from their councils on several occasions to object, particularly when it involved her knowledge of the business and accounting practices of Berry Association, Inc., but were overruled more often than not. Even when they were successful, Kane merely rephrased the question and continued.

Regina was required to spell out every single detail she knew, each incident and piece of information, to the letter. The interrogation went on and on until it seemed she had been in the stand for hours, a lifetime. Kane wanted, it seemed, exactly what the oath she had been given demanded: the truth, and nothing but the truth.

As that realization sank in, she caught a fleeting, prescient glimpse of where he was headed. Goose bumps prickled her skin and panic clutched at her throat. No, surely not. He couldn't. He wouldn't, not in here in a public courtroom. Not in front of so many witnesses and in the midst of such important proceedings. It was impossible.

Surely he wouldn't expose everything that they had been to each other, all the things that they had done? He didn't dare use the tender, wanton desire they had shared to prove the perfidy of the man who had tried to ruin his grandfather. There was no way to bring it up without laying himself open to censure.

But if that wasn't it, she couldn't begin to guess what he required from her. There was nothing else. And why should she think he would hold that sacred? Just as there was nothing she wouldn't do for Stephan, there was also nothing Kane wouldn't do to help his Pops.

"You may be innocent of causing bodily harm, Miss Dalton, but isn't it a fact that you used your position as an appraiser of antique jewelry to gain the confidence of Lewis Crompton? That you did this in order to discover information that would blacken his character?"

"Yes," she said through clenched teeth.

"You undertook this campaign on the instructions of Gervis Berry. Is that right?"

"That was what he said he wanted, yes."

"And did it work?"

"No."

He halted in midstride, lifting a brow as he turned slowly to face her. "No? Why not?"

"Mr. Crompton changed his mind about selling the jewelry." She added with strong irony, "I believe it was on the advice of his lawyer."

"So that avenue was cut off," Kane said with a sardonic smile. "Then what did you do?"

"I told Gervis what had happened. Someone else, Slater apparently, informed him that Mr. Crompton's grandson might be interested in me. I was directed to concentrate on him instead."

A wave of comment moved over the courtroom. Kane lifted his voice to be heard above it as he clarified, "You were told to concentrate on the grandson instead of Mr. Crompton?"

"Yes." The word was husky.

"And did you?"

She searched his face, trying to see behind the stern lines of his features. It was impossible. She didn't deserve this. Or did she? Here in this public place, the whole charade seemed far more sordid and contemptible than when it was taking place, and it had been bad enough then.

"Yes," she whispered. "Yes, I did."

"With what result?"

Did he really want her to spell it out in plain words? "We became — close."

"You pumped him for information, is that it?"

She made a small, helpless gesture. "I tried."

"You weren't successful?"

"I think he was suspicious. I've come to believe that . . ." She stopped, not quite sure she should go on.

"What did you believe?"

She looked away. "That he had reasons of his own for spending time with me."

"Even so, you continued this relationship?"

"Yes."

"Why?"

The word was bald and carried hostility behind it. Stung, she answered in kind. "Because I had no choice!"

"You had no choice? I find that hard to believe, Miss Dalton. Everyone has a choice of whether they will do right or wrong."

"No, they don't! Not when a child's well-being is at stake."

He swung to face her. "A child's well-being? Your child?"

"My son," she answered. "The only person I —" She stopped as her throat closed, choking off the words.

"Your son, Stephan Berry, who was with Gervis Berry in New York while you were occupied in Turn-Coupe?"

"Yes." She managed to force out the answer though salt tears burned in her throat.

"In what way was the child involved in this situation?"

"Please," she said as moisture gathered in her eyes. "I can't —"

Kane did not relent. "Just answer the question."

She looked toward Stephan, seeing through a blur of unshed tears the scowl on his small face. She thought that he was upset over the way she was being treated, rather than what was being said, though she couldn't be sure. In desperation, she sought for words to explain that might mean nothing to him, yet would be intelligible to the court.

Haltingly, she said, "Gervis told me that he would outline to my son, in detail, the — the criminal attack that occurred nine months before his birth and that was its cause. That is —"

"He was threatening you, holding the mental well-being of your child over your head."

"Objection!" the head of the defense team shouted.

"Yes," she said on a rush of relief at not being forced to put the humiliation of her date rape into plain terms, though she thought, from the muttering in the court-room, that it was understood well enough. For a single instant, she even felt wild grati-tude toward Kane for the reprieve he had given her in spite of all that had gone before.

He swung from her to look at the head of the defense team who, suddenly detecting the lethal nature the interrogation had taken with respect to his client, was yelling about character assassination, precedents, and a half-dozen other legalities. In even tones, Kane said, "I withdraw the question."

The judge signaled for quiet, delivered a short homily on procedure, then indicated that Kane could continue.

He approached the witness stand once more and braced his hands on the railing in front of Regina, staring down at the floor for a long moment. When he looked up, his clear blue gaze held trenchant contemplation. "According to your testimony, then," he said evenly, "you were actively seeking information to be used by Gervis Berry to counter the suit that had been filed against him. Then you suddenly stopped and left Turn-Coupe to return to New York. Why was that?"

"He sent for me." Her voice, Regina discovered, was firmer. At least the distraction had given her the chance to regain a little control.

"Did he give a reason?"

"He felt I wasn't being as effective as I might have been."

"Was he correct?"

"I — Yes, I suppose so."

"Why was that?"

She avoided his gaze, noticing instead the faintly arrogant tilt of his head, the slope of his strong neck into the width of his shoulders, the careless familiarity of the way he wore his suit, as a soldier might wear a uniform. She said finally, "I was disturbed by the tactics he was using, particularly as carried out by Dudley Slater. Also, I had begun to grow fond of — of Mr. Crompton. It made me ashamed of what I had been doing."

He pushed away from the rail. "But you didn't remain in New York. In fact, you arrived back in Turn-Coupe again within forty-eight hours. Why was that?"

"I needed help. I thought I might exchange personal services or information I had about Berry Association, Inc. for aid in freeing my son from Gervis's control."

"Was this exchange made?"

"In a manner of speaking," she affirmed, though her voice turned traitor again, almost disappearing. "I was helped to physically remove Stephan from New York and bring him to Louisiana."

"After which, in spite of your own exhaustion, you spent hours at the side of the man who was injured during the course of this rescue. Why did you do that?"

"Gratitude," she said with a helpless gesture, though she refused to look at him.

"And is that all?" he demanded, swinging closer again to add in warning, "Remember that you are under oath to tell the exact truth."

She saw what he wanted. It was simple, really. He wasn't going to be satisfied with anything less than her complete confession.

Fine. The trial would be over soon, and she would be gone. What would anything matter then?

It could even be argued that she owed him this pound of flesh. He had saved Stephan for her and been hurt in the process. He had nullified Gervis's threat. He had even prevented Slater from attacking her before sending the little man packing. He had been there when she needed him, had given back to her more than he had taken. If he wanted public restitution, then he would have it.

In fact, he was going to get more than he bargained for.

"Well?" he demanded as she hesitated.

"No," she said, her voice tight, "that isn't all."

"What else?" His gaze was intent, his mouth set in a straight line as he watched her.

She squared her shoulders and gave her head a defiant tilt. Speaking distinctly, she said, "I fell in love."

"With whom?" he demanded above the whispering from the crowd behind him. "Whom did you love?"

Her lips curled upward at one corner. "Lewis Crompton's grandson, Kane Benedict. I fell in love with you and will never care for another man in the same way as long as I live."

For a single instant, heat flared in his eyes, then his lashes swept down, wiping away all expression. Ignoring the tide of conjecture that washed around them both, he looked toward the judge. In firm tones, he said, "I have no more questions for this witness."

Turning on his heel, he walked away.

The verdict in the trial was reached a week later. It was for the plaintiff, Lewis Crompton.

Regina was not in court when it came in, but caught the news on television in her Turn-Coupe motel room where she had retreated from the stares and whispers. She immediately turned up the volume, then sat perfectly still as the familiar faces of Melville Brown and the other lawyers flashed on the screen. Melville was in fine form, calling the decision a consumer victory as well as one for his client. He also pointed out that it said good things about race relations in the South that a jury made up primarily of African-Americans could decide in favor of a white man against Northeastern interests.

Gervis's team of lawyers was not so complimentary. Its leader claimed he and his team had been placed at a disadvantage by the archaic and unique Louisiana judicial and legal system and blindsided by the tactics of the plaintiff's team of counselors. He maintained, as well, that the jury had failed to understand the broader implication of open-market competition between rival funeral service operations.

The jury foreman, a black computer engineer who had lived for years in Detroit before moving back to his grandmother's home in Louisiana, returned that disdain in kind. The high-powered lawyers from the East, he said, had miscalculated. They had expected to overawe the small Southern law firm ranged against them with the weight of their importance while using race politics to obscure the issues and conceal the crimes of their client. By the time they'd discovered their mistake, it was too late.

Gervis had no comment to make on the case, but was shown flapping his hand at the cameras and microphones in his face, then jumping into a limousine and being whisked away. Lewis Crompton said a courtly few words, giving full credit to the perspicuity of the jury and praising his law team.

As Kane's face flashed on the screen, Regina grabbed the remote and switched the TV to a cartoon channel for Stephan. She didn't want to see Kane's image, didn't want to hear his voice. She really couldn't stand it.

No word had come from him the day she left the courtroom; none had come since. She never expected to see or have contact with him again, which was exactly the way she wanted it.

If the trial was officially over, then she was free to leave. Regina jumped up immediately and began gathering the few belongings she and Stephan had accumulated. Taking the shirts and pants, skirts and blouses from drawers, she folded them into the discount-store suitcase she had bought.

"Mama?" Stephan said, sitting up on the side of the bed where he had been sprawled out playing with a book of Batman stickers. "Are we going somewhere?"

"Yes, sweetheart, we have to."

"Where?"

"I don't really know yet, just somewhere."

She had thought of New Orleans, or maybe South Florida. It didn't make a lot of difference so long as it was far away from Turn-Coupe. They would get into her rental car, she and Stephan, and just drive, turning right or left at the stoplights as whim moved them. It might be best, in fact, to have no set destination. If she had none for herself, then there was less likelihood of Gervis's finding her.

Stephan kicked his feet, staring at his toes. "I like it here."

"That's because Miss Betsy has been spoiling you."

"I like Miss Betsy, too," he said in quiet stubbornness.

"So do I." She smiled at his bowed head, thinking at the same time of how easily he had fallen into using the Southern titles of respect. She had developed a certain appreciation for them, as well, since it appeared that the respect itself often followed the form. There was much else she could have appreciated, she knew, given the opportunity, but there was no chance of it. The sooner they both faced it, the better.

Regina picked up a dirty sock from beside the bed and tossed it at the suitcase, then sat down beside her son. She took his small, square hand in hers, smoothing it, rubbing at the rough cuticles. Before she could put what she wanted to say into words, however, there came a knock at the door.

It was Betsy who stood there. "Hi, hon," she said cheerfully, then looked beyond her to wave at Stephan. "Hello there, sport. Hate to bother you, Regina, but I had a call from Mr. Lewis. He said would you mind giving him a ring."

The call had not come to Regina because

she had unplugged the phone after several requests from reporters for interviews about her affair with Kane. Now she said, "Oh, I don't know. I was just —"

"You're leaving, right?" Betsy looked toward the open suitcase on the bed behind Regina. "I told Mr. Lewis you might be. He said would you stop by at least a few minutes before you take off."

"I suppose I could do that." It was the last thing she wanted, but she had little right to deny whatever he asked.

"Good," Betsy said as she turned to leave. "I'll let him know you're coming."

If it had not been for that assurance, Regina might have decided against going after all. The idea of Mr. Lewis watching and waiting for her while she drove off in the other direction didn't sit well, however, so she turned toward Hallowed Ground. It was only as she pulled into the driveway that she realized she had never once thought of the wasted time involved in the visit. She had apparently begun to think like a Southerner, now that it was too late.

Mr. Lewis was at the rear of the house, working in the garden near the carriage house. He waved her around to the back parking apron, then took her inside through the kitchen door. Dora met them there, then enticed Stephan into stopping in her kitchen for the gingerbread man she had made just for him. Mr. Lewis ushered Regina into the sitting room next to the parlor with a promise that warm gingerbread and tea for her would be forthcoming.

"I really can't stay," she said in protest as she took the seat he indicated.

"I know, and I'm more sorry than I can say that you're leaving us. I'd hoped for a different outcome. But I did want to give you a small token of my gratitude before you go."

As he spoke, he picked up a box covered with worn velvet from a side table and held it out to her. She made no move to take it. "You have no reason to be grateful to me."

"I disagree. Without your generosity in sharing your knowledge of Berry's activities, my case would not have been so handily won. This geegaw once meant a great deal to my wife, and I'm certain she'd be happy to think someone owned it who could appreciate its value. Please?"

He opened the box this time as he pressed it on her. Regina looked down at what it held and was startled into silence. The necklace that glittered up at her was a mid-Victorian piece with bloodred stones holding a purplish tint that identified them as Bohemian almandine garnets. The workmanship was exquisite, an intricate gold-over-brass design of delicate flowers and medallions surrounding a perfect Georgian cross.

"It's lovely, truly beautiful," she said in soft acknowledgment as she touched it with a single reverent fingertip, "but far too valuable to give away out of your family."

His smile was wry. "Not at all. No one could deserve it more than you. Garnets, you know, are said to represent truth, constancy and faith."

"And you think I need those things, I see." She could feel the heat of a flush spreading upward from her neckline.

"By no means," he said in stern repudiation. "I think you have them already. Good Lord, have you no idea what you've done for this family? You shook up my grandson, knocked him out of his cynic's self-absorption and made him and his old granddad see that being afraid of getting hurt is no way to live. You taught us that the truth is a two-edged sword, that it's possible to learn more of it than you want to know. You kept me from being swallowed by a corporate python, gave me back my heritage and my trade. And that's only the beginning."

"I had my reasons, selfish reasons," she answered. "Besides, I didn't do any of it by myself."

"We all have our reasons, something I hope you'll remember next time someone needs a second chance. And none of us ever really acts alone."

Just then, Dora appeared in the doorway with a tea tray in her hand. Her face was as serious as her voice as she said, "Mr. Kane's coming up the drive."

Regina gave a low cry and sprang to her feet. "I have to go. Where is Stephan?"

"Stay, please. You and Kane should talk."

"I don't think so. There's nothing left to say."

"You may feel that way, but I don't believe —"

"No!" She moved swiftly toward the door, wondering if she could escape the back way before Kane realized she was there.

"I think it's too late, my dear. You'll have to face him. Unless you'd like to stay out of sight until he's gone?"

She hesitated, glancing toward the front windows. Beyond the curtains, she could see Kane already getting out of his car. With an abrupt nod, she said, "If you don't mind, that would be perfect."

"In here, then." He indicated the front parlor. To Dora, he said, "Take that tea tray away, will you? And keep Stephan as quiet as you can. Oh, and give us a second before you open the door, all right?"

Regina didn't pause to hear the housekeeper's answer, but slipped into the parlor, glancing around for a place to hide for a few minutes. She was considering the space behind the front curtain when Mr. Lewis followed her into the room.

"No, no," he said hurriedly as he strode to the antique coffin that had started it all and pulled a footstool forward to act as a step. "In here."

It was the last thing she wanted, but there was no time to argue. The doorbell was ringing in a sharp, imperious command. Regina climbed into the box and lay down, tucking her skirt around her knees. Mr. Lewis closed the lid and the latch clicked into place.

Panic swept over her in a wave. Locked in. Dark, smothering, dusty closeness, as black, airless and quiet as the grave. How could she have forgotten? How had she let herself be rushed into this again?

It was insane. It was also undignified and downright chickenhearted. She should face

478

Kane instead of hiding. If she could just find and release the trip latch as he had that first day, she would do that after all.

She felt for the metal closure. Her finger-tips brushed it, and she zeroed in on the mechanism, feeling for the way to release it. Surely it couldn't be too difficult since it wasn't really designed to keep people locked inside. With the promise of freedom in sight, her breathing eased.

Then she heard the baritone rumble of Kane's voice. She went perfectly still.

"Betsy said Regina was here. Don't tell me she's gone already?"

"You see her anywhere?" Mr. Lewis asked. His voice came from just outside the double parlor doors, as if Kane had caught him as he emerged.

Kane made a sound between a snort and a sigh. "I might have known. I've never seen a woman like her for making things difficult."

"I'd say you're pretty fair at that your-self."

"You could be right. I seem to have made a mess of things."

"Nothing that can't be straightened out," the older man allowed, then added, "Of course, you have to have the nerve for it."

There was no answer from Kane for long seconds, though Regina strained her ears to hear. She began to work once more at the coffin's closure.

"I don't think it will work," he objected finally. "I did everything except call Regina a prostitute in public."

Mr. Lewis made a sound of agreement. "I thought you'd gone plumb crazy for a while, until I figured out what you were doing. You were setting the record straight, weren't you? Making it crystal clear that whatever she had done was because she was forced into it. You cut off the gossips at the knees."

Regina blinked, then stared wide-eyed into the coffin's darkness as she realized what Mr. Lewis was saying. It put a different perspective on the interrogation she had endured.

"The only trouble," Kane said grimly, "is that I cut myself out of the game at the same time."

"You went a little far, I'll admit that."

"I know." Kane's voice retreated as if he'd moved away in the direction of the window. "But there she was, under oath, at my mercy. It was more than I could resist."

"So you made her say what you wanted to hear. But you couldn't do a damn thing about it, there in public, without jeopardizing the case, giving the other side the chance to yell collusion between you and the witness. You should have thought of that before you started."

He certainly should have, Regina thought. At the same time, she worked frantically at the latch.

"I did think about it. It just seemed worth whatever it might cost to know, once and for all, what it had meant to her. I was afraid that if I missed that chance, there might never be another one."

"Now you know. So what are you going to do?"

"I thought if I could see her this morning, talk to her, there might be a chance."

It was then that the latch clicked open. Regina shoved the lid away from her face with such force it flew back on its hinges and thudded against the wall behind it. Jackknifing to a sitting position, she turned at the waist to stare at the two men.

"Of all the arrogant, underhanded tricks I've ever heard, this one really takes the cake," she said in strained vehemence. "I can't believe anybody would do such a thing."

Kane whipped around. "Regina! I can explain."

"Shut up," she snapped, "I'm talking to your grandfather."

"To Pops?" Kane glanced at the older man who was trying to look innocent in spite of the amusement in his eyes.

"Exactly. Mr. Lewis Crompton, the so-called gentleman who lured me here under false pretenses and probably did the same to you with Betsy's help. He had Dora keep my son busy, tried to bribe me into sticking around with a piece of antique jewelry, then he inveigled me into hiding in this stupid coffin again while he conned you into making your case so I could hear it. It wouldn't surprise me one bit to learn he had some scheme in mind to see we wound up in this thing together again!"

Kane looked at his grandfather. "That right?"

"Guilty," Mr. Lewis said without visible remorse beyond a hunching of his shoulders. "I had the best of intentions, I swear. I've never seen a pair who belonged together quite as much as you two."

"You really had some plan for getting us back together in that coffin?"

"Crossed my mind," the older man mumbled.

"Let's hear it."

"What?" Mr. Lewis gave him a startled stare.

"What?" Regina did the same before

glancing at Kane.

"I want to know how he was going to get me back in that coffin," Kane said with a wicked gleam lurking in the blue of his eyes.

"Well now," his grandfather allowed as he rubbed the side of his nose, "I'd thought I might give you a hint that I'd finally found a use for this old coffin of mine, maybe whisper real low to you who was in it. Then I'd tiptoe off, go see if Dora has another piece or two of gingerbread in the kitchen or something. Sort of like — well, just about like this." He eased away as he spoke, then turned and walked quickly from the room.

Kane gave a low laugh and shook his head. Then he stalked to the coffin, climbed up in a quick movement, and shoved Regina unceremoniously to one side as he got in. Reaching for her, he lay back and pulled her into his arms.

"What do you think you're doing?" she asked dangerously as she struggled upward again to prop herself on one elbow.

"Finding out how we'll fit together about, oh, say, seventy or eighty years from now when they bury us side by side." He lifted his arm to cradle the back of her head, then pulled her elbow from under her and settled her securely against him.

As she shifted a little to find a more comfortable position, she asked, "And what makes you think I might be interested?"

His voice beguiling but rich with satisfaction, he answered, "That, my heart, is a matter of public record."

So it was. It was useless, then, to deny it.

With some asperity, she said, "You know, it seems to me you have a thing about wooden boxes. First this coffin, then the duck blind."

"Can I help it if you're too hard to pin down any other way?"

"You did an excellent job in court," she returned tartly.

"Witness box," he said with mock complacency. "When I find a good thing, I run with it."

She laughed; she couldn't help it. His body was warm and strong against her. In his hold was security, encompassing peace, and the slow rise of heady promise. It wasn't easy to remember why she was supposed to doubt his intentions. In something less than complete coherence, she said, "I can't believe the things you do, and get away with, too. But we can't stay shut up in a box forever."

"No, but if I can't lie with you like this through all eternity, I want to do it the rest of my days. I want to live my life with you, making up every second for all the ways that I've hurt you. I want to marry you, to tie you so tightly into my family and this town that you can never get away. I want you to have my children and to love them as you love your Stephan, to let them share your heart with your son as he will share mine. I love you, Regina Dalton, and as strange as it may sound, expect to love you even after we are both long gone and buried. Will you let me?"

It was completely impossible, she found, to stay properly irritated with a man who was proposing such a lasting future together. Still, the thought of his grandmother, who had proven to have a love very similar, drifted through her mind. "Is this preoccupation with graveyards and eternal togetherness some Southern family thing I should know about?"

"Could be," he answered on the ghost of a laugh. "What do you think?"

"It's strange, but I believe I just might fit into the program."

He kissed her, quick and fierce and gloriously. Then he reached up and began to lower the coffin lid.

"What are you doing?" she asked in tingling suspicion.

"Testing," he said, his voice gravelly in

Dear Reader,

It's my great pleasure to introduce *Kane*, the first book in a series about the Benedict clan of Turn-Coupe, Louisiana. Though the people and the place exist only in my imagination, they are as real to me as if I've known them all my life — or could have been related to them, since I'm a seventh generation Louisianian. This warm affection is the reason I've established them at the heart of my Turn-Coupe trilogy.

The fictional Benedict clan is a family whose history dates back to the earliest days of Louisiana. One branch has a Native American bloodline, another admits to Scots progenitors, while others include French or Spanish forebears in their family trees. Using these various ethnic backgrounds, I expect to explore the rich blend of cultures that is so vital an aspect of modern Louisiana. I also want to include something of the architectural diversity of my home state by giving each family line a different type of dwelling to go with their cultural history, from the grand neoclassical Greek temple so familiar as a symbol of the antebellum South, to a West Indies mansion, or maybe even a big dogtrot log house indicative of backwoods Louisiana. The common thread binding these different dwellings together will be their location on a beautiful lake which segues into a swamp: the name, Horseshoe Lake, is borrowed from a body of water that figured large in family vacations when I was a child.

The books about the Benedict clan will carry as titles the names of their heroes. This is in keeping with another of my goals, which is to explore the many sides of that mythical being, the Southern gentleman. The heroes of these books, then, will be men who embody all the virtues and faults of that fine breed, men who are slow-talking but fast to resent an insult, who never start a fight but end many, who are easygoing yet hard-loving, and who hide deep emotions behind their devil-may-care smiles. Above all, they will be men of honor. The heroes of these books have begun to live and breathe for me, lounging around my desk and bending over my shoulder to point out my errors. If I don't succeed in capturing their essence, the fault is not theirs but mine.

Food is such an integral part of the mystique of Southern hospitality that it's virtually impossible to leave it out of a story set in the region. Two recipes are mentioned in *Kane*, then, one for fig cake and the other for a fruit dip to be served with fresh strawberries. For those who may be interested in a taste of the South, here are:

FIG CAKE

2 cups self-rising flour	½ tsp ginger
1½ cups sugar	3 eggs
1 tsp baking soda	1 cup cooking oil
½ tsp salt	1 cup buttermilk
1 tsp cloves	1 tsp vanilla
1 tsp nutmeg	1 cup fig preserves
1 tsp cinnamon	1 cup pecans or walnuts (optional)

Grease and flour a 9½ x 13" baking pan. Preheat oven to 350°F. Sift dry ingredients, including sugar and spices. Add eggs, oil and buttermilk. Mix thoroughly. Add vanilla, fig preserves. Mix until figs are chopped into the batter, some chunks may remain, according to taste. Fold in nuts as desired. Bake until a knife inserted in the center comes out clean. The traditional fig preserves of the South are made with Celeste figs, an old-fashioned, candy-sweet variety that turns a dark brown when preserved. With the addition of the spices, they give the cake a distinctive dark mahogany color.

CARAMEL FROSTING (optional)

2 cups sugar   ½ cup pecans
1 cup milk   1 tsp vanilla
2 tbsp butter   heavy cream

Place 1 cup sugar in a heavy saucepan and caramelize slowly over low heat until it turns brown. In a separate pan dissolve milk and remaining 1 cup sugar thoroughly, then bring to a boil. Add caramelized sugar. Cook, stirring constantly, until a soft ball forms in cold water. Place butter in a separate bowl and pour hot mixture over it. Stir. Add vanilla, cream and pecans until spreading consistency.

FRUIT DIP

1 8-ounce package cream cheese, softened
1 cup powdered sugar
1 8-ounce can cream of coconut

In a mixer, combine all ingredients until smooth. Serve with fresh fruit — good with melons and strawberries.

I hope you enjoy the recipes — and also the first of my three Southern gentlemen,

Kane. If you have comments, please write to me at PO Box 9218, Quitman, LA 71268, or via PAMrJB@AOL.com.

Warmest regards,
Jennifer Blake